Double
Cross

Double Cross

A Novel By

MICHAEL BARAK

NAL BOOKS
NEW AMERICAN LIBRARY

TIMES MIRROR
NEW YORK AND SCARBOROUGH, ONTARIO

All rights reserved. For information address
The New American Library, Inc.
Published simultaneously in Canada by
The New American Library of Canada Limited.

SIGNET, SIGNET CLASSICS, MENTOR, PLUME, MERIDIAN
AND NAL BOOKS are published *in the United States*
by the New American Library, 1633 Broadway,
New York, New York 10019,
in Canada by The New American Library of
Canada Limited, 81 Mack Avenue, Scarborough,
Ontario M1L 1M8

Designed by Alan Steele

Library of Congress Cataloging in Publication Data

Bar-Zohar, Michael, 1938-
Double cross.

I. Title.
PR9510.9.B3D6   1981   823   81-9559
ISBN 0-453-00408-3   AACR2

First Printing, October, 1981

1   2   3   4   5   6   7   8   9

PRINTED IN THE UNITED STATES OF AMERICA

For my son, Gil, with love

Double Cross

PART I

Chapter 1

MONDAY, JANUARY 22, 3:35 P.M. An off-white Chevrolet station wagon turned the corner into the Rue Verdun in West Beirut, closely followed by a desert-yellow Range-Rover. The two cars slowed down as they approached a modern apartment house, its brown walls still soaked with the midday rain. From a second-floor window across the narrow street, a middle-aged European woman intently watched the approaching vehicles. She nervously brushed away some brown wisps that had escaped the tight bun crowning her birdlike head and were fluttering before her eyes. The sun that suddenly appeared between the clouds over St. George's Bay made her squint. But as the Chevrolet drew nearer, she spotted the youthful figure of a handsome, black-haired civilian, huddled amidst four uniformed bodyguards clutching Kalachnikov assault rifles. She noticed two more guerrillas on the front seat of the Range-Rover, also heavily armed and wearing red-spotted kaffiyehs—the traditional Fatah headdresses. She shuddered. The phone receiver in her left hand became moist with her own sweat and her arm slightly trembled as she raised it to her mouth. "Yes," she said softly into the mouthpiece.

In an apartment farther down the street a curly-haired dark man drew a deep breath as he heard the single syllable and hung up at once. From his window the approaching cars were perfectly visible, although he could not make out the faces inside. His eyes glued to the Chevrolet, he slowly reached for the remote-control radio device on the small commode to his left. The red-coated switch felt smooth and cold between his fingers. He waited one more second, watching the Chevrolet's approach.

The Chevrolet sailed smoothly past a blue Volkswagen Golf, parked by the curb. Now. The dark man pulled the switch. At that very second the Volkswagen exploded, metamorphosing into a huge ball of fire. The Chevrolet, engulfed by the blaze, blew up in turn. Chunks of metal, splinters of glass, parts of human bodies were projected violently upward as a roaring column of fire and smoke spurted from the devastated vehicles. Tiny bits of iron buzzed by the windows like stray bullets and sprayed the nearby walls with tremendous impact; the twisted chassis of the station wagon, heaved off the ground by the explosion, crashed heavily to the pavement, where the flames immediately turned it into a gigantic torch. An old Syrian street vendor, eyes wide, toothless mouth mumbling incoherently, stared with horror at the dismembered bodies of the Chevrolet's passengers, strewn about the smoldering debris. A sleek, gold-buckled Bally shoe, torn off the foot of a dead civilian, rested incongruously in the middle of the havoc, absurdly clean and undamaged.

The strident wail of police cars and ambulances broke out in the distance, and a frightened crowd warily started to assemble around the corpses. In the apartment across the street, the European woman wiped the cold sweat off her brow with a shaking hand, then slowly dialed a number on her old-fashioned telephone. The acrid smell of burning tires wafted through the window as the Mediterranean breeze gently blew away the dense cloud of black smoke hovering over Rue Verdun.

Nine miles away, the telephone rang in a public booth at the Beirut International Airport. A small gray-haired man, wearing a moth-eaten moustache and wire-rimmed spectacles, calmly picked up the receiver. "The package was delivered," the woman said in English, trying to sound casual. Without answering, the little man replaced the receiver and left the phone booth. He unhurriedly worked his way through the noisy crowd in the big departure hall, joined the line before the twin immigration desks, and patiently waited for his turn. When he finally stood before the stout Lebanese officer clad in an olive-green uniform, he neatly laid on the counter his plane ticket, boarding pass, and Austrian passport. The Lebanese examined the boarding pass. *"Vol 263 de la Turkish Airlines pour Istanbul,"* he stated pompously. He leafed through the worn Austrian passport and compared the photograph with the man's face; the square chin, the rather piteous moustache, the straight nose, the round glasses, the clear blue-gray eyes that held his with a placid, candid gaze. The large forehead was topped by a heavy mass of gray hair, combed backward. The Austrian was sixty-four years old, according to his passport, and, even though short, had broad shoulders and solid arms which must have been quite strong years ago. His thick gray overcoat was inexpensive; so was his ready-to-wear woolen suit. The outmoded blue tie was gauchely knotted. "You were here for pleasure, Mister . . . "— the officer glanced at the passport again—"Mr. Kinski?"

"Business," the short man replied in a deep voice with a clipped accent. "Electrical appliances. I am with the Siemens–Österreich export department."

The officer nodded absently and stamped the passport. "Bon voyage," he muttered and looked over the Austrian's head to the next in line.

In the Turkish Airlines Boeing 727 the little man walked straight to his aisle seat in the last row of the nonsmoking section. He deftly folded his overcoat and put it on the upper rack, sat down, and buckled his seat belt. During the short flight to Istanbul he sat still, his arms folded on his chest, his eyes dulled with a faraway look. He politely declined the refreshments served by a plump Turkish hostess. His neighbor, a bourbon-reeking Texan, tried to engage a conversation but gave up when his repeated attempts were rewarded by laconic, noncommittal answers. The man obviously wanted to be left alone, and the Texan switched his attention to a fading, black-eyed beauty on his right, who stupidly laughed at his jokes and readily accepted the drink he offered.

In Istanbul the old man collected his medium-sized suitcase and calmly walked through customs. The immigration desks were heavily manned by grim, suspicious police officers, but they did not bother with the harmless-looking Austrian. An impassive look, a quick stamp on the passport—and the old man was past the immigration desk. When the crowd of taxi drivers assaulted him in the arrival hall, he seemed to hesitate for a moment. Finally he chose a tall young man, sporting a fierce moustache, who was dressed in a black turtleneck pullover and a short sheepskin coat. The Turk took his luggage and walked out of the terminal. It had rained heavily in the afternoon, and the bright fluorescent lights of the building projected red and yellow patterns on the trembling surface of a nearby puddle. The Turkish driver threw a brief look behind him, then walked with long, easy strides to his old Ford, parked across the road. Another man sat smoking a cigarette in the front seat of the cab, but the little Austrian did not seem surprised. He gave the stranger a perfunctory nod, got in the cab, and sat upright in the back seat. The driver started the engine and smoothly maneuvered his battered vehicle into the stream of outgoing cars. Just for a second his eyes met those of the Austrian in the rearview mirror and conveyed to him a mute, anxious question. The small man nodded reassuringly.

The cab did not go all the way to Istanbul, whose fairyland skyline glittered on the horizon. Barely five minutes after setting out from the airport, the driver left the main road, plunged into a maze of narrow, poorly illuminated streets, and stopped by a tawdry apartment house in the suburb of Bakirkoy. The old man followed the driver into the building without sparing a look for the man who remained in the cab. They took the aged elevator to the fifth floor. The tall Turk fished a key from his pocket and unlocked the door on their right. They walked into a small apartment, furnished with cheap carpets and chintz-covered sofas. All the lights were on; a dark girl in a white sweater and brown slacks was sitting in an armchair facing the entrance. "Hello," the Austrian said as he closed the door behind him, and the girl nodded.

The driver turned back to face him and quickly asked in English, "Well?" The girl had half-risen from her chair, her eyes equally concerned, her small hands clutching her heavy bag.

The Austrian smiled tightly and raised a sturdy finger to his mouth. "Not now," he said, flashing a quick glance around as he crossed the living room and disappeared into the bathroom at the end of the small corridor. He closed the door behind him, removed his jacket, tie, and shirt, and busied himself with the plastic bottles and cream pots that stood on a rack over the sink. Fifteen minutes later he came out of the bathroom, slowly buttoning his shirt. Gone were the moustache and the glasses. The mane of gray hair had turned pure white and was neatly combed to one side, still soaked with water. The short man walked into the adjacent bedroom and opened the closet door. He took out a dark-red tie, a sleeveless V-neck pullover made of gray wool, and a herring-bone tweed jacket. He changed his black shoes for a pair of crepe-soled brown moccasins that added a full inch to his height, then plucked a tan raincoat from the rack. He stopped briefly before the mirror as he put on a narrow-brimmed hat made of brown felt. In the living room the girl and the cab driver were talking in low voices but fell silent abruptly as he entered. They did not seem surprised at the least by the outward change in his appearance. "Let's go," he said to the cab driver. "We don't have much time." As he passed by the girl, he paused and rather clumsily patted her shoulder. "Don't worry," he said, his voice just a shade softer. "They will be all right, all of them." She managed a wan smile. The tall driver killed his foul-smelling cigarette in a glass ashtray on the living room table and followed the old man to the door. The girl was in the bedroom already, gathering the clothes left by the visitor.

Half an hour after his arrival in Istanbul, the old man was back at the airport. As the car stopped, the man beside the driver turned around and handed him a blue plastic pouch. "Your papers," he said.

The white-haired man quickly scanned the contents of the pouch: a flight ticket, a paid hotel bill from the Istanbul Hilton, some Turkish bank notes and small change, and a Belgian passport whose entry stamp certified that its owner had arrived in Istanbul from Brussels eight days ago. He nodded to himself and got out of the cab, dragging his suitcase after him. On a sudden impulse he turned back and stuck his head through the cab window. "Thank you," he said. "Everything worked out fine. You'll read about it in the papers tomorrow." It had started to rain again, and the heavy

7

drops blossomed into big brown stains on the shoulders of his raincoat as he hurried, stooping, into the departure hall.

He boarded the biweekly evening flight of El Al to Tel Aviv that landed at the Ben–Gurion International Airport shortly after eleven P.M. In Israel the skies were clear, but an ice-cold wind was sweeping the runways, blowing the skirts of the ground hostesses who stood beside the airplane shivering in the cold and trying to hold on to their coquettish little hats.

The white-haired passenger was discreetly whisked into an inconspicuous commercial van that took him to the security wing of the main terminal building. In a small room, guarded by two plainclothesmen, half a dozen people were waiting. They were all senior officers of the Mossad, the Israeli secret service. The old man blinked uneasily at the sight of the familiar faces; otherwise he appeared unperturbed as they enthusiastically shook his hand. "Congratulations, Jeremiah," murmured a tall, balding man in Hebrew. "It was on the evening news already. The prime minister called twice. He wanted to talk to you personally."

"What about our people, David?" the white-haired man asked with a note of anxiety in his deep voice.

The bald man reassured him with a quick smile. "Everything is being taken care of. Most of them are out already, the rest will be by tomorrow. The clean-out team will get there on Wednesday, as planned." He paused, then added warmly, "I can imagine how you feel, Jeremiah. You got him at last. After all these years."

The old man shifted awkwardly, suddenly looking ill at ease. "Let's go," he said finally. "Where is Danny?" His driver, a supple, ruddy-faced young man, came forward from the far end of the room. "Let's go to the office first, Danny," Jeremiah said. "I want to drop by the Situation Room."

His assistants stared at him in wonder as he turned to go. "I told you this guy is inhuman," a towering, black-haired man with vaguely Oriental features murmured behind the old man's back as he approached two of his colleagues. "He just got Salameh himself, and—nothing! He walks by as if he couldn't care less. In his place I would have thrown the biggest champagne party since we brought back Marcelle and the boys from Egypt. How long did he work on getting Salameh? Six years?"

"Seven years and four months," the man called David whispered in return. They looked at Jeremiah Peled, the head of the Israeli secret service, as he purposefully strode away. Nothing in his behavior betrayed any satisfaction in the killing of Ali Hassan Salameh, the Red Prince, the most cunning and deadly figure of international terrorism. After seven years and four months Peled had finally avenged the massacre of the Israeli athletic team at the 1972 Munich Olympics.

Chapter 2

DAWN WAS IMMINENT when they reached Jerusalem. As far as the Trappist monastery of Latrun the road had been dry and windy; but as they started the climb into the Judean hills, Jeremiah noticed the white patches along the road and the glistening outcrops on the young firs covering the slopes. "Snow," he said in wonder.

His driver nodded. "It has been snowing in Jerusalem for the last four days. The city was even cut off for about twenty-four hours."

"As always," Peled remarked dryly.

Danny chuckled. "They are totally helpless when the snow comes. A couple of inches on the highway, and Jerusalem is isolated from the outside world. Teddy Kollek said on TV last night that he has better uses for the taxpayers' money than buying snowplows and all the equipment." He made a straight face and mimicked the mayor of Jerusalem: "Once every three years it snows for a week and we have some problems. So what? The children are happy, they build snowmen." Danny shrugged. "Maybe he is right, after all."

Peled did not answer. The headlights of the Volvo caught a myriad of snowflakes, gracefully dancing in the wind before they dropped and melted on the road. As Danny switched on the windshield wipers, Jeremiah could already distinguish the familiar skyline of Jerusalem, extraordinarily peaceful under its blanket of pure snow. He was always awed by the sight of Jerusalem under the snow when its magnificent domes, churches, minarets, and medieval ramparts acquired the appearance of a legendary kingdom. But he had never been in the right mood to properly contemplate that beauty and taste it to the full. He always had more urgent things on his mind.

Tonight, though, it was not a feeling of urgency that prevented him from enjoying the scenery. On the contrary, he had finally achieved the goal that had haunted him to the point of becoming a personal obsession, like a Sicilian vendetta. But since he had left Beirut this afternoon, he had been pervaded by a strange sensation of emptiness, a hollowness that he could not explain. He had never anticipated how he would react to the death of Salameh. Perhaps he had hoped, deep in his heart, to enjoy the sweet taste of revenge once again as he had in his younger years. But all he felt now was an apathy and a crushing fatigue that slackened his body and numbed his mind. He must be getting very old, he reflected, too old to feel again the thrill of the deadly game he had been playing all his life. He winced inwardly at the thought that only his fixation on hunting down Salameh had kept him going till now. And Salameh was dead.

Jerusalem was dark and cold, and the traffic lights were monotonously pulsating yellow flashes over the deserted streets. The Volvo overtook a police van in the Valley of the Cross. Farther up, by the Montefiore Windmill, a few shadowy figures were moving about a garbage truck, their rubber boots sloshing in the snow. The Old City walls rose like a black mass, their jagged contours blurred against the dark sky. The Volvo slowed down as it approached the familiar corner. The house was plunged in shadow and the two sleek palms seemed out of place in the snow-covered garden. Danny carried Jeremiah's suitcase through the front courtyard and unlocked the door for him. The old housekeeper was asleep in her room at the back of the house, and the living room was cold and unwelcoming. He walked straight to his den, switched on his powerful reading lamp, and plugged in the small electric stove. He absently removed his raincoat and leaned back in his swivel chair, utterly exhausted. Danny, who was also his bodyguard, was moving around the house quietly, checking the alarm system.

Jeremiah was relieved when the young man finally retired to his room, and the house became completely still. He got up from his chair, went round the desk, and crouched by a low cupboard dominated by several tiers of bookshelves. He unlocked the cupboard with a brass key he had taken from his desk drawer. One of the teak panels slid aside to reveal a small safe with an unusual dial. Frowning in concentration, the old man performed the combination and sharply turned the safe handle counterclockwise. The lock snapped, and the steel door of the safe swung noiselessly on its hinges. Jeremiah took out a thick file, whose gray cardboard jacket was worn and faded with age. It carried one name, *Salameh,* drawn in big, bold characters over the opening date, September 5, 1972. He carefully placed the file in the center of his desk and sat down. For a moment he remained completely immobile, looking at the file, as if observing a secret ritual. Then he slowly undid the straps and opened the jacket. The file was divided into several sections, each marked by a simple cardboard partition carrying a handwritten title. The first section was entitled *Munich.*

He turned the cardboard sheet and stared at the eleven photographs pasted on a rectangular leaf. There was a name under each picture: Romano, Weinberg, Berger, Friedman, Gutfreund, Halfin, Shapira, Shorr, Slavin, Spitzer, Springer. The details of the nightmare came to life in his memory. He distinctly remembered the phone call that had awakened him in the early dawn of September 5, 1972, and the urgent voice of the young duty officer. "Jeremiah, a commando team of Arab terrorists has broken into the dormitory of our athletes in the Olympic village in Munich. There has been heavy shooting, and some of our boys have been hit. The rest are being held hostage."

That was how it had started, and the hectic events that followed flashed now in his memory, a film of fragmentary sights and sounds, rolling at a maddening speed. The grim phone calls he had put to the Army Chief of Staff and Moshe Dayan, the minister of defense. The ashen face of Golda Meir, looking so old in her worn nightgown with her gray hair falling in disorder on her shoulders, the tremor of her hand as she gripped his arm. "Get them out alive, Jeremiah." The distressed voice of the director of the Bundesnachrichtendienst, the German secret service, when the overseas connection had finally been established, "We assure you we will do all we possibly can, Herr Peled. Germany will never again allow a massacre of Jews on its soil."

He now leafed through the documents in the file, his eyes quickly scanning the flimsy pink cable forms, bringing the Successive reports from the Olympic Village. The terrorists had been identified as members of Black September, the most ruthless arm of the Fatah. At noon, an official release disclosed the names of the nine athletes held by the terrorists. Two others, Joe Romano and Moshe Weinberg, had been mowed down by bursts of Kalachnikov assault rifles when they had tried to resist the attackers bare-handed. Half an hour later another list had arrived, the names of two hundred Arab prisoners in Israeli jails, whose release the terrorists demanded in exchange for the Munich hostages. The list also included Andreas Baader and Ulrike Meinhoff, leaders of the bloodiest urban guerrilla gang in Germany, who were held in a maximum security prison in Frankfurt.

Jeremiah glanced at the minutes of his frequent conversations with Golda Meir and at the top secret message from German Chancellor Willy Brandt. The German security services had worked out their own plan to free the hostages; a representative of Israel would be welcome on German soil, but strictly as an observer.

As Danny had sped to the airport pushing the Volvo to its limit, a message from the commander of the Munich police, Manfred Schreiber, had been relayed by the Motorola transceiver. His rescue plan was to lure the terrorists with their hostages to the Fürstenfeldbruck Air Base under the pretext that they were going to be flown to Cairo. Schreiber's sharpshooters were already positioned at the air base.

Haunted by an ominous foreboding, Jeremiah had boarded the Westwind executive jet. In order to lure the Palestinian desperadoes into a trap, one first had to lull them into a feeling of security so they would slacken their vigilance. How could Schreiber's people manage that *tour de force* without being familiar with the mentality of the Arab terrorists, without even speaking their language? Fooling the Arabs was a job for an expert. But Jeremiah could not bring over his experts, as he was invited to Germany "strictly in an observer's capacity,"

13

which meant that he would be nothing but an impotent by-stander.

And that was indeed what he had been: a helpless, power-less spectator in the control tower of the Fürstenfeldbruck Air Base, watching the grisly denouement of the drama. As the two Bell *Huey* helicopters carrying the terrorists and their captives had landed, the German sharpshooters had opened fire. But they missed most of the crucial targets, hitting only two of the terrorists. During the exchange of fire the police sharpshooters were clearly outgunned by the terrorists. Finally five of the terrorists had been killed, and three had surrendered; but not before they coldly shot every one of the nine Israeli hostages.

Peled did not stay in Munich to attend the memorial service for the slaughtered athletes in the Olympic stadium. He had flown back to Israel and driven straight from the airport to the modest flat of Golda Meir in a Tel Aviv suburb. She had received him standing, her face white as a sheet, her lips tightly pressed together. "I want to find the man respon-sible for this crime," he had said softly. "In the past you al-ways ruled out any act of revenge. Maybe you were right. But we cannot let our people be butchered abroad without hitting back. I shall not be a worthy head of the Mossad if I cannot crush Black September."

He did not explicitly threaten to resign; Golda knew him well enough to grasp the hidden meaning of his words. She had asked him to wait another twenty-four hours, so that she could consult with the government. The next afternoon he had been summoned to her office. She had met him standing, as she had the day before, her shoulders sagging under the burden of her decision. Finally she had spoken in a barely audible voice. "Go ahead, Jeremiah."

He had sent his best agents to Munich to gather informa-tion about the Black September commando team while his chief of operations, David Roth, formed the team that would hunt and kill the leader of the operation wherever he was. By September 15, Peled's people knew how the Munich raid had been planned with the complicity of the Libyan diplomatic missions in Europe, a Libyan architect employed in the Olympic Village, and several unnamed Germans. They also reported a rumor of a mysterious Palestinian Arab who had masterminded the devious raid from a safe headquarters in East Berlin. His code name, hinting at his bloody fame, was the Red Prince. Ten days later Peled had been able to pin a name over that vague description. Ali Hassan Salameh.

Peled leaned back in his armchair and closed his eyes. The name had come as a shock to him. He had known Salameh's father, a big, sharp-faced Palestinian who had been engaged in a ruthless fight against the Jews long before the state of Israel had come into being. On the eve of Israel's independence, he had raised a large private army that had bitterly fought against the establishment of the Jewish state. Salameh's deadly ambushes on the main roads all but cut off Jerusalem from the rest of the country. Finally, a commando team of Haganah volunteers had penetrated deep behind the Arab lines and blown up Salameh's headquarters with five hundred pounds of dynamite. Salameh and thirty high-ranking officers of his private army had perished in the explosion.

When the commando unit had returned to Tel Aviv that night in 1948, the young Jeremiah Peled, then the Haganah chief of intelligence, had closed Salameh's file with a sigh of relief. But twenty-five years later, the son had emerged from his father's shadow, resuming his bloody war against the Jews. The hunt for Salameh was on again.

Peled bent over the file again and turned to the cardboard sheet headed *The Red Prince*. Gradually the pieces of the puzzle had started falling into their places, and a portrait of the Red Prince had begun to take shape. A report mentioned Salameh's childhood in a refugee camp on the West Bank; another, his subversive training in Cairo; a third, his studies in the American University in Beirut. A blurred photograph showed him with a group of young guerrillas, cheering a rotund, unshaven Arafat. Peled remembered the excitement that had swept the Mossad intelligence department that day. At last they had a picture of Salameh! They could not know then that it would be the only one for a long time, and that the lack of a more recent photograph would result in the worst fiasco in the annals of the Mossad.

A major breakthrough in their investigation had been the

capture of a Fatah courier in Rome. After seventy-two hours of interrogation in a safe house off the Catacombs of Trasone, the man had broken down. He described Salameh as a handsome man, fluent in foreign languages, with an insatiable taste for Western women, fast cars, gourmet food, and expensive clothes. That extraordinary playboy of terrorism had established close ties with European terrorist groups, mostly in Germany. With their help, he had planned and carried out a long succession of spectacular coups, hijackings, and abductions and assassinations of Israeli citizens, which had culminated in the Munich raid. There was one question, though, that the Fatah courier could not answer: Where was Salameh now? The number one man on Peled's list had vanished without a trace.

Peled drew a deep breath as he delved into the next section of his file. It was entitled *Lillehammer.*

The news had come in the middle of July from three different sources. A Mossad reconnaissance team, roving about the Baader-Meinhoff hideouts in central Germany, had picked up the trail of Salameh in Ulm. The Red Prince had been hiding for months in a safe house with his current girlfriend, a gray-eyed statuesque blonde. They were on the move now; first, they had stayed a short while in Paris; then, they had gone north to Lille and Hamburg. The trail turned cold in northern Germany, but the direction seemed obvious: Scandinavia. That assumption was soon corroborated by a rumor the Mossad picked up about a forthcoming Black September coup in Sweden. Still, Jeremiah hesitated to give the green light to his men. But then, on July 14, another Arab was spotted heading north, a young Algerian called Youssouf al Hamid.

Al Hamid had been shadowed by Mossad operatives for more than six months. Based in Geneva, he had been followed on his flights between several European cities where he had been seen contacting Black September undercover agents and representatives of various European terrorist groups. The Mossad analysts had soon concluded that Al Hamid was a top Black September courier. His hasty departure for Scandinavia at that moment could have only one purpose: He was on his way to meet Salameh.

Hence, events began moving at a hectic pace. On July 17, Al Hamid landed in Oslo, the peaceful capital of Norway. That same afternoon in a meeting at Peled's office, the Mossad directors had agreed that Al Hamid might lead their men to Salameh. A hastily assembled Mossad hit team had flown to Oslo the very next day, July 18, and followed Al Hamid to Lillehammer, a tiny town of 20,000 inhabitants, 110 miles to the north. On July 20, two Mossad agents watched the young Algerian from a safe distance as he settled at a table on the outdoor terrace of the Karoline Café. A few minutes later, another man joined him. An Arab. The excited agents hastily compared the swarthy features of Al Hamid's companion to a seedy, enlarged photograph of Ali Hassan Salameh that they carried with them. There were some minor differences between the two faces; Al Hamid's guest sported a moustache, while Salameh did not. Still, the agents made a positive identification. The Arab that Al Hamid had met in the shade of the colorful umbrellas of the Karoline was no one else but the Red Prince.

Late that night, a coded telegram confirming the identification reached the Mossad headquarters in Tel Aviv. Without hesitating, Jeremiah cabled back: "Go."

On Saturday, July 21, Salameh walked out of a Lillehammer cinema after having seen a Clint Eastwood movie, *Where Eagles Dare*, in the company of a blond woman, wearing a yellow raincoat. At 10:40 P.M., as they walked up the Furubakken Street, a tall man and a pretty, auburn-haired girl jumped out of a rented Mazda and pumped fourteen bullets into Salameh's chest. They escaped in the car, leaving the blond girl untouched. The Red Prince was dead.

Or so they thought.

The next document in the file was a newspaper clipping, dated July 22, 1973. Jeremiah stared at the photograph of a smiling young man and the banner headline that would haunt him all his life. "Murder of a Moroccan Waiter in Lillehammer," it read. The following article described at length the strange assassination of a young Moroccan, Boushiki, who had been living in Lillehammer for the last five years. He had been married to a Norwegian girl, Torill, who was seven months pregnant.

There could be no doubt. The Mossad agents had made a fatal mistake. They had killed the wrong man.

The young Arab whom Al Hamid had met in Lillehammer was not the Red Prince. He had nothing to do with terrorism. He was just a poor North African who had wandered north in search of a better life and had been unfortunate enough to meet a coreligionist on the terrace of the Karoline Café.

Jeremiah could still feel how the blood had rushed to his face that morning in July 1973 as he read the news item over and over again, grasping the enormity of the mishap. Seething with fury, he had rushed to Operations, but his shouts had died in his throat when a grim-faced David Roth had handed him a cable that had just come from the Decoding Room. As he read the short message, his fuming rage metamorphosed into a strange weakness in the hollow of his stomach. Six members of the operational team, two women and four men, had been arrested in Oslo and Lillehammer and were presently being interrogated by the Norwegian police.

He sighed softly now, his hand lying on the telegram that had been neatly filed in the big folder in front of him. He remembered well the trial in Oslo where several of the accused Israelis admitted their parts in the operation and revealed to the world some of the most closely kept secrets of the Mossad: modus operandi, code procedures, contact rules, locations of European caches, Mossad bases, and safe houses, phone numbers . . . . When the trial in Oslo ended, five out of the six defendants were sentenced to terms of imprisonment ranging from one to six years. And Jeremiah knew that the Mossad, after Lillehammer, would never be the same again.

They had been very nice to him, personally. Neither Golda nor Rabin, who replaced her a few months later, had asked him to resign. But there was that laconic letter from the prime minister almost at the bottom of the file, informing him that "due to more urgent tasks, the Red Prince operation is to be immediately canceled." Three months later, in October 1973, the Yom Kippur War had suddenly exploded, and the Mossad had turned to more urgent tasks indeed.

The last portion of the file contained only three documents. The first was a radio-photograph of Yassir Arafat visiting the United Nations on November 13, 1974. Among the dark-skinned men standing behind him, one face had been circled with a felt-tip pen, and a single word had been jotted in fat, bold characters. Salameh.

The second document was a report from Beirut, dated November 1976. It indicated that Salameh had been promoted again and appointed chief of Fatah security. He was considered by many to be Arafat's heir. For reasons of security he never left the PLO headquarters compound, which was protected by a special unit of heavily armed Fatah guerrillas. He had even moved his wife and children to the interior of the camp.

The third document was the strangest. It was an article, clipped from a cheap Italian women's magazine that specialized in scandal stories and dirty gossip. It included a big picture of Georgina Rizak, the Lebanese-born Miss Universe. Under the luscious curves of Georgina, a saucy article told "the story of her true love." The Lebanese-Christian beauty queen had become infatuated with a dashing young Muslim, and the attraction was mutual, the article reported. The young man, although a high-ranking member of the "progressive establishment," had left his wife and children and moved with Georgina into an apartment in the fashionable Christian section of Beirut. His name was Ali Hassan Salameh.

On the margin of the article Jeremiah had written: "Check Salameh's itinerary to and from apartment. Check possibility of interception. J."

Very slowly, the head of the Mossad turned over the last document in Salameh's file and retied the canvas straps. He took his fountain pen from his breast pocket and wrote across the gray cardboard jacket: "Closed. Return to Archives."

He pushed the file to the side of his desk, took a sheet of paper from the upper left drawer, and adjusted the lamp. The letter could wait until tomorrow, of course, but for some obscure reason he wanted it written now, at once.

"Dear Prime Minister," he wrote. "I wish to inform you of my decision to resign my duties as head of the Mossad and chairman of the Commission of Directors of the Intelligence Community. I am long past the age of retirement and would have tendered my resignation long ago were it not for the murder of our athletes in Munich in September 1972. Following that tragedy I asked Mrs. Golda Meir, who was prime minister at that time, to extend my active service until I had found and punished the culprits. She agreed to my demand and stood by my side, even in my darkest moments, when I made the worst mistake in my career. I mean, of course, the Lillehammer fiasco in 1973 when my operational team killed an innocent Moroccan in Norway, having mistaken him for Salameh. I was deeply indebted to the late Mrs. Meir for her unwavering support when strong pressure was put on her to relieve me of my duties. I did not resign then, in spite of the humiliation."

He paused and frowned in afterthought, slowly rolling his pen between his fingers. Finally he crossed out the last sentence and wrote instead: "I did not resign then, even though the failure was entirely my responsibility. I felt that I had to find Salameh, the mastermind behind so many senseless bloodbaths, and execute him. I am grateful to the prime minister and to you for having agreed to my demand and allowing me to carry on my functions until I could accomplish the mission I had undertaken.

"Now that this is done, I shall gladly step aside and let somebody younger and better qualified assume command of our fine secret service. I suggest the twenty-eighth of April, Independence Day, as my official departure date. I would gladly leave my position right away, but I believe I should stay for three more months in order to thwart any possible attempt of the Fatah to avenge Salameh's death with another bloody act of terrorism."

He read the whole letter again, pursing his lips. Finally he nodded to himself, took another sheet of paper, and started copying the letter. It was personal and, as such, should be handwritten, not typed. He wrote with much care and concentration in small but neat characters, slightly inclined to the right. When he finished, he added "Yours truly" and signed his name in the same clear, tiny letters without any flourish.

He raised his eyes. The long, narrow window on the right wall of his den above the overflowing bookshelves was glowing faintly with a grayish light. A new morning had broken over Jerusalem. His eyes shifted from the window to the letter in his hand, and he suddenly felt a twinge of anguish. Three months were all he had left.

Chapter 3

A THUNDERSTORM WAS raging over Île-de-France, and a diluvial rain was pouring over the Autoroute du Nord as the black Citroën sped toward Paris. The windshield wipers could not cope with the torrent, yet the sallow-faced driver would not ease the pressure on the gas pedal, crushing it to the floor.

The glowing dashboard cast a greenish light on a gaunt face, dominated by a waxen forehead and hollow, sucked-up cheeks. The thin, pointed nose hovered over a bloodless mouth frozen in a slightly curved grin. The pale eyes, sunk deep in their dark sockets, were cold and devoid of expression. The man was in his late thirties. His sparse blond hair was plastered over his forehead and fell on the nape of his neck, brushing against a turtleneck pullover of coarse black wool. The pushed-up sleeves revealed long sinewy arms; the skin of the bony hands gripping the steering wheel was sickly white, almost transparent.

As the car sped by the Bourget exit, the driver's eyes fell on the dashboard clock. It was 5:02 A.M. He quickly turned on the radio, preset on the *Europe Un* station, and the voice of the newscaster erupted from the speaker, ". . . The other four men killed in the explosion were his bodyguards, assigned to his round-the-clock protection. Three passersby were slightly injured. The deceased Ali Hassan Salameh, nicknamed the Red Prince . . ."

A sharp intake of breath, breaking into a choked, inhuman growl, shook the chest of the blond man. His right foot smashed the brake, and the car swerved on the road, skidding on its wet surface. It swayed drunkenly as its shrieking back wheels kicked it violently to the right toward the guard rail at the freeway's edge. At the very last moment, as the car was about to crash into the massive steel rail, the driver succeeded in regaining control of the steering wheel and brought the Citroën to a screeching halt by the side of the road. He slumped over the wheel, breathing heavily, his whole body shaking.

"Ali Hassan Salameh," the *Europe Un* newscaster calmly continued, "was the son of the notorious Nazi sympathizer who was dropped by parachute into Palestine by the Germans during World War II in order to instigate an Arab uprising against the British. The son, Ali, rose to bloody fame as the chief planner of Black September, the most ruthless section of the Fatah. Posing as a swashbuckling playboy, he established close ties between the Fatah and various European terrorist groups, particularly the German Baader-Meinhoff gang."

The blond man sat still, gripping the steering wheel. The trembling of his body slowly subsided, but he repeatedly bit his lower lip, indifferent to the pain. A rivulet of blood trickled down his chin.

"Five previous attempts of the Israeli Mossad to kill Salameh failed," the speaker said. "He was the top target on the Mossad execution list. It was he who launched a letter-bomb offensive against the Israeli diplomats in Europe. He also engineered the sabotage of the Rotterdam refineries in 1971, the murder of Jordanian Prime Minister Wasfi-el-Tal in Cairo, the hijacking of the Sabena airliner to Israel in 1972, and the senseless killing of twenty-four passengers at the Ben-Gurion Airport by Japanese Red Army terrorists. But his most despicable crime was the massacre of the Israeli Olympic team in . . ."

"Monsieur!" A heavy fist was knocking on the driver's window. *"Monsieur, là, ouvrez!"* The blond man slowly raised his head, wiping his chin and mouth with his sleeve. A police car, its blue and red lights flashing, had stopped ahead of him. A bulky policeman was leaning over the front door, his face blurred by the rain splattering on the window. Another policeman, his black plastic raincoat glistening in the rain, approached from the other side and directed the beam of his

powerful flashlight at the Citroën driver. The blond man, blinded, brought up his hand to protect his eyes.

"Monsieur!" the first policeman shouted and knocked on the window again. The driver reluctantly rolled down the window, and the policeman stuck his head in, water dripping inside from his soaked *képi*. *"Que faites-vous ici?"* "What are you doing here?" he shouted. His breath reeked of garlic and cheap tobacco. "Don't you know that it's forbidden to stop on the freeway?"

". . . escaped death in 1973," the radio went on, "when an Israeli hit team killed the wrong man in Lillehammer, Norway . . ."

"Why don't you turn off the radio and answer my questions?" the policeman growled.

The blond man tried to compose his features before answering. "There was a very strong gust of rain, *Monsieur l'agent,"* he said respectfully. His French was correct, but it carried a foreign accent with a faint German intonation. "I just couldn't see anything, so I decided to stop for a couple of minutes."

The policeman examined him closely with his small, suspicious eyes that were set in a heavy-jowled, red face with a bulbous nose. "You haven't been drinking?" he inquired, his head slightly cocked.

The blond man smiled tightly. "No, *Monsieur l'agent,* I never drink."

The second policeman, who had been checking the car's license plates, approached his partner and murmured something in his ear. The blond driver picked out the word "papers." His right hand imperceptibly slid to his side, reached under the seat, and gripped the butt of a loaded Thompson submachine gun, his fingers swiftly releasing the safety catch.

But the policeman did not ask for his papers. Perhaps he was satisfied with his explanation, or more probably had had enough of standing in the cold rain, and wanted to get back to the cozy warmth of his car. "Well, the rain is not as strong now," he remarked in a less belligerent tone. "Do you think you can proceed on your way? Where are you going?"

"To Paris, *Monsieur l'agent,"* the driver politely answered. "I can drive now, it's clearing."

"All right," the policeman said and straightened up, raising

23

his fingers to his *képi* in the customary salute. "Drive slowly and take care. *Au revoir, Monsieur."* He moved back, threw a look in the opposite direction to make sure no car was approaching, then signaled the Citroën to move forward. The blond driver, bathed in cold sweat, released the submachine gun and withdrew his hand from under the seat. He shifted gears and slowly set off, swerving to the left to overtake the parked police car. He gradually accelerated until he reached a steady eighty kilometers per hour. As the flashing lights of the police car disappeared from his rearview mirror, his attention returned to the radio newscaster who was finishing his report. "Yasir Arafat himself is returning to Beirut for Salameh's funeral. Arafat, who used to call young Salameh his adopted son, has threatened to avenge his death upon the Zionists and American imperialists."

The pale young man turned off the radio. His hand was steady. As he entered Paris through the Porte de la Chapelle, he spotted a public phone booth. He parked the car by the sidewalk, leaving the engine on. He walked out in the drizzle, bareheaded and coatless. He fed a coin in the slot and dialed.

A concord of heavenly music echoed in the receiver, and a mellifluous woman's voice cooed sweetly, *"Air France, à votre service."*

His voice was grating, harsh. "I want to know when your next flight to Beirut is."

Peled usually arrived at his office in the Mossad headquarters in Tel Aviv at eight o'clock sharp. But this morning, before leaving Jerusalem, he gave Danny the address of a decrepit stone house behind Herod's tomb in the old quarter of Yemin Moshe. A white-haired woman, her narrow face withered and creased like old leather, opened the door. She shivered in her shabby robe, her fleshless hands wrapping the thin brown fabric tightly around her flat chest. She looked at Peled searchingly without speaking. Her big brown eyes had the inward look of one who had learned to live with raw, everlasting pain. Behind her, in the obscurity of the bare living room, Peled made out the figure of an old man, slumped in a wheelchair. "I came to tell you," he said to the woman, "that we found the man responsible for the murder of your son in Munich. Our boys discovered him and killed him."

For a moment she stood still. Then a spark flashed in the weary eyes, and the woman grasped his arm, her lips trembling. "Who are you?" she rasped, and stepping back, quickly added, "Please, come in." There seemed to be a sharp, quick movement in the darkness behind her, and the wheels of the invalid chair squeaked shrilly.

Peled awkwardly touched the woman's shoulder with his free hand. "I am with the government," he said. "I have to go now. I thought that you should know."

"Wait," she said. "Please, wait. Don't go." There was a poignant plea in the old voice. The woman disappeared inside and he heard her quick steps on the bare tiles of the corridor. In seconds the woman was back, pressing to her chest a framed photograph. Now that she stood on the doorstep, holding her precious possession against her breast, she seemed to hesitate. Finally she timidly handed the photograph to Peled. "That's him," she said. "My boy, Ami. Look how handsome he was." The athletic boy in the photograph, wearing only a pair of boxer's trunks, was grinning widely, his hands on his hips.

Peled nodded in compassion as he looked at the smiling dark youth. He had been shot by the terrorists on the Fürstenfeldbruck runway before they surrendered. Peled sighed. The woman stood close to him, looking intensely at his face. He gently patted her arm and gave her back the photograph. "I must go now," he repeated uneasily. He saw the tears welling in her eyes, then abruptly turned and walked away, leaving her immobile on the threshold.

In the car he sat silent for a long while as Danny drove through the narrow, empty streets, avoiding the congestion of central Jerusalem. When he finally spoke, Danny perceived a slightly apologetic note in his voice. "Their son was all they had. He was an only child and left no wife, no children. I had to tell them personally." He paused. "They were very proud of him when he was picked for the Olympic team, you know."

He did not speak again all the way to Tel Aviv. Danny concentrated on the driving that had become a daily routine for him. Since he had moved to Jerusalem, shortly after the 1973 war, Peled commuted daily to Tel Aviv except in emergencies when he would sleep on a cot in his office. On the top floor of the Mossad building, various rumors circulated about the Old Man's motives for leaving his villa in a garden suburb of Tel Aviv and moving to Jerusalem. Some maintained that the war had strengthened his patriotic feelings and that he wanted to demonstrate that fact by settling in the much disputed Jewish Quarter in the Old City. Others slyly hinted that Peled's position had been so severely shaken by the Lillehammer fiasco that the old fox wanted to be close to the prime minister's office and especially to the Parliament in order to cultivate his personal lobby, keeping watch over his interests.

The strangest theory, though, had originated among the elderly ladies of the Allocations Department, nicknamed the Witches as a tribute to their benevolent treatment of the expense accounts of Mossad senior officers. Two of the Witches doggedly contended that the Old Man had moved to Jerusalem because of his need to be close to his family, or what remained of it. The poor man had been living alone for more than twelve years now, they pointed out, since his son Omri had been killed fighting in the Sinai and his wife had died, brokenhearted, a year later. In recent years Peled had been seen frequently visiting the Jerusalem apartment of his niece Edna, the daughter of his late sister. The visits had multiplied after the birth of Edna's child, a curly-haired little girl named Sharon. Peled was reported to bring home a present for Sharon every time he made a trip abroad. One of the Witches, the buxom, red-haired Vera Herzog, even claimed to have seen Peled strolling with little Sharon in the Biblical zoo one Saturday, buying her cotton candy and making funny faces to amuse her. Although told with great conviction and interspersed with appropriate sighs in the right places, the Witches' preposterous tale was unanimously dismissed. Only an addled mind, indeed, could visualize tough Jeremiah, whose cold stare gave one the creeps, clowning in public like an old fool.

Young Amos Hefner was waiting for him this morning when he entered his sparsely furnished office on the ninth floor of the Mossad building. A handsome lean man in a checkered-woolen shirt, Amos was leaning over Peled's desk, gloomily frowning as he examined the files piling in the IN tray. Since his appointment as Peled's chief of staff, six months ago, this former commander of the special antiterrorist unit seemed to be fighting a losing battle against the formidable amount of paper work connected with his new functions.

Peled greeted him curtly, crossed the room, and banged his bunch of keys on the desk before settling in his upright chair. "What's new, Amos?" he inquired.

Hefner straightened up, brushing a black lock of hair off his forehead. "We are closing Quest, as you know." Peled nodded. Quest was the code name for the Beirut operation. "The operational team left Beirut without any problems, two via Damascus, two via Cairo, and the rest directly to Europe. The Fatah succeeded in identifying three of our people, but . . ."

"Who?" Peled quickly asked.

"Erika Chambers, who rented the first apartment on the Rue Verdun, and Peter Scriver and Roland Kolberg, who rented the cars." Following Mossad standard regulations, Amos was using the cryptonyms of the Israeli agents. "As you certainly remember, we had assumed that their cover would be blown anyway, therefore they were the first to leave, using their escape papers. By the way, we left Kolberg's Simca on Mameltein Beach and it worked fine. The Fatah are convinced that our men escaped by sea aboard one of our gunboats." He chuckled.

Peled ignored the last remark. "I want those three back here and kept on ice for six months at least. No trips abroad, not even a holiday. I don't want another Jacob Gindi on my hands."

The words hit Hefner painfully, stronger than a physical blow. Jack Gindi had been a member of the advance team sent to Beirut three years ago to prepare for one of the most daring coups of the Mossad: the bombing of the headquarters of the Popular Front terrorist group. It had been a combined operation of the Israeli Mossad and the special commando squad of the Army. Hefner himself had commanded the raid that had succeeded beyond expectations. But when Gindi, back in Israel, had come to him two weeks later and asked for a short leave in Europe, Hefner had disregarded regulations and let him go. A Palestinian reconnaissance agent had identified him in Lucerne and followed him across Europe, down to

Barcelona. Jack Gindi lay now, his skull shattered by a 9 mm bullet, in the military cemetery on Mount Herzl.

Peled seemed unaware of the effect of his remark. "What about the equipment?" he asked. The sophisticated remote-control devices could provide the Fatah with vital clues about the modus operandi of the Mossad.

Hefner cleared his throat. "The equipment is in the Verdun Two apartment, which has not been discovered yet. The Fatah agents were quite excited when they got to Erika's flat, and they stopped the search. We have been watching Verdun Two since H-hour, and it's still safe. The clean-out team will get there this afternoon, and all the instruments will be destroyed."

Peled nodded. "What about reprisals? Do we have any forecasts on that?"

Before Hefner could answer, there was a knock on the door, and a small, auburn-haired woman stuck her head in. "Yes, Mally?" Peled said.

"Jeremiah, the funeral is about to start in Beirut." She had a confident, unceremonious manner, and her voice was surprisingly melodious. "They are transmitting it live, and we are monitoring it in Operations. I think you'd better come."

"Certainly." Peled was on his feet. "Come, Amos," he said as he turned to his young assistant. A strange, joyless note muffled his voice. "We can't miss our final encounter with Salameh."

In Operations, several people were already seated in a half-circle facing a big color television set. The sound had been turned off, and the plump face of a speaker, sporting a bushy moustache and dark glasses, filled the screen. Two technicians, equipped with headphones, were busy checking a complex video recorder that softly purred as it projected a black-and-white image of the Lebanese speaker on a smaller television monitor placed on a lower stand. The perky, petite Mally Segev, whom nobody would even suspect of being the director of the Fatah intelligence department, was checking some photographs in a big blue folder beside the TV set. Peled crossed the big room and sat in the empty chair beside David Roth, the narrow-shouldered, balding man who had welcomed him on his arrival from Beirut. Hefner sensed the spark of sympathy that flashed between them. Roth, director of operations and therefore second in command in the Mossad hierarchy, had been Peled's friend and companion since the days of the underground resistance against the British before the State of Israel had been established. Russian-born, like Peled, but ten years younger, this skeletal, shy, clumsy Muscovite, rather amusing in his ever-baggy trousers and loose shirt, was one of the coolest field operators Hefner had ever met. The ninth floor grapevine had long ago reported that the Old Man had chosen Roth to be his heir at the helm of the Mossad.

As Peled swerved to the right, Hefner noticed the cold reserve that settled on his features. The man next to him looked attired for a wedding in a dandyish blazer with shining buttons, flashy tie, and impeccably creased gray trousers, with neatly combed salt-and-pepper hair and a small, suspiciously black goatee, trimmed to perfection. Rafael Avizur, director of research and analysis, who exuded conceit and pompousness, was the prime minister's protégé. His appointment had been nothing but political. He was cordially loathed by the other department heads and was held by Peled in icy contempt, which he returned wholeheartedly. The man was the very image of an outsider by his behavior, his clothing, his mannerisms. Yet Peled's hands were tied. Avizur was cunning as a fox, and his incisive mind produced solid intelligence analyses. The Old Man had no choice but to swallow his pride and carry on under the cool, ironic stare of the prime minister's watchdog.

The liaison officer of Army intelligence, a sturdy AMAN colonel, was placidly smoking a thin cigar at the far left. Peled nodded at him and bent slightly toward Roth, who was whispering something in his ear. At that moment the image on the television suddenly changed, and a multitude of faces distorted with hatred filled the screen. Clenched fists were furiously brandished in front of the cameras; Fatah guerrillas in leopard-spotted uniforms, their red kaffiyehs wrapped around their faces, swung their Kalachnikovs above their heads. One of the technicians turned up the volume, and strident shouts in guttural Arabic echoed in the room. As the TV newscaster started to speak, little Mally came forward and stood beside the television, holding a chewed-on yellow pencil in her right hand. "More than fifty thousand Palestinians," she quickly translated, "have flocked to the funeral of Ali Hassan Salameh, whom PLO chief Yasir Arafat used to call his adopted son."

The round, unshaven face of Arafat appeared on the screen, ravaged by pain. "This is his first appearance in public since Salameh's death," Mally pointed out. "He had gone into hiding with the other PLO leaders as soon as they heard the news. They feared their lives were also in danger."

Arafat's voice rose over the roar of the electrified crowd. His harangue erupted in shrill, uneven outbursts. The cords of his neck bulged against the taut skin; his fist punctuated his shouts with violent thrusts upward. "We bury a martyr!" he shouted. "Good-bye, my hero! Our revenge will be terrible! Terrible! Let the Jews tremble!"

The camera shifted to the black coffin that seemed to ride the roaring waves of a demented human sea. A big portrait of a smiling, handsome Salameh was plastered to the front of the sinister wooden box. Arafat grasped one of the front palls of the coffin as his bodyguards tried to clear a path through the screaming crowd. The other pallbearers appeared on the screen in a swift succession of close-ups. Mally calmly pointed with her pencil and called the names of the Fatah chiefs. "Abu Ayad, chief of operations . . . Al Nimer, the rising star of Black September . . . Omar Tariki, leader of the Popular Front . . ." She was interrupted by a sudden exclamation from Peled, who had half-risen from his chair and was pointing at a face in the upper left corner of the screen. "Who is that one?"

A stranger had moved into the frame and replaced the pallbearer right behind Arafat. For a short moment the camera focused on him. He was not an Arab. The nose was sharp, the eyes were hidden behind dark glasses. Yellow uneven teeth were biting into the colorless lower lip as a tear slowly trickled down the ashen skin. He was wearing an old duffel coat over a black turtleneck pullover. "Who is he?" Peled repeated impatiently. "Mally, you should know."

The little woman shrugged, her eyes glued to the screen. "I don't know," she admitted. "I've never seen him before."

Peled shot a quick glance at the four other people seated

in front of the television set, but all of them shook their heads in puzzlement. "He might be a foreign volunteer," the AMAN colonel began tentatively. His prominent Adam's apple moved up and down his throat, as if it had a life of its own. "There are quite a lot of Germans and Irishmen in the Fatah camps. A few Swedes too."

"You don't give a simple volunteer the honor of carrying the coffin together with Arafat," Peled snapped. A deep frown appeared on his forehead, and he shifted restlessly in his chair throughout the rest of the funeral. "Here he is again!" he exclaimed angrily as the ceremony drew to its end. Indeed, after the coffin was lowered into the ground, Arafat was seen closely embracing the blond man. Surrounded by armed bodyguards they got in Arafat's car together and slowly plowed their way through the crowd. Two jeeps laden with guerrillas quickly moved behind the black Mercedes of the PLO chief.

"Show me that man again," Peled said. One of the technicians crouched by the video recorder and fumbled with the switches. The images of the funeral flashed before them in accelerated playback, accompanied by a shrill, squeaking blabber of voices. Then the tape stopped, and the ascetic face of the blond stranger froze on the screen.

Peled closely studied the unknown face, his thick eyebrows joined in concentration. "I want to know who he is," he snapped.

In Arafat's small office in the very center of the Palestinian camp of Junieh, the blond man sat stiffly in an armchair, facing the PLO leader. "You should not have come to Beirut," Arafat said in clipped English, taking small sips from his tiny cup of sweet Turkish coffee. "Nobody should have seen you here."

The blond man took off his glasses. The pale blue eyes stared coldly at Arafat. "I had to," he said finally. His voice was strained, high-pitched. "Ali was more than a brother to me." He let his gaze wander around the walls, ornamented with Palestinian flags, posters, and black-framed photographs of deceased Fatah leaders. A slightly contemptuous grin touched the edges of his mouth as he spotted the loaded Kalachnikov propped against the wall within arm's reach. He despised Arafat's obsession with displaying weapons, although he had never fired a single shot in his life.

"Nobody knew of your part in the Munich operation," Arafat said. He put down his unfinished coffee and propped his elbows on the table, clasping his hands. "They didn't even suspect that you were in the Olympic Village all along."

The blond man shrugged. "Nobody knew that I saved Ali's life either. When the Israeli hit team set out after him, I put them on the false trail to Lillehammer. Did he tell you that?"

Arafat nodded. He was slowly rubbing his soft palms against each other. "Who was the man they killed instead of Ali?"

"A Moroccan waiter." The blond man's voice was emotionless. "As soon as the Jews killed the wrong man, I alerted the Norwegian police. They had most of them behind bars in a matter of hours."

A tight smile fluttered on Arafat's lips. "That was their worst failure ever. It turned the Mossad into the laughingstock of the whole world." He ran his small hand over the bristle covering his plump face and his eyes clouded. "But they got him in the end."

The blond man leaned forward, and an eerie flame lit his opaque eyes. "This is not the end," he whispered. "They are going to pay for this." His voice lashed with sudden fury. "A terrible price. We'll avenge every drop of his blood. Every single drop."

"I have already instructed Abu Ayad . . ." Arafat began, but the blond man was shaking his head. His face was a mask of hatred. "No, no," he blurted. "Not your people. Not another bombing or killing. Not that kind of revenge. The Jews murdered the only friend I had. And I have another personal account to settle with them, a private account. I'll bring the most terrible revenge upon them. But,"—he suddenly smiled, a distorted, chilling smile—"this must be an operation planned to the smallest detail. The French say that revenge is a dish that should be eaten cold."

Arafat involuntarily recoiled. "I think we can find the killers, every one of them."

"No!" the blond man spat with contempt. "Not just the killers. I want every single Jew to pay for that murder."

32

Noticing the puzzled look in Arafat's eyes, he quickly added, "You think that I am mad, don't you? I am not, believe me. I've gone over this plan in my head a hundred times. And when I carry it out, the world will vomit the Jews, wherever they are."

"How?" Arafat shifted uneasily in his chair.

The blond man leaned forward. "I shall need your help," he started.

An hour later, he left Arafat's office. Outside, machine gun nests and heavily-armed guerrillas kept watch over the flat, oblong building. A double-wire fence kept out the refugees inhabiting the camp. Beyond the fence, children were marching, chanting slogans, and brandishing wooden rifles. At the sight of Arafat, a crowd of youngsters rushed forward, waving and cheering wildly. Several guerrillas quickly deployed along the fence, unslinging their weapons. Arafat's bodyguards, who had been chatting by the entrance, swiftly flocked around him, shielding him with their massive bodies.

The PLO chief walked his guest to his car. "Take him to the airport, Fuad," he told his driver. He embraced the younger man warmly. "Remember," the blond man said, his hands gripping Arafat's shoulders strongly, "this will be the ultimate revenge. The most terrible one. We owe that to Ali."

Arafat tilted his head slightly, and his folded kaffiyeh fell on his shoulders. "But you will need a Jew for that," he observed gravely.

A cold smile bared the blond man's teeth. "Don't worry, I have one in mind. I'll get him, and he will do it. Afterward, nothing will be the same."

Arafat nodded, his face a mixture of admiration and anxiety.

The black Mercedes slowly moved forward.

Chapter 4

PURE, PLAYFUL, MELODIOUS, the last golden notes of the harpsichord were echoed by the rich concords of the orchestra as the musical dialogue culminated in a lively finale. At the far end of the room two girls applauded with enthusiasm, and the thirty-odd people in the audience exchanged approving glances. Most of them were elderly European ladies, but the few men were predominantly Arab. The frail narrow-shouldered European sitting behind the chairman's table quickly got up and turned off the stereo record player. He cleared his throat, twice, and timidly surveyed the audience, wiping his round spectacles with a blue handkerchief. He was almost bald; only a few tufts of gray fluff still survived on the egg-shaped pink skull. His pale blue eyes blinked several times, and the small pinched mouth twitched nervously before he started to speak.

"This was the *Concert Champêtre* for harpsichord and orchestra," he said in French in a low, hesitant voice. "I chose it as an example of the extraordinary versatility of Francis Poulenc. He wrote the concerto in 1928 at the suggestion of the great harpsichord player, Wanda Landowska." His soft hand crawled over the narrow lapels of his worn black suit and touched, as if seeking reassurance, the knot of a blue tie nestling under the collar of his white nylon shirt.

"Imagine, *mesdames et messieurs*, the genius of this extraordinary French composer. When the divine Landowska played his *Concert Champêtre* at the Salle Pleyel in Paris, he was barely thirty years old! As a matter of fact, at the age of twenty-one he was already known for three major works and was an outstanding member of the famous group of 'The Six' those most promising young composers of French music." A note of enthusiasm slipped into his voice that became louder, more confident. "Who were 'The Six'? Arthur Honegger, Darius Milhaud, Georges Auric, Germaine Tailleferre, Louis Durey, and Poulenc, the composer of magnificent melodies like the collections *Poèmes de Ronsard* and *Chansons galliardes*. His songs were impregnated with the purest lyricism and were an example of the sensitive integration of voice and accompaniment. For the lyrics of his songs, he turned to poets like Louise de Vilmorin, Paul Eluard, Guillaume Apollinaire. He also composed a ballet, *The Houseparty,* whose production by Diaghilev's Ballet Russe de Monte Carlo met with considerable success.

"And then," he paused briefly, his pink skin coloring with excitement, "came the *Concert Champêtre.* Soon, very soon, Poulenc was to give another proof of his magnificent talent with his religious works of the thirties, like . . ."

"La Vièrge Noire de Rocomadour?" a portly, gray-haired lady in the third row suggested.

He turned to her, beaming with pleasure, "That's right, *chère madame. Litanies à la Vièrge Noire de Rocomadour."* Somebody on her left raised his hand, but he disregarded it. "The forties were marked by his surrealistic comic opera *The Mamelles de Tirésias."*

The girls in the back giggled softly, and the younger of the two quickly covered her mouth with her hand. He shot her a reproachful look and concluded, "But Poulenc was to reach the peak of his career with his magnificent opera *Les Dialogues des Carmélites.* That will be the subject of our next meeting." He took a deep breath and added forcefully, "When we savor and analyze this great opera, I am sure that you will agree with Poulenc's biographer, Henri Hell, who wrote: 'Poulenc was one of the masters of the French music in the twentieth century, and the last of the great melodists.' "

He stopped. A young man in the second row got up. "I have a question," he said with deliberate aloofness. "Will you agree with the description of Poulenc by Colette in the article she wrote in 1941 . . ." As his voice trailed off, the young Lebanese pompously leafed through the pages of his notebook.

Before he could continue a small, stout man rose to his

feet and stood beside the speaker. *"Mesdames et messieurs,"* he said with natural authority, "I am afraid that tonight we shall have no time for questions. I suggest that we reserve the last half hour of our next meeting for a concluding debate on Francis Poulenc." He turned to the speaker, who nodded hastily, his hand fluttering over the knot of his tie. The little man pivoted back to face the public again. "Allow me, therefore, on behalf of the Cercle Culturel de Beirut, to thank Mr. Armand Mesurier of the Saint Joseph University for his excellent lecture on Francis Poulenc. We shall look forward to your forthcoming lecture next Wednesday at six-thirty P.M. Thank you." A ripple of polite applause followed his words and the audience slowly dispersed.

Fifteen minutes later, dressed in a dark-blue overcoat and a wide-brimmed gray hat, Armand Mesurier stepped out of the Centre Culturel Français. The pleasant Rue de la Republique was deserted, and a cold wind swept the empty sidewalks. Mesurier tucked the bunch of newspapers, notebooks, and the two Poulenc records under his left arm and, with his right hand, clutched the collar of his coat, tightly wrapping the rough fabric against his scrawny throat. He shivered in the bitter cold and quickly walked down the street. The civil war had not spared the fashionable street. Several facades still bore the fresh scars of recent street fighting and the once impressive Hotel Imperial was nothing but a pile of rubble. Mesurier turned right at the first intersection, then right again. He seemed to hesitate a moment before the illuminated facade of Le Café de L'Orient but finally made up his mind and stepped in. The spacious café welcomed him with a wave of pleasant warmth, some measures of monotonous Arab music, and a blabber of voices. He slowly unbuttoned his overcoat. The place was half empty. There were no women in sight. Only men, most of them Arabs, sat on dark-red, velvet-upholstered sofas and armchairs around copper-topped tables, sipping their coffee and eagerly arguing. Most of them did not pay any attention to Mesurier. Two of the waiters, dressed in embroidered black trousers and vests, recognized him and grinned broadly as he clumsily moved between the tables; the owner himself, a huge fat man in a gray suit, left his seat at the cashier's booth under an old portrait of President Sarkiss and came forward to shake

Mesurier's hand. Le Café de L'Orient had a mainly Muslim clientele; but the habitués had gotten used to the eccentric Frenchman—*Fransawi* in their lingo—who appeared punctually as a Swiss clock every Wednesday night after his lecture at the Cercle Culturel. Mesurier shook the owner's damp hand, bashfully murmured a few banalities without raising his eyes, and walked awkwardly to his usual place at the farthest corner of the café. The old-fashioned radio, standing nearby blaring plaintive Oriental melodies at full blast, did not seem to bother the French musicologist. He sat stiffly at the edge of the sofa, arranged his newspapers and records in a neat pile beside him, straightened his tie, and accepted with a shy smile the tiny cup of Turkish coffee that a waiter placed on his table. Left alone, he slowly relaxed and picked the *Nouvelles Littéraires* from the top of the pile. Engrossed in an article about Jean-Pierre Rampal, he did not raise his eyes even when somebody sat at the adjacent table and ordered some coffee in guttural Arabic. And he stayed perfectly immobile when the newcomer spoke in a low voice, almost totally covered by the languid Arab song, yet distinct enough to be picked up by him, and him alone.

"On Monday, after Salameh's funeral, I drove a man from the Martyr's Cemetery to the chief's office," the stranger murmured in Arabic. "A blond man, about thirty-five years old. On the way to the office they spoke about Salameh. The blond man spent an hour alone in the chief's office. When he left, the chief accompanied him to the car, and I heard their conversation. They hugged each other, and the blond man said to the chief, 'This will be the most terrible revenge. The ultimate revenge We owe it to Ali.' They were speaking in English."

"Repeat that," came a quick whisper from the corner where Mesurier was studiously bent over his magazine.

"The ultimate revenge," the Arab said again. "Then the chief said to him, 'You will need a Jew for that.' And the blond man answered, 'I know a Jew who will do it . . .' No, wait, it was not exactly that." He paused for a second, then spoke again. "He said, 'I know a Jew, I'll get him and he will do it.' And the blond man added, 'Afterward, nothing will be the same.' "

"Repeat."

37

"Afterward, nothing will be the same."

Mesurier raised his cup of coffee to his lips and imperceptibly nodded.

"Then I drove him to his hotel to pick up his luggage and to the airport. He boarded the Air France afternoon flight to Paris. He had an overnight bag, and I carried it to the counter."

"Did you see his passport?"

"Yes. A German passport in the name of Alfred Mueller."

"What did you do then?"

"I drove back. The chief spent the rest of the afternoon with Abu Ayad. He seemed concerned."

"Nothing else?"

"No."

"Who else heard them talking?"

"Nobody. They were alone in the office."

"Did you speak with anybody about this matter?"

"No."

"Did you overhear the conversation between the chief and Abu Ayad?"

"No, not a word."

"Where did Abu Ayad go after he spoke to your chief?"

"He went to Saida. I was sitting outside with his driver when he came out and said, 'There has been a change of plans. We are going to Saida.' "

The melancholy song flowing from the radio ended, but Mesurier did not seem to care. He tucked the *Nouvelles Littéraires* under his pile, picked up *L'Express,* and buried his nose in a review of the last performance of the Concerts Pasdeloup. Soon an oily masculine voice started lamenting a lost love over the radio, accompanied by the tones of the *el-ud* and the rhythmical sighs of a male chorus. And the whisper, cold and insistent, again reached Fuad's ears.

"Where did Mueller stay in Beirut?"

"Hotel Phoenicia."

"How long did he stay there?"

One of the waiters passed by, his eyes sweeping the tables for new orders, and Fuad asked for some sweet baklava stuffed with pistachio. "I don't know," he cautiously began as the waiter hurried to the kitchen. "I think only one or two nights."

There was a pause, then the Frenchman said, "How did he get to the funeral in the first place?"

"I don't know."

"But your chief . . ." The words died in midair as the waiter brought the sweets and placed them before Fuad.

"Would you like something more, *monsieur?*" the waiter asked Mesurier. The Frenchman did not seem to hear. *"Monsieur?"* the waiter said louder.

Mesurier started, raised his eyes, and a bewildered expression settled on his face. "What?" he stuttered. "I . . . I didn't hear you." The waiter repeated his question and Mesurier shook his head, blushing in embarrassment. "No, thank you, I am all right. Thank you indeed." He readjusted his tie and returned to his magazine. Once the waiter was gone, he smoothly resumed his interrogation.

"Your chief, was he surprised to meet Mueller at the funeral?"

Fuad hesitated. "No," he whispered finally, munching his baklava. "The chief was upset, but not surprised. Somebody must have told him before the funeral that Mueller had arrived in Beirut."

No more whispers came from the corner, and the Arab felt that this was the end of the interrogation. The *Fransawi* always got on his nerves with his questions, but he had to admit that he knew his job. Fuad had worked with three other Frenchmen before, almost since he had gotten his job as Arafat's driver; but this one, who looked the most ridiculous and unsuitable for the job, had turned out to be the best. He never omitted a question, never missed an appointment, always left him precise instructions about the alternate rendezvous routine, and once had virtually vanished into thin air the moment an agent of Fatah security had walked into the café.

As the Frenchman sat still, Fuad turned toward him and said loudly, "Excuse, *monsieur*, I can look this newspaper?" He was pointing to the *Paris-Match* weekly lying on top of the heap of Mesurier's papers.

"Yes, of course," Mesurier smiled and politely handed him the popular magazine. On its glossy cover Brigitte Bardot was stretched languorously, displaying her still intact endowments under a tight, thin blouse.

The Arab leafed through the magazine till he found the

familiar envelope, stuffed with Lebanese bank notes. As he slipped the envelope into his pocket, Fuad smiled to himself. The fat wad of bills that the French spy slipped him weekly with his sheet of coded instructions was roughly equal to what he earned in three months as Yasir Arafat's driver.

Five minutes later, he returned the magazine to the *Fransawi*, paid his check, and left. Fuad would not have been surprised to learn that late that night at the *Fransawi*'s house his report would be written down, then coded, broken into five-letter groups, copied on a rectangular slip of paper, photographed, reduced to a microdot, and pasted under the stamp on an innocent postcard to be sent in the morning to a private address in Paris. Fuad had seen a movie once about the way spies operated. But he would have been utterly astounded to learn that neither that postcard, nor any of the others Mesurier sent, ever reached the offices of the SDECE, the French intelligence agency.

Mesurier himself would have been even more baffled. The musicologist had been convinced that he was working for his beloved France since the night he had been recruited three months before his departure to Beirut on a sabbatical. The man who had knocked on his door in the quiet Paris suburb of Colombes had introduced himself as Mondy. He had displayed the credentials of a high official of the Middle East Bureau of the Service One Department of the SDECE. Reminding Mesurier of his wartime past in his native Algeria as an anti-Nazi *résistant*, Mondy had convinced him to undertake "a mission vital to our country" while teaching in Beirut. His experience and his fluency in Arabic made him a perfect choice for the project, Mondy had said. A week later, he had introduced Mesurier to a young woman, Michele, who had become his instructor in a crash course in basic undercover techniques. The shy, lonely Mesurier had soon fallen in love with his young and pretty instructor. He suspected that Michele knew it, although he had never dared to open his heart to her. On the eve of his departure for Beirut, Mondy had come to see him again. He had briefed him on the nature of his assignment; then he had made him sign an official paper wherein Mesurier undertook not to reveal his secret functions to anybody, not even another SDECE official. The only exception to that rule would be a man who would use three secret passwords, successively slipped into their conversation. That was done for his own security, Mondy had told Mesurier.

Since, the musicologist had done his job as best he could. Every week at a prearranged drop, called in the spooks' jargon a dead-letter box, he would find an envelope containing money and instructions for Fuad, his only field agent. He would meet Fuad once a week to get his report. Paris seemed to be very satisfied with his work. The lovely Michele, impersonating his real-life niece, would often compliment him in her warm, sensual voice during long-distance phone calls from Paris. He never told her that those short conversations and the silvery echo of her laugh over the phone were much more important to him than the substantial salary deposited on the first of each month in his account at the Banque Worms in Paris. His undercover activities did not seem particularly dangerous to him. Once a week, after meeting Fuad, he would process the information in his small apartment and send the postcard with the tiny, concealed microdot to a Madame Leroy, 27 rue Chardon Lagache, in the sixteenth arrondissement of Paris. He did not know what happened afterward.

What really happened would have amazed him. The kind old lady who received his postcards in Paris had no connection whatsoever with the SDECE. She would briefly contemplate the lovely photographs depicting Baalbek or the majestic cedars of Lebanon; then she would seal the postcard in a plain envelope and drop it at her usual dead-letter box.

That was what happened to the postcard carrying the report about Alfred Mueller. Four days after it reached Madame Leroy in Paris, the microdot was removed, developed, magnified, and decoded at the Mossad laboratories in Tel Aviv.

"The ultimate revenge," Peled slowly said. "Now I wonder what that means." He did not look up from the single sheet of paper that lay before him. The ceiling lamps that had burned through the long, dreary afternoon cast a yellow illumination on the six people gathered in Peled's office.

"It might be just a figure of speech," David Roth suggested in his calm manner. "Perhaps he had a particularly cruel sort of revenge in his mind."

"So why use the word 'ultimate'?" Peled insisted, thoughtfully rubbing his knuckles along his jaw. "And that phrase here, 'Afterward, nothing will be the same.'" He raised his eyes and surveyed his audience. "It can't just be another terrorist attack. What does he want to do? Start a war? Drop an atom bomb on Jerusalem?"

For a moment, nobody spoke. Avizur sat aloof in his corner, watching the head of the Mossad with a slightly sarcastic smile. David Roth, frowning, leaned back in his chair and vacantly gazed at the low, leaden sky stretching beyond the rain-splattered windows. Mally Segev, her head cocked to one side, was chewing the edge of another yellow pencil from her seemingly unlimited supply. She was waging another of her hopeless give-up-smoking campaigns, Amos Hefner noted. His eyes shifted to the Old Man's sturdy fingers, impatiently drumming on the glass top of his desk.

Dr. Noah Bergmann, the Mossad psychiatrist, broke the silence. "There certainly are some inconsistencies here," he started uncertainly, taking his crooked pipe out of his mouth. A large man with a shock of silvery hair, bushy eyebrows, a fleshy face, and big, chunky hands, he always became meek as a lamb in the presence of Peled, and his cavernous voice faltered with deference as he addressed the Old Man. "This Mueller is a fanatic, no doubt about that. A balanced mind would not use expressions like 'ultimate revenge' or 'nothing will be the same again.' These expressions hint at some sort of apocalyptic scheme." He paused and stared fixedly at Peled, his hand frozen in midair, as if wanting to make sure that he had made his point clear. The director of the Mossad nodded impatiently. "Yet," the psychiatrist went on, "I rather doubt if Mueller has in mind one of those crazy schemes that a deranged imagination may produce. He speaks about a certain operation, to which Arafat seems to agree. And he needs a Jew for it."

"Yes, yes," Peled muttered, his restlessness growing. "But why a Jew?"

David Roth joined the tips of his spread-out fingers, leaning his elbows on the armrests of his chair. "A Jew could easily get into the country," he pointed out, "and approach the target of the operation without arousing suspicion."

Peled moved his chair, obviously irritated. "Yes, I could

guess that myself," he said belligerently. He was very high-strung today, Hefner thought, or maybe his ulcer was bothering him again. "You speak about the target of an operation," Peled went on, looking at Roth. "But what kind of operation? And he says that he has a Jew in mind who would do it." He perused the report again, as if hoping to discover a clue that had escaped him until now. "As far as I can remember, we never had a case of a Jew taking part in a terrorist plot before."

"Well, Jeremiah," Hefner said uneasily, "as a matter of fact we did." He was standing across the room, casually leaning on the doorframe; under Peled's sharp look he hastily straightened up. "There was the Jacobi affair last year, the guy who smuggled the explosives for the Fatah over the Lebanese border."

"Nonsense," Peled peevishly waved his hand. "Jacobi was a common criminal who did not even know for sure what he was carrying. And he lived in Israel." His hand came to rest on the report. "If Mueller says that he knows a Jew, he must have somebody in mind who lives abroad. Mally," he turned to the neat little woman, "do we have anything on Jews in Europe or America connected with the Fatah? Could you check that?"

"I checked it as soon as the report arrived." She took the pencil out of her mouth. "We have about a dozen names of leftist activists in France and Denmark and a couple in England. But they are not the kind who would go beyond speaking at a pro-PLO rally. We don't have anything on Mueller either," she added, anticipating the next question.

"We are groping in the dark," Peled said, annoyed. "This report is too fragmentary. We should ask for more details. Who is the source?"

"Spider," Mally said, slowly shaking her head. "That would be a waste of time, Jeremiah. He is very thorough. All he could possibly get is in the report."

The Old Man was not satisfied. "And you are sure that this Mueller is the same man we saw at the funeral?"

"Yes," she said. "It all matches—description, time period, visit to Arafat. It's the same man, Jeremiah."

The uneasy silence that followed was finally broken by

43

David Roth. "I agree with Dr. Bergmann," the head of Operations said, crossing his long legs. The Mossad psychiatrist, who was trying to relight his pipe, shot a quick glance at Roth. "I agree," Roth went on, "that Mueller does not plan to drop an atomic bomb or trigger some other holocaust. That happens in spy novels, not in real life. If he wants revenge, the most likely project would be an assassination."

Peled took his time before answering. When he spoke, his voice was slightly ironic. "Assassination?" A wry smile touched the corners of his mouth. "Whom would they murder to avenge Salameh?"

Roth thoughtfully pursed his mouth. "They tried to kill Ben-Gurion back in seventy-one when he was in Scandinavia, remember? They might try the prime minister, or somebody like Dayan, Weizmann . . ." He paused, then added softly, "Or you, Jeremiah."

Chapter 5

"THESE SNAILS WERE absolutely delicious," the girl sighed, sadly contemplating her earthenware plate where half a dozen empty shells lay in their tiny pools of garlic butter. "How I would love some more . . . May I, Michael?"

The young man beckoned the waiter, who laboriously worked his way through the noisy crowd of students and artists to reach their table. *"Encore une demi-douzaine d'escargots pour mademoiselle,"* Michael said. The silver-haired Frenchman gravely nodded and moved away. Michael switched back into English, leaning over his lovely companion. "Isn't that indulging, Maureen? For a revolutionary like you?"

She had a soft, melodious laugh, and her eyes sparkled as she tossed back her strawberry-blond hair. "It's not me who's the real revolutionary, Michael. It's Patrick, and his friends, and . . ." she hesitated, "and you."

"I am trying," he frankly admitted, frowning, "but they won't have me."

"But Patrick . . ." she started.

"Patrick is my best friend, but he won't even invite me to one of their meetings. Except for Patrick and Alfred, I don't know anybody in the group, though I've been in Paris for almost a year now."

The lively green eyes watched him in amusement. "So since you failed with Patrick, you're trying to approach him through his sister. You are a very stubborn man, Michael Gordon."

"Oh, come on, Maureen," he said earnestly and put his

glass on the table. "You know that I've been trying to take you to dinner since the moment I laid eyes on you. This has nothing to do with your brother. I just happen to like you, that's all."

"Yes, I know," she conceded, her cheeks slightly coloring. Michael's utter honesty could be confusing at times, yet it pleased her. "So, let's postpone the revolution for a while and enjoy our dinner, okay?"

She grinned with delight at the waiter who brought her second plate of snails, and the Parisian's stern face melted into a captivated smile. That little *Irlandaise,* she is really something, he said to himself, as he hovered unnecessarily about her, pouring some more wine, moving the plates and silver. Even in her worn-out jeans and bleached sweater, she looked like a princess in the middle of the crowd. And the spacious cellar restaurant, with its vaulted ceiling and long rustic tables of rough wood, suited her to perfection, enhancing her beauty. The dancing flames of the torches, riveted to the stone walls, colored her hair with a multitude of reddish-gold shades. Some vague memory of his youth made his heart twitch. But his face remained impassive as he bowed toward the young American sitting across from the girl. The American was wearing a smart blue-gray jacket over a dazzling white shirt. The heavy lock of black hair that curled over his forehead made him look quite young. "Your pepper steak is coming, *monsieur,*" the waiter said. "And for *mademoiselle,* it was the sole meunière, right?"

"Now," Maureen said, expertly picking a snail out of its shell. "Tell me some more about you, Michael. Why are you so determined to join Patrick's people? I didn't suspect that Americans were so concerned with what happens in Europe."

He sat still for a moment before answering. "No," he said seriously, "most Americans are not very concerned. As a matter of fact, I wasn't involved either till last year." He pushed his plate aside, speaking earnestly. "I was raised in the most conventional milieu, you see. A nice Jewish boy from a nice, square, well-off family in Westfield, New Jersey. My parents had my life programmed for me. Bar mitzvah in a synagogue . . ." he paused, looking questioningly at the girl. "Do you know what a bar mitzvah is?"

"Of course," she said. "Didn't I tell you I was raised in

46

America? I grew up in Boston, and there were quite a few Jewish families in our neighborhood. I was invited to a couple of bar mitzvahs."

He nodded. "After my bar mitzvah my road was planned: a Zionist youth organization, then college, then a cozy future as a nice Jewish doctor, lawyer, or public relations executive. A Madison Avenue tiger, that's what I was going to become." The waiter brought their main courses, but Michael did not seem to care. "I think that Vietnam threw me off the track, so to speak."

Maureen frowned. "Vietnam? But you must have been a kid during the war. How old are you?"

"Twenty-five," he answered and absently started carving his steak. "I was a teenager when the peace marches and the protest movements were going on. I didn't take part in any. I was just a high school kid, as you said, but I started to ask myself all kinds of questions, and I discovered some ugly truths about my country and my society."

"What sort of truths?"

"For instance, that American foreign policy was not as chivalrous and noble as I had been taught. That we didn't always defend freedom and democracy. That we supported some of the most corrupt and bloody regimes in Asia and South America. That we had dictators and military juntas on our payroll. That we just pretended to ignore the existence of torture chambers a few hundred yards from our embassies. And so on." His voice had grown loud and impetuous, and two young men at a nearby table turned and stared at him.

Maureen studied him with new interest. Michael's coal-black eyes were ablaze with an inner fire and his face colored with excitement. She suddenly realized that he was very handsome. His burning eyes, high forehead, and passionate mouth were those of a romantic dreamer. You remind me of somebody I used to know in Belfast, she wanted to say. The same fervor. The same candid dedication. And where did all that lead him? Are you also heading for a bloody death in some savage shoot-out, Michael Gordon? Will I cry at your funeral as well? She suddenly shivered, but managed to keep her voice low, controlled, as she asked, "So what did you do?"

He laid his fork beside his untouched food. "For a while I

tried to organize my fellow students on campus. I was studying political science. Before long I was labeled a radical activist." A note of self-mockery rang in his voice. "And then one day I sobered up and realized that all that was rubbish. Protest marches, rallies, sit-ins, that was very nice and very exciting, and all the college kids would join us for a couple of hours. But as soon as it started getting late, their revolutionary fervor would evaporate, and everybody would hurry home for dinner and the late show. So I decided it was time for me to stop blabbering and start doing something real."

A trio in medieval troubadour costumes entered the cellar and started walking between the tables, singing an old French ballad. The two male singers accompanied their melancholy song with a lute and a zither. The girl, wearing a low-cut velvet dress, had long flaxen hair, and her voice was clear and pure like a choir boy's.

Michael lowered his voice. "I went to South America. There were five of us: two guys from Chicago, one from Dallas, a girl from California, and myself. We spent about a year in Argentina, Bolivia, and Guatemala. We wanted to join the revolutionaries there and fight on their side."

"And did you?" Maureen asked doubtfully, tilting her head.

"No, not really," he said bitterly. "We had no trouble getting in touch with the guerrillas there. But we had a lot of trouble convincing them that we were on their side. They just hated Americans, that's all. For them all Yankees were bloody imperialists, and we were no exception to the rule. They just didn't want us." He shrugged. "Finally we split. Two guys remained in Nicaragua, and I came home with one of the Chicago boys. The girl, Janet, had returned to L.A. earlier. She had gotten into trouble with a man in Buenos Aires, and her parents brought her back."

Maureen watched him thoughtfully over the rim of her glass. "So you never saw any real action," she concluded.

"No, I didn't," Michael conceded. "I stayed at home and went back to school for a while, but mostly I read—Sartre, Marcuse, Gramsci, that sort of stuff. Finally I realized that the real struggle for a new society was taking place in Europe —in France, Italy, Germany. That's why I came here. Officially, for my parents' sake," he smiled faintly, "I'm writing my Ph.D. thesis on the radical student movements in Europe. Actually, I'm trying to get into something. I met Patrick and Alfred through some New Left activists. They seem to like me," he smiled again, a rather sad sort of smile, "but I have the distinct feeling that like the South Americans, they don't really care for my services."

And rightfully so, Maureen thought. There was something pathetic in Michael's efforts to join the active cells of the IRA and the German group. He was so candid, so determined. And yet, so immature. She could not visualize this romantic boy who radiated such a genuine kindness committing an act of deliberate violence. He was not cast in the same mold as Patrick and his friends. They saw him as just a spoiled American boy from a rich family trying to play the part of a revolutionary. She felt an urge to reach out and grab him by the shoulders and shake him awake. It's not for you, Michael, she wanted to scream at him, it's deadly dangerous, it's a cruel, violent life. Take my word, I tasted it. It's not a game. People maim, kill, and get killed. Why don't you go back to America and get yourself a secure job, why don't you become a Madison Avenue tiger, for Christ's sake? "But you haven't given up?" she asked instead, concealing her emotion.

He smiled again. "Of course not." There was something enchanting in his smile. It made all his face light up. She suddenly wanted to touch the tiny dimples that emerged on both sides of his mouth, to feel the full, beautifully curved lips.

Michael did not grasp the meaning of her look. He was still with Alfred and Patrick. "Sooner or later they'll ask me to join them," he said stubbornly.

All at once, she felt tired and old, much older than Michael. He was so vulnerable. She wanted to warn him, to protect him. But could she? Once before she had tried, and she had failed. Yet, if she had only tried harder, maybe Kevin would not have been killed that night in Belfast. Maybe Patrick would have let things be and managed to die of old age in his bed. But Kevin was dead and buried, and her half brother would probably never live to celebrate his fortieth birthday. She was the only one who had started to doubt if their cause, any cause, was worth so much useless killing. "Don't . . ." she started softly, but Michael was leaning back in his chair, surveying the almost empty restaurant, as if coming out of a dream.

"Look," he said in wonder, "everybody's gone home, and I didn't even notice. I guess I got carried away. Sorry, Maureen." He leaned over and confessed boyishly, "That's not what I had planned. I wanted to charm you with a first-class dinner in a beautiful restaurant and . . ."

"But you did charm me," she protested, trying to sound amused, but feeling a strange tremor deep inside. Was he going to ask her, she wondered. "I was fascinated by your story. And the food was *magnifique.*"

"Yes," he said in mock exasperation. "And now you'll say that it's very late, and you should hurry home because you have a rehearsal tomorrow."

She looked straight into the intense black eyes. "It's not so late," she quickly said, struggling to conceal her growing turmoil.

He had not expected that kind of answer. "I . . . I wanted to offer you a drink at my place," he started, confused. "I wanted to show you . . ."

"I'd love that," she blurted, surprising him with her readiness, surprising herself with her own temerity. But she did not want to hear the usual clichés about a collection of paintings, or the view from the apartment window, or a bottle of rare Scotch. She wanted it to happen the way she felt about it, the way it would suit Michael's character. Honestly.

Still, there was a moment when she felt a surge of panic and wanted to turn and run away: the moment when he closed the door of his small apartment behind them, cupped her face in his hands, and kissed her very gently, very lovingly. She was not prepared for such tenderness, and his caress brought back raw, painful memories from her past. She felt again Kevin's mouth, Kevin's touch, Kevin's lithe body, and the same body flashed before her eyes as it lay naked, bullet-ridden, on that cold stone slab in the Belfast morgue. He had been the only man she had ever loved, and she had wanted nobody else, not until she had met Michael. But even now, two years after it had happened, the memory of her slain lover still haunted her, crushing her with his presence even now when, for the first time, she wanted to be left alone, to be free.

Michael sensed that something was wrong. "Maureen . . ." he started, but she gently placed her hand over his mouth, tracing the edge of his full lips with her fingertip. "It's okay, Michael," she whispered, and he felt her whole body tremble as she pressed against him. He kissed her again, and his lips moved over her mouth, her cold cheeks, and her closed eyes. His hands softly stroked her throat and slipped down her firm swelling breasts. They kissed and caressed with infinite tenderness, slowly undressing each other, their warm mouths exploring each other with growing audacity. Yet, after he gently laid her on his bed and when she opened herself to his hardness, she turned her head into the pillow, trying to conceal the tears that streamed down her cheeks.

She moaned only once, briefly, as he exploded inside her and his warm, thick juices spurted deep into her body. Then it was all over, and he held her tight, burying his head in the hollow of her neck. He moved his hand and ran his fingers through her hair, pressing her face close to his. "I am sorry," she murmured, "I was not too good." As he did not answer, she added in a small voice, "I've made love to only one man before you, Michael." He did not ask her who her lover had been but kept stroking her hair. She felt his hardness dissolve between her legs and tried to prop herself up on her elbows, but he would not let her. "Don't move," he whispered. "I like to hold you this way. It feels wonderful."

They lay for a while, closely entwined. His lips were soft and warm against her neck, and she liked the weight of his body over hers. His bedroom was small with big, old-fashioned French windows, and the pale moonlight that filtered through the lace curtains painted it in soft, milky illumination. The night was quiet, and she started to feel a pleasant, relaxing drowsiness. Michael slightly changed his position, and his hands began caressing her again, touching her thighs, hips, and breasts. This time she felt her body respond, and her breath quickened as Michael slid downward and his warm lips moved on her breasts and down her belly. Her hands reached for his head to guide his mouth as her body arched upward to meet it. "Yes, Michael," she panted. "Oh, yes. Oh, yes."

The strident ring of the telephone jolted them both like an electric charge. "Shit," Michael cursed furiously as he rolled over and groped in the dark. Some heavy object—an ashtray or a book—fell from the night table and landed with a thud on the carpet. She snuggled in the far corner of the bed, her face on fire, feeling furious and humiliated. He should have let the phone ring. Michael cursed again, and his eyes fell on the luminous dial of his watch. "Two-fifteen," he rasped. "What a time for a phone call!" Finally he got hold of the receiver and brought it to his ear, struggling with the cord. *"Allo, oui?"* he said tersely into the mouthpiece. "Yes, speaking," he growled, his voice still heavy with irritation. He shifted the phone to his right hand, and his left found the lamp switch. As he listened, Maureen noticed the sudden change in his expression. His face became puzzled, then pleased. "Oh, hello, Alfred," he said eagerly. "No, I wasn't sleeping. You didn't disturb me at all, really."

Maureen watched him closely. She did not know all of Michael's friends, of course, but somehow she was sure the caller was Alfred Mueller. He had that particular habit of calling in the middle of the night. More than once he had summoned Patrick long after midnight for an urgent meeting.

The voice asked something, and Michael threw a quick glance at Maureen. He seemed to hesitate a split second, then made up his mind. "Yes," he said, "I am alone."

He listened attentively, nodding his head. "Of course, Alfred. I've told you already. I'm with you, all the way."

Alfred went on, and Michael repeated after him, "Tomorrow morning, eight-thirty, at the buffet of the Gare de Lyon. Fine, I'll be there." He paused, then asked: "Will Patrick also . . ."

The voice cut him off brutally, and Michael's voice grew apologetic. "Okay, I understand. You can count on me. Good night, Alfred."

He replaced the phone on the hook and stretched his arms. He seemed thrilled and elated. "Tonight is my lucky night," he said to Maureen, grinning broadly. "First, that wonderful evening with the delicious Maureen, and now . . . this phone call. They do want me after all." He paused and added, "All my dreams seem to have come true."

The delicious Maureen looked at him intently but was clever enough not to ask any questions.

A torrential rain was furiously lashing the Galilean Mountains as the light-gray Volvo sped toward the Lebanese border. From the back seat of the car, Amos Hefner leaned forward and lightly touched the shoulder of Jeremiah Peled, who sat beside the driver. "This rain is bad news and good news," he observed. "It's bad because the boys will have a hell of a time getting through all that mud and across the Litani River. Good, because nobody will spot them. In such weather the Fatah sentries won't even show their noses outside their bunkers."

Peled shook his head. "I wouldn't count on that," he said dryly.

They entered the border village of Metula. The low, slate-roofed houses on both sides of the road were dark. A long line of tour buses, painted bright orange and yellow, was parked beside the road. The Volvo slowed down as it reached the gate of a large courtyard. A solitary figure, huddled in a military windbreaker, appeared beside the car, and the beam of a powerful flashlight briefly danced over the faces of Peled and Hefner. The soldier stepped back and waved them in. The Volvo parked by the entrance of a big warehouse beside two military Dodge Aspens, a jeep, and a halftrack laden with antennas. A thin beam of light filtered under the side door, but otherwise the building looked dark and peaceful.

Peled was the first out of the car and through the door. He was wearing a heavy lambskin coat and a soft fur hat, a memento from a secret visit to the Iranian-Russian border a couple of years ago before the Shah's downfall. Hefner followed him, shivering in his light raincoat. Danny, the driver, stayed in the car. Somebody had to be by the Motorola set and the short-wave radio that insured access to the head of the Mossad twenty-four hours a day. Danny wrapped himself in a blanket and curled his long body on the back seat.

The Old Man threw open the warehouse door and cast a quick, sharp look about him. The place was swarming with soldiers. Most of them lay on the floor, dressed in their army fatigues and combat boots, their weapons and gear at arm's reach. Some were sleeping, huddled in their windbreakers;

others, smoking or conversing in low voices. A few wandered around in search of a cigarette or a box of combat rations, moving with the lazy, casual calm of combat veterans.

"This way, sir," said the dapper lieutenant waiting by the door who then led Jeremiah and Amos to the back of the warehouse. Behind a tarpaulin partition a War Operations Room had been set up. A large-scale map of South Lebanon was pinned to a large board fastened to the wall. The map was covered with a transparent plastic sheet, and a paratroop major was drawing intricate patterns on it with a grease pencil. Several wireless transceivers were humming on a folding table, and a young, curly-haired soldier, almost a kid, was whispering into the telephone receiver plugged into one of them.

Peled removed his hat and walked purposefully to the small group of officers standing beside the map, mugs of steaming coffee in their hands. They turned to him as he approached, and the first to shake his hand was General Eytan, Commander in Chief of the Army. He was a small man too, about the same height as Jeremiah. He had a stern, weather-beaten face and calm, humorless eyes. The oversensitive skin on his nose and under his eyes, burned by the sun, had a raw, reddish color. His grip was firm; the hard, callous hand was that of a farmer. Eytan still worked on his farm at Tel-Adashim on weekends and built his own furniture in his small carpenter's workshop. *"Shalom, Jeremiah,"* he said curtly and moved aside. Even though he was one of the most legendary fighters of modern Israel, he was a shy, withdrawn man, and eloquence was not his forte.

Peled was warmly greeted by the chief of operations, General Adam, a tall, broad-shouldered officer whose Bukharan origin showed in his slightly slanted eyes and drooping moustache. "You guys did a good job in Beirut last week," Adam drawled. "I was rather proud of my brother." Abner, Adam's younger brother, was with the operational department of the Mossad. Adam turned back to a willowy girl in khaki shirt and trousers. She had enormous, clear eyes and wore lieutenant's bars on her epaulets. "Miriam, will you please get some coffee for Jeremiah and Hefner? They look like they need it."

The third senior officer beside the map seemed to be out of place in his slack, ill-fitting uniform. He had a weak, flabby body, a receding chin, and his short-sighted eyes were grotesquely magnified by his powerful glasses. One couldn't but wonder at first sight how that man had become a general. But Peled knew. General Granit was a shrewd, highly intelligent man. As chief of AMAN, the Army intelligence unit, he had been Peled's trustworthy ally, but also his redoubtable rival in many a high-level controversy over covert actions. Still, despite the almost traditional feud between the Mossad and Army intelligence, the two men were close friends.

"How are you, Jeremiah?" The tranquil voice was cultivated and controlled. "You are just on time. The boys are to leave in five minutes. We have briefed them in general terms, but I'd like you to fill in Rami Levin more thoroughly. After all, he is in charge of the operation and must know what it's all about."

Jeremiah looked at him sharply. "Rami and nobody else, agreed?"

Granit smiled reassuringly. "Of course, Jeremiah."

"Fine." Miriam brought him the coffee, and he smiled at her gratefully. She was looking over his shoulder, her cameo face flushed; as he glanced back he saw young Hefner staring at the girl, his mouth curved in a half-smile. Granit beckoned to a tall, bony colonel, who wore jump boots and a windbreaker. A red paratroop beret was neatly folded and tucked under his epaulet. He greeted Jeremiah with a casual wave of his hand and walked to the map. Eytan and Adam joined them, while Amos Hefner lingered behind, talking excitedly to a middle-aged sergeant major. Hefner had done his military service in that very outfit, the Special Commando Company of the Paratroop Corps.

Peled was talking in a low, urgent voice to the senior officers clustered around him. "As some of you know, we have had an early warning of a terrorist plot to avenge Salameh's death. We still have no idea where and how they are going to strike, but we have reasons to believe that they are planning something of unprecedented magnitude." Levin and Adam exchanged glances. "We must therefore disrupt their plans at all costs. The man in charge of the operation seems to be a

European by the name of Alfred Mueller, probably a German. We don't know anything about him yet. He met Arafat after Salameh's funeral before leaving for Europe. Immediately after their meeting, Arafat summond Abu Ayad who, as you know, is the Fatah's chief of operations. We learned that when he left Arafat's office, Abu Ayad cancelled all his plans for the day. He was supposed to take part in the testing of a new 105 mm field gun that the Fatah had just received from Russia. Instead he drove to the training center of Saida south of Tyre."

"Saida is the camp where all the European volunteers get their advanced training," Granit pointed out. General Eytan was listening, his arms neatly folded on his chest. Adam took a chunky cigar from his pocket, removed the cellophane wrapper, and stuck it in his mouth.

"We don't know what Abu Ayad did in Saida," Peled went on, "but we are pretty sure that he met with some of the Europeans there. As far as we know, there are practically no Fatah units in Saida—only Europeans."

"There is a Fatah battalion, hightly trained," Rami Levin said coldly.

Peled shook his head impatiently. "As far as we know, it is there only to protect the foreign volunteers."

"How many foreigners are there?" General Adam asked, chewing his cigar.

"Between twenty and thirty," Peled said. "There are quite a few Germans, some Dutchmen, Irishmen, four Swedish girls, and four Italians."

"I think there were some Japanese also, Jeremiah," Granit said softly.

The Old Man took a sip from his mug. "That's correct," he said, "there are some members of the Japanese Red Army." He ran the fingers of his left hand through his hair. "It seems that Arafat plans to use the volunteers in the Mueller project." He turned to Rami Levin. "And that's why I asked you guys to go there. I want you to get hold of those foreign volunteers—all of them if you can—and bring them back here. And any documents you can find, of course. Foreigners are not so easy to recruit, and it would take them time to find and train a new team."

56

Adam took his unlit cigar out of his mouth and thoughtfully examined its moist tip. "If Arafat finds that we know about the project," he said slowly, "would he cancel it altogether?"

Peled shrugged. "That's a possibility."

"I don't get you," Colonel Levin said, his voice overtly belligerent. "Why should we go through all that trouble of capturing those people? It complicates the whole operation, and it might cost me quite a few lives. Why not just storm the camp and liquidate everybody there? Can you imagine us herding back twenty or thirty prisoners? That's foolish."

"You are right," Peled said. "I wouldn't have hesitated to do away with all that scum there, in different circumstances. They are more fanatic and more dangerous than the Fatah. But I need them for interrogation."

"So why not kill as many as we can and bring back one or two?"

A note of contained anger slipped into Peled's voice, "I guess you don't know the basic principles of undercover work. They might have been assigned different roles in the operation, and each one knows about his own part only." He shot a quick glance at Eytan, then looked back at Levin. "Anyway, you've got your orders," he said calmly. "I didn't come here to discuss them with you. You'd better tell me how you intend to execute them."

Anger flashed in Levin's eyes, but before he spoke General Eytan intervened. The low, neutral voice of the Commander in Chief had a soothing effect. "You know that you're not going to bring them back on foot, Rami. We'll get you back by helicopters." He turned to Peled. "I would have used choppers both ways, Jeremiah, but you insisted on a surprise attack, so we must get there by foot. So far, the Fatah doesn't suspect that anything is cooking. We've been listening to their radio exchanges; it's pure routine stuff. We brought the boys over here in buses."

Adam chuckled. "Some clown at headquarters had big signs saying *United Jewish Appeal—Annual Convention* plastered all over the buses."

Eytan smiled dryly and resumed, "We are carrying out two diversionary attacks with gunboats and naval commandos on

57

the camps of Tyre and Rabia on the coast. They'll start in an hour." He turned to the sullen-faced colonel. "Rami, tell Jeremiah how you're going to proceed."

Levin, still sulking, took a folding metal ruler from the paratroop major and pointed at the map, "We are here, right?" The stick touched the village of Metula on the very border. "Now, we are going to take this direction, across the Christian enclave." The stick followed an arrow that curved to the northwest. "This part is the easiest, of course. They have been notified and they'll let us through. Then,"—the stick zig-zagged through a hilly region—"we shall have to cross the strip held by the United Nations. We'll pass between the Irish and the Poles. I don't think they're going to be any problem. They're scared shitless of all the fighting that's been going on, and all they think about is how to keep out of it. We'll cross the Litani, here." As the stick touched the thin blue line of the river, heavy thunder crashed outside and the rain pounded on the warehouse roof with increased intensity. Levin looked up briefly before resuming, "From the river we'll have four more miles to go to reach the camp. That's the most difficult part because it's pure Fatah country. All the Lebanese civilians deserted it months ago. Anybody who moves there is a com-batant." He looked at his watch. "I reckon we'll be there in about two hours, so we'll storm the place ten minutes before first light." The stick pointed at a rectangle marked in red. "That's Saida. We'll have two advance squads ambush the access roads, here and here,"—the metal stick glided quickly on the map—"and we'll attack simultaneously from the north and the west. We have timed the operation to take seventeen minutes exactly. The boys have been rehearsing the assault since yesterday morning. After seventeen minutes everything will be over, and we'll be expecting the choppers smack in the middle of the camp, with hot coffee and sandwiches."

"Thank you," Peled said. He did not like the cockiness of the paratroop colonel but kept his opinion to himself. Levin was an intrepid fighter and a born leader; his utter confidence in himself and in his men certainly contributed to the success of his coups.

Eytan looked at his watch. It was 2:30 A.M. "Get moving, Rami," he said.

The colonel's good spirits had been restored. He playfully threw his red beret to the girl, Miriam, who stood beside the wireless operator. "Keep that for me till I'm back, lady," he said and pulled the tarpaulin aside. "Okay boys, let's go," he called, clapping his hands. The soldiers were on their feet almost at once, reaching for their gear and weapons. A red-headed giant swung a PN machine gun on his back. Two medics passed by carrying their folded stretchers. The company jester shouted something, and a wave of laughter rolled through the warehouse. In a minute the place was deserted.

"Are you going back, Jeremiah?" Eytan inquired.

"I'd rather wait," Peled said, his eyes still glued to the map.

By the warehouse door, Granit gave Levin's shoulder a friendly slap. "Good luck, Rami," he said. He hesitated briefly, then added in a whisper, "And bring back those people. It's serious. The Old Man seems real worried."

The colonel nodded and vanished in the rain.

They had set up a cot in a corner of the warehouse for him, close to the improvised communications center. He had covered himself with his sheepskin coat, his head resting on a folded military blanket that smelled of human sweat and tobacco. Somebody had plugged in an electric stove nearby, so his feet felt warm. Eytan and Granit had left for headquarters; only General Adam had stayed in case a high-level decision had to be made during the operation. The general had gone to sleep in his car.

Jeremiah dozed and awoke time and again. Most of the warehouse was dark now. He could hardly make out the silhouettes of Amos Hefner and the attractive lieutenant, Miriam, who were sitting on a blanket in the opposite corner, smoking and talking quietly. The big wireless set on the table beside him whined softly. At times, Jeremiah could hear far-away voices interspersed with crackling static; that was the commando unit, reporting on its progress through Lebanon. The dials of the transceiver cast a soft yellow hue on the face of the soldier who operated it. It was a very young face, smooth, fresh, with soft lips and a curled lock of hair playfully hovering over the forehead. But the boy's expression was very grave. It suddenly reminded Jeremiah of another face—

thinner, more angular, but carrying the same solemn expression as it bent over the large book in the yellowish light of a candle—the face of his father, Rabbi Piladski, as Jeremiah would always remember it from those long nights at Sepetovka in the Polish Ukraine. His father came from a family of scholars and holy men, famous for their shrewdness and their sharp minds. And being the only son of Rabbi Piladski, Jeremiah seemed chosen to embrace the same vocation. But he had become a Zionist, immigrated to Israel, and the Piladski tradition had been broken. Even the name of Piladski—which Jeremiah had hebraized to Peled—was bound to vanish soon, as his only child, Omri, had been blown to pieces by a hand grenade when he led his platoon to the assault of the Abu Ageila Fortress in 1967.

He moved restlessly on his cot. As he grew older, the pain for his dead son and wife was becoming unbearable. He had never suspected that solitude could be so tormenting. For most of his life he had chosen to be alone, free to plan his operations in detail without interference. But in the last few years things had changed. Even his frequent visits to Edna and little Sharon did not help much. Now that he had made his decision and his retirement was so near, he contemplated the inevitable solitude with a growing concern. He was not much of a reader; he did not enjoy the theater, music, or social life. For almost half a century his work had been all that he cared for. What was he going to do now?

Most of the people around him did not even suspect how vulnerable he was. Funny, only the KGB assessed him correctly when they had decided to set him up with that woman two years ago. They did not send him any young sexpot, though. They were too clever for that. They knew that an attractive girl would immediately arouse his suspicion, as he would not believe for a single moment that she might be interested in him. Therefore, they chose for the job that sweet, middle-aged widow, Ruth Bronfman. She had bumped into him one Saturday in Independence Park in Jerusalem when he was strolling with little Sharon. She had given some sweets to the child, then they had struck up a conversation. She was an American Jewess, owner of a bookstore in Brooklyn. Her husband had died of a heart attack two years before. The year before her daughter had gotten married to a young state department official, and Ruth had felt free to fulfill her dream of visiting Jerusalem.

He had felt at ease with her. They had gone out several times, and he had discovered that movies and concerts and even restaurants could be very pleasant. And sex too. She was the only woman he had slept with after his wife's death. He had been very shy and inhibited at first, but she had gently led him through some new experiences which he had never had with Sarah. He had come to look forward to the nights they would spend together and, more than once, caught himself longing for her slim, well-preserved body.

She had proceeded as a first-class operator. She had manifested a very mild interest when he had vaguely told her that he worked for the government. When she occasionally spent a night in his house, he never found any signs that she had touched his papers. She would discreetly leave his study whenever he made a phone call. He had run a thorough check on her, of course, and had cabled the CIA for a Grade-One report. Her story had been verified in all its details.

That was the time of the Ultima operation, and when it aborted, nobody could explain how the Russians had identified and arrested nine out of the twelve Jewish dissidents as they were about to cross the Finnish border with their forged papers. Then the Sandstorm project was blown in its turn, and the British chemical engineer, Selby, was caught by the KGB with all the documents on the SS-18 missiles that awaited shipment to Syria in the Russian port of Odessa. For the first time Jeremiah began to suspect that a mole had worked his way up his own service. He ordered an internal Mossad inquiry and secretly dispatched two of his most trusted men to America. They were to check Ruth Bronfman's background in depth and go over her apartment with a fine-tooth comb. Only if they found something tangible were they to contact the CIA. It was highly irregular to carry out an operation in a friendly state, but he had come to doubt the efficiency of the CIA routine investigations. Still, he was convinced that nothing would come out of the inquiry, which he had ordered only because of his mania never to leave a stone unturned.

If not for that mania, he might never have learned the

truth. His men would never have found the incriminating evidence and rushed it to Washington. He would never have received the urgent report from Langley—*Top Priority, Top Secret, For Your Eyes Only*—telling how the plot against him had been hatched. He would never have learned of the thorough KGB planning, of the wild pot and sex orgy into which Ruth Bronfman had been cunningly lured, of the films and photos and recordings which had enabled her Russian seducer to blackmail her into anything he desired. There would not be much of a future for her son-in-law in the state department, the KGB blackmailer had told Ruth, if his superiors were shown some glossy photos of what his wife's mother had done with two Russian agents in a Brooklyn apartment.

Jeremiah did not press any charges against her. It would have been difficult to prove anything, and she had been burned and exposed anyway. Furthermore, he knew what awaited her in America. He drove her to the airport and escorted her to the plane without a word. Still, there was a question he wanted to ask her; he desperately strove to read its answer in her dark brown eyes when he looked at her for the last time before handing her over to the CIA agents who had come from Washington. Had it all been sheer acting? Could she be such a consummate performer, or did she really feel some of the things she told him, some of the things she did to him? He did not ask her for he knew that no matter what she said, he would never believe her.

Now as he restlessly turned on the narrow cot, he felt the old pang of self-recrimination. A commission of inquiry, appointed by the prime minister at Jeremiah's demand, had cleared him completely. The commission had unanimously blamed the CIA for issuing a Grade-One clearance on the woman and failing to detect her Russian connection. Nevertheless, that did not put his conscience at rest. The affair had been hushed up, and even some of his closest collaborators at the Mossad did not know about it. Still, the Bronfman case had taught him to be more tolerant, more understanding toward his men. Nobody was infallible, and he was no better than the others.

He must have fallen asleep at this point, for the next

moment Adam's swarthy face was leaning over him as his hand gently shook his shoulder. He looked concerned. "Get up, Jeremiah, they're coming."

He awkwardly put on his coat as he followed Adam to the door. The young radio operator was still by his instruments, but Amos and Miriam were gone. He found them outside, sheltering from the rain under the narrow slanting overhang of corrugated iron that surrounded the building. He ran his fingers over the bristle on his face. His mouth was thick and sticky. The rain had turned to a drizzle, and the approaching dawn had painted the low clouds a murky gray.

In the middle of the vast courtyard, two soldiers were lighting flares that spewed thick yellow smoke. And then, flying low, the first chopper emerged from behind the dark Lebanese hills. The big Sikorsky S-58 landed neatly in the middle of the courtyard. The first to alight was Rami Levin. In his right hand he held a package, hastily wrapped in brown paper. He stopped by the open hatch and shouted something at the soldiers in the helicopter, then turned and walked with his quick, long strides to meet Peled and Adam. His face was gaunt, gloomy, and he looked at Peled with open hostility.

"We got there all right," he said, indifferent to the rain drops that were splashing on his face. "But your volunteers were not in Saida. They had already left, twenty-four hours ago. All we found were some papers." He thrust the package into Peled's hands.

Peled tilted his head, contemplating the bundle and weighing the information. "Well, that's also news . . ." he started.

"But the Fatah batallion was there," Levin muttered furiously, turning back to the helicopter. The soldiers were silently hauling out two stretchers, covered with blankets. Peled glimpsed a lock of red hair protruding from under a dirty army blanket. "We lost two men," Levin said, "a high price for your news."

He angrily kicked a stone into the thick mud. "Shit," he growled, "who the hell needed that fuckin' raid?" He abruptly zipped up his windbreaker and walked away. Miriam ran after him, waving his red beret.

63

Chapter 6

IT WAS ONE of those unique Paris dawns sung by generations
of poets. An eerie gray light softly filtered through the low
clouds, and a trembling mass of white mist formed a blanket
over the dark waters of the Seine. Then the early morning
winds gently chased the layer of mist from the river, and the
vaporous patches of fog soundlessly invaded the adjoining
streets, sticking to the centuries-old facades and hovering over
the cobblestones of the pavement, bestowing upon the city
the fleeting aura of a dream. Michael Gordon always felt a
new fascination with Paris when wandering the empty streets
in the early morning hours as the crawling brume blurred the
outward signs of modern times—cars, neon lights, television
antennas—and revived for a brief moment the spell of past
centuries. He had once met a couple of lovers, emerging from
the mist, hair disheveled, faces spent from the long night, eyes
weary yet shining with happiness. They were very young—
the boy tall, narrow-shouldered, with a trim beard and a
passionate mouth, the girl with long black hair and almond-
shaped eyes. He had turned to watch them as they walked
past him, clinging to each other, but they had dissolved into
the mist like a mirage. He had entered a small bistro and,
over a cup of strong black coffee, had composed a poem
about the Paris lovers. Back at his apartment, he had copied
the verses into his notebook of poems that he had kept in
the bottom drawer of his desk under his university papers.
Nobody knew that he was writing poetry, and he was somewhat ashamed of it, hiding his romantic streak like a guilty
secret. In the life he had chosen, his sentimentalism would be

regarded as a weakness. Last night, when he lay beside Maureen in his narrow bed, he had felt the urge to read the poem about the Paris lovers to her, knowing that she shared his passion for poetry. But finally he had decided against it. She might tell Alfred about it, and Alfred might not understand. He needed men of action, not amateur poets. Alfred might even change his mind about the mission he wanted to entrust him with.

He had left Maureen sleeping in his bed, her golden hair fanned over his pillow and a serene expression painted over her lovely features. His attraction to her had grown even stronger after the night they had spent together. He had not lied to her last night, he had wanted her since the first time he had seen her. As a matter of fact, he had become infatuated with her even before he saw her face. As he unlocked his small Renault, parked in the Rue Dauphine, and gunned it along the river banks, he let his mind wander to that summer afternoon, six months ago. He had spent a couple of hours at a corner table at the Select–Montparnasse, delighting in a bottle of cool, fragrant rosé wine and listening to Patrick's fiery discourse on the struggle of the IRA. That evening Michael was flying to Ireland for a week, and he had asked Patrick for a briefing. Patrick was a huge, brown-eyed young man, always dressed in a crumpled corduroy jeans outfit. His curly hair, unkempt beard, and clumsy manners made him look like a harmless, good-humored bear. His movements were slow, phlegmatic even, and Michael had been wondering if there was any truth in the stories about his miraculous escape from a British ambush in the very center of Belfast. Yet, when Patrick spoke, a hard expression settled on the tranquil face, and a wild fire erupted in the gentle eyes. It had taken four meetings before the Irish rebel had opened up to his newly acquired American friend. But now he spoke to him freely, describing in great detail his past operations and expounding the Irish cause with a quasi-religious fanaticism. Religious indeed, Michael reflected, for like all his comrades in the IRA, Patrick O'Donnell was a devout Catholic.

Patrick had suddenly glanced at his watch that looked tiny and toylike on his bulky wrist and had drained his glass. "Sorry, Michael, I've got to go," he said, embarrassed. "We'll talk again when you get back." As Michael threw a French bill on the table, Patrick suddenly asked, "Hey, when is your plane leaving?"

"Seven-thirty from Charles de Gaulle."

"So you still have plenty of time." The pleasant smile transformed the hairy face. "Why don't you come with me? I promised to drop by and see my sister. She's having her first rehearsal today. It's quite near, behind Saint-Sulpice."

"I didn't even know you had a sister in Paris," Michael remarked as they walked out into the stifling August afternoon.

"Didn't I tell you?" the bearlike man was moving with enormous strides, and Michael realized that his appearance of slowness was deceptive. "Actually she is my half-sister. Same father, different mothers, you know. She came here a couple of months ago. She's an artist." Michael could not tell if it was irony or respect that rang in Patrick's voice. "She is studying pantomime with Marcel Marceau." He suddenly burst out in cavernous laughter, crushing Michael's shoulder with his immense paw. "Don't worry, the princess doesn't look like me. No sir, not like me at all."

When they reached the tiny theater behind the Saint-Sulpice church, the rehearsal had already started. The theater was plunged in darkness except for the brightly illuminated stage. As they groped their way toward the front row, Michael had a first glimpse of the four figures in black body stockings performing on the bare stage. There was something strange about their heads; they were big, marble-white, faintly glowing in the darkness with an unearthly incandescence. Patrick pushed him into a seat, and Michael took a better look. The pantomime performers were wearing white masks, representing mythological gods and goddesses. The show was some sort of allegory, and the young artists were gracefully moving in a closely knit group to the musical accompaniment of a flute. A fifth figure emerged on the stage, and Patrick touched his arm. "Here she is," he whispered.

The girl's face was hidden behind a mask of Aphrodite. Her body stocking was of a different cut; held by a single strap, it left her left shoulder bare. A heavy golden-red braid escaped from under the mask and was gracefully tossed over the smooth, milky shoulder, hovering over the rising swell of her breast. She was long and lithe, and the tight fabric did not leave anything to the imagination. It even enhanced the contours of her exquisite legs, round hips, narrow waist, and high breasts struggling against the black cloth. But more than the perfection of the body, it was its movement that stirred Michael. The girl glided on the stage in sensual, feline motions that aroused him sexually and tightened his whole body in involuntary response. He was unable to follow the story that her movements tried to convey. The few other men in the audience seemed to be as fascinated by the girl as he was. Nevertheless, it occurred to him that she would never become a good mime. Like a model, a mime's body was her working tool. The attention of the viewers should focus on the story she acted, as it should on the model's dress. But the femininity this girl exuded was too strong for anybody to care about her acting.

The lights came on, and Patrick was on his feet, enthusiastically applauding. The girl saw him and came down the stage stairs to meet him, removing her mask. For a split second Michael did not want her to take it off. She seemed too good to be true; he feared that under the mask she would have a plain, ordinary face, a too big nose, or a sullen mouth. And the magic would be dispelled.

Then the mask was off, and he stared at the high cheekbones, the ripe mouth, and the sprinkle of freckles over the delicate, upturned nose. For a second he thought he discerned a hidden sadness in the smoky green eyes. Then he heard Patrick's voice, "Meet the princess, Maureen."

A tense, nervous crowd was streaming through the gates of the Gare de Lyon, jamming the entrance to the underground station, clustering around the bus stops and hurrying toward the long line of taxis. The morning wave of suburban trains had just discharged its load of commuters, coinciding with the arrival of the night express from Marseille and the *rapide* from the Riviera. The buffet was tightly packed, mostly with weary night passengers who had spent long hours in the crammed second-class compartments and were now trying to warm up with a quick *café-crème* before confronting the big metropolis.

As he pushed the glass door, Michael noticed a girl sitting

alone by the entrance. Her old suitcase, strapped with a leather belt, stood beside her. The girl seemed worried and nervously toyed with her empty coffee cup. She was rather good-looking, but her clothes were ill-fitting and quite old-fashioned. A country girl, Michael concluded, escaping the dullness of her village and heading for the glamor of Paris. But once here, at the gates of the big city, her courage had run out, and she had suddenly realized that she had nowhere to go. A dark, skinny man in his early thirties with the sharp profile of a ferret stopped by the girl and ceremoniously asked if he could share her table. She nodded shyly. The man sat down, smiling pleasantly, offered the girl a cigarette, and lit it with an expensive Dupont lighter. Michael knew that kind of a man only too well. He would sweet-talk the girl, offer to help her, find her a room, promise her a job, seduce her. Then in a couple of weeks, when she became dependent on him, force her to prostitute herself in the back streets behind the Pigalle. She'll end up a cheap whore, and her fate will be no different than that of so many inexperienced girls who got picked up daily in the railroad stations of Paris by the sleazy little pimps. Here is glamorous Paris for you, he thought sadly.

Alfred Mueller was sitting alone by a corner table with his back to the wall so that his field of vision covered both the railroad platform and the Boulevard Diderot entrances. Barely five yards to his left, overwhelmed waiters were hurrying in and out the kitchen door. As Michael made his way by the brass-topped bar toward Alfred, he remembered the first time Patrick had talked to him about undercover contact techniques. "You should always make your contacts in fairly crowded places," Patrick had stated. "Cafeterias, railway station buffets, popular restaurants are the best. Always have your back to the wall to prevent any assault from behind. You should be able to watch all the entrances simultaneously, and make sure of an escape route in case of emergency— toilet, service entrance, kitchen." As Michael, taken by Patrick's discourse, was nodding eagerly his Irish friend had bitterly smiled and said, "You learn those rules, and believe in them, and live by them. Until the day when the cops charge at you from all the entrances at the same instant, and there you are like a sitting duck with your back to the wall, and they blow your guts all over the fuckin' place." He shook his head sadly. "That's how we lost Sean Graham at Brannigan's in Belfast. The goddamn bastards have been reading the same manuals as us."

Mueller had an untouched cup of coffee in front of him. He was sitting completely still, hands flat on the table, eyes hidden behind dark glasses. He was dressed in black, as always, and in spite of the heat he had kept his coat on. Michael wondered if he was armed.

"Good morning, Alfred," he said, trying to sound cheerful. Mueller nodded but did not attempt to shake hands. "Sit down, Michael," he said softly. Michael pulled up a chair and playfully caught a passing waiter by the sleeve, "A double espresso," he ordered. "And a couple of croissants."

"Don't do that again," Alfred said in the same low voice, but it had a hissing note that sent a chill through Michael's spine. "Now you can be sure that the waiter will remember you. You should never attract attention. Don't spill your coffee, don't shout, and don't pull the waiters by their sleeves."

Michael nodded. An uncomfortable feeing made him stir uneasily in his chair. This the first time he had been alone with Alfred. He did not like him; he even feared him a little. Alfred was not like Patrick. Patrick was human. Dedicated, ruthless, ready to kill—but human all the same. Alfred was weird. A lone wolf, keeping mostly to himself, ugly, silent, secretive, cold. Nobody even knew where he came from and what he had done in the past. He would often disappear for weeks and then suddenly reemerge in a group meeting. But he was the one who called the shots, and Patrick spoke of him with admiration. He said Alfred was the best. Nobody could plan and direct a coup like Alfred did. The revolution needed people like that, Michael thought. Without them it would never win. But afterward, it was people like himself and Patrick who were going to take over to build a better society.

"You asked to join us, Michael, and we have a mission for you," Alfred said without preliminaries. "You will not be alone, of course. There will be quite a few other men taking part in this project. You'll meet some of them, not all. You know what compartmentalization is all about. You will know

69

only what is essential for you to know. That's the best way to protect our people and carry out the project successfully."

"Yes, I understand," Michael said. The waiter brought him his order, and he started absently munching the tip of a fresh croissant.

"We shall meet once again before you go, for a final briefing," Alfred continued, "but now I'll give you the main details of the plan." He paused and raised his head. Michael could not see his eyes behind the dark glasses. "The operation is going to take place in Jerusalem," he said.

It took Michael a moment to grasp the meaning of the single name. Then the blood drained from his face, and his lips blanched in fury. "What?! Are you out of your mind? Send me against my . . . "

"Don't raise your voice," Alfred hissed quickly, reaching across the table and placing his clawlike hand over Michael's. "Keep cool. I am not sending you against your people, if that's what you think. This is going to be a nonviolent operation. Do you hear me? Nonviolent. Nobody is going to be killed, nobody is going to fire a single shot."

Michael withdrew his hand and eyed Alfred sullenly.

The blond man's face remained impassive. "I know that you are Jewish, Michael. I respect your faith and your identification with your people. I will not send you to do anything against Israel. Do you trust me?"

Michael did not answer.

"But you'll agree with me that Israel practices an imperialist policy right now. You know it has unilaterally annexed Jerusalem and denies freedom to the Palestinians. You know that thousands of enlightened Israelis are opposed to that policy."

"Yes," Michael conceded despite himself. "But the PLO . . . "

"This has nothing to do with the PLO," Mueller said forcefully, and for the first time there was a note of anger in his voice. "Those PLO fanatics are murderers. We are freedom fighters. Don't you forget that!"

"I don't like it," Michael said stubbornly, but his voice was not as belligerent. He agreed with the distinction between the PLO and the real freedom fighters.

"I believe you'll change your mind if you listen to what I have to say." Alfred's voice was low again and dispassionate. "But tell me first, do you agree with me about the Palestinians? About their right to have their own homeland?"

Michael shrugged. "Yes," he admitted. "Yes, I do agree. The Jewish people cannot deny to others what has been denied to them throughout the ages."

"That's what I'm trying to say." A tight smile, rather a spasm, flashed briefly on Alfred's lips. "And because of all the past sufferings of the Jewish people, I oppose violence in the Middle East. There are places where violence is the only way—Germany, South America, Ireland. But not Israel. That nation has been bled almost to death."

Michael felt relieved. There was something sincere and even noble in Alfred's attitude. He was not as ruthless as he had seemed before. He took another bite of his croissant and sipped his espresso. The thick, bitter liquid was strong and stimulating.

"We believe," Alfred resumed, "that we can achieve a much better result with a nonviolent operation, and the impact on world opinion will be tremendous." He removed his glasses, wiped them with a paper napkin, and replaced them on the bridge of his nose. Michael caught a brief glimpse of the opaque pale eyes.

"We want to organize a peaceful march on Jerusalem by one hundred thousand Palestinians," Mueller quietly said.

For a long moment Michael did not speak. Then the meaning of Mueller's idea slowly dawned on him. "One hundred thousand Palestinians," he murmured. "God, that might turn into a bloodbath! They'll clash with the police, somebody will start shooting and . . . "

"Not if it's kept under control," Mueller countered calmly. "And not if the march is led by women and children. I don't believe that there is a single Israeli soldier who will open fire on a peaceful demonstration of unarmed civilians. And we are going to take care that they are peaceful and unarmed."

Out of the corner of his eye Michael saw the country girl who had been sitting by the entrance get up and walk out, clumsily smoothing her cheap coat on her hips. The ferret-faced pimp took her suitcase and followed her. There were fewer people in the buffet now, and the atmosphere gradually became more relaxed. Mueller took a package of cigarettes covered with a strange yellow wrapping out of his pocket and lit one of the thin cigarettes. An odd, sharp odor spread about. "What's that?" Michael asked, making a face.

"Eucalyptus leaves," Mueller said curtly. "I like them." He exhaled some thin, yellowish smoke. "Well, what do you think, Michael?"

"I think this might be a hell of a project," Michael admitted. "It would show the world that the Palestinians really want independence, and that they don't identify with terrorism."

"It's more than that," Alfred pointed out. "Just think, Michael. That march might turn out to be the mortal blow to the PLO and Black September and most of all Yasir Arafat. It would be as if the Palestinian people as a whole were standing up and proclaiming, 'We want our freedom, but we don't want violence. We don't want bloodshed, and we don't want Arafat.' "

Michael nodded earnestly. "That makes sense," he agreed.

Mueller smiled again, that crooked, twitching smile. "So you will join us?"

"Yes," Michael said firmly, "I certainly will."

"Good. Now let me give you some details." Mueller leaned over the table. "This is a huge operation, as you already said. We shall have to set up quite an organization in Jerusalem in utmost secrecy. We shall have to coordinate and direct the whole project. We already have undercover people there. I want you to know that there are quite a few Israelis working with us as well."

"You speak about secrecy," Michael remarked. "How can you possibly keep secret a project where one hundred thousand people are involved?"

"Oh, but they won't know. The idea is that they'll go on Friday morning to the mosques like they always do, all over the West Bank. The moment the prayers are over and the crowds are in the streets, our people will take over with short speeches and slogans. The crowds are always electrified when they come out of the mosques. If we are well organized, then in a matter of minutes we'll have thousands on the roads, converging on Jerusalem."

It seemed simple, and yet it was an idea of a genius. It could work. "What am I supposed to do?" Michael asked.

"You must go to Jerusalem as soon as possible."

"Next week?"

Mueller thought for a second, then nodded. "Next week will be fine."

"What will my cover be?" Michael felt singularly thrilled by the idea of going to another country with forged papers under an assumed identity.

"No cover," Mueller said. "You don't need it. On the contrary, you are Michael Gordon, an American Jew, a Zionist at heart, who is coming to spend a few months in Israel, maybe even stay there for good. You'll have two assignments. First, you should pose as an ultra-nationalist Jew and join the organization of Rabbi Kahane."

"Why?" Michael asked, frowning. Kahane was a notorious right-wing extremist. A New York Jew, he had created the Jewish Defense League, and after a long series of clashes with the law, he had immigrated to Israel. There he had become the leader of a tiny group of fanatic extremists.

"You are not supposed to ask questions," Mueller said acidly. "But I'll tell you, this time. Kahane's people are obsessed and irresponsible. They will be happy to turn the march into a bloody confrontation. We must have someone inside to warn us of any violent move they might attempt to stop the march."

"That sounds logical," Michael agreed. "And what's the second assignment?"

"I'd like you to rent a room in the Arab Quarter of the Old City. We shall need quite a few rooms and apartments all over Jerusalem to serve as observation and control posts. It's quite natural that a Kahane follower would rent a room in the Arab Quarter. They pretend it belongs to them."

Michael pursed his lips, skeptical. "Now wait a minute. How can I get a room? I don't think the Arabs over there are all that willing to rent rooms to Jews."

"Don't worry," Alfred said, pulling the sleeve of his black pullover and glancing at his watch. "A friend of ours, an

73

Arab from East Jerusalem, will get in touch with you. You'll get all the help you need."

"Okay," Michael grinned, trying to sound confident. "You've got yourself a deal."

Mueller took some five-franc coins out of his pocket. "You leave first. I'll take care of the check."

"When shall I see you?" Michael asked.

"I'll call you."

Michael remembered Alfred's call last night, when he had been in bed with Maureen. "By the way," he said, starting to stand up, "I guess I can talk to Patrick and Maureen about the project?"

"No!" Mueller snapped in sudden anger. "Not a word to anybody, do you hear me?"

"But . . . " Michael protested, "Patrick and Maureen are not anybody. They are your closest friends."

"I said not a word!" Mueller grunted vehemently and furiously crushed his cigarette in the ashtray. "They are not supposed to know."

Michael looked at him in disbelief. "I thought you always worked with Patrick. What's wrong with him, Alfred?"

"He will not participate in this operation," Mueller exploded. Michael had never seen him so furious. His hands were trembling, and he nervously chewed his lower lip. An old lady, wearing a turban, stared at them from her nearby table. "No Patrick," Mueller muttered. "No Maureen. No ka . . . " He suddenly stopped in the middle of the last word, took a deep breath, and placed his hands, palms down, on the table.

"I am sorry," he said. "You just do what I say. Go now."

"Monsieur Cavaletti," Rodrigo, the Portuguese mechanic stuck his head in the door, "we are leaving. Shall I lock the workshop?"

"No, I'll lock it myself," the old Corsican grumbled back. "And shut that door, *merde*, it's freezing." He heard the quick footsteps of the Portuguese workers splashing in the mud of the parking lot. They were laughing over something Rodrigo said in the thick accent of Algarve. Cavaletti rubbed his big red hands over the electric stove and stuck them under his armpits to get some more warmth from the lambskin vest he was wearing over his overalls. A coughing fit turned his round face more scarlet than ever. He cursed under his breath. Bloody weather, and getting worse every year. Or maybe it was his age. Although he wore long woolen underwear and two pairs of socks under his rubber boots and the hand-knit scarf that Séverine had wasted her eyes on, he still could not stand the fierce cold.

He should have retired, of course, on his sixtieth birthday. The junkyard and the night business in the toolshed were bringing in good money, and his house over Bastia had been ready for over two years. But that *bon à rien* son of his had gotten collared in Hyères with two half-pound packages of heroin, and there was nobody else to run the business till he got out of the Toulon Penitentiary. How many times had he told him, "Émile, don't touch those drugs, the risk is too big, and, anyway, we are not starving." But that good-for-nothing was after easy money and was now stuck in jail for at least three more years. The son of Boniface Cavaletti serving a sentence for drug peddling. What a shame!

It was true that his own business was not as lucrative as dope smuggling, but the risk was smaller, the income steady, and, in exchange for some good tips now and then, the cops didn't bother him more than necessary. Since he sold his first gun, a German parabellum, to a small-time gangster thirty-five years ago, he had made himself quite a name in the arms business. Most of the hit men of the Union Corse came to him for their weapons; and quite a few big shots in the Parisian underworld would visit him here, after working hours, when his hired hands were long gone to their *bidonville* slum. The place was very convenient; the big junkyard was right off the cluster of highrises on the east side of Nanterre. Anyone who wanted to visit him discreetly could leave his car in the parking lot of the apartment complex, cross the road, and walk to his small office by the gate. The toolshed was right behind. The customer could choose his gun and be off in fifteen minutes. If a bigger delivery was needed, like lately, since he had started supplying those Irish crazies with the M-16 automatic rifles, they would come late at night with a van, and the arms would be loaded and away in minutes.

That's also how he got his supplies in from a German heavy truck that smuggled them from the American base at Ramstein.

The French police did not know about the M-16s, of course. But they assumed that he dealt occasionally in small weapons, and he would often throw them a bone, some information about a suspicious character who turned up at his place looking for something unusual. Like those guys of the right-wing FANE who came to inquire about explosives. Quite young they were, stupid jerks who tried to act tough, especially the balding guy with the silk scarf who called himself "Consul" and seemed to be an aristocrat. They were eager to buy four crates of dynamite and hand grenades, enough to blow up half of Paris. Well, he asked them to come back a week later, and when they did, the police had quite a welcome committee waiting for them. Boniface Cavaletti was too clever to get mixed up with terrorists in French territory. And there was also a practical side to the whole affair. The Corsican police inspector, the son of the Widow Perrini from Ajaccio, promised him to arrange an early release for Émile.

He uncorked the bottle of calvados that stood on the side table beside his empty lunch box and took a long slug that warmed up his belly. Maybe Émile will change and settle down after he gets out, he said to himself. He had no one else to leave the business to. There were, of course, the husbands of Nicoletta and Marie-José, but he would never trust them. A good Corsican should always leave his business to his direct bloodline.

A low, menacing growl reached his ears and the German shepherd tied by the toolshed started tugging on its chain. Cavaletti frowned, got up from his armchair, and walked to the window. Somebody must be out there; otherwise Solo would have kept quiet. He cupped his hands around his eyes and stared out the window, but it was too dark to see a thing. To get to the toolshed, the man must have passed by his office, and yet he had not heard a thing. He wrapped his scarf around his throat and opened the door. A cold, damp wind was blowing outside, and he felt it immediately in his bones. The dog kept snarling and pulling on its chain. "*Qui est-ce?*" Cavaletti called.

For a second nothing moved, then a shadow detached itself from the toolshed wall. "Cavaletti?" The voice was low and cold.

"Yes. Who is it?"

"I am a friend of Cleary," the voice said. Cleary was the man who bought the M-16s for the Irish.

"Clearly? *Connais pas*," Cavaletti said, straining his eyes to see in the darkness.

"Oh yes, you know him," the voice said matter-of-factly. "Are you alone?" The stranger's French was good, but it carried a trace of a foreign accent. Another Irish lunatic, Cavaletti thought. "Yes, I am alone. Come in, it's cold out there."

The stranger walked noiselessly across the muddy lot. Cavaletti backed up and looked at him suspiciously as he appeared in the yellow rectangle cast by the open door. He saw a light flicker briefly, and the wind carried the pungent smell of a eucalyptus cigarette. The man was thin, almost skeletal, and was dressed in a black duffel coat over a black turtleneck. He wore a cheap *apache* cap, and his eyes were hidden by dark glasses. He had a repulsive, sallow face resembling a skull; his sideburns and the few strands of hair hovering over his forehead were of a yellow-blond color. He slowly walked into the office, closed the door behind him, and leaned on it. The thin lips avidly sucked on the foul-smelling cigarette.

"So, who are you?" Cavaletti asked, still on his guard.

"I told you, Cleary's friend. He'll be here next week. He will need another crate of M-16s and some R-40 hand grenades. Did you get the M-60 that you promised him?"

Cavaletti hesitated. The purchase of the M-60 machine gun was a secret, shared by him and Cleary alone. If the visitor knew about that, he must be a close friend of the Irish terrorist. On the other hand, what if Cleary had been caught with the shipment of arms? He was a tough guy, but even some of the toughest quickly collapsed under torture.

"I don't know what you're talking about," Cavaletti murmured stubbornly.

The skull-faced man kept calm. "He told me that if he has the time he will stop in Glasgow and bring you a bottle of Glenlivet. It's better than your Rémy Martin he says."

Cavaletti relaxed. When he had started doing business with Cleary, they had agreed that the brand names of Glenlivet and Rémy Martin, used in a conversation, would serve as identifying passwords. "*Bon,*" he said wearily, "so you are a friend of Cleary. What do you want? The M-60? I will have it only on Monday as I told him."

The stranger drew on his cigarette. "I came for something else," he said. "I need a sniper's rifle. A small one, easy to carry, with a telescopic sight."

"You're paying cash?" Cavaletti inquired warily.

"Yes."

The Corsican nodded. "That won't be a problem. I can get you a Winchester Special. I even have one here. A first-class weapon, very accurate. Trigger as smooth as butter. Or, if you want something smaller," he made a sucking sound with his teeth, "I can get for you the Ruger Mini-14 carbine. It's very good too. Semiautomatic, uses 5.56 cartridges like the M-16. It's less than one meter long. You can carry it in a photographer's tripod case."

The man in black shook his head. "No, I don't want that. I have something else in mind."

"Oh, do you?" Cavaletti asked, mildly irritated. "And what's that?"

The stranger dug in his pocket and handed Cavaletti a tiny photograph the size of a business card. The Corsican walked to his desk, put on his wire-rimmed glasses, and adjusted them on his nose. He peered at the photograph and grimaced in puzzlement. He had never seen anything like that before.

The photograph showed a curious firearm, something between a pistol and a rifle. To some extent it resembled the strange pistols that shot laser beams in those science-fiction movies they showed on TV. It had a nicely carved pistol handle and a pistol trigger. The short barrel made him think of a sawed-off shotgun; but the barrel was smaller and it carried an adjustable gunsight. Its most peculiar trait, though, was the oblong square butt that projected behind the pistol's handle. Cavaletti took a closer look at the photograph. "That's a bolt," he said, surprised. "A pistol with a bolt!"

"That's right," the man in black said. "Remington XP-100 bolt action pistol. Single shot with bolt action, exactly like a rifle."

"What kind of cartridge does it use?" Cavaletti frowned, intrigued.

"A Fireball .221."

The exotic name was new to him. "Never heard of it," he grunted.

"It shoots a fifty-grain bullet." The man in black spoke in a neutral tone, blurting his facts like a computer. "The muzzle velocity is two thousand six hundred fifty feet per second, faster than any other pistol cartridge."

The Corsican tried to estimate the dimensions of the strange weapon. "How long is it?" he inquired.

"Seventeen inches, which makes it about forty-two centimeters."

"So you can easily carry it in a briefcase!"

The stranger nodded. "Even when fitted with a telescopic sight," he said.

"What's the range?" Cavaletti asked, removing his glasses.

"With a telescopic sight, the effective range can be up to two hundred yards, or one hundred eighty meters."

Cavelleti nodded, impressed, and handed the photograph back to the stranger. "That sounds fascinating, Monsieur, but but I have no idea where I can get that pistol for you."

"You get your American-made weapons from the U.S. Army Base in Ramstein," his visitor said. "You have a couple of sergeants on your payroll there. Now, there's a weapons testing center in Ramstein where they have been experimenting with the XP-100 for the last ten months. They have several XP-100s there, kept in the same armory where they keep the M-60 you are going to get for Cleary." He pointed at the telephone. "Call your man there, now. Pay him as much as he wants and get me an XP-100 with a case of cartridges and a Leidor ff telescopic sight by next Tuesday."

A tiny alarm bell started ringing in the back of Cavaletti's mind. This man knew too much about his business. "Why don't you go get it yourself?" he asked tartly.

The man in black disregarded the question. "Get it for me," he repeated. "I'll pay you double what Cleary is paying you for the M-60." He took a thick roll of francs out of his pocket and handed it to Cavaletti. "That's half the money. I counted it."

As the Corsican stretched out his hand, the stranger withheld the bills for a second. "But this is an affair between you and me," he said, and the cold voice was suddenly filled with menace. "If the story leaks, I might get upset."

Cavaletti involuntarily shivered. He knew nothing about the man, yet the veiled threat sounded ominous.

"Nobody else should know about this, not even Cleary. Understood?"

Cavaletti nodded and pocketed the money. "I can't promise anything," he said cautiously, "but you can call me or come on Tuesday. I hope I'll have it for you."

"That's fine," the stranger said, "I have your phone number."

Cavaletti could not suppress his curiosity. "Why do you want a bolt action pistol?" he asked. "It's quite a risk, you know. You will not normally have time to reload. And if your first bullet doesn't do the job . . . "

A twitching, crooked smile briefly appeared on the bloodless lips. "Don't worry about that, Cavaletti. The first bullet will do the job."

He opened the door and walked out without trying to close it behind him.

Cavaletti took a few steps after him. "You didn't tell me your name," he called, almost certain that the stranger would not even bother to answer.

To his surprise the man stopped and turned back. "The name is Michael Gordon," he said. "Michael Gordon."

Chapter 7

THE MAN WHO was bound to die got up as usual at five that morning. Being deeply religious, he started his day with a morning prayer, then washed and dressed. The weather was chilly, so he slipped a sleeveless woolen cardigan over his French-cuffed white shirt. He quietly walked down the stairs and into the garden of his residence. He had always been a great nature lover and used to spend hours, sometimes days, in walks about the countryside. But since his election, that was not possible anymore. He could not spare the time for anything but a short morning stroll in the peaceful garden behind his official residence. He stopped for a moment at his favorite spot, a cluster of low shrubs beside a solitary palm tree. He knelt down and removed some dead leaves with loving care from the flower beds. The climate was mild in this part of the world and tolerated greenery and flowers even in winter. In his native country the winter cold would mercilessly smother any small plant; a palm would never survive the snow and blizzards.

On his left by the stone wall, a uniformed guard jumped to attention. He smiled at him. He still could not get used to that aspect of his public life—bodyguards and sentries everywhere, following all his moves, scanning the crowds with watchful, suspicious eyes. He had not liked it from the start; and ever since his surprising ascension to office, he had been busy destroying the wall that his subordinates were striving to build around him. On the very night of his election, while still dismayed by the unexpected outcome of the vote, he had driven incognito in an unmarked car to visit a sick friend in the hospital. And ever since his inauguration, he would not miss an opportunity to mix with the crowd, shake hands, pat children's heads, warmly kiss infants. His entourage was horror-stricken; he was exposing himself to unnecessary dangers and breaking deep-rooted traditions. But the people loved him for it.

Their first reaction to his election had been one of apprehension and reserve. His predecessor had been born in the country and was a quite obvious choice; he, on the other hand, was an outsider. He still spoke their language with an accent and was considered to be tough and conservative. That was quite true. He was a conservative, and some of his critics even called him a right-wing reactionary, belonging to another age, unfit for the twentieth century. But his eloquence, his confidence, and most of all the spontaneous empathy he created with the people soon turned the tide. His unorthodox behavior won him the support of the press. The papers wrote that he had a casual way with the media that his predecessors had totally lacked. It was true that he respected journalists and liked to chat with them on any occasion. On his first trip abroad, instead of keeping aloof and distant in his compartment like his predecessor, he had spent half an hour in the press section of the aircraft, informally talking and joking with the newsmen. When his press secretary had tried to intervene, he had tactfully ignored his nervous hints. The reporters liked his fluency in foreign languages and interest in a wide range of subjects remote from his official duties.

He had been adamant that once a week visitors to the city should be allowed to meet him and talk to him. He had won that battle, to the deep consternation of his security men. Sometimes those impromptu talks with ordinary people moved him deeply. He smiled to himself, remembering last week's chance encounter with Regina Reisenfeld, whom he had not seen for forty years. As he had walked out of his office to meet the visitors, she had called to him, "Do you remember me?" He would not have recognized her face, but he immediately recognized her clear voice. "Is that you, Yanka?" he had asked, using her nickname from their high school days. She had nodded her head, too moved to speak. He had felt tears running down his cheeks. In their youth they had played the parts of two young lovers in an amateur theater production. "What happened to you?" he had asked. "Where have you been all these years?" She told him that she had immigrated to Israel after the war and was living in Tel Aviv now, a grandmother of four. "Remember my mother?" she had asked. "She was murdered in Auschwitz." He had warmly grasped her hands, unable to control his emotion. Two days later the story of their meeting was published in the papers. The German *Bild* magazine had even used an old photograph of himself and Yanka on stage. The paper, of course, made quite a fuss about his past as an amateur actor.

There was a sudden gust of wind, and he quickly reached for his skullcap to keep it from being blown away. Yes, he had loved acting on stage when he was young. Actually, he had toyed with the idea of becoming an actor or maybe a playwright. He had even written several plays, mostly on Biblical subjects. His best play, in his eyes, had been a drama about the tragic fate of Job. When he had gone to the university, he had chosen drama and literature as his two main subjects. He was already spending entire nights in his spartan room writing poetry, while his fellow students were gorging and guzzling about town. Then the war had started, and everything had changed.

The terrible tragedy that had savagely crippled his people had affected him profoundly and made him abandon his studies and the dreams of his youth. By the end of the war, he had found his true vocation and was preparing for his new life that would bring him to this part of the world and to his present position.

A fine drizzle started to fall, and he slowly walked back into the residence, humming an old religious song to himself. He took his breakfast alone, poring over his daily schedule that had been typed by his secretary. It was going to be a very busy day. He had to receive four ambassadors by lunchtime. There were also several appointments for the afternoon, one of them with the visiting foreign minister of Luxembourg, Gaston Thorn. He expected Thorn to raise the subject of Jerusalem, which was his main preoccupation lately. He sighed. Those were the burdens of his office, and he could not escape them. On the other hand, he still had a lot of work to

83

do before his forthcoming trip to the United States. He looked forward to this trip and to his meeting with the large community of his people who had settled there.

His private secretary was waiting for him in his office. He had brought with him a thin blue file concerning the Jerusalem project. They had been working on it secretly for quite a while but had not agreed yet on the final dates.

"I have made my decision," he said without preliminaries. "We'll do it on April the seventh."

His secretary frowned. "I wanted to warn you," he said, "that this year the dates of the Jewish Passover and the Christian Easter coincide. The city will be full of pilgrims."

He shrugged. "So what? I don't mind."

His secretary smiled nervously. "I know you don't," he started with deference, "but . . . "

"No buts," he stated firmly. "April the seventh is the final date." Then he grinned and said in a milder voice, "Please, stop worrying. Everything will work out fine."

He could not know that by his decision he was signing his own death warrant.

As soon as Jeremiah entered the small restaurant, Olga hurried forward to meet him, her moonlike face beaming. She moved lightly, not without grace, in a flurry of undulating double chins over ripe breasts and generous haunches, barely restrained by the folds of her long brown dress. "Jeremiah! How good to see you!" she exclaimed, wiping her bloated hands on a white towel. The mischievous brown eyes twinkled merrily at him between layers of soft fat. "Where have you been hiding lately?"

He smiled back in embarrassment and shook her damp hand rather formally. He always felt ill at ease in the presence of women, especially when they treated him with such familiarity. Yet, it was only natural for Olga to behave that way. She had known the Peleds for more than forty years, since she had sailed to Palestine as a child aboard the same old boat that had carried Jeremiah's mother and sister; and she still remembered him as a young khaki-clad pioneer, hungrily spooning his soup in the remotest corner of her father's workers' canteen.

Even in those long gone days Olga had suspected that he

was involved in "affairs of security," although he never spoke about his work. Sometimes he would quietly disappear, and then she would read in the papers about some spectacular feat of arms carried out by the Haganah underground: the holdup of a British convoy carrying arms and ammunition, the escape of Zionist activists from a closely guarded fortress, the blasting of a Royal Navy radar station tracking Jewish refugee boats en route to the Promised Land. Olga, then barely a teenager, firmly believed that the shy, taciturn Jeremiah was up to his neck in those coups, but all her attempts to make him talk were in vain. Even today, thirty-five years later, she did not know what the small, secretive man was doing exactly; still, the deferential respect that his occasional companions manifested toward him made her suspect that he had become somebody very important. And yet, in a way, this was the same Jeremiah of old days, who liked her home-style cooking and preferred her modest restaurant to the flashy places patronized by senior officials and important businessmen. And that made her very proud.

She pretended not to notice his confusion and cheerfully led the way. "Will you be lunching alone?" she chirped and squeezed her palpitating bulk between the tables. "No," he said and awkwardly nodded to a waiter who swiftly moved aside to let him pass, almost dropping the steaming bowl of soup he was carrying on a plastic tray. "A friend will join me in a moment."

"Good," she threw over her shoulder, stepping out of the congested room into the narrow corridor. "Your table is free." That's Jeremiah all over, she thought, inwardly chuckling. No matter how important he had become, he would always be five minutes early for an appointment.

The unique advantage of Olga's restaurant, besides its food, of course, was its site. It occupied the ground floor of a small apartment house and had originally been built as an apartment. It was therefore divided into five dining rooms. The smallest one, in the back, had once served as a child's nursery and could barely contain a table for four. It suited Peled perfectly, as he could discuss sensitive matters with his guests without a curious neighbor lending an ear to their conversation. The Old Man placed his tidily folded raincoat on the chair beside him and took his usual seat in the corner opposite the window. Olga quietly drew the curtains and sailed out of the room, noting that Jeremiah seemed rather pre-occupied today. Under his clumsy politeness, she could sense the edge of contained irritation.

Irritated he was, indeed, after the prime minister's phone call in the early morning. He had expected a letter in reply to his own asking him to withdraw his resignation or at least to "reconsider it in view of our grave security situation." He knew the formula; he had used it himself more than once. Instead, the prime minister had congratulated him again for the successful outcome of Quest and had added: "I understand that your decision to resign is irrevocable. Therefore I have no choice but to accept it with deep regret." Peled's sharp instincts had quickly grasped the real meaning of those words. The prime minister was quite satisfied, maybe even relieved, to let him go. Furthermore, the prime minister had not even asked him whom would he recommend for his successor, which was disconcerting.

He was aware, of course, of Peled's preference for David Roth. But if so, how could one explain the curious item in today's evening paper? Jeremiah unfolded the paper and read again the short newspiece on the front page. "Major personnel changes are to be carried out soon in one of the institutions dealing with national security," said the lead. "Sources close to the prime minister's office indicate that a new appointment will be made at the highest echelon of the institution. The names and functions will not be disclosed for security reasons. The personnel changes will take place on Independence Day." The prime minister was moving quickly, too quickly. Perhaps he had played into his hands with his letter of resignation, Jeremiah thought. Perhaps the prime minister had no intention of appointing David Roth at all but would seize the occasion to put his own man in command of the Mossad. For a moment the arrogant face of Avizur with his sardonic grin and cold, disdainful look floated before Peled's eyes.

"Shalom, Jeremiah."

He raised his eyes and put the paper down. His lunch guest stood in front of him, his plump, swarthy face cracked by a wide grin. He wore a well-cut but not gaudy tweed suit that artfully concealed the droop of his shoulders and his considerable paunch, which Peled surveyed critically. His crisp shirt was light blue, and a finely knit woolen tie, expertly knotted, blossomed over his tight vest. "I apologize," the man said in his pleasant baritone voice, his right hand loosely fluttering over his attire, "working clothes. I came straight from a meeting with our American friends."

"Any problems?" Jeremiah quickly asked.

His guest shrugged, drawing up the chair facing Jeremiah and slowly settling down. "They are still in a state of panic, I'd say. They still don't know what to do about Iran."

"That's their own fault," Peled spoke tersely. "They should have listened to us when we warned them what was coming. If they had just done their job properly, all that mess would have been avoided. When did I first send you to Langley with that report for Congdon?"

"In June," the swarthy man promptly answered, somewhat surprised by Peled's quick flare-up.

"June," Peled repeated, "I remember the report, I signed it myself. I don't think they ever read it. They were too busy running from one congressional committee to another negotiating the status of the CIA." He made a deprecatory gesture with his hand. "Well, what's bugging them now?"

"They're worried about Saudi Arabia and Kuwait," his guest said. "They see a Khomeini in every mosque. I told them there was no immediate danger . . . yet. They were not satisfied and asked for facts. So I gave them the facts." He corrected himself. "Some facts."

Peled nodded anxiously, then leaned over the table. "All right. Now listen, Robert . . ."

They were interrupted by Olga, who discreetly stuck her head in the door. "Would you like to order now, Jeremiah?"

The Old Man nodded. "Sure. Come in, Olga. Meet Robert. He's a very close friend of mine." She smiled at the swarthy man, taking in in one look the pleasant, smooth face, the strong nose, the candid eyes, and the jet-black hair. Then her eyes fell on the big brown hands, and she almost gasped in horror as she saw the ugly pinkish scars in the place of fingernails. But Robert's broad face was relaxed, reassuring, and she scrutinized it in vain for any reflection of the terrible mental ravages so often left by torture. For there could be no doubt; it was the torturer's tongs that had pulled out the fingernails and scarred the hands of this big, gentle man. She shivered, the blood draining from her face.

"Well, Olga?" Peled was watching her closely, his half-smile frozen. She pulled herself together and quickly recited the main items on today's menu. Jeremiah ordered his favorites: a soup with kneidlach, the traditional Jewish dumplings, and Russian pirushki with sour cream. After some hesitation Robert followed suit, and Olga retreated to the kitchen.

The two men ate their soup in silence. Peled ventured a quick look at the big dark head bent over the bowl. He had noticed the horror in Olga's eyes at the sight of Robert's scars. Suddenly he felt a surge of warmth for the younger man. Warmth and deep, genuine admiration. Robert Benn was one of the bravest men he had ever met, a man with a unique kind of courage, more moral than physical. But it had taken a tragedy to prove it.

He pushed away his bowl and leaned back while Olga silently served the next course. He still remembered that sultry Passover, fifteen years ago, when he had sent Robert to Baghdad to establish a new spy network for the Mossad after the Temple Ring had been decimated. Robert was a young man then, shy and soft-spoken. He had been born in Cairo and spoke Arabic perfectly; he had been given the cover of an Egyptian lawyer, a fiery opponent to Nasser's regime. Egyptian dissidents were very popular in Iraq, as she was waging her traditional subversive war against Egypt for the leadership of the Arab world. Benn had succeeded beyond expectations: he had recruited a corrupt Iraqi pilot and convinced him to defect to Israel aboard his super-sophisticated Mig-21, hitherto a mystery to the West. The operation had been a stunning success, but Benn's cover had been blown in the process, and most members of his ring had been apprehended. Jeremiah could still recall, to the smallest detail, that nightmarish afternoon in Communications when the flashes about the arrest had started coming in. He was standing behind a middle-aged, balding radio operator, gripping the back of his chair with both hands to conceal his trembling from the four white-faced officers in the room as

the names poured from the tickers: Benn . . . Robards . . .
Fawzi . . . Hamid . . . Selima Tawil . . .

The Iraqis had dragged them to the torture chambers of
the secret police in the cellar of a grim stone building off
Huriyet Street. Selima had died under torture and Robards
had gone mad. Fawzi and Hamid were sentenced to death and
hanged in the courtyard of the Baghdad Central Prison.
Robert was sentenced to life. He was too precious a prize for
the Iraqi secret service to be done with so easily. They
continued to torture and question him for months in the
notorious Basra Prison, whose other inmates were mostly
murderers, awaiting their death sentences.

For more than a year, David Roth had worked solely on
the Benn case. Using complicities, double agents, bribery,
barter deals, he had succeeded in smuggling a message to
Robert in his prison cell. "Don't despair," the message said.
"We'll get you out." But Roth knew that Robert's liberation
was almost impossible, that sooner or later his nerves would
crack in the living hell of Basra; so he sent, besides the
tiny piece of paper, a vial of poison.

The vial was never used. For a while all contact with
Robert was lost. And then, a year later, a strange rumor
reached the sensors of the Mossad. It came from Basra.
Robert, said the rumor, had become the "gallows judge" of
the prison.

"What the hell is a 'gallows judge'?" Peled had asked,
frowning. He was standing in his old office at the former
Mossad headquarters in Jaffa. Behind him, the heavy drops
of the December rain were drumming on the window, and the
sudden gusts of wind shrieked and moaned as they sneaked
through the cracks of the rotten window frames.

Roth had helplessly motioned toward the black-eyed woman
and the little boy sitting in front of Jeremiah's desk. Some
fool in the Dependents Department had summoned Robert's
family to the Old Man's office as soon as word had come that
Robert was alive and seemingly well. As Roth frantically
signaled now, Jeremiah changed the subject and rather
abruptly sent away the woman and the child. "What, for
heaven's sake, is a 'gallows judge'?" he had repeated, seething
in anger when he was left alone with Roth.

And Roth had told him. All year round, convicted murderers and rapists were being executed on the gallows of Basra Prison. And the venal hangman had worked out a perverse scheme to earn a side income from his grisly job. According to the way he fastened the noose on the condemned man's neck, he could snap the vertebrae as soon as he pulled the rope and thus grant a quick, almost painless death; or he could make the victim writhe in horrid agony and pain for long minutes before he expired. The families of the condemned were ready to pay a heavy bribe to the executioner to spare their beloved ones the most cruel of deaths. But how could they make sure the hangman would not cheat them and would fulfill his part of the macabre bargain? That was how the position of "gallows judge" had come into being. With the complicity of the prison authorities, who also shared in the bribes, the prisoners would elect a man of integrity and rectitude from among themselves. He would become the trustee of the convict and his family. In his hands the bribe money would be deposited. And he would be called to the gallows to witness every single execution. Only after the hanging, if truly satisfied that the executioner had kept his word, would he hand over the money. And Robert Benn had become the "gallows judge" of Basra Prison.

"This is the most important position among the prisoners," Roth had added. "It means that Robert has gained the respect of prisoners and jailers alike. He is practicaly immune to any further harassment by the prison authorities."

Peled had not heard Roth's last words. A shiver ran up his spine as he visualized the gentle, timid boy he had sent on his mission two years ago, standing in the wee hours of morning by the Basra gallows, a wad of bank notes in his hand, expertly judging the hangman's morbid performances. Could he still be sane? Could he remain normal in that living hell, in that macabre function? That day Peled had vowed to get Robert out, no matter what the cost.

He tried everything. Yet, the opportunity had come only two years later when the Mossad uncovered a conspiracy by a group of officers to assassinate the president of Iraq, General Zaim. Stubbornly disregarding the advice of his colleagues, Peled had flown to London in person and met Zaim's personal counselor. He had offered him a deal: the names of the would-be assassins for the release of Robert Benn. A week later, Robert had landed at Lod Airport.

Peled was waiting for him, alone. The family had not been notified yet. The Old Man expected to meet a wreck, a man broken physically and mentally by what he had undergone. He was amazed to meet a calm, cheerful man with an easy smile, his hair still black, his manner confident. Robert looked older, more mature, he had gained some weight; but basically he had not changed. Jeremiah had felt tears choking his throat and had stood speechless in front of his subordinate. Only later, after the debriefing, after the joyful reunion of the liberated agent and his family, after the party the Mossad had thrown in his honor, did Jeremiah dare to ask him, "Robert, how did you manage? How did you . . ."

The swarthy man had grasped the unspoken question, and, just for one instant, sharp, unfathomable pain had flashed in the black eyes. His reply was puzzling. "I ate bread," Robert said. "Whole loaves of bread. I love bread, you know. I would eat for hours, every day, chew it and swallow it and repeat to myself: 'They'll get me out of here. They'll do all they can to get me out of here.' So I kept eating." He pointed at his thick waist, and the old candid smile flourished on his large face. "And here I am."

Eat bread? Peled had repeated the puzzling answer to the Mossad psychiatrist, who had nodded knowingly. By sticking to the most elementary occupation of eating, Dr. Bergmann had explained, by holding on to the bread which was something tangible, Robert had found a sort of life buoy to keep him afloat. "Like many people in a state of great tension, he found a compensation, an outlet for his anguish, in eating. He unconsciously blocked a part of his brain and banned the most disturbing thoughts from his mind. He managed to identify the hope and the food. He convinced himself," Dr. Bergmann concluded, "that as surely as the bread arrived in his cell every morning, his friends were working to save his life. Do you understand, Jeremiah?"

But Jeremiah had understood another truth. The friends, the Mossad, had become the lifeline of Robert Benn. He could not be discharged now, even with honors. For if Robert suddenly lost that support, that tower of strength that had kept him sane for so many years, he might easily crack and go under. And so, Jeremiah Peled had decided to keep him in the Mossad. Robert could no longer do undercover work; his pictures were in the files of all the Arab secret services. Therefore he had appointed him head of the Foreign-Two Department that dealt with friendly foreign agencies. In this capacity he had become Jeremiah's personal ambassador at large; in this capacity he would be employed in the Mueller case.

He suddenly became aware that Robert had finished eating and was watching him in mild puzzlement. "Would you like some more bread?" Peled asked.

"No," Robert raised his hand spontaneously, then suddenly understood the question and laughed softly. "I should have never told you about that, Jeremiah," he said good-humoredly.

Peled became his brisk old self again. "Let's talk business," he said. "Did you check on what I asked you about? Mueller?"

"Yes, I did." Robert took an envelope from his inner pocket and handed it to Jeremiah. "That's my report, but I guess you want to hear the main points."

Peled nodded.

Robert shifted his massive bulk on the straight-backed chair. "I sent the Mueller file—the television photographs and all the details we got from Beirut—to the main European services."

"What about the Americans?"

"I brought the file to Jim Nolte myself." The Defense Intelligence Agency had a representative in the Tel Aviv embassy, buried in the political section. "They checked with all the agencies—FBI, Narcotics, DIA, Langley, of course. They don't have anything on him."

"They have those computerized photo archives," Peled pointed out quickly. "He might be listed under a different name."

Robert shook his head. "They checked that too, Jeremiah. Nothing, as I said."

Peled sighed. "What about the Europeans?"

Olga appeared with a tray of strong, fragrant Russian tea. Robert waited for her to clean the table and place the cups in front of them. Before she left, she smiled warmly at him and he smiled back. "Go on," Peled urged him, suddenly irritated.

"The answers were negative. Mueller is unknown in Italy, England, Switzerland, and all the Scandinavian countries."

"Did you check with the Irish?"

"No," Robert said. "Lately there have been several leaks in Dublin. I didn't want to take the risk. If he learns that we are searching for him, he might duck under cover, and we'll never find him." He lighted a filter cigarette, disregarding the disapproving grimace of the Old Man.

"I didn't check with Spain and Portugal either for similar reasons," Robert went on, exhaling some bluish smoke. "Their services are bad, and you can never rely on their discretion." The Old Man nodded. "That left me with France and Germany."

"And they cooperated?" Peled's voice was doubtful.

"No, of course not," Robert said bitterly. "They would readily sell us to the PLO for a few barrels of oil." He paused. "The French did not outrightly refuse, though; they were more subtle."

Peled tilted his head inquisitively.

"The SDECE rerouted our request to the DST. The DST advised us to contact the police. The police transferred the file to Interpol. And Interpol said they had nothing on that particular *monsieur*."

"Nonsense," Jeremiah said angrily. "Mueller flew from Beirut directly to Paris. His ticket was in the same name as his passport. They just had to go over the disembarkation cards from last Tuesday, and they would have found him."

Robert shook his head in disagreement. "I hate to be the devil's advocate, Jeremiah, but there are two other possibilities." He leaned forward. "First, he might have booked a flight from Paris to another destination beforehand so that he would not have to go through immigration. All he would have had to do was to go to one of the airline desks in the transit lounge, show his second ticket, and proceed on his flight. He could've even made them reroute his luggage."

Peled sat still for a moment, considering. "Yes, that is a possibility," he admitted. "And what else could he have done?"

"What else? Switch identities, of course. In De Gaulle Airport it's a child's game. We do it ourselves very often. The passengers from all the flights flock to the immigration booths. There are only six of them. Nobody ever asks the passengers for their flight tickets. Mueller could have easily pocketed his German passport and gone through immigration with a second set of papers. He could have written any flight number he wished on his disembarkation card. It would take them months to trace him."

"All right," Peled said, placed a sugar cube between his teeth, and drank his tea the Russian way, sucking it through the sugar. Robert was watching him with an amused smile. "You win, Robert. Now what about the Germans. They just said *nein*?"

"Not only *nein*," Robert said morosely. "They also told us why they wouldn't cooperate."

"Did they?" Peled snapped angrily.

"Remember the *Spiegel* article three months ago? The one about our two experts who questioned the PLO terrorist in Munich?"

"But that was at the Germans' request!" Peled exploded. "Wurthmuller,"—he had some difficulty in pronouncing the name of the BND deputy director—"he asked us in person to send somebody. They needed us, not the other way round!"

Robert shrugged. "Yes, but it leaked, and they had some explaining to do, and the Arabs didn't like it. So, when I asked for help on this, they said very plainly: Sorry, we cannot cooperate."

Peled slammed his clenched fists on the table. The teacups clattered in their saucers. "The . . . " he started angrily but checked himself and brought his head down, his lips tightly compressed.

"You haven't heard the end of the story yet, Jeremiah," Robert remarked, lighting another cigarette.

Peled looked up sharply. "What do you mean?"

"What I mean is that the Germans do have a file on Alfred Mueller," Robert softly said.

For a second the Old Man sat still. "You could have said that in the first place," he said accusingly. "I don't like that kind of game. You are not on stage, and the Mossad is not a theater." His voice carried a sharp edge. "Let's have the whole story."

Benn took the reprimand quietly. "Remember Joachim Scherz?" he asked after a momentary pause. "He was once with the Zentralstelle in Ludwigsburg."

"The guy who tracked down all those Nazis? Of course I remember him. Why, we carried out quite a few operations together. But it was years ago. Wait . . . " Peled leaned back and closed his eyes. "My, he must be about sixty-five now. I thought he was retired."

"No, not yet. He works in the archives of the Bundesnachrichtendienst in Pullach now."

"He was a true friend," Peled said spontaneously.

"He still is," Robert corrected. "After I got the official refusal from the BND, I called him at home. I asked him only one question: Did they have anything on Mueller in their archives? I didn't want to ask for more; it would have been unfair."

"And the answer was . . . " Peled said impatiently.

"The answer was yes. They have a file on Alfred Mueller."

Peled nodded, then sank into a long brooding silence. Robert knew well the remote expression on his boss's face. He could almost visualize how deep down there, behind the large forehead and the sharp blue eyes, little wheels were turning and a cunning, ingenious scheme was slowly taking shape.

And then Peled laid his hands on the table with finality and looked at him. He was not angry anymore; the blue eyes were twinkling with secret amusement. "You are flying to Bonn, my boy," he said, pointing his forefinger at Robert. "You are going to get that file. And I'll tell you exactly how."

Chapter 8

MICHAEL GORDON BURIED his face in the abundant silken hair, breathing Maureen's fresh fragrance, and his lips followed the smooth curve of her neck. He felt the contour of her ear under his mouth. For a second he hesitated, then, knowing he had to say it sooner or later, he murmured, "I shall have to go away next week. For quite a while."

He felt her stiffen, then she slowly disengaged from his embrace, backed off, and looked at him. The gentle winter wind played with her hair, blowing thin golden streaks across her face. It was a Sunday morning, and the Luxembourg Park was almost deserted. Only one other couple of lovers was strolling by the low shrubs, the girl's blissful face offered in abandon to the man's caress. An old lady in black was sitting in an iron chair, and plump Paris pigeons flocked around her, drawn by the handfuls of seeds she scattered at her feet. By the still pond, a young mother was laughing softly as her small boy repeatedly tried to shove his toy sailboat away from the shore.

"You are going away?" There was pain and surprise in the green eyes. "Where, Michael?"

He shifted uneasily and took her by the shoulders. "Let's sit down, Maureen." There was a bench beside them, painted light green.

"No," she tossed her hair and nervously brushed the loose strands off her face. "Where are you going?" she repeated.

He drew a deep breath. "I have to go," he said vaguely, looking away. "But I'll be back in a couple of months, I guess."

Maureen was silent for a moment, her eyes riveted to his face. "It's Alfred Mueller, isn't it?" she whispered at last.

He tried to evade the question. "What do you mean?"

"It's Alfred Mueller." It was not a question any more. "He called you that night and asked to meet you, and now he is sending you away."

There was no use lying. "Yes," he said, looking straight into her eyes. "Alfred asked me to participate in an operation of his group, and I accepted. Gladly. Anything wrong with that?"

She shook her head. Her lips were trembling. "No. That's what you wanted, Michael, isn't it?"

As he looked down at her, a strange lump suddenly materialized in his throat. "I guess so, yes." he muttered.

She brushed her hair off her face again, holding it with her right hand. A lock fell on her sleeve, forming a red-gold pattern on the coarse blue fabric. Her voice was low, almost inaudible. "Where will you be, Michael?"

"I am not supposed to tell anybody." He averted his eyes. The boy by the pond was clumsily jumping about and giggled loudly as his tiny fist plunged into the water, splashing silvery drops on his clothes and face.

Maureen followed Michael's look, then turned to face him again. She sounded surprised. "You are not supposed to tell anybody? But you can tell me. Patrick keeps no secrets from me."

"Well," he did not know how to put it. "You see, Patrick is not in on this either," he blurted.

She tilted her head and looked at him in bafflement. "I don't understand. Are you telling me that you are to take part in a project that Patrick doesn't know of? Is that what you're saying?"

He sighed miserably. "Oh, Maureen, for God's sake. Don't make it harder for me, please. I told you already how much I want to take part in Alfred's struggle. Finally I've got my chance. I was accepted, do you understand?" His voice grew more passionate, more heated as he talked. "Do you see what it means to me? I was told not to divulge anything to anybody. That's what I'm trying to do. If I tell you anything, I might blow my chance. Why don't you stop this interrogation?"

Her face still puzzled, she started to say something, then changed her mind and lowered her eyes. "I'm sorry," she finally spoke without looking at him. "I guess I got too sentimental about the whole thing. I told you that I had loved only one man before you. His name was Kevin Leamas. He was Irish, what they call a freedom fighter. He was killed in Belfast. Since he died," she swallowed, desperately fighting the tears that choked her, "there has been no man in my life. Until you, Michael. And I don't want to lose you like I lost him." She raised her face. Her eyes were flooded. "When you come back from your revolution, look me up, okay?" She suddenly turned and ran down the white gravel alley.

Michael remained motionless for a moment, absorbing the impact of Maureen's words. Then he came back to his senses and darted after the lonely figure, as she merged with the crowd on the Boulevard Saint-Michel.

On his right, the small boy was bitterly sobbing. His ship had finally sailed away, but a sudden gust of wind had overturned it, and it lay on its side in the middle of the pond, slowly sinking. "I lost it!" the child was crying in French. "It's gone away, I lost it!"

"Something's wrong," she kept repeating to herself as she ran down the boulevard to the corner where she had parked her motorbike. She was angry at herself, at her tears, at her sentimental outburst that prevented her from thinking clearly. Something was wrong, otherwise, how come Patrick didn't tell her anything? Or perhaps Mueller was indeed preparing a private operation and had approached Michael secretly without telling Patrick? It was amazing. He had never done that before, at least since he and Patrick had started working together. But maybe he had, and Patrick simply didn't know about it? As a matter of fact, what *did* Patrick know about Mueller? Where did that weird man come from? Where did he live, where did he vanish to so often?

She kicked her motorbike to life and darted up the uneven pavement of the Rue Soufflot. The crisp February wind cooled her flushed face, touseled her hair, and swiftly dried the stinging wetness on her cheeks. It made her feel better. Before her the Corinthian columns of the Pantheon rose in their stern splendor, crowned by the looming dome of the huge monument. She rode around the cruciform temple, squeezing between an old blue Peugeot and a Cityrama tourist bus, and turned into the narrow Rue de Clovis. On the corner, a red-faced woman, wrapped in a black shawl, was roasting chestnuts on a portable stove and packing them in small brown paper bags. As she saw Maureen approaching, she called without much hope, "*Chauds, les marrons!*" then shrugged and returned to her stove.

Patrick O'Donnell lived in a tiny ground-floor apartment in the Rue Mouffetard, the famous market street of the fifth arrondissement. His two rooms were unheated, damp, and dark. The noise of the busy market would wake him at dawn and would not fade away before nightfall. In summer, the stench from the garbage cans in the backyard was unbearable, and the oversexed cats of the fat, sloppy concierge would moan amorously under his windows. Still, the drab lodging suited Patrick perfectly. The house had two exits, which could be very useful in case of a police raid. Barely three blocks away, Ilich Ramirez Sanchez, better known as Carlos, had earned his bloody notoriety in 1975 when he shot his way out over the bodies of an Arab informer and two French police officers. Patrick often used to say that if Carlos had been living in his apartment, he could have slipped away quietly and disappeared. True, he might not have become a terrorist celebrity overnight; but then, he would not have to run for his life like a hunted animal for the rest of his days.

In his Paris exile, Patrick had established a clandestine liaison office between the IRA and other revolutionary organizations in Europe. He would meet almost daily with messengers from the Italian Brigate Rosse, the German RAF, and the Basque separatists. His efforts to establish working ties with the Swiss radicals, who had lately sacked the center of Zurich, had failed so far. On the other hand, he had succeeded in forging an alliance with the distant cousins of his people, the French Bretons. The Bretons were now busy collecting money and had established a whole network of safe houses in France for the use of the IRA. There was also some talk about stealing arms from the French Army arsenal in Brest and smuggling them to Ulster aboard fishing boats based in Saint-Malo.

Patrick used to spend most of the day in his flat, so his visitors could slip in unnoticed, using the protective cover of the crowded street. In the evenings or on Sundays when the street cleared and strangers became conspicuous, he would shift his headquarters to the busy Café des Amis off the Pantheon square. It was there that Maureen found him, sipping a late-morning anisette with another Irish exile, a middle-aged man with greasy hair and an acne-pitted face. "You'd better split now, Liam," Patrick said softly as he saw the distressed face of his half-sister. He worshipped Maureen for her beauty and her talent; deep in his heart he felt a gnawing remorse for having dragged her into a world of cruelty and bereavement. He had come to realize, albeit too late, that she should have been spared all that, despite being an O'Donnell.

The O'Donnells were something of a legend in Ulster. Generation after generation of Irishmen would resent them for their vanity, envy them for their wealth, yet admire them for their stubborn, defiant struggle against the Brits. The O'Donnells had made their fortune the ugly way, by exploiting their own. Many a poor peasant had worked himself to death in their fields, many a hapless colleen had destroyed her eyesight sewing cheap garments in their gloomy workshops. The inhabitants of Upper Kavanagh would eye with open hostility the familiar limousine crossing their tiny village en route to Kavanagh Manor, the magnificent Victorian mansion of the O'Donnells. And yet, when an O'Donnell spoke in public, fearlessly exhorting the Irish to fight for their freedom, he filled their hearts with pride. When old Ivor O'Donnell had died in a British prison as the First World War was drawing to its end, a crowd of eighty thousand walked behind his coffin. When his son, Sean O'Donnell, went underground during the Second World War, the Irish activists willingly accepted his leadership. He proved to be a daring fighter endowed with a rich imagination. It was he who contrived and directed the notorious theft of the crown jewels of the kings of England from Westminster Abbey to focus the world's attention on the plight of the Irish nation. His wife, the feverish, red-haired Margaret, did not lag behind him. She was a sharp-tongued, iron-willed lass, as good with a rifle as any Irish patriot. If it weren't for that tragic car accident at Enniskillen in which Margaret lost her life and Sean the use of his right arm and leg, he would still be leading the Ulster Republicans in their uneven battle.

Patrick was four years old when his mother died. He grew up to resemble his father—a burly, heavy man, yet swift and agile; from his mother he inherited the stubborn chin and a total, all-consuming devotion to the cause. Yet he was not a born leader like his forefathers. In vain would one seek the tough determination of the O'Donnells in his smiling eyes or in the good-humored grin that rarely deserted his moonlike face. Patrick was easy-going and cheerful, always inclined to see the funny side of things, always ready to burst into his rolling laughter. His pleasant manner was erroneously interpreted by his comrades-in-arms as a sign of weakness. Only after he had made his bones in the Ballymena ambush and showed exceptional courage during the Blue Night in Belfast were they satisfied that some real O'Donnell blood was running in his veins.

Maureen was a different story. Her mother, Deirdre, was the youngest daughter of Eoin MacMurrough, the famous poet and most outstanding apostle of nonviolence in Ulster. The slender, neurotic woman had grown up in her father's shadow, wholeheartedly embracing his principles. A lover of art and music, she kept away from politics and abhorred violence in all its forms. One could hardly imagine two more contrasting individuals than the fierce Sean O'Donnell and the gentle Deirdre MacMurrough. When they got married, two years after Margaret's death, Sean's numerous followers had been shocked and infuriated; their leader had brought an enemy into his own house. The only way they could explain the incongruous union was by the irresistible sexual attraction between those two passionate, romantic people.

The truth was that Sean and Deirdre had been in love since their early youth when they used to ride together in the thick Tullymore Woods joining their family estates. Sean had proposed to Deirdre long before he had even met Margaret, but the girl had refused, troubled by the violent streak in his character. Only after the accident had turned Sean into an invalid did Deirdre agree to marry him. She knew that he would not fight anymore, not with his shattered limbs and broken body.

His body had been broken, but not his spirit. Deirdre O'Donnell was soon to discover that, though disabled, Sean went on preaching violence and rebellion, holding secret meetings in his house with the leaders of the IRA, bringing up his son to carry on the bloody struggle which she regarded as senseless and suicidal. When her only child, Maureen, had reached the age of ten, a lively, happy little girl full of admiration for her father and her half-brother, Deirdre had panicked. She felt that she was too weak to check her husband's overwhelming influence over the girl. If the child grew up in the atmosphere of the O'Donnell house, she might become like Sean and Patrick. Deirdre had decided, and had won her point over Sean's objections, to send the girl away for several years. Maureen had been flown to America to live with a distant cousin of the MacMurroughs in Boston.

What Deirdre did not realize, though, was that Ireland looked quite different from across the ocean, glorified and idealized as she was by the Irish-Americans. The ugly reality of fratricidal strife and a grim, hopeless succession of bloody atrocities became strangely embellished and justified when it reached the shores of the New World. For the nostalgic Irishmen of Boston, Chicago, and New York, Ireland was the land of dream and beauty, of "Danny Boy" and the "Forty Shades of Green," of pride and poetry and passion, of a noble struggle against terrible injustice that made one's blood boil. And that was more than enough to turn the head of a young, romantic girl, still bearing in her memory the breathtaking beauty of the nine Glens of Antrim and the lakes of Fermanagh, still recalling the poignant verses of Angus O'Gillan and the sweet melody of "The Star of the County Down." When she finally returned to Ireland eight years later, she fell like ripe fruit into the hands of Patrick O'Donnell. Their father had died a few weeks before, but Patrick was already an active member of the Provisional IRA. His fiery rhetoric fascinated Maureen, and there was nothing that the prematurely aged

Deirdre could do about it. The unhappy woman easily recognized the familiar signs. Glancing at the flushed face and the enthralled eyes of Maureen as she listened to Patrick, Deirdre knew that she had failed. She had finally lost her daughter to the O'Donnells.

Deirdre did not notice, though, how distressed Patrick himself was by his reunion with his half-sister. Maureen had left Kavanagh Manor only a child. She had returned a strikingly attractive young woman, and Patrick soon realized that she was getting under his skin. Her virginal charm, her burgeoning womanhood triggered a response in him that he could hardly control. Before long her very physical nearness became an unbearable torture for him. Sometimes he would wander all night long in the park surrounding the mansion, afraid to confront her; at dawn, when he sneaked into his room, he would sink into erotic, incestuous dreams and would awake bathed in cold sweat.

Horrified by his feelings toward his sister, he all but pushed her into the arms of his best friend, the darkly handsome Kevin Leamas. Kevin was a passionate, sensitive boy, tall, lithe-bodied, with the burning black eyes of a poet. Born in Dungarvan in the Republic of Ireland, he had been sent to the north by his officers after three long years of underground activity and many a gunfight with Irish gardai and Special Branch men. Before coming to Belfast he had carried out several bombings in London and narrowly escaped a CID raiding party after an aborted sabotage attempt in a Liverpool shipyard. In Ulster, he had met Patrick shortly before the Ballymena ambush, and since, they had become inseparable. They had been together in the Lisburn raid, in the attack on the railroad at Coleraine; and after the Blue Night massacre Patrick had dragged his wounded friend to safety through the old sewers of Belfast.

Kevin carried about him the aura of the romantic Irish rebel, as depicted in poetry and prose. Maureen could not remain immune for long to the spell of the young hero; neither could he resist her stirring sensuality. Still, as a fervent love affair sprouted between the two young people, Patrick started having doubts about their involvement with the underground. They were too handsome not to be noticed, too outspoken not to be identified as IRA supporters. Kevin started neglecting the elementary security precautions when he was with Maureen. They both behaved with that candid confidence of young lovers all over the world, obsessed with each other, oblivious of people around them, certain that no force on earth could harm them. It did not take long for their names to join the list of CID suspects in Ulster.

Patrick also noticed the first signs of disillusionment in Maureen's attitude. As long as she served only as a courier, carrying small arms under her skirt or coded messages on flimsy paper taped to the inner sides of her thighs, her initial enthusiasm did not subside. But when she witnessed the bombing of the Orange Arms pub in Belfast and saw the bloody corpses and torn limbs scattered amid the debris, she had hastily retreated to the neighboring backyard and thrown up, her whole body shaking. She had seen cruel, senseless death for the first time in her life. When she later asked Patrick a one-worded question—"Why?"—he realized that he had been mistaken to drag her with him into his struggle, and that sooner or later she would desert them. She did not ask him any further questions in the following months, yet he read her unspoken torment in her red-rimmed eyes, in the bitter creases on both sides of her mouth, in the slight trembling of her hands. She did not join them in their operations anymore, and when Kevin was away, she would become a nervous wreck and sit for hours before the fireplace in their Belfast house, staring ahead with haunted eyes. When Kevin sneaked into the house in the wee hours of morning, she would cling to him with her whole body and hold him tight, as if she knew they were living on borrowed time. When he stole a glance at them, Patrick would feel a pang of anguish. Gradually a vague, ominous premonition settled in his heart, and his innate Irish foresight told him that tragedy was near.

Still, Kevin's fate was not sealed until six months later when he caught the attention of the Moore mob.

Even among the Protestant militants in Belfast Billy, Moore and his Butchers gang were considered despicable sadists. Former members of the outlawed Ulster Volunteer Force, Moore and his cronies had set a bloody goal for themselves: to torture and kill as many Catholics as they could. The ten members of the gang would start their evening drinking in a tavern in Shankill, a predominantly Protestant neighborhood. Later, bolstered by the liquor, most of them would pile into a black taxi that their leader had had shipped from London and set out to kill their man. At times, they would cruise the streets of Belfast at random, determined to kill any *taig*—their disdainful term for a Catholic—who would chance to cross their way. Mostly, though, they would mark well ahead a suspected member of the IRA and stalk him till an opportunity presented itself.

Billy Moore and his men left a grisly trail behind them. In an empty lot they shot a young university student, then left Billy Moore, actually a butcher, to slice his throat open and play on him with his knife. In a machine-gun attack on a Catholic pub they slayed five people before escaping in their London-style cab. Suspected IRA members were blown to pieces by rudimentary bombs. Butcher Billy Moore considered as the peak of his career the "public execution" of a purported traitor to the Protestant cause. The nineteen-year-old boy had been apprehended in a bar, tied to a chair, savagely whipped with a pistol butt, and shot in front of scores of terrorized witnesses.

Kevin Leamas was to be their fourteenth victim. On that soft, peaceful spring evening, he had come to meet Maureen in the blooming Dixon Park. The thousands of rosebuds, the pride of Belfast, were starting to open and their sweet, intoxicating scent wafted in the cool evening air. Kevin's mouth had barely caressed Maureen's parted lips when he was brutally wrenched from her arms by three men who dragged him to the sinister black car parked nearby, while two others held the hysterical, screaming girl. Her eyes wide-open with horror, she saw her lover knocked out by a vicious blow with a nail-spiked cudgel.

That was the last time she had seen Kevin alive. The next morning she identified his bullet-ridden, mutilated body in the Belfast city morgue.

The Moore butchers were apprehended by the police on Christmas Eve, thanks to the testimony of their twentieth victim, the young Gerard McLaverty, whom they had left for dead after a savage beating. They stood trial in the Royal

Court of Justice in Belfast. Most of them got life sentences. Fourteen life sentences went to Billy Moore alone, who confessed to eleven killings and three attempted assassinations. But the trial had another, unexpected consequence. During the proceedings, a witness formally identified Patrick O'Donnell, Kevin's closest friend, as an IRA officer. With half the Ulster police on his heels, Patrick managed to escape to France aboard a fishing trawler. Some months later, Maureen followed him to Paris.

She never mentioned Kevin's name in his presence again.

This Sunday morning the Café des Amis was packed with excited Parisians, clustering around the tobacco counter to place their bets for the afternoon horse races in Vincennes. Maureen made her way through the crowd, exchanging quick smiles with Liam Higgins, Patrick's companion, who vacated his seat and slowly moved toward the exit. Patrick got up and kissed her cheek. "You've been crying," he said uneasily. He still felt embarrassed in Maureen's presence.

She nodded sullenly and sat down, opening her coat. The sight of her young breasts, molded by her tight sweater, troubled him, and he lowered his eyes. He was still desperately, hopelessly in love with her. She lit a cigarette with short, nervous gestures, wasting several matches. "Patrick, I . . . " she hesitated, "I just saw Michael."

He tried to behave casually. He had called her several times the night she had dined with his American friend. Since she had not picked up the phone, he had understood. "Yes, how is he?"

She looked at him closely, "Tell me the truth, Patrick. Did you ask Mueller to let Michael participate in your next operation?"

He frowned. "Me? On the contrary . . . " he paused in midsentence to let the waiter take Maureen's order. "On the contrary, I advised him against it. Frankly, Maureen, I like Michael very much, but I don't think he is our kind of man. I told Mueller not to involve him." He ran his fingers across his bushy beard. "Don't tell Michael," he added hastily.

He read a deep concern in the clouded green eyes. "Do you

106

know," she asked, "that Mueller met Michael and asked him to take part in some secret project he's planning?"

The dull-faced waiter brought her a small cup of espresso, but she absently pushed it aside. "Do you know that?" she repeated.

He blinked in bewilderment. "A secret project?" He raised his eyebrows, and the furrows in his forehead grew deeper. "What kind of project?" He slowly shook his head. "Never heard of any project. Are you sure?"

"Yes, I am sure," she said furiously, raising her voice. "Patrick, you're not hiding something from me, are you? Tell me the truth, I want to know what is going on."

"Now, take it easy," he said quickly in a low voice, throwing a look around them. "I told you, I know nothing. I don't know about any secret operation, and I can't believe that Mueller has asked Michael to participate."

"Well, he has," she continued in the same heated voice. "He asked Michael to meet him last Thursday. They met at the Gare de Lyon, and he is sending Michael away next week. Michael refuses to talk about it. He only said,"—she crushed her half-smoked cigarette in the plastic ashtray—"that you are not to take part in that particular operation."

He looked at her in amazement. "Mueller told Michael that I am out of the operation?"

She nodded.

"I . . . I can't believe it," he stammered. "I am Mueller's right hand. He hasn't done anything without me, ever."

"Are you sure?" Since he did not answer immediately, she went on, speaking quickly. "Patrick, I want you to find out what Mueller has in mind. Please, talk to him. You can make him talk. I want to know what he wants from Michael."

He flared in sudden anger. "What do you want me to do? Ask him why he called Michael and not me? Tell him that my sister wants to know? Good heavens, Maureen, I'm as surprised as you, I can't understand it."

She was shaking her head impatiently. "No, Patrick, please. Talk to Mueller. Don't mention Michael or me. Just lead him on, make him talk about your next operation. Maybe he'll tell you something."

107

He shifted impatiently on his seat, but her eyes were riveted to his, and they had a beaten, almost desperate look. "Please, Patrick," she whispered, and her words sent a shiver through his spine. "I don't want to lose him. Not again."

He drew a deep breath and hesitantly reached across the table to stroke her cheek with his fingertips. "All right, princess," he said.

Chapter 9

THE EL AL BOEING 707 landed at Munich Airport barely minutes before a TWA jumbo laden with noisy Getaway vacationers. Robert Benn was lucky to pick up his lightweight suitcase and clear immigration just a few yards ahead of the stampeding Americans on their thundering way to Romantic Bavaria and Its Legendary Castles. He spotted Sammy Rosen in the arrival hall, dressed in a too long winter coat, the eternal cigarette dangling from his lips. As he waved to him, he noted that Sammy had gained some weight since he had seen him last. There was not much exercise in the functions of the chief security officer of the Israeli consulate in Munich.

They exchanged greetings. "What's new at home?" Sammy inquired. He had the unpleasant habit of speaking with his cigarette stuck in his mouth. It made him look like a Chicago gangster out of an old Hollywood movie.

Robert shrugged. "Jeremiah is on his way out, and it seems that they intend to replace him with Avizur."

"We heard some rumors about that," Sammy said gloomily. "Avizur at the head of the Mossad, can you imagine that?" He shook his head. "They must have gone nuts over there." He led Robert out to his BMW sedan that was parked in the diplomatic lot.

"And how are things here?" Benn asked.

"Bad," Sammy stated, his half-consumed cigarette freely swaying on his lower lip. He gunned the car forward and cursed as a Mercedes Spider, driven by a stunning blonde, cut across his path and roared past him. "Bad," he repeated. "They are obsessed by oil and scared of the Arabs. They won't even talk to us. Your schedule has been changed too."

Robert glanced at him sharply. "What do you mean?"

"You were supposed to meet good old Wolfgang Kruger in Pullach, right? Well, I got a phone call this morning. They were terribly sorry, but the visit to Pullach must be canceled. Something urgent has popped up, and they will be very busy. They suggested that you drive straight to the Vierjahreszeiten Hotel, and they will meet you there. Unfortunately, Herr Wolfgang Kruger is tied up, so somebody else will come talk to you."

"Who?" Robert asked, his face flushed in anger.

"They didn't give me any name," Sammy said morosely. "What do you make of it?"

"It's clear, isn't it?" Robert looked distraitly at a row of small, graceless cottages on the right side of the road. "They don't want me in Pullach. If somebody inquires later, they'll be able to confirm that no Israeli has been admitted lately to the headquarters of the BND. And they don't want me to meet their top man in the Middle Eastern Department for the same reason."

"So your visit has failed even before it started," Sammy said glumly.

Robert grimaced. "I don't know yet," he muttered. They drove in silence the rest of the way. As they made the last turn and the exquisite facade of the Vierjahreszeiten Hotel appeared before them, Sammy asked, "Should I stay, Robert?"

The swarthy man shook his head. "I'm afraid not, Sammy. Highly confidential, et cetera et cetera."

"Sure." There was no change in Sammy's face, and a new cigarette already hung on his cracked lower lip. "Just call me before you fly back and let me know if you got anything."

"I'll do that," Robert promised, gave Rosen's shoulder a friendly squeeze, and nodded at the uniformed doorman, who pompously opened the car door.

As he was signing his form at the reception desk, a little man approached him and coughed discreetly to attract his attention. Benn turned to face him. The man was in his late forties, dressed in an adequate brown suit, beige shirt, and a narrow, outmoded tie. He bowed formally, "Herr Benn?"

Robert handed the registration form to the tall Valkyrie behind the counter. "Yes?"

"May I introduce myself," the little man said. "My name is Hellmut Wegner. I am with the BND. My colleague, Herr Kruger, could not come, unfortunately, and I was asked to meet you in his place."

They shook hands. "May I see your credentials?" Benn asked politely.

"Of course. That's my ID and here is an introductory letter from Herr Kruger." As he handed the papers to Benn, Wegner noticed the ugly scars on his fingers and averted his eyes. Benn carefully examined the special card of the Bundesnachricttendienst and the handwritten letter from Wolfgang Kruger containing the routine apologies.

"Would you have a drink with me in the bar?" Wegner suggested in the same formal tone.

"With pleasure."

As they walked into the cozy half-dark room, Robert asked, "What are your functions with the BND?"

Wegner weighed the question for a long moment before answering, "I take care of foreign visitors at headquarters."

"I see," Robert said, hardly controlling his anger. They had sent him an underling, a subaltern functionary who was not even involved in secret work. He decided to carry on, though, and stick to Jeremiah's original plan.

They ordered their drinks and waited for them in an uneasy silence. As the waiter placed their whiskeys and a small bowl of roasted nuts on the table, Robert opened his attaché case. "One of our army units raided the camp at Saida in Lebanon last week," he said, taking out a brown file. "Saida is the center where the Fatah trains foreign volunteers and members of friendly terrorist organizations. The volunteers had cleared the camp twenty-four hours before our attack, but we found a bundle of interesting documents in one of the offices."

He leafed through the papers. They were handwritten in English and German. Some of them had been slightly damaged by water, and one document was sprinkled with ugly red-brown stains. Wegner did not ask what the origin of the stains was.

"Here we have a complete list of the German terrorists who have been trained in Saida in the past two years," Robert proceeded matter-of-factly. "Most of them are active members

111

of the Baader-Meinhoff gang. Here are the terrorists' individual sheets, describing the part each of them has taken in former operations, the training he—or she—has gone through in Saida, the missions he may undertake in future operations, and the date of his return to Europe. We believe that you would be interested in this material."

Wegner's face was flushed with excitement. "May I have a look?" he asked quickly.

"Sure," Benn said pleasantly and handed him the file. He leaned back and lit a cigarette, suddenly feeling more relaxed.

Wegner rapidly went through the file, his thin brows joined in concentration. "Oh yes," he eagerly said, his eyes still riveted to the last report in the file, "we are definitely interested in this information."

"Good," Robert Benn said and gently took the file from Wegner's hands and replaced it in his attaché case. "Then all you have to do is call Wolfgang Kruger at headquarters and ask him to come see me as soon as he can with the personal file of Alfred Mueller."

Wolfgang Kruger was a tall, lanky man in his early fifties. His face was ruggedly handsome with a strong jaw, a straight nose, and a pair of sharp blue eyes. His dark blond hair, turning gray at the temples, contributed to his distinguished looks. He was impeccably dressed in a pinstriped charcoal suit. He slowly rose from the corner armchair in Robert's hotel room where he had been reading the Saida papers.

"Sorry, Robert," he said quietly. "We don't have a deal."

Benn looked at him in amazement. They were facing each other across the large double bed. "Are you trying to tell me that you are not interested in that?" He pointed his scarred index finger at the file in Kruger's hands.

"Of course we are interested," Kruger said, tossing the papers on the bed, where they fanned irregularly on the velvet spread. He stuck his thumb in his vest pocket. "This is first-rate stuff, and we want it badly. The point is, I have no authority to make any deal with you."

"Even for . . ."

"Even for something of this importance," Kruger completed his phrase. He looked bleak.

112

For a long moment Robert looked at him without speaking. "Are things so bad?" he finally asked in a very soft, very friendly voice.

Kruger sighed. "Yes, they are." He paused, and Robert felt that an inner struggle was taking place behind the bright blue eyes. "Look, Robert, we are friends, and we have been working together for quite a while. You know exactly where my sympathies are and what I think is best for the interests of my country." He hesitated, groping for the right word. "But I have orders from higher up. We are to limit cooperation with you to the strictest minimum. The official policy of this country is to develop a close and trusting friendship with the Arab world. I personally . . ." he stopped in midsentence.

"I understand," Robert Benn said. The first stage of Peled's plan had failed, and he had to try the fallback tactics. "Well, we feel that we should continue cooperating with you, even under the present circumstances." He bent over the bed and collected the Saida documents. Then he walked around the bed and handed them to Kruger. "No deal, Wolfgang," he said gravely. "Just a one-sided gesture for old times' sake. The file is yours."

Kruger frowned, puzzled. He seemed to hesitate, then an uneasy smile slowly spread on his handsome features. "Well, thank you, Robert. I . . . I didn't expect this. Thank you very much. I'm sure that the director of the BND will be extremely grateful . . ."

"Oh, forget it," Benn said and suddenly remembered Peled criticizing his tendency for dramatics. He could not help dramatizing, but did not try to as he said in a casual voice, "By the way, I guess you've heard about the Mogadishu story."

Wolfgang raised his eyes and looked at him sideways, intrigued. "Mogadishu? What story about Mogadishu?"

Benn shrugged. "So you don't know yet. I thought that your embassy in Tel Aviv kept you informed." He lit a cigarette and continued in the same offhand manner, "Israeli television is preparing a special program about skyjack rescue operations. They call it 'From Entebbe to Mogadishu' and tell the inside story of those two rescues, which they consider the most spectacular in recent history."

"That's a fine idea," Kruger approved. "Of course, one can't compare Mogadishu to Entebbe. In Entebbe you carried out a really fantastic operation. Mogadishu was much simpler. Those Arabs hijacked the Lufthansa plane to Mogadishu; our special unit just landed there and stormed the plane. It was more or less the same pattern you used when you rescued the Sabena plane in Ben-Gurion Airport."

"That's it!" Robert exclaimed cheerfully. "That's what they're trying to show. How your rescue in Mogadishu followed the same pattern of our attack on the Sabena airliner. Of course, they also explain why; they reveal that four Mossad agents actually took part in your Mogadishu operation."

"What?!" Kruger gasped, utter amazement painted all over his face. "The Mossad agents? Who the hell told them?"

"That's why I asked if you knew already," Benn kept on amiably chattering, ignoring Kruger's outburst. "The producer of the special was very excited about it. He claims that he got his story in Germany where an Israeli reporter interviewed a retired member of your Mogadishu team. The producer, though, told us that he wanted to get the official comment of the German government and intended to get in touch with your embassy. We, of course, refused to comment. The Mossad never comments on covert operations."

Anger flushed in Kruger's blue eyes. "Stop this comedy, Robert," Kruger muttered, his features drawn. "You must be out of your minds. The participation of Mossad agents in the Mogadishu raid is a state secret. You have no right to divulge it, you know that. If that story is disclosed, it might destroy our whole relationship with the Arab world!" He paced toward the window, his back ramrod stiff, his arms rigid. "My God," he said without turning back, "I can see the headlines in the world papers: Israeli Agents Landed Secretly in Muslim Somalia, Helped Germans Kill and Capture Arab Terrorists."

"Let's not exaggerate," Robert said, trying to sound casual but feeling that he had pushed the comedy a little bit too far indeed. "The Israelis did not actively fight at Mogadishu, they were there only as advisers. That will be clearly stated in the program."

Wolfgang Kruger strived to regain some of his self-control and failed. "What's your game, Robert?" he exploded. "What are you trying to do? Compromise us? Hurt us? What is this, revenge?"

Robert Benn's smile disappeared from his face. He was not acting anymore. "No, it's not revenge, Wolfgang," he said wearily, but firmly. "It's sheer blackmail. We asked your help in something quite marginal, I'd say even unimportant. A dossier on a common terrorist who happens to be engaged in I-don't-know-what crazy scheme against Israel. You refuse obstinately because you tremble for your oil. You even avoided meeting me until I tempted you with that file. Okay then, you play the Arab card, we play the Arab card. If you help us as we ask, in exchange for the information I brought you today—there will be no television special. But if you go on treating us as lepers and selling us down the river—the special will be broadcast. And I can promise you that even in twenty years time you won't be able to convince the Arabs that there are no Israeli agents swarming behind every closed door in Pullach."

Wolfgang Kruger stood erect, his fists clenched. "You are talking like that to me?" he said in indignation. "Don't you know how I feel about this whole mess?"

Benn took a deep breath. "I know how you feel, and I appreciate it. Still, you refused to help us, even though that Mueller could be a real danger to Israel. You are obeying orders, aren't you?"

Kruger's lips blanched. The expression "obeying orders" used by Nazi officers to justify the massacres of Jews during the war was intended to hurt, and it did. For a moment, both men stood still, their eyes locked in angry challenge.

Finally Kruger sighed and his shoulders sagged. "Will you excuse me for a moment?" he asked formally. "I have to make a phone call."

"By all means," Robert Benn said. "Use my phone, I'll wait for you outside."

He stepped out and lit a cigarette. A young maid, dressed in black, hurried past him carrying a covered tray to a room at the far end of the corridor.

A couple of minutes later, Kruger opened the door. "Alfred Mueller's file will be delivered to you before midnight," he said, bowed coldly, and walked away.

* * *

115

It was not a file. It was a long computer printout that covered four pages of coarse yellow paper. Since the establishment of cooperative operational ties between the Western secret services in the early sixties, each service had its files computerized in two languages, the official language of the country where the file originated and English. Kruger had delivered both the German and English versions of the BND file to Robert Benn.

Tonight, photocopied and numbered, both versions of the Mueller file were distributed to a few Mossad department heads, who had convened at Peled's office. The select group, known as Forum One, was Peled's inner circle. A hush descended upon the spartan room as Jeremiah's closest collaborators unhurriedly studied the terrorist file.

MUELLER ALFRED-ALSO KNOWN AS HOLLANDER EGON AKA BORGSENIUS REINHARDT AKA RIELKE JOACHIM AKA SODERSTOM PER XXXXX *DATE OF BIRTH*-ESTIMATED BETWEEN 1942 AND 1947 XXXXXXXXXXXXXXXXXXXXXXXXXXXXXXXX *PLACE OF BIRTH*-UNKNOWN X POSSIBLE GERMAN ORIGIN BUT ACCORDING TO SEVERAL SOURCES BORN AND RAISED ELSEWHERE X SOURCE SCHUBERT (REPORT XW 735-21-GTT-45/77) AFFIRMS SUBJECT BORN TALLINN ESTONIA XXXXXX SOURCE HONNEGER (REPORT XL-220-001-GTT-23/78) AFFIRMS SUBJECT BORN PRAGUE CZECHOSLOVAKIA X SOURCE WAGNER (REPORT XM 1007-1107-202-GTT-08/79) REPORTS RUMORS SUBJECT BORN FINLAND (OR) POLAND (OR) NETHERLANDS XXXXXXXXXXXXXXXXXXXXXXXXXXXXXX *CRIMINAL RECORD*-NONE XXXXXXXXXXXXXXX *THUMBPRINTS ON FILE*-NONE XXXXXXXXXXXXX *PHOTOGRAPHS ON FILE*-NONE XXXXXXXXXXXX *CURRICULUM*-(FOLLOWING CURRICULUM BASED ON FRAGMENTARY REPORTS BY SOURCES SCHUBERT HONNEGER WAGNER MOZART GRIEG DEBUSSY) SUBJECT FIRST REPORTED PARIS JUNE 1968 DURING STUDENT RIOTS SAID TO BE CLOSE TO LEFTIST STUDENT LEADER DANIEL

COHN BENDIT AKA DANNY LE ROUGE/UNCON-
FIRMED X SEEN BERLIN SAID TO HAVE TAKEN
MAJOR PART STUDENT DEMONSTRATIONS 1970
SAID TO BE CLOSE STUDENT LEADER RUDY
DUTCHKE AKA RED RUDDY/UNCONFIRMED X
WHEREABOUTS UNKNOWN 1971-1974 SOURCE
SCHUBERT AFFIRMS CLOSE TIES ARAB TERROR-
ISTS IN EUROPE THAT PERIOD/UNCONFIRMED X
SOURCE MOZART REPORTS PRESENCE IN MUNICH
AUGUST SEPTEMBER 1972/UNCONFIRMED X 1974
REPORTEDLY HIGHLY ACTIVE MEMBER GANG
ANDREAS BAADER AND ULRIKE MEINHOFF
SEEN IN KARLSRUHE BONN HAMBURG FRANK-
FURT REPORTED TO HAVE TAKEN PART
MURDER CHIEF FEDERAL PROSECUTOR OF
FEDERAL REPUBLIC OF GERMANY SIEGFRIED
BUBACK IN KARLSRUHE STREET APRIL 1977/
UNCONFIRMED X REPORTED INVOLVED IN
MURDER BANKER JURGEN PONTO TOGETHER
WITH FUGITIVE SUSANNE ALBRECHT JULY
1977/UNCONFIRMED X REPORTEDLY PARTICI-
PATED TOGETHER WITH FIFTEEN OTHER TER-
RORISTS OF SO CALLED RED ARMY FACTION
IN KIDNAPPING OF INDUSTRIALIST HANNS-
MARTIN SCHLEYER AND MURDER OF HIS
BODYGUARDS AND CHAUFFEUR IN COLOGNE
SEPTEMBER 1977 AND LATER MURDER AND
TRANSPORT OF BODY OF SCHLEYER TO FRANCE/
UNCONFIRMED X SOURCE DEBUSSY AFFIRMS
SUBJECT SEEN IN PARIS ON AT LEAST EIGHT
OCCASIONS DURING 1978-1980 IN COMPANY OF
IRISH TERRORISTS MEMBERS OF IRA AND
ITALIAN MEMBERS OF RED BRIGADES XXXXXXX
QUALIFICATIONS-SUBJECT CONSIDERED HIGHLY
DANGEROUS SAID TO BE WELL TRAINED
KILLER X OPERATES SELDOM IN GROUPS
MOSTLY ALONE X SPECIALIST DECEPTION &
DIVERSIONARY TACTICS XXXXXXXXXXXXXXX
SEXUAL BEHAVIOR XXXXXXXXXXXXXXXXXXX
REPORTS CONTRADICTORY X SOURCE MOZART
REPORTS HOMOSEXUAL TENDENCIES X SOURCE

HONNEGER REPORTS SEXUAL IMPOTENCY X NO
REPORTS OF ANY LASTING INTIMATE RELATION-
SHIP WITH MALE(S) OR FEMALE(S) XXXXXXXX
PROFESSIONAL TRAINING-NO INFO XXXXXXXXX
THIS FILE HAD BEEN COMPILED WITH THE
ASSISTANCE OF THE FEDERAL REPUBLIC DOMES-
TIC INTELLIGENCE AGENCY HAMBURG OFFICE
SERVICES OF THE DIRECTOR DOCTOR HANS
JOSEF HORCHEM FILE OPPENING DATE DECEM-
BER 19 1977 XXXXXXXXXXXXXXXXXXXXXXXXX

When he finished reading the printout, Amos Hefner cast
a quick look across the room. Behind his desk Jeremiah
Peled was busy filling his small black notebook with his neat
handwriting. He always had one of those leather-bound notebooks in his pocket, and although everybody in his entourage had seen him on endless occasions scribbling reli-
giously into them, no one had ever had a chance to steal a
glimpse of their contents. Hefner had heard somebody in
Operations once hint that the black notebooks were the Old
Man's life insurance, kept to keep his enemies at safe distance. There could be no doubt indeed that there was enough
dynamite in those black books to blow the lid off the Israeli
intelligence community and the government as well. There
could be no secret in the country that had not been recorded
in Jeremiah's diaries.

At Peled's right, Mally Segev was still engrossed in the
documents, now and again checking cross-references in two
thick files she had brought over from her department. She
was not chewing a pencil tonight. Roni Amir, the Mossad
permanent representative in the U.S., had brought her a
handful of "the newest anti-smoking device" from Washington, a plastic cigarette containing some bits of menthol that
sold at drugstores for ninety-nine cents a piece. She was now
sucking at her new toy with commendable zeal.

Hefner was seated between David Roth and Rafael Avizur
and felt utterly miserable. The rumors about Peled's imminent resignation and his replacement by Avizur had thrown
the Mossad into turmoil. Roth was considered to be the
natural successor to Peled and the best possible choice for

head of the Mossad while Avizur owed his position to dirty political maneuvers. The snooty braggart, Hefner thought, glancing at Avizur's sardonic profile, how dare he worm his way into Jeremiah's position! Roth must be ready to strangle him with his bare hands.

But if Roth was furious, he did not show it. He was softly chuckling to himself as he simultaneously read both the English and German versions of the Mueller file. He was fluent in six languages, and, as a rule, would never accept a translation without comparing it with its original. Amos looked at him searchingly. "What's so funny, David?" he whispered.

"It's so typical of those Germans," Roth whispered back, grinning, "to use composers as cryptonyms for their sources. Did you notice? Mozart, Wagner, Grieg, Debussy. We wouldn't have even thought of that."

"Well, Mally?" Jeremiah's voice cracked from across the room. He had laid aside his black notebook and was leaning forward earnestly, his folded arms propped on his desk.

The pleasant face of the Fatah expert was pensive. "This file is rather vague, Jeremiah," she started slowly. "And yet . . . I checked the few dates mentioned against Salameh's file and they seem to match. Mueller is reported in Paris in May sixty-eight during the student revolt. At that time, Salameh was there too. He had set up a Palestinian stand in the court of the Sorbonne and was very active in propaganda activities on behalf of the PLO." She consulted her notes. "In 1970, Mueller was with Rudy Dutschke in Berlin." She looked up from her papers. "Salameh was in Germany as well, forming pro-Fatah cells among German left-wing students. He traveled twice to Berlin at that time." She marked another pause. "In July, sorry, in August seventy-two Mueller was sighted in Munich. That was the time when Salameh was planning and preparing for the murder of the athletes. The Olympics took place in September, as you remember."

Robert Benn, who was sitting at her left, quickly turned toward her. "After Munich there was talk of some German terrorists who helped Salameh in his operation," he said. "Remember that, Mally?"

She nodded. "There were some rumors, yes, but nothing

119

was clearly established." She turned back to Peled. "Finally, between seventy-four and seventy-nine Salameh went to Paris very frequently. He was the case officer of Hamshari, Boudia, and the other Fatah agents there." She shrugged rather apologetically. "I don't know if that amounts to anything, but it seems to me that Mueller and Salameh have been following quite similar travel patterns in Europe for more than ten years."

Peled pursed his lips and hastily jotted a few lines in his notebook. He raised his eyes and looked at David Roth, who was still comparing the two versions of the file. "What do you make of it, David?" he asked.

Roth raised his egg-shaped head, leaned back, and laid his hands on the table. He took his time before answering. "Frankly, Jeremiah, I don't make much of it," he finally said. He took the printout with his left hand and lightly tapped it with the back of his right. "This thing here looks more like a gossip column than an intelligence file." He adjusted his glasses and peered closely at the paper, quoting aloud: "Unknown . . . unknown . . . rumors . . . said to be . . . reportedly . . . unconfirmed . . . unconfirmed . . . unconfirmed . . ." He placed the report on the table and removed his glasses, performing his gesture in his characteristic slow motion. "Nothing about this Mueller has been proved; not a single shred of evidence has been confirmed."

"And what about all those murders?" Peled asked belligerently. "Don't you believe that he had a part in them?"

Roth nodded calmly. "Oh yes, I do believe. I guess he was involved in the murders. But he wasn't the brains behind the operations, we know that. He was not the main killer either, otherwise the Germans would have found out more about him. So what do we have here? A second-class terrorist, who might be a killer, like about fifty other Red Army Faction German terrorists."

Peled was restlessly moving in his chair. "That qualifies him as highly dangerous," he pointed out tersely.

Roth raised his hands, palms up. "Okay, so he might be dangerous. But how dangerous? Since Salameh's funeral, all we think about is this Mueller. Now, Jeremiah, what can he do?" As he saw Peled about to speak, he went on hastily, "I agree, I was as surprised as you when he turned up at the funeral. I read Spider's report about what he said to Arafat. But I told you then, and I tell you now, I don't believe in those theories about doomsday machines, apocalyptic revenges, small men carrying nuclear bombs in small suitcases, mad scientists with death rays, and weird biologists with vials full of deadly microbes. All that is Hollywood nonsense. So Mueller spoke to Arafat about the ultimate revenge. I don't believe in that. I don't believe that some Alfred Mueller, or any terrorist in the world, can bring about the ultimate revenge. The facts are that he was a friend of Salameh—I think Mally made that point very clear—and that he is a killer. My conclusion is that he plans a murder, with the help of a Jew."

"But . . ." Jeremiah started, an angry frown stamped on his forehead.

"Let me finish," Roth said calmly. "If he plans a murder, let's prepare to prevent a murder. But let's not exaggerate the danger. There is no person on earth whose death might be fatal to the very existence of this country. So let's bring the affair down to its proper proportions. Let's stop running around as if we were preparing for doomsday."

"I absolutely agree," a voice on Hefner's right said, and to his surprise Amos saw Avizur smiling suavely at Roth. The director of research and analysis was deliberately ignoring the unwritten rule of the Forum One meetings that nobody spoke without being recognized by the Old Man. "David is right," Avizur went on, his eyes holding Jeremiah in an overtly accusing focus. "The Mueller affair has been blown out of proportion. It has already cost us two lives in that dubious raid in Lebanon. I believe the Mossad has more urgent tasks to attend to than worrying about Mueller."

Peled's hands had clenched into white-knuckled fists. "Are you suggesting canceling the investigation of Mueller?" His voice was loud and hostile.

"No, I am not," Avizur said in the same urbane voice. "We should definitely try to find out what he intends to do and how. We should take some preventive action if we can. We should tighten the internal security measures and keep an eye on the points of entry into the country. I think that covers the subject quite adequately."

Out of the corner of his eye, Amos saw Roth's bald head nod in agreement. He noticed the perplexed look that appeared on Mally's lively features. What was going on? Was this the beginning of a new alliance between Roth and Avizur? Were they already preparing Jeremiah's departure?

Jeremiah did not even glance at Avizur and behaved as if he had not spoken at all. "I don't agree with you, David," he said to Roth, his voice thick with contained anger. "I consider Mueller as utterly dangerous. We shall redouble the efforts to find him and thwart his plan before it is too late." He swept the room with a hard, challenging look. "Any further questions?"

Nobody spoke.

"All right then. I shall personally take charge of the Mueller case." He slammed his hands on the table to indicate that the meeting was over. "Mally, could you stay? I must talk to you."

As they walked out of the room, David Roth sadly shook his head. "He is getting old, Amos," he murmured, throwing his hand over Hefner's shoulder. "For years he was obsessed with getting Salameh. Now that he's gotten him, he can't just simply step down and go away. So he found himself a new enemy. Alfred Mueller."

There was genuine sorrow in his voice, but young Hefner realized that the long, close alliance between Peled and Roth was quickly fading away.

Chapter 10

BONIFACE CAVALETTI REARRANGED the worn-out cushion on the seat of his armchair and painfully settled down behind his desk. It had rained all day long, and he felt the dampness in his very bones. He cautiously stretched his feet toward the electric stove and grimaced in pain. The damn rheumatism was back, worse than ever. His whole body was falling apart. His coughing was getting worse, and that good-for-nothing Dr. Bellanger called it chronic because he was afraid to admit that he did not know how to cure it. His last liver attack had been twice as painful as the one before, and there was also the trouble with his heart. He might kick the bucket any moment, he had told Séverine, maybe even before they could move to Bastia. Mumbling to himself, he spread the checkered napkin on the desk and laid on it a round loaf of peasant's bread, some butter, a piece of coarse garlic sausage and an overripe camembert cheese. The bottle of beaujolais that he had brought over this morning was still half-full. It was the fear of dying, of never again seeing the green hills of his native Corsica, that had made him agree so easily to that bastard Perrini's request for "another small service" before Perrini would do something for his jailed son.

He was a real bastard, Inspector Perrini was. His mother would be ashamed of him, if only Cavaletti could tell her the full story one day in Ajaccio. The Widow Perrini was a fine woman, always as faithful to her word as she had remained to the memory of her late husband, may he rest in peace. But her son could not be trusted. Didn't he promise last time, when Cavaletti delivered the band of fascist thugs to him, to help

Émile get an early parole? And yet, last Friday, here was Perrini again, hanging about the junkyard, prying in his office, opening his files, and looking into the desk drawers. It's not so easy, the son of a bitch had said, there were still problems, the prosecutor would not countersign, the prison authorities were reserved, the drug squad of the *police criminelle* threatened a scandal. . . . In short, Perrini had told him bluntly, another small service was needed before a new approach to the authorities could be made on behalf of Émile.

Cavaletti understood there was no use arguing with him. Perrini held all the aces. So he meekly gave in and told him about the creep who had ordered a sniper's gun for tonight. That man must be a hired killer, Cavaletti had knowingly confided to the inspector, and he definitely was going to get a lot of money for that single shot. His target must be somebody very important, he felt in his bones, and he was ready to swear to that on his mother's grave. That kind of man did not go for small-fry. Who knows, he had whispered conspiratorially, maybe there was a plot to assassinate the president himself. Boniface did not tell Perrini what made him think so. He had had a customer like the blond creep years ago, in 1963. He had been the same sort of man, cold, evil-looking, rather inhuman. He had sold him a Winchester Special, the same gun he had offered to the skull-faced guy. Two weeks later they had caught him on the roof of the École Militaire in Paris, lying in ambush for De Gaulle. Boniface had gone through some sleepless nights, but it turned out that he had had nothing to fear. Later he learned that they had given the assassin the third degree, but he had never told where he had gotten his weapon.

The man who had ordered the Remington XP-100 was of the same stock. He seemed to be a loner, and a tight-lipped one, not the kind who might blabber around that he had ordered an assassin's gun from Boniface Cavaletti, which meant that the risk Cavaletti ran by betraying him was not very big. He doubted that anybody would inquire about him later, and if they did—he knew nothing, absolutely nothing. He did not tell Perrini the blond man's name, of course; neither did he mention the Irish connection. Nonetheless, Perrini had been very excited and had immediately decided to set up a trap for the blond stranger.

Boniface took his Swiss folding knife out of his pocket, pressed the loaf of bread against his chest like his father used to do in their small farm over Bastia, and cut a thick slice. He spread a nice layer of butter and some slices of sausage on it and started munching slowly. "Sit down and eat," Perrini had instructed him, "so that anybody who looks through the window will see that you're having dinner. That will reassure your man."

The blond man had called shortly before noon. Cavaletti had recognized his voice as soon as he had picked up the receiver. "This is Michael Gordon," the slightly accented voice had said. "Did you get the merchandise I ordered?"

"Yes," Cavaletti had said.

"I'll be there at seven," the man had stated and had hung up abruptly.

Cavaletti had immediately dialed the direct number of Perrini's office at the Quai des Orfevres. Perrini had been delighted with the news, and his eager, thick voice had quickly poured detailed instructions over the phone. "We'll prepare a cozy welcome for your client," he had declared confidently.

Soon after dark, Perrini and half a dozen of his plainclothesmen had arrived. Two of them had hidden in the junkyard, the others had taken positions around his office and behind the toolshed. Cavaletti himself had been instructed not to leave his office. "We'll get him as soon as he gets inside the office," Perrini had said.

He glanced at the cheap oval clock hanging on the wall. It was 6:55. He suddenly remembered the impassive face of the blond man and his cold voice warning him to keep his mouth shut. "I might get upset," he had said. Cavaletti felt a sticky dampness on the palms of his hands, put the open sandwich on his napkin, and wiped his hands on his trousers. He had no appetite anymore, and the lump of half chewed food stuck in his throat. He washed it down with a long slug of beaujolais.

The phone rang. He hesitated a second, then picked up the receiver.

"*Oui?*"

"Gordon," the familiar voice said. "I cannot come tonight. I'll come tomorrow, same time."

"Now, listen . . ." he started to say, but the line was already dead.

He cursed furiously and slammed the receiver down. He slowly extracted his body from the armchair and walked to the door. "Perrini!" he shouted into the darkness outside, "Inspector Perrini!"

Quick as lightning a shadow materialized on his left. "Stop yelling," Perrini savagely hissed. "Are you out of your mind? You'll blow the whole thing, you old fool."

"Will you let me speak, *bon sang?*" Cavaletti grunted. "The guy just called. He isn't coming." He repeated word for word the short phone conversation.

Perrini cast him a suspicious glance. "Is that true, Boniface? You are not trying to fool me, are you? Because if you are . . ."

The old Corsican raised his hands in exasperation. *"Nom de Dieu, Monsieur l'Inspecteur,* you heard the telephone ringing, didn't you? And why should I lie to you?" His chin trembled. "You are the only one who can get Émile out of that mess."

Perrini watched him for another moment, then nodded. *"Ça va, ça va,"* he muttered. He whispered a few words into the tiny walkie-talkie in his right hand, and some figures detached themselves from the deep shadows and moved across the vacant lot in front of the office on their way out. "We'll be back tomorrow then, at the same time," Perrini said to the old man. "Stay in your office for another ten minutes. I don't want you to be seen with us. Then you can go." He quickly strode behind his men.

From the dark window of an empty ninth-floor apartment in the highrise across the road, Alfred Mueller watched the departing detectives with his German-made night glasses. As he saw them getting in the two unmarked cars in the nearby parking lot, he swiftly walked out of the apartment and pressed the elevator button. The taillights of the two police cars were still visible when he crossed the road and headed for Cavaletti's office. The German shepherd barked furiously, but he didn't care. As he stepped on the small concrete platform in front of the office, the door opened and Cavaletti looked out. "What, again?" he asked irritated. He had heard Solo barking and had assumed that one of the police officers was back.

Mueller was on the old man before he even recognized him. He violently shoved Cavaletti into the office and kicked the door shut behind them. As the Corsican gasped in fear, he raised his right hand and dealt him a vicious blow on the side of the neck. Cavaletti collapsed heavily on the stone floor. Mueller grabbed his sheepskin vest and dragged the Corsican to his armchair. "What . . . Why . . . ." Cavaletti mumbled, breathing shallowly, his eyes slightly glazed. Mueller hit him twice, in his soft underbelly and on his exposed face. The old man wailed in pain, and blood spurted from his smashed nose. Mueller still did not say a word. With eyes hidden behind the dark glasses, the sallow face looked impersonal, even calm. From the pocket of his duffel coat he took a spool of thin nylon cord and tied the panting Corsican to his chair, yanking his arms behind his back. He neatly moved the food and the bottle of beaujolais to the side of the desk, rolled the checkered napkin into a ball, and stuffed it in Cavaletti's mouth. For a second he paused, contemplating the results of his work, then slowly straightened up. Finally he spoke. "Where is the pistol?" he asked calmly.

Cavaletti was choking, and shrill strident sounds escaped from his chest as he fought for air. He jerked his head toward the opposite corner where a brand-new attaché case was partly visible under a few layers of dirty work clothes hanging on some nails in the wall. Perrini had told him to keep the weapon handy in the office, just in case the blond man succeeded in getting in and had to be kept busy until the police could corner him.

Mueller unhurriedly picked up the attaché case, whose black vinyl coating was scratched on the right side. The small keys were dangling from a plastic ring fastened to the handle. He put the case on the desk and unlocked it. His expression did not change, but the clawlike hands avidly sprung toward the evil-looking weapon that lay before them. The Remington XP-100 pistol rested in the middle of a tray of tan plastic foam tightly fitted into the case. The oblong gunsight, a tube that gradually expanded at both its extremities, fitted into another compartment carved in the foam. A third slot, deeper than the others, contained a round tin, stamped with a purple inscription: ".221 Fireball / 25 cartridges."

Mueller's long bony fingers gently caressed the short, dully gleaming barrel, the strange oblong butt, the old-fashioned trigger guard. They touched the crooked trigger and moved backward, following the contour of the beautifully carved grip. His right hand slowly closed on the grip and with a sudden, quick pull jerked the weapon out of its tray. Mueller grasped the gnarled knob of the steel bolt with his left thumb and forefinger and pulled it up and backward. The bolt slid back with a dry clang, exposing the gleaming chamber. The blond man carefully laid the pistol on the desk, took the cartridge tin out of its compartment, and unscrewed its top. He fed a snub-nosed cartridge into the chamber and drove the bolt into the breech, snapping it shut. He then dislodged the telescopic sight from its slot and expertly fitted its spring clips into the narrow grooves neatly chiseled along the barrel. He thoughtfully weighed the weapon on his right hand, then turned back to face the Corsican. "You didn't by any chance remove the firing pin, Cavaletti?" he asked softly and without waiting for an answer took two steps back, grasped the grip with both hands, and slowly pointed it at the old man. With his right finger he deftly adjusted the tiny knobs controlling the distance between the lenses. The round face of the half-suffocated Corsican appeared huge and grotesque in the magnifying scope, his eyes rolling in utter terror in their sockets, each tiny bead of sweat clearly outlined on his low forehead. Mueller held the pistol steady for a second, the cross hairs of the sight meeting at the bridge of Cavaletti's nose between the small, inflamed eyes. Finally he lowered the gun, unlocked the bolt, and caught the cartridge as it sprung out in his cupped hand. He rammed the bolt shut again, raised the pistol, and pulled the trigger. At the faint click he nodded in satisfaction.

He quickly removed the scope and replaced it together with the pistol and cartridges in the attaché case, which he snapped shut. He put the case by the door, then kneeled in front of Cavaletti. With neat, precise gestures, he pulled open the flaps of the sheepskin vest and unzipped the old man's coveralls, slid his hand under the nylon cord that bound the Corsican to the chair, and pulled the zipper down to the waist. He meticulously rolled up the two pullovers and undershirt of his writhing victim, revealing the pink bare belly and the lower part of the hairy chest. The Corsican, still gasping for air, watched him with horror-stricken eyes, but the blond man was too preoccupied with his strange activity to even glance at Cavaletti's face. He raised his left hand up to the level of his eyes, and his fingers deftly explored the edge of his duffel coat sleeve. They repeatedly rubbed the fabric close to the seam, and with a slow, precise motion his thumb and forefinger pulled out something long and thin that glistened with a silver gleam in the electric light. It was a slender sharp needle about seven inches long. He held it now before his eyes, repeatedly rolling it between his fingers. Cavaletti wriggled in his chair in boundless panic, his bulging eyes riveted to the evil instrument. His throat contracted in repeated spasms, frantically struggling to reject the gag, as his maddening horror strove to explode in a scream. His brain, albeit stunned, shot a message of recognition. He remembered having seen that kind of needle in a television program about Chinese acupuncture. Another convulsion of fear cramped his bowels as he felt the bony fingers crawl on his chest and suddenly stop on the left side of his rib cage, tightly pressing the skin against his bones. The blond man removed his glasses and laid them on the floor beside him. For the first time the Corsican saw the pale cold eyes as they locked with his. "You shouldn't have called Perrini," the blond man murmured, and Cavaletti felt the cold sharp tip of the needle piercing his skin.

The needle smoothly penetrated between his fifth and sixth ribs, easily progressing as Mueller continuously rolled it between his fingers. It entered the pleural cavity, tore the pericardium, and pierced the inferior left chamber of Cavaletti's madly hopping heart. Mueller ran the needle back and forth several times, piercing the pericardium again and puncturing the aorta. Cavaletti's muffled sobs turned into a raucous gurgle, and he slumped in his chair. The last thing he saw before he died was the face of the blond man barely inches from his own. The opaque eyes, suddenly bloodshot, stared at him in demented ecstasy, and a pale pointed tongue was feverishly licking the bloodless lips.

An irrepressible shudder shook Mueller's body as Cavaletti's bulk jolted for a last time and lay still. As the tremor gradually subsided, he remained immobile, breathing heavily. Then he carefully pulled the needle out of the dead man's chest. The fat and tissue quickly closed behind the needle, and only a tiny droplet of blood appeared at the point of entrance where the needle had initially broken the skin. Mueller knew that only a very thorough autopsy would detect the clot in Cavaletti's pleural cavity, and even then there would always be somebody to insist that the Corsican had died of a heart attack. Not that it made much difference, once they found that the pistol was missing.

He wiped the droplet of blood off Cavaletti's chest and rearranged his clothes. He removed the rolled napkin from the corpse's mouth and threw it on the table beside the unfinished meal; then he untied the nylon cord and stuffed it back in his pocket. The long needle was almost spotless, but he rubbed it clean against Cavaletti's trousers and adroitly inserted it into the improvised sheath in his left sleeve.

On his way out he picked up the attaché case before turning off the light.

Shortly after eight P.M., Mueller walked through the swinging doors of La Coupole, the huge world-famous Left Bank restaurant. He used the door on the extreme left that allowed him, after passing the narrow bar, to come into the restaurant from the side. By doing so, he evaded the couple of formally attired *maître d*'s standing by the main entrance and escaped the curious looks of hundreds of diners on the watch for celebrities. Many movie and television stars, outstanding painters, singers, and musicians were regular patrons of La Coupole, and every newcomer was devoured by hungry, inquisitive looks. That was an honor which Mueller could dispense with, especially tonight.

He ordered a Perrier from the deferential silver-haired bartender who stood erect in a white jacket and dark tie behind the old-fashioned bar. He paid for his drink and slowly walked toward the shoulder-high wooden partition that separated the bar from the vast dining room. On the bench to his right, a hirsute, fierce-looking young man was fondling a plump blond creature under a 1927 Picasso poster. Mueller

130

squeezed past their table and looked over the dark partition into the restaurant. The place was packed, as always, and hummed like a giant beehive. The dim memory of the drab workers' dining halls in his homeland flashed through Mueller's mind. His gaze slowly swept the restaurant. At the far end, a Welsh soccer team that had won this afternoon's game against the Paris team was shouting and singing wildly around a table laden with empty bottles. A group of young people in jeans, boots, and leather jackets merrily made their way along the aisle, heading for the discotheque downstairs. Straight ahead of Mueller, three models were gobbling their oysters, sipping champagne, and cooing in delight under the excited gaze of their escorts, a couple of impeccably dressed black officials from some undernourished African republic.

Mueller spotted Patrick at one of their usual tables, absently munching a chunk of French bread, which he was dipping in his pot of yellow mustard. He crossed the hall casually, holding his drink in his right hand, and settled in the chair facing Patrick. He slid the attaché case under the table against his right leg. *"Bonsoir,* Patrick," he said curtly. "You wanted to see me."

Patrick was used to Mueller's abruptness. *"Salut,"* he replied. Two men speaking French, even inadequately, were less conspicuous than strangers conversing in a foreign language. As for their outward appearance, La Coupole was used to shabby, extravagant artists; Mueller's black glasses and Patrick's unkempt beard rather melted in the scenery. "Will you have dinner with me?" Patrick asked. "I'm starving."

Mueller shook his head. "I'm not hungry, and I haven't got much time; you can go ahead and order. I'll just finish my drink." He lit an acrid-smelling cigarette and watched Patrick order onion soup and a pepper steak with a bottle of burgundy.

The waiter scribbled Patrick's order on his pad, tucked a copy of the slip under the ashtray, and headed for the kitchen. Mueller leaned forward over the table, scrutinizing the Irishman's face. The bulky man seemed rather high-strung tonight. He toyed nervously with his fork before speaking. "The Bretons want me to go to Brest for a while to prepare the raid on the arsenal," he said.

131

Mueller continued watching him in silence. "The thing is," Patrick went on, "that I'll have to be away from Paris for two or three weeks." He paused again, but there was still no reaction from Mueller. "Last month you told me that you have a couple of projects on the drawing board. Now, I don't want to be away when you are ready."

The waiter was back with a tray. He uncorked the bottle, and poured some wine into Patrick's glass, waiting for his nod of approval. He then filled the glass nonchalantly and served him a big bowl of onion soup, covered with a thick layer of bread crumbs and melted cheese. *"Attention, c'est chaud,"* the waiter chanted and hurried away.

Patrick uneasily plunged his spoon into the bowl. "Before deciding, I wanted to ask you if you needed me," he said without looking at Mueller. "Brest can wait, you know."

Mueller was watching him closely, and took his time before answering. "You can go to Brest," he said finally.

Patrick took a spoonful of the steaming soup. "But those projects you mentioned . . ." he started.

"There is nothing immediate." Mueller's voice was cool and reserved. He emptied his glass and poured himself some water from the carafe standing on the table. "Our instructions are to lay low for another couple of months. The French are still investigating the Bouvier affair. They seem to have quite a few descriptions, and we shouldn't run any risks now."

Patrick raised his brows in puzzlement. The Bouvier affair—the killing of Commissaire François Bouvier, the chief of the special anti-terrorist squad of the French police—had been their smoothest operation ever. They had carried it out together with two guys and a girl from Action Directe, the French extreme leftist organization. It had been planned as a retaliation for the squad's murder of Gaulnier and Pavard, two Action Directe members who had been extradited by the Italian police after being apprehended in a Brigate Rosse safe house.

The girl, a sexy little slut who had been screwing all the Action Directe male members, had succeeded in seducing Bouvier one evening as he was sipping his cognac in the Rosebud bar on the rue Delambre. Bouvier, who was a married man, had taken her to the Latin–Studios, a discreet establishment off the Boulevard Raspail, where horny businessmen

132

could sneak in quietly at any time of the day or night to enjoy the charms of their secretaries. The night clerk had given them a key without asking any unnecessary questions. The girl, Catherine, had opened and closed the curtains twice to indicate the room to her accomplices who were waiting outside.

Fifteen minutes after they had gone up the stairs, Mueller had walked into the hotel and shot the night clerk, using a gun with a silencer. Patrick and the two others had broken into Bouvier's room and pumped fourteen slugs into his naked body while Catherine squatted in a corner, huddled in a blanket she had snatched from the bed. Patrick remembered watching with fascination Bouvier's huge erection which continued to stick up from his sprawled, dead body while his blood spurted from his multiple wounds. Nobody had seen them as they came and left; and nobody could possibly have identified Catherine who had worn a wig and false eyelashes at the Rosebud. He knew about the false eyelashes from personal experience because that night the tight-assed little nympho had ended up in his bed. The killing must have turned her on for she had given one of her best performances ever, sucking, drawing, and squeezing every single drop of liquids his glands were able to provide.

"Descriptions?" he now asked Mueller skeptically. "Who the hell could have given them any descriptions? Nobody was caught, and no outsider knew that we did the job."

Mueller shrugged. "I don't know who their witnesses are," he said evenly, "but the instructions are clear, and we should comply. No operational activity in the next couple of months." He wiped his rubbery lips with his sleeve and shook his head coldly as an old woman selling cellophane-wrapped roses caught his eye. "So you can go and prepare the Brest operation as long as you keep indoors and don't take any active part in it."

Patrick slowly nodded, although now he was almost sure that Mueller was lying. "All right," he said. For a second he toyed with the idea of asking a straightforward question about Michael but decided against it. "I'll go to Brest. But if anything changes, you call me. You know how to get in touch with me."

"Of course," Mueller said. "You know that I can't do

anything without you." He gave Patrick a last long look, then rose, and took his attaché case. "Enjoy your dinner," he said and walked away.

He slowly walked out of the restaurant. The early movies had just ended, and the dozen or so cinemas on Boulevard Montparnasse were spilling their lively crowds on the sidewalk. Mueller stopped to light another cigarette and purposefully walked toward the Boulevard Raspail intersection. He did not notice the shadow that emerged from a dark porch and stealthily moved behind him. Liam Higgins, Patrick's most devoted lieutenant, had been thoroughly briefed this afternoon. As he merged with the night crowd, Higgins was determined not to let Mueller out of his sight, come what may.

The telephone was ringing when Patrick unlocked the decrepit door of his apartment. As he hurried toward his bedroom in the dark, he threw a quick glance at the luminous dial of his watch. It was barely 10:05, so it could not be Liam. They had agreed on a phone call every hour, at twenty-five minutes past the hour, starting at 10:25, as during the first two hours Liam would be too busy tailing Mueller around the city. Patrick hurled himself across the bed and groped for the phone on the night stand. *"Allo?"*

It was Liam, though. Patrick recognized his heavy brogue even before he detected the note of urgency in his voice.

"It's me." The voice was quick, the respiration shallow.

"What's wrong? Where are you?"

"At Charles de Gaulle Airport." Liam paused to catch his breath. "Our friend has just boarded a flight bound for Rome."

"Rome?" Patrick failed to digest the stunning news. "What are you talking about?"

"You heard me," Liam said tersely. "After he left you, he wandered around town for a while, taking the usual precautions, then he got in a blue Renault 16 that had been parked off Place des Ternes and drove here. He paid for his ticket in cash. His flight is boarding now and will take off at 10:20."

"Christ!" Patrick exclaimed, frantic thoughts rushing through his mind. "What name did he use?"

"I don't know," Liam said. "I didn't want to get too close to him. Before he went through immigration he left a black attaché case in a luggage locker."

Patrick remembered the attaché case. Mueller had had it with him at La Coupole. "I didn't know there were such late flights to Rome," he said. "What's that, Air France?"

"Air Afrique, flight forty-one. It's the weekly Paris–Abidjan flight with a stopover in Rome."

"What's the arrival time in Rome?"

"Eleven-fifteen. It's a fast one. A DC-10."

"Shit," Patrick cursed furiously, but a rough plan was already shaping itself in his mind. "I have to run. I'll talk to you tomorrow." He hung up and darted through the dark apartment, stumbling on a chair in the tiny living room. Out in the street he broke into a run contrary to the most elementary security rules. A running man was bound to attract attention and was easily remembered; but he had no choice. He had to make a phone call but could not do it from his apartment or from his usual hangouts. The number in Rome might be under constant surveillance, and the police could trace it to him.

He turned left on the Rue Lacepede, which emerged on the Rue Monge. That was students' territory, the huge complex of the *Faculté des Sciences* looming barely a few hundred yards to the south. The Royal Monge café was still bustling with activity, a young crowd hanging around the oval brass counter and clustering by the pinball machines. He spotted the neon sign *Téléphones et toilettes au sous-sol* and took the narrow winding staircase to the basement. There were four phone booths beside the men's room, but only one was equipped with a new automatic phone adapted to direct long-distance calls. A tall girl was standing inside, her back to him. She was talking excitedly, rolling the ends of her long black hair around the fingers of her free hand. He moved impatiently behind the glass partition, trying to get her attention. The girl turned back, smiled at him, and continued blabbering into the phone.

He suddenly remembered he didn't have enough coins. Swearing savagely under his breath, he ran back up the stairs and elbowed his way to the counter. *"Un espresso,"* he told the middle-aged, faded blond who was pouring two draft beers into big glass mugs, *"et des pièces pour le téléphone."* From experience he knew that she would not give him change if he did not order something. He handed her two ten-franc coins. She calmly nodded and turned to the espresso machine. The small cup of bitter coffee was in front of him before she even walked to the cash register. He gulped the burning liquid and scooped up the one-franc coins the blond brought back in a tiny saucer.

In the basement, the black-haired girl was just leaving the booth, and a fat, sturdy boy was about to get in.

"I was next," Patrick blurted angrily and shoved the youngster out of the way. The boy was about to protest, but took a quick look at the huge bulk of the bearlike stranger and gave up the idea. Patrick quickly fed the coins into the slot and dialed the international automatic line, the code of Italy and Rome, and finally the six digits of the private number which he knew by heart.

He got his party on the first ring. *"Pronto,"* a girl's voice said.

"Luigi, please," he said in French.

There was a pause, and then the lilting voice of his friend echoed in the receiver. "It's a long-distance call," Patrick said quickly. "Do you recognize my voice?"

"Of course," Luigi said. They quickly went through the routine of exchanging casual greetings in which the necessary passwords were included. "This is rather urgent, Luigi," Patrick said, throwing a quick look at his watch. It was 10:35. "Somebody is arriving in Rome in forty minutes, and we must know where he is going."

"How is he arriving?" Luigi asked quickly.

"By plane. To Fiumicino Airport, I guess."

The Italian let out a long whistle. "You must be crazy. Fiumicino is twenty-six kilometers from town."

"I know, I know." Beads of sweat popped out on his brow, and Patrick angrily wiped them with his sleeve. "It's really an emergency, Luigi. If we lose the guy, we'll never find him again."

"Let's see if I can send anybody. Let me think . . ."

"No!" Patrick felt his insides contract at the thought that Luigi might send somebody who knew Mueller and could later report that Patrick was tailing his best friend. "Could you go in person? Please, I need this favor very badly." Luigi, he knew for sure, had never met Mueller.

136

There was a moment of silence on the other end of the line. "Luigi? Do you hear me, Luigi?"

"Yes, yes, I hear you," the Italian lilted. "I was just try-ing to think. Okay, I'll . . ." Three soft beeps cut through Luigi's words, and Patrick feverishly fed some more coins into the slot. The line cleared. "What flight?"

"Air Afrique, flight 41." He gave him a quick but detailed description of Alfred Mueller. "You can't miss him."

"All right," Luigi said. "I'm leaving right away. Should I call you?"

"No," Patrick snapped, making a decision on the spot. "I'll be in Rome tomorrow on the first flight."

"That's fine. *Arrivederci.*"

He hung up, bathed in sweat. It was 10:39.

Barely five minutes before and two thousand miles away, a thrilled Michael Gordon had disembarked from an El Al 707 in Ben-Gurion Airport on his way to Jerusalem.

Chapter 11

A HOSTILE, LEADEN sky lay low over Rome, and shapeless patches of fog glided across the runways when the Air France Boeing 727 landed on the wet tarmac. The plane had circled over Fiumicino Airport for almost half an hour before the pilot had found an opening in the clouds enshrouding the city. Patrick crushed his empty package of Gauloises into a crumpled ball and tucked it into the pocket in front of his seat. He had been chain-smoking since the takeoff from De Gaulle, and his mouth was bitter with the taste of the strong French tobacco. He yawned, unbuckled his seat belt, and hurried toward the exit. At the plane door he blinked several times, his puffed eyes itching from lack of sleep. He had stayed awake all night, too tense to go to bed. Before boarding the flight, he had called Maureen. "I am going to Rome," he had said dryly. "Mueller flew there secretly, last night. Maybe you were right after all; he does behave strangely indeed."

His sister had sounded puzzled and worried. "Is Michael mixed up in this?" Her voice was heavy with anxiety. "He has left his apartment, and nobody knows where he is."

"I don't know," Patrick had admitted. "Mueller boarded the flight alone. But I have a hunch that Michael might be tied in to this trip. I'll call you as soon as I find out what dear Alfred is up to."

But he was not sure, not sure at all that he was doing the right thing. What if Mueller's trip had no connection to Michael Gordon? What if Mueller found out that Patrick had spied on him and chased him across Europe? Wouldn't that destroy their whole relationship?

He drew a deep breath. For once, his good-humored grin deserted his face, and the parting smile of the French hostess was not returned by the tight-lipped, bearlike man who looked at her sourly before stepping off the airplane.

Patrick went smoothly through immigration with his forged English passport in the name of Terrence Fleming and then squeezed his heavy bulk into the first available phone booth. He dialed Luigi's number, and the phone was picked up by the same girl who had answered his call from Paris the night before. They exchanged the recognition formulas. Luigi was not there, the girl said, but had left a message for him. Luigi would meet him at an espresso bar, the Tramontana, on Piazza Farnese. If Patrick did not find him there, he should wait for his phone call. The girl hinted that Luigi was on the move, but he was calling her every half-hour for messages. Under what name was the *signore* traveling? The *signore* chuckled in spite of himself. "Fleming," he said, "Terry Fleming."

He hailed a taxi and gave the address to the driver. The florid-faced Italian took in his rumpled corduroys in an expert look and sullenly nodded, as his hopes for a good tip swiftly evaporated. He gunned his cab into the huge traffic jam in the center of Rome and thirty-five minutes later unloaded his fare by the small sidewalk café. The nasty weather had driven the patrons of the open air terrace to safer havens. Patrick quickly walked past the deserted iron tables and into the espresso bar. Luigi was not there. He ordered a double espresso, which he paid for in advance, and settled down at a small side table.

He did not have to wait long. About ten minutes after his arrival, the mousy, gold-toothed owner brandished the telephone receiver and announced theatrically, *"Signore Fleming! Telephone for the signore Fleming!"*

Patrick walked slowly to the counter and took the receiver from the Italian's hand. "Terry Fleming," he said softly into the mouthpiece.

It was Luigi. "Trattoria Borghese," he whispered urgently. "Via Tunisi, opposite the entrance of the Vatican Museum." Patrick grunted in acknowledgment, hung up, and was on the sidewalk flagging a cab in a matter of seconds.

The small Fiat 127 had no meter, but Patrick was not in the mood for bargaining with the driver who demanded a flat fee of 2,500 lire. Obviously satisfied, the driver plunged into a maze of small streets and made his way to the Tiber. He crossed the muddy river by the Vittorio Emanuele Bridge, and a few minutes later Patrick walked into the Trattoria Borghese. Luigi was morosely sipping some cheap red wine at a table covered with the inevitable checkered cloth. His seat, facing the trattoria window, offered a good view of the Vatican Museum entrance.

Luigi was a tall, very skinny young man with sharp features, a hawkish nose, and prematurely graying straight hair that fell almost to his shoulders. He did not wear a tie, and his old brown jacket hung loosely on his skeletal frame. He was deeply indebted to Patrick, who had smuggled him out of Italy the previous summer when all the Italian police were looking for him in connection with the murder of Aldo Moro, the former prime minister. Since his return, four months ago, he had taken over the coordination of the urban operations of the Red Brigades, but for the time being he refrained from any direct participation in the underground *coups de main.*

He stretched out his dark-skinned hand to Patrick, his eyes still focused on the crowds of tourists clustering at the entrance of the Vatican. He glanced briefly at Patrick and without asking poured some wine into a second glass. "I hope that what you asked me to do is important," he said, resuming his intent watch of the street outside. He looked as tired as Patrick was. His eyes were bloodshot, and his creased, leathery face was unshaven.

"It's important," Patrick confirmed. "One day I'll tell you all about it. You did me a great favor last night."

Luigi nodded vaguely. "Sure." His voice was suddenly brisk and purposeful. "Your friend arrived last night as scheduled. Looks rather creepy, doesn't he? Who the hell is he?" He paused for a reaction but, getting none, smiled and went on, "First he drove around Rome, changing cabs four times. The last cab left him on the Via di Monserrato. He entered a villa with a big garden, quite isolated, on the very corner of the Piazza Farnese. By the way,"—he threw a quick but inquisitive glance at Patrick—"the house belongs to the second secretary of the Libyan embassy, Said Boupacha. Boupacha is in charge of the Fatah activity in Rome, but he's out of town right now."

Patrick nodded, puzzled. He had not suspected that the Fatah was involved in Mueller's secret project.

"I spent the whole night on the sidewalk, waiting for your friend to come out. In the morning I moved into the Tramontana. Its side windows overlook the entrance to the villa. At ten-thirty the guy came out, and we went through the same routine all over again."

"What routine?" Patrick tilted his head, cocking an eyebrow.

"Changing cabs a couple of times, in and out of buildings with several entrances. The guy is good, believe me, and he knows his way around Rome. I almost lost him twice."

"That's why I asked you to do it, why I didn't want somebody else," Patrick lied.

"We got here at about eleven-fifteen. He walked into the museum and I followed him. I kept my distance and for a while it was fine; but there was a crowd in the Etruscan rooms, and I lost him."

Patrick stiffened. "What the hell do you mean?" he fiercely muttered. "You lost him just like that?"

Luigi nodded, keeping calm. "Just like that," he said softly, snapping his fingers, his eyes still riveted to the museum entrance. "One moment he was ahead of me, the next he had vanished."

"You think he saw you?" Patrick asked quickly. The wine tasted sour in his mouth.

Luigi slowly shook his head. "No, definitely not. The man was careful, that's all. He was on his way to make contact with somebody and used all the tricks in the book."

"So what did you do?"

"The only logical thing." Luigi stretched his long arms, yawned, and rubbed his red-rimmed eyes. "I made a quick search around, and when I didn't see him anymore, I took the shortest way out. I'm sure he didn't make it out the gate ahead of me. He's still somewhere inside." He yawned again. "So, here I am, waiting for him to come out. He'll show up. Don't worry."

Patrick was seething but mastered his anger. "You tell me not to worry? We'll never know whom he met there."

Luigi was busy lighting a cheap Swiss Mecarillo. "I'm not so sure," he said. "I think he'll make at least one other contact with that guy, or the contact will lead him to a third party. We'll catch up with him all right." He cast a quick look at Patrick and, noticing his incredulous expression, went on in an explanatory tone. "Look, your friend is a very careful man, right? I'd say even extremely careful. He definitely isn't the sort of man to complete a contact on a first meeting. You know the technique. He asks for an appointment, usually by phone, at a prearranged place. Still, he has to make sure that the phone hasn't been tapped and that the other party wasn't followed. Therefore, the first contact is very brief and serves only to check security and fix a second meeting. The follow-up meeting is the important one."

Patrick watched him pensively, his right hand gently pulling his beard forward, as if trying to gather it at the edge of his chin. "And that's why you ran back out so quickly?" he inquired.

Luigi nodded in confirmation. "Your friend won't be late, believe me. He'll be out any moment now."

The Irishman drained his glass, smacking his lips. "Thank you, Luigi. Why don't you go get some sleep? I'll take over from here."

Luigi yawned again. "You sure? He might recognize you, you know. That creep is a professional."

Patrick smiled reassuringly. "Don't worry. I'm a professional too."

The thin Italian spread his bony hands, palms up, and slowly got on his feet. The glowing Mecarillo was stuck in the middle of his face. "Okay. But do me a favor. Call us at one-hour intervals if you can. I want to keep track of you. If you wish, I'll get one of the guys to replace you tonight."

Patrick nodded and stretched a hairy hand to Luigi. "That's a good idea. We might have a bite together."

"Ciao," Luigi quipped and was gone.

Patrick had barely taken his friend's seat by the window when Mueller appeared in the middle of a group of Swedish tourists emerging from the Vatican. Luigi was right, Patrick conceded, following the black-clad figure with his eyes; Mueller did look weird indeed. As he contemplated the skull-like face, the thin, clamped lips, the sickly white skin, Patrick suddenly realized that there was something utterly ruthless, inhuman, in the gaunt blond man. He put his glass on the table and walked out to the street, falling in step behind Mueller. Yet, at that very moment he knew he had made a mistake. He should have let Luigi shadow Mueller across Rome. He should not have taken over. A chilling shudder shot up his spine, as it occurred to him for the first time that he might be in danger.

For Mueller knew his face.

Mueller spotted Patrick O'Donnell barely twenty-five minutes after the chase through Rome had begun. Mueller had started his slow, deliberately tortuous journey toward the site of his follow-up rendezvous, meticulously executing the successive stages of his routine security procedure. He had changed cabs twice, on Piazza Navona and Via Veneto, then sneaked in and out a big department store off Piazza Venezia before plunging into the throngs streaming down the Corso. As he checked behind him in a shopwindow mirroring the narrow pedestrian street, he caught a brief glimpse of the familiar bearlike figure, hulking behind a party of twittering young women. He gasped, dumbfounded. Patrick was too far back to notice the short pause in Mueller's purposeful walk, the sudden stiffening of his shoulders. Only a little boy, unhappily trudging behind his mother, grimaced in fear at the sight of the sudden spasm that contorted the ugly man's face, baring his foul yellow teeth.

Mueller continued walking like an automaton as a film of cold sticky sweat formed on his forehead and wild, frantic thoughts rushed through his mind. The Irish bastard had followed him all the way from Paris. Why? Did he know something? Had Michael spilled the beans before he left for Jerusalem? But Michael knew nothing about the real project, he had only been told the cover story. Mueller furiously gnawed his lower lip. How long had the Irish son of a bitch been following him? Had he seen him with Caruzzi in the Vatican library? Was he alone, or did he have a whole team on his track?

Behind the dark glasses, his eyes darted madly, shooting frenzied glances around him. The Plan, a panicked voice screamed inside his head, the Plan, the Plan, the Irish traitor might blow the Plan! O'Donnell was trying to rob him of his final revenge, of his glorious design to crush the Jews like vermin. The bloody Irishman had to be stopped, now, at once! As if moved by an independent will, his bony fingers curved inward, and his thin hands stiffened into crooked, deadly claws, ready to close on his enemy's throat. The blood pounded in Mueller's temples, sending waves of throbbing pain through his head. He made an effort to regain control of himself. First—he tried to reason, sinking his nails in the palms of his hands—first he had to find out if the Irishman was alone. And as he managed to gradually overcome the trembling of his arms and legs, he feverishly schemed his next moves.

He forced himself to walk at a leisurely pace to the next intersection. He did not see O'Donnell anymore, but he knew he was close behind him. He let two cabs pass by and hailed the third one, a brand-new Autobianchi. "Stazione Termini," he hoarsely muttered. He threw an oblique glance at the driver's side mirror and caught a glimpse of a bulky figure entering a second cab at the intersection. The man seemed to be alone. Since nobody had stopped the first two cabs that he had let go on purpose, he could assume that there was not a front tail either, a second pursuer who moved ahead of him watching him in a rearview mirror.

The Piazza Cinquecento, the largest in Rome, was swarming with people. Crowds of commuters clustered around the terminals of the buses connecting Rome with the suburbs. The entrance of the Metropolitana, the underground, was gaping like a big black mouth, spewing out multitudes of harried Romans and peasant women laden with shopping bags. The Stazione Termini, the main railroad station, loomed stolidly on the south-east side of the square, a huge, ugly block of dirty-white stone stretching over the 250 yards that separated the Via Marsala from the Via Giovani Giolitti.

He paid the cab and walked in through the tall main gate. The place teemed like a giant beehive and droned with the incessant hum characteristic of train stations all over the world. He walked quickly by the newspaper stands and the fast food kiosks, heading for the departure platforms. The dial of the big electric clock hovering far above the tracks read 2:07 P.M. Mueller purposefully paced along the main platform, glancing sideways at the signs displaying the destinations and departure times of the next trains. Several trains were boarding, but he disregarded them, brushing aside some eager, olive-skinned vendors and avoiding the noisy families parting from a relative in a typical Italian effusion of kisses, tears, and shouts. The eleventh track seemed to be a good one. The train for Milano, Genoa, Ventimiglia, and Nizza was scheduled to depart at 3:45 but was already waiting in its place, a gigantic green metal snake, stretching still and dark between two deserted stone platforms. Mueller quickened his pace as he walked beside the train. When he reached the fourth car, he took the steps in a single jump and turned the door handle. The iron door opened smoothly and he was inside, his heavy breath the only sound in the half-darkness that enveloped him. After a moment, he moved. His steps sounded abnormally loud in the narrow corridor. He sneaked into a compartment on his left and crouched behind the open sliding door. And waited.

Patrick had watched Mueller's moves from his improvised observation post, a gaily painted sandwich stall by the main entrance that offered an adequate view of the main platforms. Munching a coarse bun stuffed with slices of mozzarella cheese and sliced green peppers, he stayed put until he saw Mueller board the Nizza train. Only then did he make his way toward Platform Eleven, cautiously walking on the far side of the concourse and using the crowd of commuters as a protective shield. He stopped behind a newsstand facing the platform and plunged into the cluster of Italians who were browsing through the paperbacks and illustrated magazines on display. He repeatedly sneaked quick glances at the deserted platform, but nobody followed Mueller into the train.

Half an hour later, nothing had changed. Platform Eleven remained deserted, except for a pair of cleaning women, who slowly walked toward the far end of the train, giggling foolishly as they swayed their brooms and empty pails.

As he watched the dark train, pretending to examine an old copy of *Playboy*, Patrick stirred uneasily. Half an hour was a long time. People did not usually wait so long for a contact in an empty place because of the danger of being accidentally discovered. And what if Mueller's contact had been the first to arrive and was already waiting when Mueller boarded the train? And what if . . . Suddenly a new thought struck him, triggering a tiny alarm bell in the back of his mind. What if Mueller had used the railroad station and the empty train merely as one more precaution to cut off any possible pursuers? Mueller might have left the empty car by the second door, then walked across the tracks and out of the station while he had been waiting here, leafing like an idiot through outdated men's magazines. He slowly closed the glossy publication and put it back on the rack. It dawned on him that he had no other choice but to go after Mueller on that train.

He quickly strode toward Platform Eleven, keeping as close as possible to the cars. The door of the third car softly creaked under his pressure, and he noiselessly climbed inside, holding his breath. He stealthily moved toward the next car, the one Mueller had entered. His rubber-soled shoes made no sound as he advanced along the corridor, flattening himself against the metal wall and glancing into each compartment before proceeding to the next. The car was empty. With utmost caution he went through the connecting doors and the tiny passageway between the cars. He was in the fourth car now, standing in the small entrance space, his back leaning on the narrow door that he had closed behind him. He tried the door of the lavatory on his right. It was locked. The car was silent as a tomb. He took a quick step toward the first compartment and chanced a glance inside. There was nobody in it. A sudden noise outside attracted his attention, and he shot a quick glance out the train window. An old porter in a faded blue uniform slowly walked up the platform, pushing a cart laden with mailbags. The cart wheels clattered on the stone pavement. This was good luck, he thought. The outside noise would drown the noise of his steps. He quickly moved forward to the second and third compartments. Empty.

The clatter outside slowly subsided. Yet it was still loud enough to cover the faint, almost inaudible, rustle behind him. He jerked his head back just a fraction of a second too late, too late to avoid the vicious chop on the exposed side of his neck. He collapsed heavily, his unprotected skull crashing against the iron wall of the car, and everything went black.

Mueller jumped him like a demented animal. His breath

came in quick, rasping bursts as he grabbed Patrick by the collar and ferociously battered his head against the wall. The prostrate Irishman did not react, stunned by the shattering blows. Panting, quivering with his whole body, Mueller smashed the huge man's head over and over again, his force redoubled by hatred, his vision blurred by a red veil. His dark glasses slipped and fell, close to Patrick's right hand stretched on the floor, fingers grotesquely splayed. He blinked in the diffuse light and let go of Patrick's shoulders. The big head rolled down and came to rest against the wall. The Irishman's eyes were closed and blood gushed from a deep cut on his forehead, trickling down over his left eyelid and painting the bushy beard red.

Shrill, whining sounds erupted from Mueller's contracted throat as he gulped air in quick spasms. With trembling fingers he felt the rim of his sleeve and pulled out the long, glistening needle. But his hands were shaking badly, and the slender needle caught in the lining and broke. He desperately growled and threw the useless pieces aside, then his claws closed on the Irishman's throat and ferociously dug into his Adam's apple, choking him. The massive body jerked in tremendous convulsions. A gurgling sound escaped from the Irishman's throat, and his eyes opened, bloodshot and unseeing. O'Donnell's legs kicked the air, and his hand blindly groped about, opening and closing with the last flickers of life. The massive paw came down on Mueller's glasses and crushed them into smithereens. Mueller's face was red with effort, his opaque eyes glowed with yellow fire, and his tongue flicked about his rubbery lips. "Die, die," he groaned in German, desperately squeezing his friend's throat. "Die, die, *du Schweinhund,* die!"

He continued to strangle his victim long after the neck had gone limp in his iron grip and bloodied fragments of glass rolled out of the now open, inert hand.

He slowly emerged from his trance and drew his hands back inch by inch. For a while he leaned over the corpse, rocking back and forth in quasi-orgasmic oblivion. After a final shudder, he moved away from the corpse and squatted by the compartment door. As he wiped the froth from his mouth with the back of his sleeve, a crooked grin gradually settled on his face. He had done it. The traitor was dead. The Plan was safe.

His hands were steady now, the trembling gone. He meticulously collected the fragments of his smashed glasses and the broken needle. He rolled the dead body on its back and went through the pockets, removing identity papers, plane ticket, and personal objects that could help identify it. He stuffed all the items into the inner pocket of his duffel coat, then slowly got up on his feet. He felt exhausted, spent; yet a delicious feeling was spreading through his whole body, and his hammering headache was gone. He walked noiselessly to the end of the corridor and left the train by the far door, landing on the adjacent platform. He quickly merged with the outgoing crowd and hailed a taxi on the Via Marsala. For more than an hour he traveled around Rome, taking re-doubled precautions. But this time nobody was shadowing him.

As he walked, at exactly 4:00 P.M., into the magnificent Church of Santa Croce in Gerusalemme for his follow-up meeting with Caruzzi, he was sure that he was not followed.

But Caruzzi was.

The Archbishop Innocent Caruzzi was a tall, lean man with a very erect carriage. His black cassock, falling almost royally from his broad shoulders, and his full black beard, streaked with gray, made him look very distinguished. The intense black eyes, over which the salt-and-pepper eyebrows made an almost unbroken line, exuded power and authority. The strong nose and the large forehead completed the impressive face that bore a striking resemblance to the late Archbishop Makarios, the charismatic first president of Cyprus. Still, the photographs of the handsome Caruzzi had, not so long ago, been displayed on the front pages of the world press, and they still adorned the active files of the Israeli Mossad. For a very special reason.

The distinguished Archbishop was a terrorist.

A Maronite Christian, born Pierre Houri in the Lebanese village of Bint Jubail, he had embraced the religion as a boy and had quickly risen in the hierarchy of the Eastern Province of the Church. After several years as a high dignitary in the

Lebanese Catholic Church, he had been transferred to a choice post in the very cradle of Christendom, Bethlehem. He was the bishop of the tiny town, nestled on the eastern flank of the Jerusalem mountains, when the Arab-Israeli War of 1967 suddenly erupted and the Israelis became the new masters of the West Bank. Four years later, in the spring of 1971, the Pope bestowed the title of Archbishop on Innocent Caruzzi.

Strangely enough, the Israeli occupation changed the status of the Church for the better. Conscious of world public opinion and of the wary attitude of the Vatican toward the Jewish state, the Israeli government spared no effort to protect and even expand the rights of the Church in Jerusalem and the West Bank. Archbishop Caruzzi had no cause for complaint as far as his functions were concerned. But in the seventies, especially after the October War, he began to feel a growing identification with the Palestinians. He was a passionate man. He disliked the Israelis intensely and gradually developed a deep sympathy for the Fatah underground. Being an extremist, he even found reasons to justify the massacre of women and children by the Fatah.

Caruzzi had always been an outspoken man. He did not mince his words in public, and his radical opinions soon became known all over the West Bank. In the fall of 1974, while he was in Beirut for a conference with the heads of the Maronite Church, he was approached by two young Arabs. They introduced themselves as Fatah officers. After thanking him warmly for his "courageous" statements, they made a strange request. The weak spot of the Palestinian resistance, they pointed out, was its short supply of arms. The Israeli Army and security services had sealed the country's borders. An electrified fence, supported by land patrols, minefields, radar units, and electronic sensors, had been built all along the Israeli frontier. The security measures at Ben-Gurion Airport and the other points of entry into the country, including the bridges over the Jordan River, were tough and efficient. The Fatah headquarters in Beirut had almost no way to smuggle arms and explosives into occupied Palestine.

But Monsignor Caruzzi, the younger of the two anonymous visitors said, could cross the border as often as he wished. He came to Beirut quite often, about once a month. As he enjoyed diplomatic status and a privileged position as a high Catholic dignitary, his car was never searched. He could provide the Palestinian freedom fighters with invaluable help by agreeing to carry some shipments of arms for the resistance over the border. Would he do it?

Caruzzi did not hesitate for a second. The following afternoon, when he crossed the Israeli border on his way back to Bethlehem, he carried a heavy crate in the trunk of his Peugeot sedan. Soon he became the main Fatah courier between the Fatah headquarters and the West Bank, carrying letters, reports, and messages to Beirut, returning with carfuls of weapons, hand grenades, and explosives. He never asked what happened to the weapons which were collected at his home by a carpenter from Jenin; but even if he were told, his conscience would have remained at peace. He sincerely believed that violence and terror were a necessary means to achieve a noble goal.

It took the Israeli services two years to discover the unorthodox activities of the handsome priest; and it took the various echelons of government forty-eight hours of feverish, embarrassed deliberations till they decided to make the story public. Caruzzi was arrested *in flagrante delicto* while transferring Kalachnikov assault weapons and Katiousha rockets from his car to the van of his Fatah contact. In a rudimentary cache in his home, the police found an impressive array of Russian-made weapons and explosives. Arrested, Caruzzi was sentenced to ten years in prison; but six months later, he was expelled from the country. In the secret negotiations engaged in with the Vatican shortly after the verdict, the Israeli government had obtained assurance that Caruzzi would never again come to the Middle East and would make no more political statements. That promise was enough for an uneasy Israeli government to get rid of the embarrassing presence of an important Catholic priest in its maximum security prison.

For a while Caruzzi behaved. Appointed roving ambassador of the Vatican secretariat of state, he spent many months in South America and the Philippines. But in the summer of 1978 he suddenly appeared in Syria and in October sojourned in Beirut for three weeks. At the beginning of the next year he was seen successively in Teheran, Baghdad, and Tripoli.

When Mally Segev brought Peled a detailed report from Lebanon describing the election of Caruzzi to the Supreme Council of the PLO, Jeremiah had sighed. "Well, Mally, it seems that we should keep an eye on the monsignor."

Instructions were sent to the Mossad resident agent in Rome to place the archbishop under close surveillance and to report any unusual contact he made. And so it happened that an Israeli agent witnessed the brief meeting of Caruzzi with a strange blond man in the Vatican library that morning. When Caruzzi left the Vatican in the early afternoon and was driven to the ancient Roman church, appropriately named The Holy Cross in Jerusalem, he was followed inside by a middle-aged bald man, carrying a worn leather case. The case contained a highly sophisticated camera, its lens secured against a narrow crack in the old bag, its shutter activated from the outside by a concealed switch. The bald man hesitantly stepped into the church and joined a small group of Italians from the country flocking behind an elderly priest who spoke in a low voice.

". . . was founded by Constantine," the priest was saying, "to enshrine the relics of the True Cross that his mother Santa Helena had found in Jerusalem. Initially a part of an antique imperial palace, the Sessorium, this church was first named Basilica Sessoriana. Rebuilt in 1144 by Lucius the Second, it underwent a magnificent restoration in 1743 when Benedict the Fourteenth added the exquisite theatrical facade and the oval vestibule." He surveyed his audience and made a gesture to the left. "Follow me, please." Sticking to the group of docile Italians, the bald man quickly glanced at the archbishop, kneeling in prayer by the left aisle. "Notice, please, the granite columns separating the nave and aisles," the priest went on monotonously. "The style is baroque, and the pavement is cosmatesque. Pope Benedict the Seventh is buried in the interior."

A blond man, his body oddly stiff, walked up the aisle and knelt beside Caruzzi. The archbishop looked up absently and sunk back into prayer. The bald agent transferred his leather bag to his right hand and pressed the switch. The clicks of the camera were inaudible. It was a classical rendezvous procedure, he reflected, as he moved back a little from the crowd and cocked his head to better contemplate the stained glass windows. First meeting in the morning in the Vatican library for establishing contact and checking security; second meeting now for the real exchange of information.

"And now we shall go to the Chapel of the Relics," the priest said, "where the pieces of the True Cross are preserved." A murmur of excited anticipation rippled through the crowd. The bald man detached himself from the group and knelt across the aisle, his forefinger repeatedly pressing the camera switch. Then he slowly got to his feet and went out. As he passed beside a vintage Alfa Romeo parked by the curb, he knelt to tie his shoelace. "Blond man in black duffel coat," he whispered to the dark-haired girl who sat at the driver's seat smoking nervously. The dandyish young man beside her was fumbling with the radio knobs. The bald man straightened up and slowly walked away. Caruzzi was of no interest to him anymore. The objective now was the blond stranger. Wherever he went, Linda and Emil would be close behind. They were first-class operatives.

Early the next evening, the Rome station report and the enclosed blown-up photographs were on Mally's desk. Barely two minutes later, she breathlessly burst into Peled's office, disrupting the weekly meeting of the Commission of Directors of the Intelligence Community.

The security officer of the embassy, a tubby, taciturn man sporting a drooping moustache, was waiting for them at the deserted Bern Airport. He shook hands briefly with Jeremiah and Mally and after some hesitation nodded noncommittally at young Hefner, who lingered behind them. "This is Amos Hefner, my new chief of staff," Peled said. "I don't think you've met before. Amos, Israel Brand."

"Let's talk in the car," Brand said laconically. Outside the terminal, the snow was piled high on the sidewalk, but the night air was dry and clean. The heavy man led the way to the parking lot, his galoshes squeaking on the powdery snow. Peled and Mally followed, and Hefner closed the rear. He did not like the cold arrogance of Brand, but then, he was not in a sociable mood either. He had set up everything for a nice, sinful weekend with Miriam, the girl he had met during the night of the ill-fated raid on Lebanon. He had gotten a friend's apartment in Eilat on the Red Sea, had convinced his wife that he was on an urgent assignment, and then at the last moment an urgent assignment had come up indeed. After spending most of the day on the scrambler phone making arrangements with Rome, Bern, and Paris, he had been informed by Jeremiah that he had to come along to Switzerland that very evening. He had sulked during the four-hour flight, distractedly leafing through reports and memos. Across the aisle, Peled and Mally were too immersed in their low-voiced conversation to notice the morose expression stamped all over his face. As he glanced at them, they suddenly looked to him like a pleasant, aging couple on their way to a hard-earned vacation. The thought of Jeremiah and Mally as a married couple brought a brief smile to his pinched mouth, yet it made him wonder. On second thought, they really suited each other, he said to himself.

He slipped into the front seat of the Citroën CX beside Brand who was speaking concisely, half-turned toward Jeremiah and Mally in the back. "I guess you know the main points. Your blond man arrived here from Rome night before last. We had been alerted and were waiting for him at the airport. He bought an open ticket, Geneva–Paris. Open, no reservation," he stressed, waving his fat forefinger like a teacher. "Then he rented a car at Avis. He used the name Bernard Ross and gave an address in Linz, Austria. His Air France ticket was issued under the same name."

"Driver's license?" Peled asked quickly.

"Austrian. He paid the deposit in cash and said that he was going to drop the car in Geneva."

"So he intended to drive to Geneva and board a flight to Paris there," Peled concluded.

"Right." The heavy winter coat hindered Brand's movements and he unbuttoned it, shifting uneasily on his seat. "I sent Teddy, my assistant, after him and alerted our people in Geneva and Paris. Whenever he chooses to fly, there will be somebody to see him off at Geneva and welcome him in Paris." He smiled faintly at his clumsy joke. "He took the main road to Geneva but left it about five kilometers after Payerne. He forked into a country road and arrived shortly before midnight in the small village of Lebrun. He parked the car in front of an apartment house—they have six or seven four-story houses—and spent the night there. According to Teddy's last report,"—he glanced at his watch—"filed about an hour ago, Mr. Bernard Ross is still in Lebrun."

Mally leaned forward. "Did he leave the house? Any contacts?"

"He was seen several times in the village, almost always in company of a woman."

"Who is she? What's her name?" Peled hung on Brand's words like a bloodhound, ready to leap.

Brand shrugged. "I don't know. We have a communication problem, Jeremiah. We can't use any wireless equipment in Switzerland according to standing instructions. We depend solely on the telephone. Now, Lebrun is a small village with no hotels. The only accommodation is a motor inn ten kilometers out of the place. No direct dialing, all the calls pass through a switchboard. Therefore we keep our conversations with Teddy to a strict minimum."

Peled nodded. "You can't send him any help either, that would be too conspicuous."

"Right." Brand took a cigarette case out of his pocket, opened it, then caught Jeremiah's disapproving glance and regretfully put it back. "In this kind of place a stranger sticks out like a sore thumb, especially at this time of the year. The locals—and the woman seems to be a local—would quickly spot an unknown face. I hope Teddy's cover hasn't been blown yet."

"What is it?" Hefner asked.

Brand gave him a nasty look and turned to Peled who nodded. Hefner clenched his teeth, fuming, while Brand spoke to the head of the Mossad. "We had to think of something quickly so we chose the pollster cover. He is supposed to be doing some market research for a new detergent." He chuckled. "It comes in big containers, ideal for rural areas. Teddy always has a couple hundred questionnaires in his car. For other products as well, of course."

"What about Sabi's guys?" Peled went on. Sabi was the commander of the operational team of the Mossad.

"Arriving," Brand said. It was getting warm in the car, and his heavy face was glistening with sweat. He unbuttoned his jacket and his heavy belly spilled gracelessly over his belt. "Four people arrived from Paris, three guys and a girl, and two more came from Tel Aviv on the Swissair flight an hour before you. Sabi is with them now. We expect two girls to arrive by car from Munich tonight."

"We had to take them off the Hawatma case," Hefner explained to the Old Man.

Brand could not suppress his curiosity. "Do you intend to use the operational team, Jeremiah?"

Peled marked a long pause and looked out the window at the heaps of snow, glistening in the moonlight. He rolled down the window, and some cold, dry air penetrated the stuffy interior. Two men and a woman passed beside them, chatting in German with the peculiar Swiss accent. A dry remark in a low baritone voice set the woman off into an explosion of throaty laughter.

Peled turned back. "When can we have some pictures of the man? I want to make sure that he's our guy."

Mally and Hefner looked away. The Lillehammer trauma of hitting the wrong man was still haunting the Old Man.

"We'll have photos in the morning," Brand said. "Teddy took some pictures today of both the man and the woman. A guy from the Geneva station is meeting him at midnight outside Lebrun. He'll be here a couple of hours later, so you'll have the photos by breakfast time."

Peled nodded. An uneasy, tedious silence settled in the car again, Brand's unanswered question about the operational team still hanging in the air. Finally Peled spoke in a low voice. "He is the pivot of the whole operation. If we remove him, it might be canceled, for good." Another long pause followed. "Nothing violent," he spoke again. "I want him for questioning."

"A safe house is ready as you asked," Brand volunteered. "Outside Fribourg. Good access, garage, quiet."

"Fine," Peled nodded. "There's no use driving to Lebrun now. A car in the middle of the night would alert the whole village. Let's get some sleep, and tomorrow we'll move. I want to be close when they make the snatch. I want Sabi, Mally, and you, Amos, in my room at six A.M."

Brand turned heavily in his seat and started the car. They

silently drove the short distance to the nearby Holiday Inn, where rooms had been reserved for them under assumed names. Brand escorted Mally while Peled and Hefner took the elevator to their adjoining rooms. Hefner entered Peled's room first for a routine security check. The Old Man came in behind him and closed the door. "I am afraid we won't get much sleep tonight, Amos," he said gently.

"But you told Brand . . ." Hefner started, then stopped in midsentence in sudden understanding. The Old Man did not want to disclose either the timing or the plan of the operation to Brand. He still stuck to his golden rule that nobody should know more than he must.

"Get Sabi here," the Old Man said, "with the maps and all the material. We'll have to decide on the modus operandi and send the team on its way before dawn. We'll have one of them wait by a telephone. As soon as Mally and I identify the photographs, we'll give them the green light. They must make the snatch in the morning; we are running short of time."

"Sure." His hand on the doorknob, Hefner turned back and asked on impulse, "And after you question Mueller, what are you going to do with him?"

The clear blue eyes held his with a hard stare. The placid, leathery face was devoid of expression. Peled sighed. "You should not be so high-strung, Amos. I am sure Miriam can spare another weekend."

He stared back at Peled, dumbfounded. The old fox knew, he had known all along. "But I'd like you to know," the Old Man added dryly, "that I don't approve of my men cheating on their wives. It's bad for morale."

He softly closed the door behind Amos Hefner.

The Citroën effortlessly climbed to the top of the hill and started the descent toward the valley that lay under a cottony blanket of fog. Brand was driving carefully, his face sullen. He had not said a word since he learned at breakfast that Peled had worked through the night with Sabi and that the operational team was already in place. Good for you, Hefner thought, his weary body luxuriously stretching out in the front seat. He glanced back. Peled and Mally Segev were bent over the sheaf of glossy photographs that had arrived in the morning an hour later than promised. The man was Mueller all right, dressed in the same black clothes he had worn at Salameh's funeral. The woman was old, thin, and gray-haired. She was wearing a cheap rabbit fur coat and worn flat boots. In one of the pictures, taken from the outside, they were seen sitting by a table in a crowded restaurant. Another picture showed them walking in the street, Mueller holding her by the arm. She had a haggard, sharp face. The mouth was bitter, drawn, but the eyes that stared almost straight at the camera seemed intelligent. Back in the hotel it had taken Peled only a quick glance to make up his mind and whisper "Evergreen"— the prearranged codeword for the kidnapping operation—into the phone. They had left their breakfast unfinished, hastily checked out, and left in Brand's car.

"Now, what's that?" Brand suddenly muttered. Two dark shapes appeared ahead of them, blurred by the thickening fog. Brand leaned over the wheel, straining his eyes. "Cars," he said, and half a minute later, "ours." He carefully pulled in behind the vehicles that were parked beside the road. A tall figure emerged from one of them, leaned over the Citroën's windshield, then opened the back door. It was Sabi, the head of the operational team. "Bad news, Jeremiah," he muttered as he squeezed his long body inside as the Old Man and Mally hastily moved aside to let him in. "Our bird flew away an hour ago."

"What the hell do you mean?" Peled's voice was a mixture of surprise and anger.

"He left at first light," Sabi said. His tanned, wolfish face was gloomy. "When your order was relayed to us, he was already on the road. Why were you so late?"

"The photographs weren't ready," Peled squeezed through clenched teeth, throwing an accusing glance at Brand's large back.

Sabi spread his arms. "Well, it was too late to attempt anything. We couldn't risk a shooting pursuit on the highway."

Hefner stole a look at Jeremiah. He had never seen the Old Man so angry. He was sitting still, his lips compressed, fury exploding in the hard blue eyes. "Where is he now?" he finally asked, his voice harsh.

"Teddy followed him to Geneva. He just arrived at Cointrin

157

Airport and went through customs. He's boarding the first flight to Paris."

Peled drew a deep breath and looked down at his clenched fists, shaking his head. "Damn!" he muttered hoarsely. "A whole operation aborted because a stupid technician was too slow developing a roll of film. Damn!" he repeated.

"We can do it in Paris, Jeremiah," Sabi said. "Our men are waiting for him at the airport."

"Nonsense," the Old Man snapped. "A snatch in Paris is much more complicated. Here we had him in the palm of our hand." He sunk into a long silence; the others sat still, too embarrassed to speak. Finally he raised his eyes. "Who is the woman?" he asked. "Did you find out?"

Sabi nodded and his dark eyes flashed in excitement. "I spoke to Teddy this morning before your call came through. He said that he heard the blond man call her *Mutti*. That's mother in German."

"Mother?" Peled exclaimed, astonished. "Who is she? What's her name?"

Sabi shrugged uneasily. "That will be no problem, Jeremiah. We know the address and . . ."

"Let's go," Peled said.

"You want to go to the house?" Amos looked at him in puzzlement. "Let the boys . . ."

"Let's go," Peled repeated scornfully. "Sabi, stay in the car and show Brand how to get there."

Brand started the car. They crossed the village in a hurry. Hefner sat stiffly in his place, glumly staring at the picturesque, tidy cottages and the toylike church. At an intersection the car suddenly jolted to the left to avoid a horse-drawn cart, loaded with big cans of milk. The cart driver, an elderly farmer huddled in a sheepskin coat, stared at them in dismay, struggling with the reins.

The cluster of apartment houses stood at the southern end of the village, seven ugly, yellow structures that made a sad contrast to the charming red-roofed cottages worthy of a Brothers Grimm story. "That's the house," Sabi said, pointing at the third building.

"Stay in the car, all of you," Peled said. "Mally, you come with me." Even though angry, the Old Man has not lost his

158

bearings, Hefner thought. An elderly couple walking down the street was certainly less conspicuous than a group of young strangers.

A yellow light still burned over the dark entrance of the house. "This way, Jeremiah," Mally said, but he was not listening. He had stopped on the right side of the entrance, slowly reading the names on the mailboxes. Suddenly he froze and swayed, as if he had been hit in the face. Mally caught his arm. "What's wrong, Jeremiah?"

He stared fixedly ahead, face ashen, eyes wide-open in stupor. Slowly he raised his hand and pointed at a piece of cardboard stuck in the far-left box.

"Nina Kolaichek," he whispered. "Good God!"

Chapter 12

BROWN-SKINNED, GRIM-faced, thin and wiry, Keita Senussi sat awkwardly behind his empty desk in the vast embassy lobby. He felt uneasy in the ill-fitting European clothes, the blue jacket hanging loose on his skeletal frame, his scrawny neck choked by a starched collar and a tightly knotted tie. He hated Paris: the cold, the crowds, the cars, the whoring women, the alien way of life of a corrupt nation he failed to understand. He would have paid dearly to be back where he really belonged, pacing with his brothers in the silent camel caravans across the Rebiana Sand Sea or sitting by a campfire on a rocky outcrop of the Tibesti Mountains. The fourth son of a Libyan camel driver and a black girl of the Daza mountaineer tribe, he had left his mother's home at the age of seventeen. It had been his father's wish that one of his sons become a soldier, and the obligation had fallen to Keita. Once in uniform, he did not run away from death but, to the contrary, defied it. teased it, and took the greatest risks with a tranquil indifference. Once, after an exercise with live ammunition on Darnah Beach, he was summoned to his captain's tent where a dark, intense young major with burning eyes questioned him at length about military matters and his attitude toward religion. Three months later, the fiery major, now a colonel, was the new ruler of Libya, having ousted the aging King Idriss by a brilliant coup d'etat. Keita Senussi was promoted to lieutenant and charged with the personal security of Colonel Mu'ammar el Khaddafi, the first president of the Islamic Republic of Libya.

Soon the taciturn lieutenant became one of a small, hand-picked group of hatchet men who carried out Khaddafi's secret plans far beyond the borders of his desert land. Keita Senussi was involved in the plot to overthrow President Sadat in the summer of 1972. He participated in the abortive plot to blow up the *Queen Elizabeth II* when the luxury ship sailed to Israel, carrying one thousand Jewish dignitaries to the festivities celebrating the twenty-fifth anniversary of the Jewish state. Appointed liaison officer to the Palestinian terrorist organizations, he traveled all over Europe, transforming the Libyan embassies into veritable operational bases where the commandos could find refuge, arms, funds, and false identity papers. Recently, when Khaddafi launched a bloody offensive against the leaders of the Libyan emigrés scattered in Europe, Senussi had been appointed security officer in the Paris embassy. From the big, tawny building on the Rue Keppler in the eighth arrondissement, he sent the small teams of killers on their grisly assignments. And they came back to the embassy to hide after riddling another enemy of the colonel's regime with bullets.

Still, he continued to maintain the liaison with the Palestinian commandos operating against Israel. Last week he had been instructed to expect the visit of a European. The message had been sent by Arafat himself via top secret channels. The man's name had not been disclosed. In Arafat's coded cable he was referred to as Al Sadiq, the friend. Keita was to extend "the friend" all possible help, even if that implied the postponement of any current operations. This morning the friend phoned and identified himself by a sequence of code words. Keita had instructed him how to get into the embassy unnoticed by using an inconspicuous back entrance on the Avenue Marceau that was often used by his own agents. Al Sadiq was due to arrive any minute now.

The sleek black phone, the only object on Keita's desk, buzzed discreetly. Keita picked up the receiver.

"Your visitor is here," a gruff voice said in Arabic.

"Send him over," Keita softly said and slightly eased the knot of his tie.

The double door on the far side of the lobby opened, and a gaunt blond man walked inside. He was dressed in black and carried a brand-new attaché case.

* * *

Mueller did not shake hands with the stringy Libyan who pushed back his chair and stood behind the desk, his lean face frowning. He had come here straight from the airport, where he had stopped briefly to retrieve his attaché case from the luggage locker. He strongly disliked coming to the embassy and resorting to the assistance of a Libyan diplomat. To do so went against his methods, against his lone wolf character, against the very essence of his plan. For the Plan was his own; the revenge should be exclusively his, and nobody should share either the thrill of its preparation or the sweet taste of its accomplishment. But after checking all the other possibilities with Arafat the day of Salameh's funeral, he had to admit that the help of the young Libyan from the Paris embassy was indispensable. Senussi had to be associated with the project, even if only temporarily.

"I am Al Sadiq," he said in French to the brown-skinned man. "I have a weapon in that case. It must reach an address in Jerusalem not later than next week. But first I must test fire it and adjust its sights."

Keita nodded, his face impassive. "Follow me, please," he said and led the way. They crossed the lobby and went through a side door that Keita unlocked with a key he selected from a bunch that he took in his pocket. The keyring was fastened to his belt by a thin steel chain.

They crossed a small vestibule, and Keita unlocked a second door leading to a narrow, winding staircase that descended to the cellar. The stairs ended in another vestibule, identical to the one above except for one feature: its far wall was entirely padded from floor to ceiling with a thick layer of plastic insulating material. The door in the wall was similarly insulated. A hulking, thick-shouldered Libyan with a prominent jaw and a dangling moustache quickly got up from a wooden chair propped against the door, throwing an old Arabic newspaper to the floor. Mueller glimpsed the glossy cover of a French pornographic magazine hidden between the pages of the paper. The Libyan glanced at him suspiciously with his small, porcine eyes without even attempting to conceal the heavy Tokarev revolver that was stuck in his belt. Keita nodded at him, and he unlocked the padded door. He walked in ahead of them and flipped a switch. As a multitude of fluorescent tubes flickered into a simulated daylight, Mueller entered the huge cellar that had been transformed into a compact underground shooting range. The sixty-yard-long cellar was divided into five shooting tracks, each equipped with electrically-powered target pulleys. The big steel lockers along the walls undoubtedly contained a great quantity of arms and ammunition. A gleaming array of various tools—screwdrivers, chisels, needles, and cleaning paraphernalia—was neatly laid on an oblong aluminum-topped table like surgical instruments. The place was Keita's secret pride. Here the Libyan and Palestinian commandos came for their supplies and for a quick get-acquainted course with the weapons they were going to use in their coups in Europe.

Mueller looked around him and nodded to himself. Then he turned to the Libyans. "Will you leave me alone? I have work to do." His voice was low and dispassionate.

Keita eyed him with dismay. "I can't leave you alone here," he said firmly. "Nobody is allowed alone here. This place is . . . "

"You've got your orders," Mueller hissed. "Now, leave me alone. Or do you need another cable from Abu Amar?"

The Libyan winced at the mention of Arafat's war name. Anger flashed in his liquid bead eyes. He clenched his fists and opened his mouth to speak but finally nodded in surrender. "*Ta'al*," he squeezed out in Arabic to the moustached guard and pointed at the door.

"Wait," Mueller said, stretching his bony claw. "The key."

The huge guard looked furiously at his superior. Keita nodded again, and the Arab thrust a key into the foreigner's hand, muttering under his breath. Mueller slammed the door shut behind them and locked it. He chose the far left shooting stand and placed the attaché case in front of him. He opened it and lovingly caressed the Remington before assembling it deftly, scope and all, and feeding a blunt-nosed bullet into the breech. He laid the weapon in front of him and pressed the target switch. He heard the soft purr of an electric motor across the range, and the big cardboard target slowly sailed toward him, hanging from an iron chain that slid in a groove on the low ceiling. Mueller ripped the printed target from the dangling metal frame and threw it on the floor. A tremor of excitement ran through his fingers as he took from his inner pocket a big, thick sheet of paper, folded several times. He unfolded it and fastened it to the target frame, then took a step backward and looked up.

The big glossy poster was a life-size photograph of the upper half of a man's body.

The famous face of the man who was going to die smiled at him benignly from the poster.

He pressed the reverse switch. The chain creaked above his head, and the poster quickly sailed away, gracefully fluttering like a disappearing specter. It reached the target position at the far end of the range and stopped. He took the pistol and raised it, expertly turning the distance knob of the telescopic sight. The blurred lines were sharpened by the magnifying lenses, and the face and chest of his target materialized before his eye. Now. He steadily grasped the Remington grip with both hands and squeezed the trigger, aiming for the heart. The pistol jerked in his fingers as the shot echoed in the gallery. He ejected the spent cartridge into his right palm and inserted a second bullet into the breech. Raising the pistol again, he examined his target through the sight. The slug had drilled a neat little hole in the man's chest, slightly low and to the left of the heart. He selected a sleek screwdriver from among the tools on the aluminum table and carefully readjusted the sight screws. He aimed again and fired. This time the bullet pierced the paper a little bit too high. He eased the screw a little and fired again. The new black hole was still above the heart, and he reached for the screwdriver once more. The fourth shot made him grunt with satisfaction. He left the sight screws at the same position and fired three more bullets. They all hit the same spot, the small slug punctures merging into an ugly black hole with scorched edges at the place of the man's heart. For a fleeting second he felt the familiar pang of delicious pain in the pit of his stomach. He pressed the recall switch, and the target returned to him on the moving chain. He removed it carefully and laid it on the instrument table, closely examining the hits. The Remington was fit now, zeroed to perfection. He poured some droplets of quick-drying cement on the sight screws to keep them in position. On the right side of the table he saw a small tin of red paint and a brush used for drawing outsized targets. He dipped the brush in the viscous red liquid and with quick, bold strokes painted three concentric circles on the poster around the man's heart. As he raised the poster, some tiny rivulets of red paint trickled down around the scorched black hole. His mouth quivered in a twisted smile, and he moistened his dry lips with the tip of his tongue.

Mueller disassembled the Remington, cleaned its parts, and packed them back in the attaché case. He locked it and put the tiny keys in his inside pocket together with the folded poster. In the outer room Senussi and the moustached guard were talking in low tones but stopped abruptly as he came out. "Let's go," he said to Senussi. When they reached the landing, out of the guard's earshot, he handed Senussi the attaché case and a slip of paper. "That case must be in Jerusalem next week," he said. "No later than Thursday. The courier has to call that number. They are expecting him."

Senussi nodded sullenly. He loathed being bossed around by the repulsive stranger and hoped to get rid of him as soon as possible. "Anything else?" he asked, scowling.

"Yes. I might have been followed to the embassy. I must be absolutely sure that when I leave nobody will tail me."

Keita nodded. "That will be no problem."

It was easy indeed. During the six months crash course in Dzerzhinsky Square in Moscow, he had learned the routine KGB method for such an emergency. He even remembered the title of the procedure: "Agent dispatch in foreign city, under surveillance." Ten minutes after he took the attaché case from Mueller, everything was ready. In the inner court of the embassy, five cars warmed their engines, ready to depart. Two of them carried four passengers each, the three others were apparently empty except for their drivers. Mueller was in one of them, lying down on the floor. As Keita gave the order, the massive gates of the embassy suddenly opened and the cars darted out one after the other, immediately heading off in different directions. Mueller was in the third car.

The two Israeli agents who had followed Mueller from the airport to the back entrance of the embassy had called for reinforcements and watched both entrances closely. But they were totally overwhelmed when the fleet of diplomatic cars emerged from the embassy. The Israeli surveillance car followed one of the Libyan limousines at random; but the Mossad agents had to acknowledge their failure as the four swarthy passengers flocked into a North African restaurant on the Grands Boulevards. Mueller's track was lost.

Before Mueller had left the embassy, he had briefly squeezed Senussi's hand. He did not mind the small gesture. He knew that he was seeing the Libyan for the last time in his life. Senussi was a marked man already, as good as dead.

Keita Senussi was the first to disembark from the next morning's Air France flight to Beirut. He flashed his diplomatic credentials at the immigration officer and was quickly whisked through formalities. He morosely nodded at the third secretary of the Libyan embassy who had rushed to the airport to meet him; his glum face and monosyllabic answers promptly discouraged the diplomat's nervous attempts to engage in a casual conversation.

"Have you got the car I asked for?" Keita asked as they walked out of the terminal.

"Yes. We rented one according to your instructions. A Ford Fairmont. I shall be delighted to drive you wherever . . . "

"I shall drive myself," Keita cut him short. "Just give me the keys and tell me where the car is, then you can go back to the embassy."

Five minutes later he was speeding south on Route One in the direction of Tyre. The gearbox screeched in protest under his brusque handling of the shift. He had had no choice but to fly to Lebanon himself. Until a few months ago he had sent the weapons by diplomatic mail to the Beirut embassy and let his opposite number there take care of the rest. But last November *Paris-Match* magazine had published the memoirs of Lieutenant Colonel Leroy-Finville, a former top official in the SDECE, the French intelligence and counterespionage agency. With amazing candor Leroy-Finville described how his department, the Service 7, opened and thoroughly examined all diplomatic cargo, starting with sealed pouches and ending with locked crates, that was sent through the French airports. Keita had shuddered at the thought that the sly French had read all his top secret reports and inspected the arms and explosives regularly smuggled in and out of France as diplomatic cargo. A new means for smuggling arms had yet to be devised; so for the time being he had to act as a courier and bring Al Sadiq's weapon to Lebanon personally. Fortunately, they still did not search diplomats at Charles de Gaulle Airport.

Barely an hour after leaving Beirut, he reached the headquarters of the Nigerian batallion that was part of the United Nations peacekeeping force in Lebanon. "Major Balewa," Keita said to the black sentry, smart in his freshly pressed uniform. "He is expecting a friend." The athletic corporal saluted and picked up the phone in his booth. Barely two minutes later, a jeep stopped by the gate; an obese, profusely sweating officer jumped heavily out of the driver's seat and entered Keita's car. They exchanged a casual greeting, and Keita handed the major the attaché case, the note with the phone number, and a thick wad of bills in a sealed envelope. They did not have to discuss the current assignment. Balewa was an old hand and had accomplished several such missions in the past.

By the late afternoon, Keita was back in Beirut, where he checked into the Hotel Meridien. He was booked for the next morning's flight to Paris.

That same evening Major Balewa reached Jerusalem after a four-hour drive. He had no trouble crossing the Israeli border. The soldiers at the checkpost, acting according to strict standing regulations, waved him through as soon as they identified the UN plates on his white Chevrolet. In his room at the King David Hotel, Balewa gulped a late snack and dialed the number he had gotten from Senussi. It was in East Jerusalem. A voice with a thick Arab accent answered him. "How is your family?" Balewa asked in English. He did not have to say anything about his mission. His interlocutor asked him to drop in for breakfast the next morning at Abu Bakar's, a picturesque Oriental café in the Old City, which was a favorite tourist spot.

In the morning Balewa shaved, dressed, paid his hotel bill, and drove to Abu Bakar's. He had a leisurely breakfast on the beautiful terrace of the café that offered a breathtaking view of the Mount of Olives. Nobody approached him, but when he got up to leave, the attaché case was no longer by his chair where he had left it. As Major Balewa started his long drive back to Lebanon, the black attaché case was delivered to the modest room of a student called Nawaf, an active member of the Fatah organization.

The weapon was in place, fit and ready, according to plan.

Also according to plan, a deplorable accident took place at the same time in Beirut. As he walked out of the Hotel Meridien to his rented car that was parked on the street, Keita Senussi was hit by a huge GMC truck that suddenly emerged from a nearby parking lot. It was a hit-and-run accident, and the heavy machine had disappeared down the street before anybody could note its license number. The Libyan diplomat was killed on the spot.

Arafat was taking good care of his friend Al Sadiq. The link between the blond man who practiced shooting in the cellar of the Libyan embassy in Paris and the deadly pistol smuggled into occupied Jerusalem had been definitely removed.

In the late afternoon dusk, the gently undulating slope, covered by a thick layer of immaculate snow, looked utterly peaceful. Half a mile to the north, the thick pine forest had already lost its fresh green glimmer and stretched in a dark, blurred line to the shores of the Lac de la Gruvère. The frozen lake, shaped in the strange form of a long, sleek dagger, dully reflected the soft light of the fading day.

Mally slowly walked down the path leading from the safe house to the wooden jetty. Jeremiah had decided to set up the operational command post in the safe house, a big, ugly replica of a traditional Swiss chalet, and to await there the news from Paris. Most of Sabi's people were in France already, and they were very few left in the isolated cold house —Mally, Jeremiah, Amos, a guy from Communications, and two bodyguards. Another two of Sabi's boys were staying in a hotel in Fribourg as a reserve team. The day before yesterday, news had come about Mueller's KGB-style departure from the Libyan embassy, but Jeremiah had decided to wait another couple of days in Switzerland in case Mueller returned to the Rue Keppler or to his mother's home in Lebrun.

The calm and the quiet had a soothing effect on Mally's strained nerves, and she rather enjoyed being cut off from the outside world. There was no television in the house, the phone calls were rare, no living soul was to be seen for miles around; and she delighted in the long solitary walks by the lake, wrapped in her old fur coat.

The jetty came into view, and she saw a small figure standing immobile by the lake. The man was hatless, and the evening breeze gently ruffled his shock of white hair. She hesitated. Since they had found the name of Nina Kolaichek on the mailbox in Lebrun, Jeremiah had become strangely withdrawn. He had dodged all her questions about the woman's identity, staring back at Mally with blank, vacuous eyes. He spoke very little, avoided contact with her and the others, and took most of his meals in his room. On the few occasions when she had been able to catch him off guard, he had seemed genuinely worried to her. Worse than that, tormented. She had never seen him in such a state before, and she did not know how to handle him.

She felt rather foolish now, standing in the middle of the path and staring at his back. She was about to retreat silently to the house when he turned around and saw her. He did not make any gesture toward her, just stood there watching her, and she felt compelled to walk to him.

"How are you, Jeremiah?" she asked, deciding that her question could not sound phonier.

He did not seem to have heard the question and turned back to stare at the frozen lake. After a long while he said in a very low, very insecure voice, "There are things that come at you from the past. You think they are dead and buried forever . . . and suddenly they are back in a different form. Like that bird," he hesitated, "the phoenix, that is consumed by the fire and then emerges again from its ashes." He shuddered slightly. "Faces, and names from the past. And you cannot help asking yourself if it is a simple coincidence, or . . . "—he was groping for words—"or if they were bound to return one day. As if it had been written somewhere." His voiced trailed away, faintly apologetic, as if Jeremiah were ashamed of talking such nonsense.

"It's Nina Kolaichek, isn't it?" she asked very softly. She had the feeling that he wanted to talk.

It took him a long time to answer. "She and her husband," he said finally. "Professor Kurt Kolaichek. Don't you remember the name?" He paused. "No, you couldn't remember. It was in fifty-eight, you were not with the Mossad yet."

Mally nodded. In fifty-eight she was still an agent's wife, married to Simon Segev, and did not exactly know what was happening in the organization. They took her in only after the divorce as a favor, like throwing a bone to a sick dog.

"Kolaichek came to Israel in 1957," Peled said, still without looking at her. His breath was coming out in puffs of white, frosty vapor. "He was Czech, non-Jewish, and was said to be one of the leading European experts on atomic energy."

"And the Czechs let him go?" she looked at him, doubtful.

"He was an exile. He had escaped from Prague in 1954. He had been exceptionally authorized to participate in an international congress in Paris, and he never went back. His wife and son were left behind."

"His son—Mueller, you mean."

Jeremiah shrugged. "I guess so. He was a little boy at the time." He paused. "Let's walk a little, all right?"

She silently trudged beside him along the path that followed the shoreline heading for the dark mass of the forest. "Kolaichek had spent three years as a guest lecturer in a couple of European universities, and in fifty-seven joined the physics department at the University of Jerusalem. He was also appointed fellow researcher in the Weizmann Institute of Science. They loved him there. He was an excellent scientist and a wonderful man—clever, sympathetic, immensely likeable. He charmed everybody."

"Everybody but you, I suppose," Mally ventured, trying to keep the irony out of her voice. "You suspected him from the start, didn't you?"

He ignored her question. "During World War II he had been active in the underground, something to do with rescuing and hiding Jewish scientists. The Gestapo arrested him, and he was imprisoned in the Theresienstadt ghetto."

She arched her eyebrows. "I thought that there were only Jews in Theresienstadt."

Jeremiah nodded. "Jews and a handful of Gentiles. Some of the survivors, who later came to Israel, remembered him well. They say that even in the ghetto he was quite an outstanding figure. Very warm, very human, and strikingly handsome."

"But you suspected him, nevertheless," Mally repeated doggedly.

Jeremiah sighed. "Yes, I did." His tone was oddly defensive. "I was in charge of counterespionage at the time. We were building the atomic reactor in the Negev under the camouflage of a textile plant." He chuckled dryly. "That was the most secret project we ever undertook. The Russians suspected something but had no tangible information. They had already mounted two penetration attempts. We caught one of their men on the very site of the reactor. A KGB team had also tried to break into the offices of the French company in Le Havre that was supplying us with the equipment."

They had reached the first line of firs. He bent to pick up a dry twig and forcefully snapped it with both hands. "The Russians were ready to go far to find out what we were cooking up in that textile plant. Their former attempts had failed, so they had to plant a spy at a very high level, a man who understood nuclear physics. What better choice than a renowned scientist, a notorious anti-communist, a Jew-lover, who had moved into our inner circle of nuclear experts?"

"And then . . . " Mally started.

"And then I drew a blank. For six months we sat on his tail, checked his moves, his phone calls, his mail. Nothing. The man seemed clean as a whistle. Finally I decided to dig into his past. We interviewed all the Theresienstadt survivors, in Israel and abroad. It took us another five months to get the first lead. An old man who was living in Miami told us a strange story. He had been Kolaichek's roommate for a while. And he was ready to swear that during the last year of the war Kolaichek had a secret love affair with a Nazi woman officer, a German girl from the Sudeten. Her name was Eva Schwendt. She was quite a sadist, according to our witness, and she was dreaded by the whole camp. But also, as it happens sometimes, extremely beautiful. She picked Kolaichek.

He was reluctant at first but succumbed after she saved his life. He had been selected to be sent to Auschwitz, you see, and she took his name off the list at the last moment."

He brushed some fir needles off his coat. "We started checking records, here and in Prague." He turned to look at her. "The Czechs had not closed our embassy yet and were ready to cooperate with us on Nazi crimes."

"And you found the woman," Mally said.

"Eva Schwendt disappeared at the end of the war," he said cautiously, "and was never heard of again. But three years later Kurt Kolaichek reappeared in Prague with his young wife. Her name was Nina, and she was extremely beautiful." He paused and added, "You know that Sudeten Germans speak Czech as fluently as German."

"So you broke him down," Mally said, looking away.

"I came to see him at his apartment in the Weizmann Institute and threw the facts at his face. I was bluffing of course. I had no proof that Nina Kolaichek was Eva Schwendt. But he went to pieces almost immediately and confessed everything. At the end of the war he had married Eva, using the papers of a girl who had died in the camp. They lived for a couple of years in Brno, until things settled down. That's where the boy was born. Later they returned to Prague, assuming she had nothing to fear. Most of the Theresienstadt inmates had either died or emigrated."

"He must have been very much in love with her," Mally suddenly remarked.

He looked at her sharply. "He was a weak man," he snapped with vehemence, "to fall in love with a Nazi after he had seen all those horrors." She did not answer, so he went on, "Anyway, it took the Russians a few more years to find out. In 1952 some KGB agents came to see him in his laboratory. They had all the proof that he had married a war criminal, they said. They could have Kolaichek and his wife arrested, tried, and hanged in a week—her for her crimes, him for his complicity. But they offered him a solution."

"Of course," Mally said. "If he would defect to the West and spy for them, they would let his wife alone. Elementary."

They were slowly walking back toward the house. It was almost dark, but the snow was glowing with a strange incandescence. The sky was clear and starry. Jeremiah was silent, so Mally said matter of factly, "You didn't arrest him, though. If there had been a trial, I would have known. So you must have turned him."

He nodded.

"So what happened, Jeremiah?" He seemed to retreat once again in his shell, reluctant to speak.

"I turned him," he finally confirmed. "He didn't want to. He implored me to arrest him and to put him on trial. He kept saying that he was unable to play a double game. He claimed that the Russians wouldn't hesitate to kill his wife and son if they found out that he had betrayed his mission. But I needed him. I needed him to feed them with false information. I had to turn him, you see? The reactor was all that counted." He had raised his voice much more than necessary, Mally decided.

She did not speak but fumbled nervously in her bag and produced a package of cigarettes. She had not smoked for a long while, but now she felt she badly needed a cigarette. She lit it and inhaled deeply, expecting one of his biting remarks. But he just watched her in silence. "How long did he work as a double agent?" she asked with forced indifference.

"A couple of months, no more. In April fifty-eight a KGB debriefing team came to Israel. They used the cover of a delegation of the Soviet Academy of Sciences. We knew, of course, that the Academy was a KGB front organization. They were running quite a few agents in Jerusalem."

"And they found out about him?"

"No," he said after another pause. "They established contact and set a meeting with him. We had him thoroughly briefed—what to tell them, how to tell it. We even cooked up a phony research file for him to give them."

She sucked her cigarette nervously.

"The night before he was to meet them, he asked to see me," Jeremiah's voice was very low now. "We met in my car outside the Weizmann Institute. He told me he couldn't do it. He was sure they would see through him immediately. He asked me again to arrest him, to put him in prison for life, just to save his wife and child. He begged. I couldn't do that. He was desperate. Such a nice man, but how weak."

Night had fallen, and the dark shape of the house loomed

ahead of them. A single light made a yellow rectangle on the ground floor. She had never before felt so close to Jeremiah. She moved closer and looked at him. His face was in shadow, and he was staring away from her. "He went home," he said, "and hanged himself."

She threw the cigarette away, and it fell on the snow, still glowing.

"It was my fault," Jeremiah blurted, as if confessing a crime. "Entirely my fault. He was a fine man, and I liked him."

She took his arm spontaneously and pressed it. "Let's go back, Jeremiah."

After dinner she lay on her bed for hours, chain-smoking. She had never seen Jeremiah so exposed, so vulnerable. He must have spent many a sleepless night, haunted by his guilty conscience. Not that he cared about what could have happened to Nina Kolaichek, of course. She was a Nazi, and he hated all Nazis. But he had come to like Kurt Kolaichek. He must have felt responsible for the fate of Kolaichek and his little boy, until day before yesterday, in Lebrun, when he had seen the name Nina Kolaichek on that piece of cardboard, and had suddenly understood that he had been beaten at his own game.

For the Russians had been much more devious. They had not killed Kolaichek's family or sent it to one of the gulags within the Arctic Circle. Planning for the distant future, they had set their eyes on the young boy. They must have indoctrinated him, patiently, thoroughly, molding him into an instrument of violence. They must have told him that the Israelis had humiliated and kill his innocent father. They must have instilled in him a burning hatred for Israel and the West while sowing in his soul the seeds of radical, violent communism. And his mother . . . Mally suddenly shuddered, imagining how Eva Schwendt, alias Nina Kolaichek, had raised her boy in the privacy of her own home. As long as his father had been alive she must have kept her Nazi opinions to herself. But after his death in Israel, the fanatic anti-Semitism of the former concentration camp officer must have erupted, more hateful and violent than ever. How many times

174

must the boy have heard that the Jews were responsible not only for all the evil on earth, but for the death of his own father—a man who loved them, lived among them, and rescued so many of them during the war at the risk of his own life!

The gaunt, skull-like face of Mueller materialized before Mally's eyes, as she had seen him on the television screen. And his parting words to Arafat, as overheard by the driver, suddenly acquired an ominous meaning. "This will be the ultimate revenge," he had said. "Afterward, nothing will be the same." The Mossad psychiatrist had called Mueller a fanatic, a man of unbalanced mind and deranged imagination. She did not have to be a psychiatrist to understand how insanity had overtaken the mind of the boy, crushed between ruthless Russian indoctrination and the raw anti-Semitism of his mother. He had grown up, obsessed with the idea of a terrible revenge. As soon as he was ripe for the task, the Russians had turned him loose. They had let him and his mother emigrate to the West and settle in Switzerland. That was also a calculated move of the KGB. The man had grown to be a fanatic, consumed with hatred, craving violence. They did not want to be associated with him anymore; and they did not have to be, as he had been almost programmed for what he had to do. Mueller's file in Germany proved it. The young man had chosen the only path open to him. He had become a radical terrorist, a cold, scheming killer. He had made his bones with Baader-Meinhoff and the Red Brigades, and then he had met Salameh and joined Black September's bloody war against Israel. The KGB could be proud of him.

Still, she had the feeling—although it was pure intuition, nothing tangible—that the Russians had no part whatsoever in Mueller's present project. The man was a loner, confiding in no one, taking no one's advice. During the years the obsessive idea of revenge had shaped itself in his mind, and now he was carrying it out. Even Arafat and the Fatah seemed to be only an instrument in his scheme to take his own, terrible revenge against the Jews.

But what revenge? Her Mossad colleagues had ruled out any insane plot. All of them, except Jeremiah, had agreed that Mueller was most likely planning an assassination. That had been her opinion too, but now she doubted it. True, he had certainly been told since childhood that Peled was responsible for his father's death. In the light of his past, an attempt against the Old Man's life seemed even more plausible. And yet . . . The man was an obsessed fanatic, seeking a terrible, unprecedented revenge. Could the assassination of Peled, or anybody on earth, satisfy his blind hatred? Or maybe he planned something bigger, some new form of holocaust that only a demented mind could conceive?

She moved restlessly on her bed till dawn, unable to rid her mind of the nagging, alarming questions. And she was still at a loss when the faint morning light filtered through the curtains and somebody knocked on her door. "Get up, Mally," it was young Hefner. "We are going home. They lost his trail in Paris."

In Paris, a grim, worried Liam Higgins repeatedly knocked on the door of Maureen O'Donnell's flat on the fifth floor of an eighteenth-century house in the Latin Quarter. She finally opened the door, still fumbling with the belt of her robe. Her eyes were heavy with sleep, and her silken blond hair spilled on her shoulders, some golden strands sticking to her cheeks. She did not recognize him immediately and stared at him in apprehension.

"I am Liam Higgins, Patrick's friend," he mumbled uneasily. "We last met at the Café des Amis behind the Pantheon."

"Oh, yes," she whispered, and the blood drained from her face. "What's wrong? Has something happened to Patrick?" Her voice was suddenly laden with fear.

"I don't know," he said, trying to avoid her eyes. "We lost all contact with him. He flew to Rome for a couple of days and . . . "

"Yes, I know," she said. "He was following Mueller."

"He disappeared," he admitted flatly. "He didn't get in touch with me, nor with our friends in Italy. We are worried, and I wanted to ask you . . . "

"No, he hasn't called me since he left," she spoke quickly, anticipating his question. "You think that something happened to him, don't you?" Her trembling hand jerked to her mouth.

He shrugged. "I don't know, I really don't. Only . . . " he hesitated but finally made up his mind, "only if Mueller did find out about him, you might be in danger too."

"Me? Why? I mean . . . "

"Mueller knows that you and Patrick are very close. If he found out that Patrick was following him, I say if, you understand, he might come looking for you. I think you should go away, Maureen. Immediately."

"Oh, God," the distraught girl buried her face in her hands. "You are hiding something from me, Liam, tell me!"

He did not answer, and she slowly removed her hands, fighting her tears. "Tell me!" she repeated.

He shook his head. "We don't know where Patrick is," he said again, stubbornly. "But you must go away for a while."

Her hand blindly reached for the door, seeking support. Her lips were colorless. "But," she stammered, striving to regain control over herself, "where should I go? Michael is away and there is nobody . . . "

Liam took a deep breath, as the luminous green eyes gazed at him in unspoken terror.

PART II

Chapter 13

As the sun slowly rose over the gentle slopes of the Mount of Olives, its rays caressed the huge Dome of the Rock, majestically hovering over the Old City of Jerusalem. It was like the touch of a magic wand. The gilded dome, caught in the sunbeams, metamorphosed into a half-sphere of liquid gold, sparkling like a fabulous gem in the limpid morning air. A minute later, as the sunrays slid through the luscious greenery of the Garden of Gethsemane, the onion-shaped golden domes of the Mary-Magdalene Church erupted in their turn into a dazzling radiance. Below them, the Church of All Nations, built in the style of a Greek temple, slowly emerged from the night shadows in its immaculate whiteness. First in a murmur, then in a ringing, melodius chorus, the pure din of the thousand churches of Jerusalem responded to the birth of a new day.

On the outer landing of his apartment in the Jewish Quarter of the Old City, Michael Gordon paused to contemplate the magnificent sight. The unique beauty of Jerusalem stirred deep emotions in his heart and created a strange feeling of belonging which he could not explain, even to himself. Something unexpected had happened to him in this country. Since his arrival in Israel, ten days ago, he had been wandering about Jerusalem as a man possessed, captivated by the magic of the eternal city. He had explored every crooked alley, every shady bazaar of the Old City, crawled into the ancient Tombs of the Kings of Israel, sloshed in the knee-deep waters of the millenary Tunnel of Siloam, rambled about the domed mosques and the serene churches. He had followed cross-bearing pilgrims along the tortuous path of the Via Dolorosa, had watched religious Jews, wrapped in their prayer shawls, murmur holy verses by the Wailing Wall, and had paced, livid, through the horrid exhibitions at the Memorial of the Holocaust. Jerusalem had awakened in him dim recollections from his childhood; with every day that passed, more words he had learned for his bar-mitzvah prayer and more Hebrew letters from the holy scriptures were surfacing from the recesses of his memory. At times he had the feeling that he had inadvertently started a pilgrimage to his own faraway roots. One night he had called his parents back in New Jersey and spoken with enthusiasm about his experiences. He had felt that he had to share his feelings with somebody, and they were the only ones he could talk to. He was not allowed to call Maureen, whom he badly missed; and in Israel he practically did not know a soul.

His father's enthusiasm over the phone had matched his own. Herb Gordon seemed relieved that his son had abandoned his radical friends, even if only for a few months—as Michael had repeatedly said in the mouthpiece—and had gone to Jerusalem. The old man had immediately volunteered to pay the rent for the small apartment Michael had found in the restored Jewish Quarter.

Michael had not been so lucky, though, in the mission he had undertaken on Mueller's instructions. The Muslim friend of Mueller, who was supposed to find a second room for him in the Arab Quarter, had not shown up as yet. That worried him a lot, as he could not be sure that the cable containing his address had reached Mueller at all. He had sent it a week ago, according to Mueller's instructions, to a post office box in Paris; but he had no means of verifying if it had reached its destination. Furthermore, he had failed in his efforts to penetrate the Jewish Defense League, the extremist organization of Rabbi Kahane. True, he had already assisted at two public meetings organized by Kahane's supporters, but that did not advance him much. To his surprise, most of the speakers and the members of the audience were young American Jews, wearing short beards and yarmulkes. Only a few Israeli-born youths assisted at the meetings. Three out of five speakers even addressed the audience in English. They spoke

at length about their ideology, preaching the unilateral an-
nexation of the West Bank—Judea and Samaria—and the
uprooting of all the non-Jews living there. The speeches,
bombastically delivered and interspersed with fiery slogans
and Biblical quotations, were tirades of religious fanaticism
seasoned with a Brooklyn accent.

At first he had thought that being an American Jew himself
would make it easier for him to work his way up the organization; but he had soon given up that hope. When he had approached several of the speakers at the end of the meetings,
they had been willing to discuss their ideology and to provide
him with leaflets, brochures, and stickers. But when he had
volunteered for action, all he had gotten in return were cold,
wary stares and evasive answers. "We don't need volunteers,"
a tall, scrawny guy named Barney had snapped. "Our activity
is purely ideological." Barney seemed to be the main spokes-
man of the group. Only when he had struck a conversation
with a stooping, thick-waisted boy from Forest Hills did
Michael discover the real reason for Barney's reluctance. The
boy from Forest Hills told him that Rabbi Kahane had been
arrested barely a week ago and placed under administrative
detention. He seemed to be the main suspect in a plot to
blow up the Al Aksa Mosque, one of the holiest shrines of
Islam. The mosque was built on top of the Temple Mount on
the very spot where Solomon's Temple had stood three millenniums ago. The extremists had considered the presence of a
mosque on the Temple grounds as a supreme sacrilege, therefore they had planned to remove it by a spectacular act of
sabotage. Fortunately, the police had discovered the explosives
in time, arrested several people, and placed Kahane under
administrative detention. But the other Kahane followers
who had remained at large were haunted by the fear
that the police might be after them as well. They suspected every newcomer to their meetings as being an undercover police agent planted to spy on them. Michael realized
that he could court Barney and his friends for weeks on end,
but they would not let him into their secrets. If he wanted to
infiltrate their ranks, he had to conceive a different approach.

That was the reason for his stepping out of his apartment
at 5:35 A.M., shivering in the early morning chill. He raised

183

the collar of his denim jacket, took the heavy plastic bag that he had prepared last night, and hurried down the steps. As he strode along the narrow Street of the Jews past the ruins of the once splendid Hurva Synagogue, he pondered his plan's chance of success.

The idea had germinated in his mind two days ago when he was strolling in the New City, enjoying the serene beauty of Ethiopia Street. The houses on both sides of the short street were set in a checkerboard pattern, each of them surrounded by four square gardens of equal size. As he had walked along, peering through the wrought-iron gates into the lush gardens inside, he had come to a strange, circular building. A sign on the wall, supported by two lions of Judea carved in stone above the entrance, announced that this was the Ethiopian church. But the beautiful facade of the church had been viciously vandalized. Somebody had smeared black paint over the immaculate marble slabs; the walls on both sides of the entrance were covered with hastily painted Stars of David and hateful slogans against the bloody *goyim* in Hebrew and English. "Gentiles, go home!" screamed one inscription. A sad-faced, dark-skinned man sat on a chair by the entrance. He turned out to be the Ethiopian key keeper. "Hotheaded young people, sir," he had said with a shy smile when Michael asked him for the identity of the vandals. "The police say that they were Kahane's followers." He had shaken his head repeatedly, spreading his narrow, creased palms. "They are young, they don't know what they're doing."

Michael had thanked him and started walking away when he had had a sudden inspiration. He had come back and copied the inscriptions into his small notebook. Yesterday he had entered a shop on Jaffa Street and bought a can of black paint and a brush. And now he hurried across the Old City of Jerusalem, determined to beat Kahane's boys at their own game. He was pained by what he was going to do; but he had been charged with a mission, he was committed to carry it out, and today's ruse seemed to him the only way. Besides, he hoped that he would not do any substantial damage before he was caught. For that was what he wanted—to be caught.

He turned left into Suq el-Bazaar Road, the busiest market

lane in the Old City. This portion of the market was covered and was still plunged in darkness. At that early morning hour the customers and most of the merchants were still fast asleep in their beds, and the narrow stone-paved street was almost empty. Still, the nearness of the bazaar was heralded by the sharp, exotic scents of Oriental spices that wafted from a narrow alley to the right. The exquisite sign painted at the entrance of the alley read Spice Market Street. Michael hastened his step. He had now come in the open, into David Street. A few early-rising Arab shopkeepers were already moving about, opening their shops, arranging their merchandise on display in front of their tiny boutiques. An old man was assiduously rubbing large brass plates before propping them against the wall while his son was dragging out of the dark shop a small Damascus stool, inlaid with mother-of-pearl. Farther down, two small kids, trembling in their thin shirts, stood on their toes on dilapidated chairs, hanging richly embroidered peasant dresses from a rusty rack. The sheepskin coats piled on the other side of the lane gave off a pungent odor. Michael moved to the left to avoid a group of street vendors, squatting around tiny cups of Turkish coffee. They looked at him in puzzlement. What was a Jew doing in the market at such an unholy hour? One of them instinctively called after him, "You want beautiful souvenir, sir?" But his voice lacked conviction and he crouched back over his coffee without even waiting for Michael's reaction.

A tantalizing smell caught his nostrils as he emerged on Omar Ibn el-Khattab Square. From the illuminated bakery at the corner a couple of ragged youngsters were dragging a cartload of oven-fresh loaves, topped with sesame seeds. On the left, above the steep walls of the Citadel, rose the sleek David's Tower, already bathed in the morning sun. Michael crossed the square and hurried along the Citadel walls. He was now on the Armenian Orthodox Patriarchate Road. His heart thumped quicker as he approached the huge Armenian compound. The splendid building spanning the street ahead of him was the residence of the Armenian patriarch. He walked under the arch and came out on the other side. In the thick wall on his left he saw the big iron gate controlling the entrance to Saint James Convent.

He stopped by the gate and threw a quick look around him. The street was empty. He knelt by the plastic bag and took out the brush and the can of paint. His fingers were trembling slightly, and he broke a fingernail struggling with the lid of the can. Finally it gave way and the can opened, the liquid black paint mirroring Michael's drawn, tense features. He grasped the can in his left hand, the wooden handle of the brush in his right, and straightened up. He dipped the brush in the paint, splashing tiny black drops all over his clothes, and with swift, bold strokes sketched a big black Star of David on the wall. Far behind him he heard footsteps, but he did not look back. He dipped the brush again, and another star, even bigger, blossomed on the white wall beside the first. The brush was in the can again. "Gentiles, go home!" in English. And now in Hebrew. He remembered the inscription he had copied at the Ethiopian church; actually he did not mind making a mistake. He smeared the Hebrew letters from the right to the left. There was not enough paint for the last word, dammit! As he dipped the brush in the can again, he heard a sharp metallic sound above his head. He looked up. The iron shutters of a window on the first floor were open, and a face was looking at him. He glimpsed a pair of dark eyes and a white beard. *"Qu'est-ce que vous faites là?"* the bearded man asked in astonishment. Michael lowered his eyes and furiously painted the rest of the stupid slogan. And suddenly it was all over. He had achieved what he wanted and had no desire to do any further damage. All he wanted now was to be arrested. So he just stood there, feeling foolish, the viscous paint slowly dripping from the brush and forming a tiny puddle at his feet.

The iron gate squeaked and a figure clad in black noiselessly stepped out. It was an Armenian monk, dressed in a long black robe. An odd triangular hood covered the top of his head and cast a shadow over his eyes. Michael recognized the long white beard. It was the man who had spoken to him from the window. The Armenian ignored Michael and stared at the fresh inscriptions on the wall, wringing his hands. Finally he turned to Michael. Just for a moment, his eyes glinted beneath the hood, but when he spoke, his voice was soft, devoid of hostility. *"Pourquoi avez-vous fait cela?"*

186

"English," Michael grunted, feeling ridiculous.

"Why did you do that?" the monk asked in the same mild voice. "We do no harm to anybody."

For a fleeting instant, Michael thought of delivering a speech like those he had heard at the Kahane organization meetings. But even in this situation he could not force himself to repeat that nonsense. "I shall give my reasons to the police only," he said sullenly.

The monk seemed at a loss. He stepped closer to Michael, scanning his face intently. Three or four Arabs, coming from the direction of Omar Ibn el-Khattab Square, stopped beside them. One of them cupped his face with his hands and sadly shook his head; the others were urgently whispering. A young man in a tan sweater and crumpled trousers, his eyes puffed with sleep, came out of the convent gate and looked in horror at the inscriptions on the wall. He had a typical Armenian face, round, bulging eyes, a thin and slightly curved nose, a smooth, dark complexion.

After some hesitation the monk spoke again. "Do you want me to call the police?" he asked.

Michael shrugged. He had not anticipated that such an absurd situation would develop. Why, the Armenians might even let him go! He nodded his head. "Call the police," he mumbled.

The monk turned to the young man behind him and spoke quickly in a strange language which Michael assumed was Armenian. He only grasped the boy's name, Aram. The youngster nodded and broke into a run toward the square. In the meantime some other men and old women gathered around them. Somebody angrily shouted at Michael in Arabic. "Come!" the monk said, suddenly making up his mind. "We shall wait for the police inside."

Michael followed him through the gate, still holding the can of paint and the brush. The entrance to the convent was stone-paved, and a single lantern hung from the vaulted roof. The wooden guardian's room, to the left of the handsome iron gate, was empty. Michael assumed that young Aram was tonight's guard. A decorative drinking fountain made of marble stood by the entrance. Farther down, on the wall opposite the courtyard, Michael saw several ornamental flagstones, artfully decorated in patterns of the cross. Each of them carried an inscription in Armenian. Michael had read about those stones. They were Khatchkars, offerings of pilgrims who had come all the way from Armenia to Jerusalem. The oldest, he recalled, dated from the twelfth century. Two huge clappers that had served to call the faithful to prayer until the Turks had lifted the ban on church bells in 1840 still stood by the main entrance to the cathedral.

The monk stopped, still wringing his hands. "Why did you do it?" he asked Michael again. His voice was shy, almost apologetic. "We worship God, we do no harm."

Michael was spared the answer by the sound of an engine by the gate. Aram, his face flushed and moist with sweat, hurried into the courtyard and pointed at Michael. Two policemen peered inside, obviously hesitating to enter. "You, come here," one of them called in Hebrew. As Michael approached, the policeman angrily wrenched the can and brush from his hands. A police van stood behind them, its engine running. "Get inside!" the policeman snapped. He was a frail, thin man with a moustache. Michael climbed the steps into the back portion of the van. Inside were two wooden benches, facing each other. The floor was a mess, strewn with chewing gum wrappers and cigarette butts. The vehicle smelled of disinfectant and tobacco.

From the window of the van Michael saw the moustached policeman nod vigorously as the Armenian monk softly spoke. The other policeman, a large man with a notable paunch, lit a cigarette while looking at the inscriptions on the wall. He took off his hat and wiped his brow with the sleeve of his dark-blue uniform. Then he got in the driver's seat, slamming the door behind him. The moustached policeman deferentially shook the Armenian's hand, stepped into the van, and sat facing Michael. Somebody had found the plastic bag and the lid of the can. He snapped the can closed, packed it with the brush in the bag, and put it at his feet. As the van moved toward the Zion Gate, he looked at Michael and said something in Hebrew.

"I don't understand," Michael said in English.

The policeman stared at him suspiciously. He seemed to doubt that Michael did not speak Hebrew. Michael decided to start his charade. "Rabbi Kahane," he said forcefully, brandishing his fist. "Jewish Defense League!"

"Oh, yes," the policeman said, his face brightening. "Oh yes," he repeated, lightly tapping his temple with his index finger to illustrate what he thought of Rabbi Kahane and his boys, then made a spiteful gesture with his left hand. He lost all interest in Michael and for the rest of the drive gazed vacantly out the window. He did not seem to fear an assault or even an escape attempt by his prisoner.

Michael got out of the van at the police headquarters in the New City. As he walked up the steps, he caught a glimpse of the massive, stolid bulk of the neighboring Russian Cathedral, incongruously topped with a multitude of green domes. In the big, drab hall a score of petty criminals were sitting on a long bench set against the wall, their faces unshaven, their eyes lost in the absent, vacuous gaze of people used to spending hours and days in the idleness of a prison. The three police officers sitting behind an elevated counter across the hall would raise their eyes occasionally to gaze at the first catch of the day. There was a night's stubble on their jaws, and their faces were slack with fatigue. Michael looked at his watch. It was barely 6:25.

He was ordered to approach the counter. A police sergeant who spoke heavily-accented but adequate English noted his name and address and checked his papers. Another policeman escorted him to an inner office where his thumbprints were taken. A brisk, redheaded girl who wore a lieutenant's insignia on her epaulets questioned him for fifteen minutes. He gave her a full account of his deed and repeated the slogans of the JDL. The pompous clichés sounded hollow and phony in the small police office, and the ironical expression on the redhead's face changed into puzzlement, as she seemed to doubt that he really believed in what he said. He refused to sign his statement and proudly declared that he had no means to bail himself out. He was escorted to a cell where six other men sat in a circle, playing with some coins. He squatted in the opposite corner, wondering if his gamble would work.

It did. At 7:25 A.M. the news of his arrest was on the tickers of the Israeli press agency. At 8:00 it was broadcast on the morning news bulletin. At 9:30 a fat, aging policeman unlocked the cell door and beckoned him with his short, chubby finger. As Michael followed the policeman down the narrow corridor, he passed the redheaded lieutenant. "Goodbye, Jewish defender," she quipped mockingly. "Your friends have come to bail you out."

In the entrance lobby two young men wearing knitted skullcaps were signing some papers. The taller one turned to him and nodded in recognition. "Next time you'll do that only when I tell you to, painter boy," Barney said. Then he added with a grin, "And welcome to the club, Michael."

Dusk was settling over the city when he finally got home. He was tired and cold, but his spirits were high. He had spent most of the day with Barney and his friends from the Jewish Defense League. They had had lunch together in a small restaurant, whose windows offered a nice view on the Old City wall. Barney had mildly reprimanded him for his "Armenian adventure" as he called it, and Michael had answered with the speech he had rehearsed beforehand. He had started by saying that he could not stand that Jerusalem was full of mosques and churches which had all the rights while the Jews had to walk about on their tiptoes. Jerusalem was Jewish, he pointed out, it belonged to Israel, and it was time for a change. The world should know that Jerusalem would become a purely Jewish city. "Besides," he had added, "I saw that you guys did the same thing at the Ethiopian church."

"That was before," Barney had replied. "Now the situation is different. Meir Kahane and two other guys are in prison. Everybody is after us, even the religious establishment. The police are just looking for a pretext to wipe us out completely. We should be very careful."

"But we must act, not talk!" Michael had exclaimed heatedly. That was a good one, he reflected. He was really getting into his role.

"No action for the moment," Barney had stated. "Now we just lie low and wait. When the moment comes, we'll act, don't worry. And I can promise you that we'll do much more than paint slogans on churches."

The fanaticism of Barney and his friends had worried him,

but he comforted himself with the thought that they were just a handful of people, no more than fifty or sixty in the whole country. What really counted, though, was that he had been accepted in their innermost circle. If anything happened, he would be among the first to know.

When they had parted, he had exchanged telephone numbers with Barney, and they had agreed to maintain a daily contact.

Michael was now certain that if the JDL decided to take any action against the forthcoming march on Jerusalem, he would be at the right spot to forewarn Alfred and his friends. Alfred would be proud of him, he thought, as he strolled back home through the beautiful squares and alleys of the renovated Jewish Quarter.

Some children were playing in the open space before his house. By the outer staircase he passed a dark girl, probably an Arab, who stared at him intently with her coal-black eyes. She wore a brown cardigan over a shapeless, dark-red dress, but even the shabby, outmoded clothing could hardly conceal the curvaceous lines of her body. Some locks of heavy black hair escaped from under the scarf she wore over her head, tied under the chin as peasant women used to.

She could be quite pretty, in different clothes and in a different place, he absently thought for a second, reaching for his key. Then he was home. He poured himself a glass of dry Avdat wine, lit a filter cigarette, and stretched luxuriously in the low, well-padded armchair. God, he was exhausted. But it had been a day well spent.

He had barely taken a sip of the fragrant red wine when there was a knock on the door. He got up, puzzled. The rapping was repeated, quick and urgent. He hesitated another instant, then got up and opened the door.

The Arab girl he had seen before stood on the landing.

"Let me in, please," she said breathlessly in English. "Alfred sent me."

He looked at her in amazement as she stepped in quickly and leaned on the door that snapped shut behind her. He had expected a man, not a young girl. But did Alfred ever say he would be contacted by a man? He tried to recall their conversation at the Gare de Lyon. "We have an Arab friend in East Jerusalem," Alfred had said. A friend could be a girl as well.

She seemed to read his thoughts. "You didn't expect a woman, did you?" she suppressed a cold smile. "Well, in our group women are equal to men. I was instructed . . . "

"Which group?" he broke in sharply.

She hesitated for a split second, her eyes hostile. "The group that is helping Alfred with his project," she said dryly.

"Do you know what the project is about?" he asked. He suddenly realized that they were both standing by the door. "Please sit down." He motioned toward the chairs and the sofa. "Would you like a drink?"

She shook her head vehemently. "No, I prefer to stand. I don't want a drink."

Michael was taken aback by the overt hostility in her behavior. He shrugged, sat down, and took his glass of wine. "You didn't answer my question," he said. "Are you acquainted with Alfred's project?"

She had removed her scarf, and as she shook her head, a ripple ran over her mass of luxurious black hair. She was a beautiful girl indeed. Yet the hostile expression stamped on her face distorted her lovely features. "The answer is no," she replied. "I don't know what the project is about. I only know that I have to find a room for you in . . . in our part of the city." The last words were loaded with hatred.

He looked at her, frowning, pervaded by a growing feeling of uneasiness. He had an impulse to ask her why she was so hostile, but on second thought decided not to. They both had a mission to accomplish, and her feelings were her own business. "Did you find the room?" he inquired.

"Yes," she said. "It was not easy. People in East Jerusalem are very reluctant to rent rooms to Jews. That's why we did not get in touch with you earlier. We found a room only yesterday. I have been waiting for you downstairs for more than an hour. Come, let's go there."

"Now?" he asked surprised. "What's the hurry? We can go tomorrow morning."

She shook her head. "No. We must go there tonight. They

192

are waiting for you to sign the lease. If we wait until tomorrow, the deal might be off."

He sighed, slowly getting up. "Okay." He put on his jacket. "Where is the room?"

"It isn't far, about ten minutes walk. It's off Saint Helena Road."

"Saint Helena?" He tilted his head. "Isn't that the Via Dolorosa?"

"Almost," she said, lowering her voice as they went out and down the stairs. "You may consider yourself lucky. Your window faces one of the most famous places in the world, the Church of the Holy Sepulchre."

He nodded. "What's your name?" he inquired pleasantly.

She hesitated for a moment, then gave in. "Latifa," she said in a low voice.

Latifa Husseini had never had such a long conversation with a Jew in her whole life. Not that she had not had the occasion. The Jews who used to shop or stroll in East Jerusalem seemed eager to engage in a dialogue with young Arabs. But she did not want to talk to them. She had been raised in hatred, total, overwhelming hatred, and felt it in her very bones, in the blood that was pulsating through her body. She had not been born in 1948 when Israel had become an independent state at the cost of nearly one million Arab refugees who were scattered all over the Middle East. Her schoolbooks contained many chapters on the terrible injustice the Jews had done to her people. The Jews were a gang of barbarians and murderers, the books said. It was also written there that one day the Arab nation would rise, strong and united, and would crush the Zionist state once and forever.

But the opposite had happened. When she was ten years old, in 1967, the war had broken out, At first all the inhabitants of their village were crazy with joy. The radio promised that the Jews would soon drown in the rivers of their own blood. They were still rejoicing when the Israeli columns suddenly appeared at the outskirts of their village. It could not be, they said to each other, the Jews were cowards, they were unable to fight properly. Maybe it was

193

just a temporary fallback until Hussein sent fresh troops from across the river, until Egypt and Syria launched their decisive offensive that would lead them to Tel Aviv. And then the bits and pieces of terrible rumors started to flow into the village. Hussein's army had been destroyed and so had the armies of Egypt and Syria and even the formidable air force of Iraq. Israel had defeated all the Arab states and now occupied all of Sinai, the Golan Heights, Jerusalem, and the West Bank. How could that have happened? she asked her older brothers. The Arabs had failed because of their corrupt regimes, they said. In order to wipe out Israel the young Arabs had to become revolutionaries and join a new organization, the Fatah, that would fight the Jews as well as the rotten regime of Hussein. And after the victory, the Arabs would establish a revolutionary Marxist state on the ruins of Israel. Both her brothers had joined the Fatah, and she had been very proud, although she could not speak about it to other children in the village.

And then, one day, Israeli soldiers in command cars and half-trucks came to their village and surrounded their house. In one of the cars were both her brothers, their hands manacled. The officer had come in and said that her brothers had blown up a car full of explosives in the center of Jerusalem and killed several people. They had to go to prison for many years. Furthermore, according to a law existing since the time of the British Mandate, their house had to be destroyed. She was fourteen at the time, and she writhed in her mother's arms, screaming and crying, as they stood on a nearby hill and watched a tremendous explosion turn their house into a smoldering heap of rubble. Then she told her mother, "When I grow up, I too will join the Fatah!"

She had grown up, and her hatred for the Jews had grown deeper. Their family had moved to East Jerusalem, and she was free to associate with other young Arabs who were ready to risk their lives for the destruction of Israel. She joined a cell of the Fatah and took part in organizing demonstrations, riots, strikes, and protests against the Jews.

She worked during the day at the East Jerusalem daily *Al Fajar* as a secretary and met with the other members of her Fatah cell in the evenings.

194

Yesterday Nawaf, the chief of their cell, had called her and instructed her to visit a room in the Arab section of the Old City. The room had been chosen already, he had said. He had spoken to the owners and had assured them that the Fatah wanted them to lease the room to an American Jew and that they would serve their people well if they did as they were told. She was to arrange a meeting between them and the Jew and make him sign the necessary papers. His name was Michael Gordon, and he lived in the Jewish Quarter. Nawaf had also told her the passwords: Alfred sent me.

Well, after tonight she would not see him again, she thought, as she led him through Suq el-Hussor and Muristan Road toward the big Christian church. He seemed nice and friendly, but she did not want his friendship. She even felt humiliated walking with him in the street. Maybe he was on their side, as Nawaf had explained. She did not care. The Jews were all the same.

They walked through a small porch and emerged on the big square facing the church. The restoration work was still going on, and there were chunks of wood and broken stones strewn all over the place. She stumbled in the darkness over a block of concrete and would have fallen if he had not caught her by the arm. She shook her arm free, and he noticed the same expression of hatred etched in every line of her beautiful face.

"It's here," she said, "on the first floor. The family name is Masri. Go up, they are expecting you. You'll sign the lease, and you can have the room."

"Aren't you coming up?" he asked, surprised.

"No," she shook her head. "You don't need me anymore."

"Wait," he called after her. "If something goes wrong, I might need you. I don't know how to get in touch with you."

The house was a part of a huge facade, built of rough Jerusalem stones, that rose on the southern edge of a middle-sized square, about one hundred yards wide. Across the square loomed the sturdy structure of Christendom's most sacred shrine, the Church of the Holy Sepulchre. A faint glow was coming from its big arched porch, and Michael heard the low murmur of people praying. He followed Latifa through the small entrance above which a Greek inscription was carved in the stone. They went up an outer staircase and reached a small, beautiful terrace, spotlessly clean. Two ancient lanterns, fixed on the walls, bathed the terrace in soft, yellow illumination. Big pots full of plants and flowers lined the walls. Some steps on the western side led to a bigger terrace, whose wrought-iron balustrade was covered with greenery. Several doors and windows opened on the landing. One of the big, brown doors had frosted-glass panels. Over its stone frame there was a small stained-glass window with a star in the middle and another Greek inscription formed an arch over it. The door opened, and a woman clad in a black robe and a strange headdress that left only her face visible walked out. She smiled at them and noiselessly disappeared into the stairwell. Michael looked at Latifa quizzically.

"She is a Greek nun," the young woman said dryly. "All this building belongs to the Greek Orthodox Church. Only these two rooms," she pointed to the doors behind them, "have been leased to the Masri family. Adnan Masri is the custodian of the church over on the square. Since his sons left home, he lives here alone with his wife. So he rents the second room."

At the sound of her voice, one of the doors opened. An aging, fat man came out, peering at them with short-sighted eyes. He held a pair of glasses in his hand. He was wearing an old jacket over a woolen shirt, a pair of crumpled brown trousers, and shiny black slippers. He adjusted his glasses and, recognizing Latifa, smiled nervously. "Good evening," he said in hesitating English, addressing Michael. "Come in, please." They entered the big, overstuffed room. Masri's petite wife came forward from the shadows. As her emaciated face cracked in a toothless grin, her left hand shyly jerked upward to conceal her mouth. Michael and Latifa sat down in deep, shabby armchairs facing the narrow bed. The thin woman brought some coffee, while Adnan Masri produced a sheaf of papers held in a nylon bag. "I understand that you want to rent the room," he articulated with difficulty.

The negotiation that followed was short. Michael did not argue about the rent, which was rather modest. He was told where the toilets were situated, where he could shave and take showers. He nodded absently while the explanations

196

were being given. He was not going to use the shower anyway, as he did not intend to sleep in this room. Alfred's instructions were clear. The room had to be rented in his name but kept unoccupied, for it was to serve only for the purposes of the march on Jerusalem. He just had to drop in once a week to check if everything was all right.

He signed the papers, paid Adnan Masri a month's rent in advance, and pocketed the handwritten affidavit in which his landlord confirmed that he was his new tenant. The only formality left was to stop by the nearby police station the next morning to get the certificate stamped and authenticated. As he got up, he asked, "May I see the room?"

"Of course," Masri said. He took a big key from the top drawer of his dresser and invited Michael and Latifa, with a sweeping motion of his hand, to follow him. He unlocked the first door on the left and switched on the light. Michael blinked, surprised. The room was a draftsman's study, complete with drawing boards, lamps, slide rules. A multitude of pencils and nibs were strewn on a big table beside a pile of drawings.

"This used to be an engineer's study," Latifa explained after a short exchange in Arabic with Masri. "He is leaving tomorrow morning. The room is yours starting tomorrow at noon."

"Fine," Michael nodded and approached the window. It faced the entrance of the Holy Sepulchre Church straight across the square. He decided to come here during the day. The sight must be really fascinating in daylight with all those pilgrims swarming about. He was certain now that Mueller had insisted on a room at that square, even if it took longer to find. The place was ideal for their purposes. In the crowd that always filled the square, nobody would notice people coming in and out of the narrow entrance.

He thanked Masri and followed Latifa down the stairs. In the square he stretched his hand to her. "Thank you very much, Latifa," he said, smiling. "It was nice meeting you."

She barely let him touch her fingers, then abruptly withdrew her hand. "Good-bye," she said in a muffled voice and quickly walked away.

* * *

A week later, Alfred Mueller walked into a post office on Rue des Saussaies in the eighth arrondissement of Paris. By a side door he entered the room of the post office boxes. From a bunch of strikingly similar keys that he took out of his pocket, he chose one and unlocked a box. Inside were several envelopes of various sizes. He tucked them into the inner pocket of his duffel coat and walked out. He entered a modest café on Rue Montalivet and slid behind a corner table. The waiter who brought him his black coffee wrinkled his nose as the pungent smell of the eucalyptus cigarette irritated his nostrils.

Mueller neatly slit the envelopes with a pocket knife and systematically went through their contents. Two of the envelopes came from Israel. They had been sent by the men Arafat had put at his disposal. The first was an innocent letter full of nonsense about the beauty of Jerusalem in the spring and the health of some imaginary grandmother. That letter contained another message, but it was coded, and Mueller decided to decipher it when he would be alone. The second envelope contained no letter, just a clipping from the *Jerusalem Post*. Mueller quickly read the short news item. It described the despicable act of vandalism against the Armenian Convent of Saint James committed by a fanatic Jewish Defense Leaguer named Michael Gordon.

For a second he stared at the clipping, then all of a sudden his whole body contorted in soundless, convulsive laughter. The stupid sucker! In his zeal to carry out his mission that idiot Gordon had done him an invaluable service. He would never live to know how much he had helped Mueller by that initiative. He went into a second fit of laughter that distorted his skull-shaped face in an ugly rictus, baring his uneven yellow teeth.

From his position behind the brass counter, the waiter watched the black-clothed stranger writhing in laughter in disgust. He had seen many freaks in his life, but this one was in a class by himself. Creeps like that should be banned from the streets like in the old times. Shaking his head, he bent back over the sink and continued wiping the wine glasses, muttering to himself.

Mueller had all the reasons to be in the best of moods. The

elements of the plan were smoothly coming together. He had gotten everything he needed in Jerusalem to Jerusalem: the weapon, the room, and the Jew. He also knew the date. It was time to launch the diversionary move that would keep the Mossad sweating while he got ready for the kill.

He took a sip of the bitter coffee and started coding a signal to Arafat.

Chapter 14

THE MAN WHO was about to die pushed aside his unfinished plate and looked out the plane window at the carpet of cottony white clouds that stretched as far as the eye could see. He felt exhausted and spent. The roar of the 747 engines was almost inaudible in his forward compartment; his aides were moving behind him on tiptoes, silent as shadows, and the reporters had strict instructions not to disturb him. Yet, the emotional strain of the last few days had left him in a state of high nervous tension, and he could not sleep in spite of his fatigue. His visit to America had been a success, and he hoped it would benefit the cause and the values in which he so deeply believed. As he closed his eyes, images from the eventful journey across America flashed in his mind. The warm welcome of the President and the First Lady in the White House. The crowds in New York, Chicago, and Philadelphia. The visit to the United Nations and his one-hour speech before the General Assembly. The point of departure for his speech had been the tragedy of Auschwitz. Except for a short paragraph about Jerusalem and the Palestinian question that stirred some mixed reactions, his address had been warmly received, and the last paragraph had triggered a standing ovation.

During his journey throughout America he had tried to mix with the people, to talk to as many groups and individuals as possible. *"Shalom*—Peace be with you!" he had shouted at Battery Park in lower Manhattan addressing the American Jews. Later he was told that Rabbi Marc Tenenbaum of the American Jewish Committee had praised his "charismatic power, intellectual sharpness, and moral persuasiveness," and defined his speech at Battery Park as "an embrace of love and respect." But the love was mutual. Wherever he went the American people welcomed him with deep affection and genuine enthusiasm. His aides told him about many of his coreligionists who had traveled hundreds of miles to see him, like the seventy-five-year-old woman from Miami who had come all the way to Boston to catch a brief glimpse of his motorcade crossing the city. In New York and Chicago, where many of his people were living, the crowds waved signs and placards written in his own language; seventy-five thousand people flocked to Madison Square Garden to greet him.

Of course, beside the triumphs, there were also some disappointments. Almost everywhere he went, he was bitterly criticized for his stiff conservatism and his refusal to budge from his rigid positions. They did not dare throw those accusations in his face, but he read them in the papers and saw the protest signs during his passage through the crowded streets. The FBI had even had to thwart an attempt on his life. Their agents in Newark had received an advance warning that he would be assassinated in Manhattan; the investigation led the federal agents to an apartment in Elizabeth, New Jersey, where a submachine gun and empty ammunition boxes had been hidden.

He suppressed a yawn and took a leather-bound, gold-embossed folder from the adjacent seat. On top of the papers inside lay a document listing the most urgent affairs he had to attend to on his return. The first item on the list was the financial crisis. The swollen staff left by his predecessor, the galloping inflation at home, and the rising prices abroad had contributed to a big deficit in the current budget. He reflected about launching an appeal to his coreligionists all over the world to contribute—as they always did—to the financing of the next budget. He would couple that effort with an austerity plan to be instituted immediately.

He had been traveling too much lately, he admitted to himself. America, France, Germany. . . . In France he had had too many meetings, although one he still remembered with pleasure was his long talk with chief Rabbi Jacob Kaplan. The man was eighty-five years old, preparing to retire in the summer, but his sharp mind was still crystal clear and his memory perfect. In Germany too he had met a quite extraordinary person, old Dr. Gertrud Lockner. The small, bashful woman, a devout Christian, had accomplished acts of unmatched heroism during World War II, risking her life daily to rescue Jewish families from the Gestapo. He had taken her with him to a meeting with the Council of German Jewry and had kissed her with admiration and respect after relating her deeds to his audience. The plight of the Jews during the World War did not leave him in peace, and his visit to Auschwitz, where he had bowed his head in prayer before the memorial to the dead, was always present in his mind. Auschwitz was the key to his deep attachment to the survival and the security of Israel.

His eye returned to the sheet of paper in his hand. He had a lot of work to do and would have to postpone several projects which he had announced not long ago. The trip to Egypt would have to be canceled for the time being, and some other plans as well.

But the one project that could not wait was the Jerusalem project. The date had been set, and the arrangements made.

But he did not know that in Jerusalem other arrangements had been made, people and weapons were in place, and death was waiting.

On the ninth floor of the Mossad the word spread quickly that something had happened to the Old Man since his return from Switzerland. He practically barricaded himself in his office where he would spend most of the day alone, avoiding visitors and refusing phone calls. The lunch trays that Nora, his gray-haired secretary, brought over from the fifth-floor cafeteria were returned untouched. To a few chosen members of Jeremiah's entourage Nora worriedly confided that the boss spent most of the day slumped behind his desk, digging in old files he had ordered from Archives or vacantly staring at a blown-up photograph of Alfred Mueller that he had fixed to the wall with long strips of cellophane tape. His office had become a mess, Nora complained—shutters closed, a single table lamp burning all day long, dusty files scattered all over the place. Jeremiah, who had always been so neat and tidy, did not seem to care. He was high-strung like he had never been before and would pester her for more and more files. If the documents did not arrive promptly he would easily blow his lid, in spite of her repeated explanations that most of the files were outdated and had to be brought from the Jaffa depot.

He was the first to come to the office and the last to leave. The duty officers who happened to pass him in the corridor would get a vague grunt in response to their greetings and would glimpse a sullen, morose face and tightly drawn mouth. Among the senior staff, many attributed his black mood to the failure of the snatch operation in Lebrun; others whispered behind his back that he could not get used to the idea of having only a few more weeks left at the helm of the Mossad. The news of his resignation was quasi-official now, and the sight of Rafael Avizur, strutting like a bantam cock in the upper-floor departments or oozing self-satisfaction at the Forum Two morning meetings, left no doubt as to the identity of the next Mossad chief.

An invisible barrier had sprung up between the Old Man and his inner circle of department heads. He became cold and detached with David Roth, who would sadly shrug and shake his head when he walked out of Jeremiah's office. Toward Avizur he adopted an icy, official attitude. With Hefner he was abrupt and impatient, and the young man finally gave in and miserably retreated to his den adjacent to the outer office.

Most of all he avoided Mally Segev. The intuitive little woman divined that he was deeply embarrassed by the fleeting moment of intimacy they had shared that evening in Switzerland. She felt that she was the only one who understood the real reasons for his distress. Of course, he had made a detailed report to Forum One about Mueller's identity and his probable obsession with avenging his father's death. His revelations had caused a good deal of excitement among the department heads. But she had been the only one to witness his bare torment for Kolaichek's suicide years ago and to sense his deep consternation about the mysterious revenge that the cunning terrorist was scheming. Therefore, she was not surprised at all when Nora conspiratorially whispered in her ear that Jeremiah had spent two long afternoons closeted with Dr. Bergmann, the Mossad psychiatrist. Jeremiah was probably striving to figure out how Mueller's psychotic mind functioned. Nora also told Mally about a worried call she had gotten from Edna, Jeremiah's niece, after a disastrous evening in their house. The Old Man had brought little Sharon a toy cuckoo clock from Switzerland, but the clock had broken in his hands when he wound it too forcefully. He had left abruptly and had not come to see them since.

Still, Mally had the vague feeling that Jeremiah was waiting for something to happen. That was merely a hunch based on her feminine intuition. But like so many times in the past, her hunch was right. Jeremiah's nerves were in a piteous state, indeed, and he was deeply into the worst crisis of his career. Yet he desperately stuck to a single hope: Mueller was bound to make the next move, perhaps a cruel, dangerous move, but one that would get him, Jeremiah, back into the game. Embittered by the Lebrun fiasco, immobilized by Mueller's disappearance in Paris, isolated among his peers in his concern about the terrorist's plans, he had no course open but to wait and pray that Mueller would show his hand.

And the Old Man waited. For three long, agonizing weeks after his return, nothing unusual happened. But finally Mueller advanced a pawn on their private chessboard—for since Lebrun it had become a private duel—and Peled was back on his trail like a bloodhound.

The phone call woke him shortly before dawn on the sixteenth of March. He had always been a light sleeper, but lately his nights were agitated and fitful. He was fully awake at the first ring of the scrambler phone and a second later was sitting erect in his bed, tightly pressing the receiver to his ear.

It was the night duty officer. "Jeremiah, we got a flash from the Amsterdam station. They say that a young Dutchman is arriving on the first KLM flight this morning. He has been seen several times with people from the local Fatah cell. Name is Rick Van Weyden. Medium height, brown hair, glasses. We checked with the computer, and the guy has spent some time in the Fatah camps in Lebanon. He was among the European volunteers who left Saida shortly before the paratroop raid in February."

He had listened without interrupting. As he heard the name of Saida, he was swept by a wave of excitement. "When is the flight landing?" he quickly asked, throwing an oblique glance at the luminous digital clock on his night table. It was 4:27 A.M.

"Eleven fifty-five. That's KLM flight 317."

"I shall be at the office at six." He tried to master the tremor of exhilaration in his voice. "Alert the Shin Beth, the Special Branch, and airport security."

"That's already done, Jeremiah," said the brisk, calm voice.

"Good. Call David Roth, Mally, Sabi, and Hefner." He paused. "And Avri Tour from the Shin Beth. Ask them to meet me at the office at six. I also want the anti-terrorist squad deployed at the airport by ten-thirty." He hung up and sat immobile for a long moment, staring in the dark.

They spotted him as soon as he reached the long row of immigration desks: a brown-haired, hollow-chested young man wearing a blue windbreaker over a woolen Lee shirt, faded jeans, and Adidas sneakers. A worn canvas rucksack was slung over his shoulder. He nervously shifted his weight from one leg to the other while waiting in line before one of the low booths where an attractive policewoman stamped entry visas on passports and disembarkation cards. He could not know that like all the other young men who had disembarked from the KLM Boeing, he was sandwiched between two security agents, posing as passengers from another flight. There were about thirty operatives of the anti-terrorist squad clustering around any suspect Dutchman, their guns concealed under jackets or loose pullovers, their eyes glued to the passengers' hand luggage.

At the early morning meeting in the Mossad headquarters, Jeremiah had ruled out any dramatic attempt to apprehend the suspect before he went through immigration. Avri Tour, director of the Shin Beth, the internal security service, had suggested throwing a security cordon around the plane and screening all incoming passengers. Jeremiah had refused outright. There was always the possibility that Van Weyden had an accomplice aboard the flight, he had pointed out. That second terrorist could slip away unnoticed and alert his local Fatah contacts. Another possibility was that Van Weyden was not traveling under his real name. In that case, all passengers vaguely fitting his description would have to be followed on leaving the terminal and kept under close surveillance till one of them made a suspect move. In both cases, any arrest had to be made quietly without attracting attention. On the other hand, extensive security measures should be taken in case the Dutch terrorist was armed and planned to carry out a massacre in the crowded arrival hall. The memory of the Japanese assassins who had slain twenty-four passengers by the airport luggage conveyors in 1973 was still present in everybody's mind.

But Van Weyden was traveling under his real name, and he was alone. As the girl in the blue police uniform stamped his passport, she nodded slightly to the dark Shin Beth agent who stood behind him, placidly chewing some gum. Rick Van Weyden was discreetly shadowed through customs where he made no objection to a routine search of his rucksack. When he left the terminal, he stopped, undecided for a moment, blinking in the glorious spring sunshine. "Taxi, sir?" a squat, bald man wearing a striped cardigan asked him. Van Weyden nodded and followed the cab driver to a middle-aged Mercedes. "Tel Aviv," he said with a strong accent, "Hotel Sabra, Hayarkon Street."

The driver nodded and started the car. After reaching the main Tel Aviv–Jerusalem highway, he slowed down and pulled off the road. "Sorry," he mumbled apologetically in bad English, "something wrong with back tire." As he killed the engine, both back doors opened simultaneously and two men squeezed in on both sides of the Dutchman.

"We'd like to ask you a few questions, Mr. Van Weyden," one of them said as the car darted forward and merged into the sparse midday traffic.

Late that afternoon, the two men were shown into the conference room at the Mossad headquarters. Most members of Forum One were there already, quietly chatting around the big horseshoe table. Shortly after his agents, Avri Tour walked in. He was a big, muscular man with a tanned face, deep-set intelligent eyes, and a receding jaw. He was mild of manner and modestly dressed; the only touch of vanity in his appearance was the excessively long hair of his temples painstakingly combed across the skull to conceal his advancing baldness. He slipped into a chair beside his men, sliding his cigarettes and lighter with a wink to Mally Segev, who was nervously chewing her pencil. She hesitated, then finally took a cigarette and lit it, exhaling the bluish smoke with apparent relief.

Jeremiah Peled was the last to take his place beside the table. He definitely looked different today, Mally noted. His step was alert, the blue eyes were sparkling again, and the deep voice was brisk and firm. "Well, Avri, what's the news?" he asked without preliminaries.

The Shin Beth director gestured toward his two men. "Elie and Jonathan did the questioning," he said in his soft voice. "Let's see if they are as good at reporting." He smiled and added, "You all know Elie, of course. I've brought him over several times. And this guy,"—he gave a friendly slap to the shoulder of the owlish young man on his right—"is Jonathan Bauman. He was born in Holland and speaks Dutch. It always pays to have somebody who speaks the customer's language."

Peled smiled politely. "Did it pay this time?"

"Definitely, sir," Jonathan said with deference. He sat woodenly in his chair, crossing and uncrossing his arms. "There were no problems whatsoever."

"It's not a terrorist you got us, Jeremiah," said Elie, the older of the two who was much more relaxed, "it's a songbird. Once he started talking, he wouldn't stop. He seemed frightened to death."

"Do you have the transcript of the interrogation?" Mally asked, tapping her pencil on the table.

"You'll have it later tonight," Elie said. "Right now, we are having the passages in Dutch translated."

"So give us the gist of what he said," Jeremiah urged with a hint of impatience in his voice.

"You tell, Jonathan," Elie said, and Avri nodded encouragingly.

"Are you interested in Van Weyden's background?" Jonathan asked uncertainly, taking a small notebook from his inner pocket.

"Later," Jeremiah snapped, his impatience growing. "First give us the main points."

"The main points are the following," Jonathan started, his

guttural *r*'s and *h*'s betraying his origins. "After the foreign volunteers had been evacuated from Saida, last month, Rick Van Weyden was sent to a camp in northern Lebanon where two other Europeans, an English girl and another Dutchman, gave him a crash course about Israel: geography, history, big cities, streets, customs, a few words in Hebrew. He also got a thorough refresher course in the use of small weapons with emphasis on Beretta and Walther handguns. Two weeks ago he was sent back home to Amsterdam and told to wait for further instructions. He met several times with the members of the Fatah cell there, two Palestinians and a Syrian girl. The names are . . ." He leafed through his notebook.

"We know the names," Jeremiah said. "Go on."

Jonathan blinked uneasily. "Two days ago, he met the Syrian girl in the tearoom of the Krasnopolski Hotel. He was told that he had been selected to take part in the most spectacular coup of the Fatah ever. He was to fly to Tel Aviv and check into the Sabra Hotel. There he was to wait to be contacted. Several other members selected for the operation were already in place, the girl said, waiting for instructions."

"What?" Mally exclaimed loudly, her hand holding the cigarette frozen in midair.

Jonathan shrugged. "That's what he said. The other members of the team have already arrived in Israel and are waiting for the go-ahead. The weapons have been smuggled into the country as well. The operation is to be carried out very soon, as Van Weyden was the last of the group to be sent here."

"Good God," Mally went on, "what if they try to contact him in the Sabra Hotel?"

Elie, the second agent, leaned toward her over the table. "Don't worry about that. A young Dutchman looking very much like our friend Van Weyden and carrying his passport has already checked into the Sabra and is awaiting contact." He grinned. "Jonathan is not the only Amsterdamer we have in the service, you know."

There was a moment of silence. "All right," Jeremiah said. "But what about the operation? Did he tell you what they intend to do?"

Jonathan nodded. "He said that they were to avenge the murder of Ali Hassan Salameh. The project is to be named

Operation Ali." His embarrassment grew and he stuttered slightly, shifting his eyes to Avri Tour, as if asking for his support. "He was told that their assignment was to ambush and execute the head of the Mossad, Jeremiah Peled."

In the surge of frenzied activity that swept the Mossad after the stunning disclosures of Rick Van Weyden, only a few noticed the strange relapse of Peled into his former dejection. His apparent recovery had lasted barely one day. While an emergency committee, headed by David Roth, launched an unprecedented dragnet operation all over the country to apprehend the members of the terrorist hit team, the Old Man quietly retreated into his office. He sank again into his glum brooding spells in the darkness of his room, and his few visitors were again confronted by a haggard face, a dull, blank look, and short monosyllabic answers. He renewed his harassment of Nora for files and documents, although he no longer seemed interested in the faraway past. Most of his requests for material were now addressed to Mally's department: the names and personal files of the foreign terrorists who had trained in Saida, the records of the various Fatah cells in Europe, reports of Mossad agents who had operated in Amsterdam during the last few years. He read the transcripts of Van Weyden's interrogation over and over again and dispatched scores of additional questions to the Shin Beth, neatly laid down in his tiny handwriting. His copy of Mueller's personal file metamorphosed into a sheaf of crumpled, tattered sheets with multiple sentences circled or underlined in colored inks, the margins jotted with unintelligible notes. Several times a day he would send Nora in person to Mally Segev with short handwritten messages, always carrying the same question: "Where is Mueller?" and would buzz her desk incessantly till she came back, shaking her head and wringing her pale, arthritic hands.

Pretending to have a cold, he asked David Roth to take his place at the urgent meeting of the government intelligence board and brief the prime minister about the Van Weyden affair. Only twice did he drop into the conference room where the emergency committee convened and listen absently to the reports about roadblocks, searches, preventive arrests, and surprise descents on the residences of Fatah sympathizers in the West Bank. He never asked any questions when Mossad, Shin Beth, and Special Branch operatives reported on the investigation of hundreds of recently arrived tourists, hotel guests, and even kibbutz volunteers. When David Roth told him that henceforth four bodyguards were to escort him everywhere and that he had to change his routine life pattern, he did not argue. He did not emerge from his apathy even in the dramatic unscheduled meeting of March 25 when Avri Tour revealed that he had almost captured one of the terrorists. A Shin Beth unit, Avri reported, had spotted a stranger lurking near Peled's house in Jerusalem the night before, but the man had escaped under the cover of darkness. Even though the chase had ended in failure, Avri pointed out, the episode itself proved that Van Weyden had spoken the truth. A terrorist hit team had infiltrated the country, and Jeremiah was the target of a forthcoming assassination attempt.

As soon as Avri's report was over, Jeremiah got up and left the room. Mally followed him with a worried look, then sighed to herself, and started collecting her papers. A hand touched her shoulder, and a soft voice whispered in her ear, "What's happening to him, Mally? This is not our Jeremiah anymore."

She turned back and stared at the long, narrow face of David Roth, stamped with an expression of deep concern. "He . . ." Mally started to say, then clamped her lips in sudden anger, killed her cigarette in the overflowing ashtray, and walked out.

It was late evening when she came home. Beduin, her slim saluki, barked joyously as she unlocked the door of her modest little house in Zahala, and gracefully stood up on his hind legs to demand a caress. She lovingly patted the desert dog's silky cream coat and let him into the garden. The night was dark and still. She opened the windows, letting the perfumed scents of the early spring waft into the house.

She carried the small transistor radio into the kitchen and turned it on for the eleven o'clock news. The last commercial jingle was on, a thundering basso praising the newest brand of pasta. The mock aria covered the barks of Beduin outside, and she became aware of the dog's excitement only when she heard the soft, but persistent, knocks on the door.

"It's open," she called, crossing the living room. The door opened, and she found herself face to face with Jeremiah Peled.

"Well, Jeremiah," she mumbled, trying to conceal her embarrassment. The Old Man had been to her house only once before. "Come in, please. What a surprise!" He stood awkwardly in the middle of the room, and she realized that he was as uneasy as she. "Sit down," she chattered, gesturing toward one of the armchairs across the living room. "How did you know that I was at home?" She felt the blood rushing to her face. "How stupid of me. You must have asked the duty officer, of course."

He nodded.

"Would you like some coffee? I've got some water boiling in the kitchen."

"Yes," he said gratefully, settling stiffly in the armchair, "some coffee would be fine. Thank you."

"I'll be back in a moment." As she turned toward the kitchen, he asked politely, "Your sons are not at home?"

"Not anymore." Her voice sounded oddly strained as she paused on the threshold. "The older one is studying architecture in Haifa. The younger, Benjamin, is in the army. He comes home only on weekends."

His anodyne question released a flux of ugly, long-suppressed recollections from the deep recesses of her mind, and she quickly turned her back to him, lest her face betray her sudden emotion. She had been living in the illusion that her wounds had scarred as time had passed; but his words, now, unexpectedly revived the raw pain and the terrible humiliation that had almost driven her out of her mind that infernal night sixteen years ago. It was a winter night, she recalled, and a tremendous storm was ravaging the coastal plain. The old-fashioned clock in the living room had struck midnight long before, but she was not sleeping. She lay awake listening to the rolling thunder and rain lashing her bedroom windows.

Since Simon had been sent on his mission to Damascus, she had become a bundle of nerves. The long, lonely nights when she would stir restlessly in her bed had become an unbearable torture for her. What was he doing now? Was he safe? Was he still free? Was he alive? The Syrians were the most cruel of Israel's enemies, and her husband, the open-faced, blue-eyed Simon, was living among them, spying on them, his life hanging on a thread. He had been dispatched to Damascus under a French identity and had opened an "officers' club" in the Syrian capital. The club included a restaurant, bar, health spa, and some discreet rooms where a few girls were providing top-ranking officers with some unorthodox services. Simon Segev—known in Damascus as Andre Perrachet—had succeeded in establishing a very close relationship with several senior Syrian generals. In the wee hours of the morning, after a wild sex experience or over a lavish meal, they would become quite talkative; and a couple of hours later the Mossad antennae would receive the short clandestine transmissions of Simon's compact set.

Three or four times a year he would fly to France "on vacation," change passports, and land in Israel for a short reunion with Mally and the boys. Originally, he had been sent to Damascus for two years. But owing to his success, his stay had been extended to four, four years of ever-present fear for his young wife. She was well taken care of; his substantial salary was never late, the Dependents Department took care of all her problems and even paid for a governess for the kids so she could continue her studies at the Tel Aviv University unperturbed. She had gone back to the university in order to keep herself busy while Simon was away. She had returned to her old love, Arabic language and contemporary history of the Middle East. She had been naive enough to believe that the intensive post-graduate studies could make her forget her harrowing fears. But she had not achieved a single moment of rest, constantly haunted by the image of Simon's predecessor, the notorious Elie Cohen, hanging on a gallows on Damascus Central Square after his capture and beastly torture by Syrian counterespionage.

As soon as she heard the knocking at the door, she had hurried across the living room, grabbing for her robe. She had always feared that moment, and had lived through it hundreds of times in her nightmares: a knock on the door, a woman from Dependents, maybe a doctor standing behind her, a compassionate hug, and a voice saying to her, "He has been caught, Mally. We are doing our utmost to save his life and . . ."

But it had not been a girl, and the small, white-haired man with the piercing blue eyes who stood on the landing did not look like a doctor. "I am Jeremiah Peled," he had said quietly, and she had moved back to let him in. She had heard his name, of course, more than once, whispered with awe by Simon or mentioned in an occasional meeting of agents' wives when they could talk freely of their husbands' occupations. She had stared at him for a moment, unable to speak. He was soaking wet, his white hair was plastered over his forehead, and his drenched raincoat dripped on the floor. "Is he . . . Is he . . ." she had stammered, and he had shaken his head reassuringly. "He is all right," he had said and had quickly added, "Your sons are not at home?"

"No," she had blurted, her voice a mixture of relief and puzzlement. "They are with their grandmother for the weekend. I have a seminar in Jerusalem tomorrow and I . . ."

As he took off his coat and hung it by the door, careful not to wet her carpets, she had nervously lit a cigarette, wondering what on earth had brought the head of the Mossad to her house at this hour of night just to tell her that her husband was all right. But something was wrong, something had to be wrong. Her heart was pounding in her chest, and she stuck her hands under her armpits to conceal their trembling.

He had sat beside her on the sofa and had started to speak. By his hesitation, by his soft voice and concerned eyes, she had understood, even before his words started making sense to her, that the news was bad.

As he talked, she was listening to him, her teeth clenched, her face chalk white. Simon was safe now, he said, stressing the word *now*. The Syrian counterespionage had been closing in on him for a long while, alerted by the coded transmissions, working hard to pinpoint their source. Two weeks before they had broken into his apartment and had found the transmitter. Fortunately, he was not at home. An accomplice of his had managed to pick him up at the club with a fast car, barely a minute or two before the police raided the place, and whisk him to safety. They had escaped from Damascus, and Simon had used an emergency procedure to notify the Mossad that he was in trouble. A rescue operation had been immediately launched, and this morning Simon had arrived in Paris, safe.

"It's wonderful. I . . ." she had started, and yet there had been something in Jeremiah's manner of speaking that had stopped her in midsentence.

"He escaped," Jeremiah had said gravely, his eyes holding hers in a grim focus, "but he was not alone. There was a woman with him."

"A woman?" she had repeated foolishly.

And Jeremiah had told her about the French woman. At the beginning, he admitted—and for the first time he had lowered his eyes—the Mossad experts had judged it best to send Andre Perrachet to Damascus as a married man to enhance his credibility. Therefore he had married—fictitiously, of course—a French girl, Denise Blanchard, who was connected with the Mossad. It had been just an operational arrangement, Peled had said, nothing more. Mally had not been told in order to be spared unnecessary torment.

Jeremiah's disclosure had not come as a total surprise to her. She had suspected for quite a while that Simon had not been alone—at least not all the time—and yet, she had never asked him about it, either because she feared the truth or because she did not want to hear lies. During Simon's short home leaves they had both, carefully, avoided the subject.

But if it was a current practice, and if the Mossad had wanted to spare her "unnecessary torment," why was Peled telling her about it? "Why . . ." she started.

Peled had raised his eyes. Deep furrows had appeared in his forehead, and his mouth was a thin bitter line. "I saw him this morning in Paris," his voice had been hoarse, loaded with anger. "He said she shared all the dangers with him. He said she saved his life." So she had been the accomplice with the fast car. "He is in love with her. He does not want to come back home, and he wants a divorce."

She had stared at him, her eyes wide, each phrase stabbing and ripping her insides.

"I don't approve of it," Peled had gone on quickly, as if eager to be through with his disgusting mission. "He will have to resign from the Mossad. Still, he is entitled to his pension, but you couldn't live on the alimony." Alimony. Dear God, why this word already? Please stop, she had silently screamed. Please. For heaven's sake, let that be another nightmare.

"I came to offer you a job in the Research Department," he had said. "You know Arabic, don't you?"

She had risen to her feet, shaking badly. She had walked to the door like a robot and opened it. "Please, not now," was all she had managed to say.

He had taken his raincoat and stopped on the threshold. His face had showed concern. "Are you all right?" he had said, disconcerted by her abrupt dismissal. "Would you like me to call somebody? Your mother, perhaps?"

She had shaken her head vigorously, biting her lower lip, the tears choking her, the room swaying before her. She had waited for him to go out and start his car. Only then had a low, desperate sob escaped from her chest and everything gone black.

When she came back from the kitchen, she was her old cheerful self. "You like your coffee black, no sugar, right?" She placed the steaming mug in front of him.

"Thank you," Jeremiah said awkwardly. He sipped his coffee in silence, his eyes roaming over the luminous abstract paintings on the near wall. Mally felt that he had come for a specific purpose but did not know how to start. "You don't seem to take that plot against your life seriously, Jeremiah," she said lightly.

He grabbed the thrown rope. "No, I don't," he said earnestly. "Tell me, frankly: Does this boy Van Weyden look like a killer to you?"

She shrugged. "I don't know. I really don't know what a killer looks like these days. Some of them look as innocent as can be. Remember Evelyne Dulong? Such a sweet girl, the classical rosy virgin fresh from the convent. When they arrested her, she carried enough explosives in her underwear to blow up everything within fifty yards."

"Yes, but this boy . . ." Jeremiah shifted impatiently. "Look, I came here to pick your brain and also to get a second opinion." She nodded encouragingly, and he went on. "You read the minutes of his interrogation. How long had he been in Saida before he was selected for the operation?"

"Three months, I think. Why?"

"Three months and three weeks, to be exact. That's your

field, Mally. How long should the basic training of a foreign volunteer in Lebanon take?"

She tilted her head, intrigued. "Six months, at least."

"Correct," Jeremiah said, gulped the rest of his coffee, and leaned forward. "Why should they select somebody who had not even completed his basic training for such a dangerous operation?"

"Well, maybe he had some experience before."

"Rubbish. He had no experience whatsoever." He paused to let his point sink in. "Now, a second point: Why did he break down so quickly? They used no pressure on him after his arrest and yet he blurted out everything. Remember what they said? They called him a songbird. Frightened to death, they said. Once he started, he couldn't stop."

She made a skeptical grimace. "You're not trying to tell me that he did it on purpose."

"Of course not. He didn't. He was genuine. But he had never been in such a situation before, and he panicked. An experienced terrorist could have walked out of Shin Beth headquarters free in a couple of hours, unruffled. We had nothing on him. He was clean, he carried no arms, no documents. . . . I think they sent him on purpose. He was a greenhorn, it was his first mission, and they knew he would crack under interrogation."

"Who is 'they'?" she asked. "And how did they know we would arrest him?"

"Exactly," Jeremiah said triumphantly. "How did they know. Let me tell you."

She remembered David Roth saying barely an hour ago, "This is not our Jeremiah anymore." Well, he should be here now to see our old Jeremiah resuscitating, she thought, and a pleasant warmth spread through her body.

"Remember how we got the tip on Van Weyden?" Peled asked. "Amsterdam station, right? And how did Amsterdam station obtain the information in the first place?"

She frowned. "There was this guy, Nawi, who penetrated the Fatah cell in Amsterdam thirteen months ago. He's still there."

"And for thirteen months we have been regularly receiving inside Fatah information from Amsterdam?"

"Let me think." She had always been proud of her memory.

"First, we got the warning about the El Al hijacking. That was last April. Then, in May, there was the report on the Syrian who had murdered the Jewish children in Antwerp and planned another killing in Brussels. In May again, the report we passed on to Egypt about the plan to take over their embassy in The Hague. And after . . ."

"Yes, what after?" Jeremiah's voice seemed to tease her.

"Now, let me see . . ." She got up and started pacing around the room, feeling his stare on her back. "No," she finally said in wonder. "I don't remember anything else."

"Because there wasn't anything else," Jeremiah said firmly. "Nothing from May to March. And you don't need me to guess why."

She lit a cigarette and blew the smoke upward. "Yes, I see," she said. "There was nothing because those three previous projects blew up and they realized that the Amsterdam cell had been penetrated." She suddenly understood. "No, Jeremiah, your theory is too farfetched."

"Oh, so you already know what my theory is." His eyes twinkled.

"Of course. Your theory is that they wanted us to learn about the assassination project. So they sent a novice, Rick Van Weyden, because they were sure he would spill the beans once in our hands. Then they leaked the information on Van Weyden to us by using their Fatah cell which they knew had been penetrated and which had been inactive for months." As he was nodding his head, she went on, "And you believe, of course, that this is a diversionary move conceived by Mueller."

"Mueller," Peled confirmed, and his face hardened. "Remember his file?" He quoted by heart, " 'Specialist in deception and diversionary tactics.' "

"So you don't believe in the assassination plot." Mally sipped her lukewarm coffee, watching him over the rim of her mug.

"Oh yes, I do believe in it. I am sure that they do have a team here, stalking me and planning my assassination. I am also sure there are no other Rick Van Weydens in the team, only professionals. We shall have a lot of trouble capturing the others, take my word. I am also sure they will try to kill me." He spread his hands. "And they might even succeed."

"But . . ."

217

"But this is not the ultimate revenge Mueller spoke about," he broke in. "The Peled assassination is the diversion, a genuine one, not just make-believe. Look, Forum One and the Shin Beth fell for it already. The ultimate revenge, though, is something else that Mueller will carry out himself. He won't miss it." He raised his hand, index finger up. "He needs a Jew for it, remember? What about the Jew? And that's not the only loose end. Why did he go to Rome? Why did he meet Caruzzi?"

"If you are right," Mally said pensively, "this revenge of Mueller's must be something really big."

He looked at her questioningly.

"If you are right," she repeated, sucking on her cigarette, "then Arafat and Mueller are deliberately sacrificing their best foreign volunteers. For whether they kill you or not, those people have no chance of getting out of Israel, not with half the Shin Beth protecting you."

Jeremiah sighed. "They are paying a very high price," he agreed. "But that brings us back to square one. What is the ultimate revenge?" His voice suddenly became softer and very tired. "Mally, would you believe that I don't sleep nights trying to guess what he intends to do? I sit all day long in my office beating my brains out speculating about this madman's revenge. You might think I'm obsessed. Well, I am." He looked at his watch and abruptly got up. "Well, I must be going now." He stopped by the door, and blood rushed to his face as he quickly blurted, "The coffee was marvelous, Mally. But after all that is over and I'm retired, we should celebrate over a glass of wine in a restaurant. What do you think?"

It seemed to her that he had rehearsed his little speech several times before coming, so quickly had it streamed from his mouth. "Yes, I'd love that, Jeremiah," she said hastily. "I'd be delighted."

"Good," he said clumsily, and she thought she saw a drop of sweat glistening on his forehead.

"Jeremiah," she called softly after him. He turned back. Beduin, the saluki, was playfully leaping around him in the doorway.

"Don't leave me in the dark," she asked. "What are you going to do now? Convene Forum One?"

"Oh no," he said and smiled for the first time. "They won't

agree with me. Not with an old fool who is halfway out any-way. No," he paused. "I am going to test my theory. I'm going to smoke out our friend Mueller and force him to show his hand."

The room was white. Totally, uncompromisingly white. Whitewashed walls, a white iron bed, a chair and a table of white wood like the door and the window frames. Even the window bars were covered with a thick coat of white paint. He could not look out the window, though, because it was too high up, a long rectangular strip running a few inches beneath the ceiling.

It resembled a hospital room. The woman who brought him his food also looked like an aging, competent nurse. She was obese, waistless, with dyed gray hair, a kind face, round spectacles, and thick legs tucked in laced, ankle-high shoes. But the man who escorted her and stood watch at the door while she carried in his trays and changed the bedsheets did not look like a male nurse. He was lean and tall with a tough face, muscular arms, and a gun openly displayed in a belt holster. He never came near him and stood by the open door, his body apparently relaxed, but his eyes suspicious and alert, following all his movements.

They did not talk to him. He had tried to speak to the woman and the guard in English and in German, but they would not answer. And when they were gone, not a sound would penetrate the white room. The silence was driving him crazy. The silence and the whiteness. They reminded him of a movie he had seen once about an insane asylum. The crazies inside lived in this kind of room. The quiet and the pure-white color were supposed to soothe their nerves. Soothe, shit! He felt he would crack and go out of his mind that way. He had never thought he could need somebody to talk to so much.

Only once every two or three days would the door open unexpectedly, and the owlish man with the glasses, the one who knew Dutch, would come and sit in the chair across the room. He would always start with the same question, "How are you today, Rick?" And then they would talk for hours. Mostly about his mission, of course, although he had told them everything about it already. He was a good listener, the owl-eyed Amsterdamer, and Rick's only human link to the outside world. The nurse and the armed gorilla were not human. So Rick would talk at length, answering each question, describing everything in great detail. He did not give a damn anymore about divulging any secrets. He was in a jam that was solely the fault of his friends, those Fatah bastards who had not been able to keep a secret. The Israelis knew all about him even before he arrived; the Amsterdamer had actually told him that. So he did not owe anything to the Fatah and should take care for his own skin. The Israelis could do with him as they pleased. He was involved in a most serious crime, the Amsterdamer had said. Premeditated murder of a high government official. If he ever got out of here alive, it would be after a long term in prison. But if he cooperated with them and told them everything, he had a chance of getting a lighter sentence. So he told them everything.

He awoke with a start as the key turned in the lock. His notion of time had become rather vague, as they had taken away his watch and the white fluorescent tubes fixed to the ceiling burned around the clock. Still, the narrow strip of sky visible through the oblong window was not black anymore, but dark gray, so he figured that dawn was about to break. He rubbed his eyes with the palms of his hands and looked at the wiry man with the snow-white hair standing at the door. The man was dressed in a pair of black trousers, a tweed jacket, and an open-necked shirt. He was rather small in stature, yet there was an indefinable air of natural authority in his carriage and in the penetrating stare of his bright-blue eyes. Instinctively, Rick got up from the bed, stood up straight, and faced the stranger.

"You are Rick Van Weyden," the white-haired man said in English. His accent was thick, but the deep voice was clear and carried a lot of power. "I am Jeremiah Peled, the head of the Mossad. You were sent here to take part in my assassination."

A lump materialized in Rick's throat, and he blinked nervously several times. "I . . . I . . ." he stammered. His mouth was dry.

"I don't believe that story," Peled went on. "I think that that plot to assassinate me is a hoax intended to deceive me, but a very clumsily executed one. You were used by the people who sent you here. They want my attention drawn to that so-called assassination plot while they prepare a much more devious operation." He paused, his piercing eyes glued to the face of the amazed boy. "I have no use for you. You will be expelled from the country aboard the first flight that leaves this morning." He looked at his watch. "In a moment they'll bring you your passport and your belongings."

Jeremiah walked out of the room and closed the door behind him, leaving the thunderstruck boy petrified in his place. As he walked down the corridor, an agitated, middle-aged man rushed to meet him. "Jeremiah, telephone. In the office, downstairs." The Old Man nodded and followed the Shin Beth duty officer to the elevator.

"Jeremiah?" The voice of Avri Tour boomed in the receiver.

"Yes, Avri," he said quietly.

"Jeremiah, is what they told me true?" Tour sounded badly agitated. "You ordered Van Weyden expelled from the country?"

"Yes, I did."

"But you can't do that! The man is in custody, and his interrogation . . ."

"His interrogation is over," Jeremiah said curtly, "and we don't need him anymore."

"We don't need him?" Tour almost choked with fury. "My dear God, do you know what . . ."

"Yes, I know very well what his expulsion means," Peled broke in, still keeping his voice even. "I weighed all the implications of such a step before I made my decision."

"But . . ." Avri paused briefly. "I am sorry I must speak formally, but you leave me no choice. The Shin Beth objects to that decision. As director of the Shin Beth I refuse to release a man who is in our custody."

Jeremiah sighed. "I am sorry, Avri. As chairman of the Committee of the Security Services, I have the power to overrule you, and that's what I am doing now. My decision is final. Of course you are free to appeal to the prime minister. He is back from New York, and you'll have no trouble getting hold of him."

He put the receiver back, left the Shin Beth compound, and told Danny to drive him to Ben-Gurion Airport.

Less than an hour later, he watched from his car window

as the discreet white van of the Shin Beth stopped beside the KLM plane that was warming its engines. His eyes followed the young Rick Van Weyden, apparently still dazed, as he climbed aboard the plane, flanked by two agents. He kept Danny waiting on the runway till the heavy passenger aircraft took off and soared over the Mediterranean. Only then did he lean back and close his eyes, wondering if his gamble would work.

In the late evening under a tedious Paris drizzle, Alfred Mueller walked into a phone booth on the Boulevard Saint-Michel and dialed a local phone number. His golden rule was never to give his address and phone number to anybody, even his direct superiors. Instead, he would ask for a contact number at the beginning of each operation and would call it several times a day, always from a public phone. That way he could get his messages without running the risk of being betrayed and cornered.

He identified himself and listened to the quick, eager voice. As the words poured into his ear, his face slackened in amazement, then contorted in fury. "A hoax?" he muttered. "Peled called the assassination a hoax?"

"That's what he told Van Weyden," the voice whispered in the receiver. "He said that the plot against him was a deception to hide a much more devious operation. And then he kicked him out of the country."

"The bastard," Mueller spat in an explosion of anger.

"What do we do now?" the whisper went on. "Should we call off the operation?"

"Call it off? You must be out of your minds, you stupid idiots!" He bit his lower lip, trying to regain control of himself. "On the contrary. Tell your people there to go ahead with it. Shoot him like a dog."

He hung up and leaned on the glass wall, blind hatred painted all over his face. His hand shook as he took a cigarette from a yellow package and lit it. The filthy Jew! He had seen through his game. But how? Could he have found out about the Plan? No, there was no possible way for him to find out. Only he and Arafat knew, and Arafat would not talk to anybody. Michael Gordon was safe, the room was assured, the weapon was ready. Peled was guessing, he must be only guessing. Everybody said he was as cunning as the devil.

Mueller straightened up and looked out at the rain-swept street. Peled will die all right, in due time. But first he had to be removed from the scene. He was the most dangerous obstacle to the Plan, he had to be stopped, neutralized, made ridiculous . . .

Made ridiculous . . . The idea suddenly struck him, and he nodded his head repeatedly as the solution quickly took shape in his mind. Oh yes, he knew exactly how he would destroy Jeremiah Peled.

It was almost midnight in Jerusalem when Michael Gordon returned from a late meeting of the Jewish Defense League. He ran up the steps to his flat, humming to himself. When he reached the landing, he suddenly stopped, and his voice died in his throat. A human figure was sitting by the door, huddled in a dark woolen cape. "Who . . ." he started, bending down to take a better look, then gasped in boundless surprise as he recognized the huge green eyes under the disheveled mass of strawberry-blond hair.

"Michael?" she whispered in a small, forlorn voice.

"My God, Maureen," he breathed, reaching for her.

Chapter 15

IN THE WELCOME darkness of his room, her head on his chest, she cried for a long time. In vain did he try to sooth her, stroking her soft hair, kissing her wet cheeks, whispering in her ear. Even when she fell silent, and her eyes dried, her chest kept shuddering in convulsive, soundless sobs. "It's okay, my love," he kept murmuring, thrown for a loss by Maureen's distress, "everything will be fine now."

She finally raised her face to him, and her lips sought his in desperate need. Her mouth was dry and hot. He gently led her to the sofa and made her sit down. He took a step toward the kitchen to get her a glass of water, but she clung to him tightly. "Don't move," she murmured. "Hold me, Michael, please. Don't . . . don't turn on the lights."

He complied, but as she gradually calmed down, his concern changed into bewilderment. "How did you find me?" he asked.

It took her a long moment to formulate a coherent answer. "I . . . I didn't know where you were," she mumbled at last. "I had to find you, I had nowhere to go." She was softly crying again. "So I decided to try your family."

"My family?" he arched his brows, baffled.

"You told me once that you were from Westfield, New Jersey, remember? I called the international exchange and asked for the phone number of the Gordon family in Westfield."

"But there must be at least . . . "

"Eleven," she said. "Eleven listed Gordons. I worked my way down the list. I called each one in turn and asked if that was the residence of Michael Gordon. The seventh number was the good one."

"And what did you say?"

"I spoke with a French accent, or what a New Jersey family would believe to be a French accent," she involuntarily smiled through her tears. "I said that I was the secretary of postgraduate studies at the Paris Faculty of Political Science, and I needed your present address to send you Professor Grosser's queries about your thesis. Your mother was very helpful."

"Clever," Michael said. "Very clever, Maureen." His lips gently brushed her cheek. "But why did you do it? I mean . . ." he stumbled in embarrassment, "when we last saw each other in Paris, you said you would wait for me to come back. What happened, Maureen?"

Her eyes faintly glimmered in the dark. "Something's wrong, Michael," she whispered in an almost inaudible voice. "Something is terribly wrong. Patrick has disappeared. I don't know," her voice faltered, "I don't know if he is still alive."

He stiffened. "What the hell are you talking about?"

She drew a deep breath. "After you left," she started, "no, after you told me in Luxembourg Park that Mueller was sending you away . . . " She spoke in quick, uneven outbursts, her narrative stilted and confused. She told him about her talk with Patrick, his decision to follow Mueller, his impulsive flight to Rome, the early morning visit of Liam Higgins at her flat.

"Liam was a kind of assistant to Patrick, you know. Did I tell you that? I don't think you ever met him. A guy about forty with black hair and a pitted face. He let me stay in his apartment for a couple of weeks. He thought that Mueller might be after me, so I had to go into hiding. I had nowhere to go, you see? I couldn't go back to Ireland after what happened there. Not ever in my life. And I didn't know where you were, so I stayed in his apartment. I thought I was going out of my mind. I hardly ever saw Liam, he was looking for Patrick all the time. Yesterday morning he came back, very early. I was asleep. He shook me awake. He was white as a ghost. His hands were trembling. He told me that Mueller was after us, that our lives were in danger. That's what he said," she slowly repeated, stressing each word, "our lives were

225

in danger! We had to leave Paris immediately, each his own way. I understood that he had found out something awful about Patrick. I asked him, I begged him to tell me the truth, but he wouldn't. He just looked at me with those grim eyes of his. Oh, Michael!" she covered her face with her hands. "I am sure Patrick is dead, Liam wouldn't tell me, but I feel it. Mueller killed him and is after me now!"

He hugged her close. "Then you called Westfield for my address and you flew here?"

She nodded, huddled in his embrace.

It took him quite a while to calm the terrified girl. He almost forced her to drink a tall glass of cognac. The liquor, combined with her crushing fatigue and her emotional exhaustion, benumbed her and blurred her senses. Docile as a child, she let him undress her and put her into bed. She fell asleep almost immediately, curled under the blankets. He lay beside her, smoking in the darkness. He was deeply disturbed by her story but did not share her suspicions, of course. She had no proof whatsoever that Alfred had harmed Patrick; she only thought he did. Alfred couldn't have hurt him; Patrick was his best friend. He would certainly surface sooner or later, safe and sound, and they would all get together and have a frank explanation.

Of course, Alfred might be mad at them. Michael would be too if he were in his place. Who asked Maureen and Patrick to spy on him, for heaven's sake? Why did Patrick follow Mueller to Rome as if he were an enemy, and not his closest companion? Who knows, Alfred might even have caught Patrick red-handed and locked him in some cellar in Rome till the march on Jerusalem was over. Alfred had his own reasons for keeping the O'Donnells out of that operation. Once he had made that decision, he was absolutely justified in protecting his secret. That's what compartmentalization was all about. Maybe that's why he was after Maureen now— if Liam's information was correct—to make sure that she wouldn't talk to anybody about the forthcoming coup.

Maureen stirred in her sleep and moved under the sheets, coming to nestle against him. The blanket slipped and soundlessly slid down to the floor. The soft predawn light caressed her skin. The sight of her perfect body, the silken touch of her smooth flesh, the sensual curve of her parted, full lips beneath the loose strands of red-gold hair suddenly aroused him. He bent over her, his hands gliding over the curve of her neck, her shoulders, and her exposed breasts. She awoke almost instantaneously and hungrily offered her body to his caress, her lips quivering. "Michael," she whispered, "I want you so much." She reached for him with her hands and her soft, wet mouth, more daring than she had ever been before. It seemed as if all the yearning, all the desire that had accumulated in them during their separation, exploded now at the contact of their bodies. They made love voraciously, both of them feverish, insatiable. Finally their bodies parted, utterly spent, and they fell asleep. But when they awoke she pulled him inside her again, although this time their raw passion gave way to a gentler, more tender lovemaking.

As the melodious peal of the church bells broke the peaceful morning silence, Maureen stretched luxuriously. A smile touched her lips. "Michael, let's go away," she whispered amorously, cuddling beside him like a lazy cat, "somewhere where we could be alone, just the two of us."

His coal-black eyes smiled back at her under his long, curled lashes. "I'd love that," he said. "But we'll have to wait a few more days."

"Why? Why not right away?"

He propped himself on his right elbow, his left forefinger playfully tracing a sinuous pattern over her nude body. He chose his words carefully. "I came here to take part in a certain operation, remember? I can't go away before it's over."

She brusquely recoiled, as if he had prodded her with a red-hot iron. "The operation?" The wild fear exploded in her eyes again. "But I told you that Mueller . . . "

"Oh, Maureen," he began cautiously, lighting a cigarette while she eyed him in growing disbelief. "I don't think Alfred is as bad as you think. I am sure that your friend Liam was exaggerating. Alfred couldn't have done any harm to Patrick. Let me talk to him. He is supposed to arrive in a couple of days and . . . "

"Alfred Mueller? Here?" She jumped from the bed, her knuckles pressed to her mouth, her eyes wide with terror.

He nodded. The Arab girl Latifa had dropped by yesterday just to tell him to expect Mueller on Thursday.

Maureen seemed on the verge of hysterics. For a moment

her lips moved, but no sound came out. "After all I told you, you still want to meet him? That murderer?" She had found the pile of clothes by the bed and started dressing with feverish, disjointed gestures.

"Now, Maureen, don't get upset, please." He stabbed his half-smoked cigarette in an ashtray and got up too, reaching for his trousers. "Wait, let's talk."

"Talk? You must be insane, Michael Gordon," she threw at him, her voice oddly rasping. He had never seen her behave that way. "You . . . you stupid, naive dupe, playing the revolutionary. When will you sober up? When he draws a gun on you and puts a bullet between your eyes?" She bit her lower lip, pulling her sweater over her head and gathering her woolen cape. Her voice fell to a whisper. "I thought you loved me."

He was beside her, taking her by the shoulders. "I do love you, Maureen. I am crazy about you. Just . . . "

"Don't touch me," she screamed at him, her cry bitter and forlorn. "Don't come near me. You admire Mueller, don't you? You must wait for him, right? Okay, so wait for him, stretch out your neck. You'll end up like all of them."

She wrung herself free of his hold, crossed the living room, and slammed the door behind her. Her face was on fire, and she was shaking badly. In the turmoil that assailed her stunned mind, her only impulse was to get out of there, to put as much distance as she could between her and Michael. She almost slipped on the stone staircase and clutched the banister, still wet with the morning dew. Under the restored arcades of the small Batei Mahse Square, some early-rising American tourists clustered around the art galleries. She tried to order her frantic thoughts. First, she had to get to her hotel, the American Colony. She vaguely remembered it was near the Tombs of the Kings. Reassured by the cheerful Americans, she slowed her pace, hesitating about the road to take. When she had come looking for Michael last night, she had entered the Old City by a beautiful gate in the wall, whose magnificent decorations and turrets were carved in the stone like lacework. What was its name? "Damascus . . . Damascus Gate," she uttered loudly. Her voice startled a bearded Jew, in a long black coat and a wide-rimmed hat, who was quickly walking in the opposite direction. He glanced at her and quickly averted his eyes. "Excuse me," she mumbled, "how do I get to the Damascus Gate?" The man looked away in embarrassment, and she recalled reading somewhere that orthodox Jews were forbidden to lay their eyes on women. Still looking the other way, the man nevertheless pointed vaguely to the north. She hurried through the labyrinth of narrow streets and covered bazaars, paying no attention to the colorful sights and magnificent monuments of thet city. She emerged in a bustling street full of souvenir shops and tiny restaurants. Suddenly she was caught in the middle of a festive crowd, swarthy Arabs in formal European clothes, tourists, nuns, and multitudes of priests in the characteristic vestments of the various religious orders represented in Jerusalem. Unable to elbow a path through the throng, she let herself be carried by it. The human river, swelling by the minute, wound its tortuous way down the canyonlike streets. It suddenly came to a stop in front of a beautiful, ancient church. Magnificent Roman columns, early Christian crosses, and ageless ruins were strewn in a deep excavation on its left. At the bottom of the excavation a patch of clear water glimmered in the sunshine. "See?" an excited father laden with cameras was explaining to his fat little boy riding on his shoulders. "Down there is the Pool of Bethesda where Jesus performed a miracle. And this is Sainte Anne's Convent. Here live the White Fathers."

"I don't see any," the child complained, tugging on his father's hair. "Where are they? Daddy, where are the White Fathers?"

But his father was too busy fumbling with his cameras. "Look, Joey, look," he suddenly shouted with a trace of an Italian accent, "here is the procession."

Maureen turned her head. A beautiful procession was entering the courtyard of the church. Nuns and monks in immaculate white vestments and young Arab girls, tidily attired, were streaming through the wide-open gates, singing a melodious hymn and waving fresh-cut palm branches.

Maureen suddenly understood. This was the traditional

Palm Sunday procession that every year commemorated the triumphal entry of Jesus into Jerusalem by the Kidron Valley. Easter was only a week away on April ninth.

She did not know that April seventh, Good Friday, was the target date of Alfred Mueller's Plan.

The party was well under way when Diane stepped out of the elevator on the eighteenth floor of the New York Waldorf Astoria. Two swarthy security agents, who looked like heavyweight champions, suspiciously scrutinized her invitation, exchanging conspiratorial whispers in guttural Arabic. The older of the two, whose shaven skull and dangling moustache made him vaguely resemble a Mongol, finally nodded in satisfaction and awkwardly gestured toward the reception line. She recognized the Saudi oil minister from his frequent TV appearances. The emaciated man next to him, clad in a loose Arab galabieh, was probably the UN ambassador, flanked by some members of the Saudi delegation.

"Diane Mason, from *The New York Times*," she said in a strong, clear voice, flashing what she thought to be her most dazzling smile.

"I am very pleased to meet you, Miss Mason." The minister's voice was cultivated and confident, carrying an unmistakable Oxford accent. His handshake was cool and firm. "I am a devout reader of your paper." The other diplomats in the line merely shook her hand with rather forced smiles. Once through the reception line, she walked into the Starlight Roof.

The big ballroom was tightly crammed with a conservative, formally dressed crowd, in whose midst the gold-embroidered galabiehs of the Saudis fluttered like big white specters. Women were rare, and the few Diane saw from afar seemed solidly entrenched on the other side of fifty—dried-up, heavily-painted females, boredom and pretentiousness etched in every line of their aging faces. The setup did not seem to herald any thrilling prospects, and now she understood why that bitch, Claire Sheen, had so kindly suggested that Diane go to the Saudi reception in her place. She had thought Claire was giving her a break, a kind of introduction to the New York diplomatic world. But Claire knew better than that. She must have guessed that the party was going to be a bore and had found in the newly hired Diane Mason the perfect solution to her problem. She must be in her Central Park South apartment now, screwing Ernesto, her oily Puerto Rican truck driver. The few times Diane had surprised her in the newsroom on the phone with Ernesto, Claire had sounded utterly ridiculous, emitting coquettish little laughs and whispering vulgar sexual hints. The gossip at the office was that she was buying Ernesto's dinners, ties, and even his evening clothes. Well, at her age and with her looks she had to work hard to get herself balled by a young virile male.

Diane shrugged inwardly and plunged into the crowd. Claire was already over the top of her career, while she was only starting hers. And if she wanted to move into something more interesting than sewage problems in the Upper Bronx or pollution forecasts for the East River, she'd better keep her eyes and ears wide open. Besides, it would be fun showing Claire tomorrow that screwing Ernesto was not the hottest game in town after all.

An hour and six glasses of champagne later, she had almost lost hope. She had joined a few groups, trying to blend into the conversation, but had been either haughtily snubbed or had not understood a thing. The main topics of the conversation were, of course, oil fields, OPEC inner politics, and Persian Gulf exports, but the secrets of the Rotterdam spot market and the properties of Iraqi crude were not exactly her forte.

She was drifting toward the far end of the ballroom, where the artistically draped windows offered a fine view of Manhattan's East Side, when she felt she was being watched. A woman could always tell when a pair of insistent male eyes focused on her, flashing the unspoken message of interest and desire. She half-turned and nonchalantly cast a look behind her. The man was standing alone by the bar, a middle-aged, heavy-bodied Arab in a dark-blue, pinstriped suit, his saturnine face slightly cracked in a sardonic grin, the small eyes watching her challengingly. She smiled at him uncertainly and was about to move away when he left his half-full glass of orange juice on the bar and approached her. His short, fat legs were out of proportion to his bulging torso, and his gait was oddly undulating.

"Good evening," he said pleasantly and stretched out his

large, puffy hand. "My name is Youssouf al Hamid. I am the second secretary of the Algerian delegation to the United Nations. And you?" His English carried a strong French accent, which she found rather amusing.

"I am Diane Mason," she smiled brightly. "I am with *The New York Times.*"

"Oh," he said, his eyes lighting with interest. "How fascinating. I have never met such a pretty journalist before."

"Thank you," she said. It was a cliché, but one couldn't expect an Arab diplomat to be familiar with the *How to Pick Up Girls* manual.

"Well, how do you like our party? Did you get any front-page scoops for tomorrow?"

Another cliché. What the heck, she suddenly thought, why not give it to him straight from the shoulder. "This is the dullest party I've ever been to. Isn't even worth mentioning."

He did not seem offended, rather the contrary. A sly smile slowly spread on his face. "My dear lady, you should know that a diplomatic party is the worst place for a good story. A clever reporter lures his—or her—prey into a bar, fills the guy with liquor, and then the scoops start pouring out. *In vino veritas*," he pronounced solemnly, and added without transition, "What about a drink in a dark, friendly bar? They serve the best French champagne on this side of the Atlantic in Sir Harry's downstairs. And it's dark enough for me to have a couple of drinks myself without being seen by my colleagues and accused of infidelity to Allah."

She glanced at him suspiciously. His eyes were teasing, faintly amused. Was the man trying to tell her something? Or just starting a deliberate maneuver to get into her pants? Both, she decided. She shrugged with studied indifference. "Okay. The party is almost over anyway."

He nodded and led the way across the dispersing crowd. They rode the elevator down with a group of Japanese diplomats, softly giggling at something one of them was saying. In the artificial darkness of Sir Harry's, he headed for the small alcove in the back and invited her to sit under a faded zebra hide pinned to the wall. A waitress in a safari jacket and hot pants nodded eagerly as he whispered into her ear and was back with a gold-sealed bottle in a silver bucket. She deftly uncorked the bottle, paused a second before the mushroom-shaped cork made its popping exit, and poured the bubbling froth into their glasses. The Algerian leaned back in his armchair and contentedly gulped down his first glass of Dom Pérignon.

"The champagne is good," she said coldly. "What about the scoop?"

She expected him to back off with another clumsy joke, but he did not.

"You are not Jewish, are you?" He was leaning forward, watching her closely.

"No," she put her glass on the low table and reached for the bowl of fried banana slices. "Half German, a quarter Italian, some Indian blood . . . Why? Why do you ask?"

"Because the Jews are sure they are the smartest nation on earth. And they pass their time bragging that they can outsmart anybody, just like that!" He snapped his fingers, his lips curved contemptuously.

"But you don't think so," she said mockingly.

"No. And I can prove it."

"Oh, really?"

He looked at her speculatively. "My name is Youssouf al Hamid. Does that ring a bell?"

She frowned. "Al Hamid? . . . No, I am afraid not. Should it?"

"In 1973 I was posted in Geneva."

"No, I've never heard your name before. I'm sorry." Her voice acquired an aggressive edge.

He did not depart from his collected manner. "Does the name Lillehammer mean anything to you?"

"What's that, a TV contest?" she said, openly annoyed. "No, Mr. Al Hamid, it doesn't mean a thing to me."

"It's a little town in Norway where a very bizarre murder took place in 1973."

"Seventy-three? . . . Wait!" A memory suddenly surfaced from the back of her mind. "Lillehammer you said? Wasn't that the place where the Israeli agents killed an Arab, a Moroccan?"

"That's right," he beamed, draining his glass and refilling it. "Good girl."

233

"As far as I can remember," she said slowly, "the Israelis were looking for a notorious terrorist, some sort of Arab Carlos."

He was nodding vigorously, filling her glass again. "That's right, a man called Ali Hassan Salemeh."

"That must be the name," she said uncertainly. "Anyway, they killed the wrong man, a waiter in a local restaurant."

"Ahmed Boushiki," he filled in, gulping his drink.

"Uh huh." She remembered it clearly now. The Israelis had made a major blunder over there. Not only did they kill the wrong man, but they also let themselves be caught by the police. The trial that followed had shattered the infallible image of the Israeli Mossad. The story had made huge head-lines in the world press for quite a while. There had also been a book, she recalled.

"They made a stupid mistake over there," she said.

"It was not a mistake," he said slowly, waiting for each of his words to sink in. "We set them up. They walked into the most sophisticated spy trap in modern times. And I played the main part in it."

"You?" For the first time since she had met him, she departed from her reserve. Her reporter's instincts, fully aroused, sensed something big; and the slowly shaping promise of a sensational story suddenly glittered before her eyes. "Tell me about it."

He downed his glass and held the bottle of champagne against the light. "Empty," he said regretfully. Then, turning to her, "Who is the idiot who told you to do your job in a bar of all places? A bar is full of people, strangers, they try to eavesdrop on you, they irritate you. My dear Diane, in order to get a scoop a reporter should work his way into his source's apartment and take advantage of the relaxed atmosphere to milk the source of all his secrets." His voice was teasing again, tinged with irony. "Let's go," he said, sticking the empty champagne bottle into the silver bucket, bottom up. "There are more secrets in this guy," he pointed at himself, "than wine in that bottle."

She slowly got to her feet. The bastard had cheek, she had to admit. Forcing her openly, shamelessly, into such a perverse deal: a scoop for a piece of ass. She had never been through such an experience before. Oh, the hell with it, she said to herself as she docilely followed him out into the pleasant spring night, why not? She could not lose her virginity anymore, and she was starting to enjoy the game. She might hit the front page, and, who knows, the guy might be a good lay.

He was a lousy lay she soon found out in his rather austere apartment on Seventy-ninth Street off Park Avenue. As soon as he closed the apartment door behind them, he had stopped playing the gentleman. He had undressed her impatiently, even brutally, dragged her into the bedroom, and hurled himself upon her. As she lay under him in the large bed, his sweaty bulk almost smothering her, his semen spurting into her unresponding body, she had bitten her lips to avoid screaming in humiliation and pain. She had never been so degraded before. But it had been her fault. She had agreed and had taken the risk of being treated this way. There was no use screaming or fighting back for he might get angry and break his promise. They had made a deal, and it was his turn now.

To her surprise, he calmed down as soon as his spasms had died inside her. He moved to the side, lay on his back, and lit a cigarette with his right hand while his left absently fondled her breasts. "In 1973," he began, "I was the labor attaché in the Algerian delegation to the UN agencies in Geneva. That was just a cover. My real assignment was to assure the liaison between Salameh and the various cells of Black September terrorists in Europe. We knew that the Israelis had been after him since Munich, so we had to take very thorough precautions."

She was listening quietly, her face sullen, but her thoughts madly rushing through her mind. There was one question she wanted to ask him, but she was afraid to interrupt his narrative. "For reasons of security, we had several undercover agents—Arabs and Europeans—watching my back on each of my trips. In May seventy-three one of my guardian angels," he smiled faintly, "spotted a suspicious character following me on a flight to London. On my next flight we had four agents with concealed cameras who took pictures of the guy. We checked them against our archives. Sure enough, the guy was an Israeli agent."

He blew a whiff of smoke toward the ceiling. His hairy hand was moving on her body like a hungry rodent, and she could barely resist the impulse to slap his self-satisfied face and run away.

"Some of our guys," he was saying, "wanted to bump off the Israeli. But a friend of ours, a European, who was also quite close to Salameh, cooked up a better idea. He suggested that we beat the Israelis at their own game. And that's what we did.

"At the beginning of July we spread the information that Salameh had been seen traveling to Scandinavia. I flew to Oslo, quite openly, taking my time so that the Mossad agents wouldn't lose my trail." He was chuckling softly. "They followed me, as they were supposed to, up to Lillehammer." He turned his head toward her. "We had chosen Lillehammer, you see, because it was a small town where every stranger would be remembered. That, we thought, would help us pin the Israelis down later. As I said, I arrived in Oslo. Once we got confirmation that the Israelis had followed me and kept tabs on me, I drove to Lillehammer. The only thing left for me to do was pick a victim for the Jews."

She was listening to him, breathless. His hand had stopped moving and had clenched into a fist, lying on her chest.

"It wasn't me who picked Boushiki," he said quietly, and she detected an apologetic note in his low voice. "It was the European guy, the one who planned the whole thing. He chose him because of his superficial likeness to Salameh. All I had to do was meet him, as if by chance, and invite him for a drink in a café in full sight of everybody, and then clear the place. That's what I did. I was already over the border when the Israelis killed Boushiki. Salameh's friend, the European, was there in a car parked barely a hundred yards from Boushiki's home. He saw them kill him. A weird guy, that one, with nerves of steel. As soon as they left the place, he called the police with full descriptions, license plate numbers, the works. Most of the Israelis were arrested the same night. You know the rest. We screwed them like nobody had ever screwed them before." He dropped his cigarette butt in an ashtray where it glowed for a moment. "Quite a story, isn't it? And I screwed you too." He guffawed in laughter, delighted

236

by his own joke. "You have a nice little round ass." He pinched her lightly.

She retreated to the far side of the bed and sat on the rumpled blanket, her arms locking her tightly drawn knees. "Who is the European?" she asked. "What's his name?"

He shrugged. "I don't know. He always used different names. A strange man. Salameh liked him, though. They had planned the Munich operation together."

Diane got up from the bed and started dressing. He was watching her indifferently. She finally asked the question that had been bugging her from the start. "Why did you tell me that story?" It suddenly dawned on her that it was not the kind of story one told a chance acquaintance, even if one was drunk as a skunk. And Al Hamid wasn't.

"I told you," he said, bursting into hoarse laughter. "I liked your ass. And besides," he grew serious, "I'm leaving the service. I've got a job waiting in Saudi Arabia as assistant director for inner-Arab relations in their oil ministry. This story will make me a hero all over the Arab world, don't you think? The man who screwed the Mossad." He definitely seemed to like the vulgar word. "And I am risking nothing for I am leaving this country next week, and the Israelis won't have the opportunity to see me again for a long, long time." He started laughing again. "Well, did you get yourself a scoop, or not?"

Only in the elevator on her way out did she realize that she was in possession of the hottest stuff a reporter could dream of. Al Hamid had given her a fantastic story. But it had not been a deal. He was ready to peddle his story to the first available journalist, and she had just happened to be there. He had screwed her just for fun.

She took a cab home, but changed her mind midway and asked the cabbie to drive her to the *Times* building. She was feeling filthy and humiliated, nevertheless, she decided to let the hot bath and the stiff drink she so desperately needed wait a few more hours. First she had to do some very thorough research in the archives and then make some phone calls to cover all possible angles.

The next day her story appeared in the *Times* under the headline "Black September Fooled Mossad in Lillehammer

Fiasco." The subtitle read: "Arab secret agent lured Israeli hit team into the assassination of the wrong man."

Al Hamid had been right. Diane Mason's story did hit the front page.

When the first edition of the newspaper reached the Times Square stalls, the bells of the Holy Sepulchre Church in Jerusalem were chiming five in the morning of April the fourth.

A fierce, bitter rain was lashing the city of Jerusalem, and thunder rolled in the black clouds smothering the Judean Hills. The torrents of muddy water and the heavy traffic of the morning rush hour had jammed the center of the New City; but the serene Ben-Maimon Street was almost deserted. As the gray Volvo slowed by the curb in front of number 19 behind a double-parked police van, two young men in civilian clothes suddenly materialized on both its sides. One of them, a close-cropped blond giant, leaned toward the side window of the car, water streaming down his face and soaking his ill-fitting brown suit. He took in the inside of the car in a quick glance and recognized the face of the visitor huddled between two bodyguards in the back seat. As the blond agent respect-fully nodded, whispering softly into his walkie-talkie, another car, a Cortina, stopped behind the Volvo, and two more bodyguards jumped out, shielding the back doors of the Volvo with their bodies. "Oh, come on guys," Jeremiah Peled groaned, extracting his body from the stuffy car, "stop this circus. Nobody is going to shoot me in front of the prime minister's house." He strode coatless on the wet sidewalk toward the prime minister's residence. A police officer in yellow oilskins emerged from his wooden booth by the en-trance, opened the small gate, and jumped to attention. The door of the two-story house was opened by another young agent of the Shin Beth detail assigned to the protection of the prime minister.

"He's in the kitchen, sir," the Shin Beth man said, "having his breakfast. He asks you to join him."

Jeremiah followed the young man across the middle-sized living room, still furnished as modestly as it had been when the late Ben-Gurion had first transferred his residence to nibbling on a piece of toast, an unfinished cup of coffee on his right. The electric clock above the sink read 7:37 A.M., and the radio morning news magazine was drawing to its end, the newscaster finishing the sports section. A pile of morning papers lay in disorder on the far side of the kitchen table.

"Come in, Jeremiah." The prime minister, in an open white shirt and a sleeveless V-neck pullover of gray wool, got up and shook his hand. "Would you like something? Toast, and maybe some coffee?"

"Coffee will be fine," Jeremiah said stiffly. He mopped a tiny rivulet of water from his forehead with the back of his hand.

"How do you like it? Black?"

"Black, no sugar, thank you." Jeremiah stood by the door, watching the prime minister's slow, confident movements as he poured him a cup of black coffee.

"Let's go to my study," the prime minister suggested, and they walked through the narrow corridor, both carrying their steaming cups. The wood-paneled study was dark and gloomy. The prime minister shivered. "It's freezing over here," he said, plugged in a small electric stove that stood beneath the window, and wearily settled in his stiff-backed armchair. His glass-topped mahogany desk was clean except for a telephone console and a single leather-bound folder. Jeremiah sat across the desk, facing him. For a moment neither spoke, the prime minister blandly watching the head of the Mossad over the rim of his cup. Finally he put his cup down, leaned back, and clasped his hands behind his neck. "I asked you to come here because I didn't want an official meeting at the office. Sorry for the short notice." Jeremiah remained motionless, as he went on, "Did you hear about the *Times* story in the morning news?"

The Old Man carefully put his cup and saucer on the desk. "I got a cable with the full text of the article, the same you got yourself."

The prime minister held his eyes for a second, then grunted to himself and opened the folder. Three pages covered with block teletype characters were on top of the documents inside. He pensively leafed through them, then raised his eyes. "This is bad, Jeremiah."

"Yes," the Old Man said curtly.

"Once again, we are being made to appear ridiculous because of that Lillehammer affair," the prime minister continued, his voice bitter. The deep lines stretching from his nose to the edges of his mouth pulling down his thin lips stamped his triangular face with a morose expression. "Seven years ago we could still pretend that the mishap resulted from the incompetence of some field agents who made a mistaken identification, killed the wrong man, and let themselves be caught with their pants down. Now it becomes clear that we had been duped from the very start."

Jeremiah sensed that the strong language in the mouth of the prime minister had a purpose: to create the right atmosphere for what was to come next.

"You can say that's an old story and water under the bridge," the prime minister went on, apparently irritated by Jeremiah's silence. "But it undermines the prestige of the Mossad, and we can't afford that." He paused. "The *Times* story will make the main headlines of the evening papers. We were asked to comment on it, but we refused."

Jeremiah nodded slightly. The official policy of the Israeli government was never to comment on covert operations.

"On the other hand," the prime minister was saying, "I am under pressure for some reaction. I got a phone call this morning from the publisher of the *Jerusalem Post*, who is acting chairman of the board of publishers of the daily press." He leaned across the desk, staring straight at Jeremiah. "He asked me, on behalf of his colleagues, if I intended to take any steps following the *Times* disclosures."

Jeremiah looked back grimly, his lips tightly compressed.

"My answer was, 'Yes, I am going to take immediate action.' " The prime minister drew a deep breath. "Jeremiah, you intended to resign from office on Independence Day which is a few weeks away. I informed the publishers that you'll cease exercising your functions as of today."

He winced. His lips trembled, and the nails of his clenched fists dug deep into his palms. The raw humiliation was worse than a slap in the face. He strove to regain control as he stared speechless at the prime minister. No, this was not the way it should have ended after all these years. But he had asked for it, he bitterly admitted to himself. He had hit Mueller, and Mueller had hit back. He unclenched his fists and slowly placed his hands on the smooth surface of the desk in front of him. He was too proud to explain, to beg, to fight for his career. He knew he had to plead his case and explain why he should stay for another week, for a few more days. But he couldn't do that. It would look like a sign of weakness. And even if he could, it was too late. The prime minister had faced him with a *fait accompli*.

"Your official departure date remains unchanged," the prime minister was saying, his voice a shade softer, "but starting this morning you are on leave. Rafael Avizur will take over. I have already talked to him."

He paused. "Frankly, I would have delayed your departure if not for your strange way of handling the Mueller case." The prime minister laid aside the cable carrying the *New York Times* story, took the two remaining documents in the folder and placed them side by side on the desk. "I have here a complaint from the Shin Beth about your unilateral decision to release a Dutch terrorist who was sent here to take part in an assassination plot against you. On the other hand," he lightly tapped the other paper, "last night the Shin Beth intercepted a coded transmission from Fatah headquarters in Lebanon to an agent of theirs in our territory. They worked on it all night and broke the code early this morning." He adjusted his glasses and bent over the document. "The message was an operational directive ordering them to carry out Operation Ali within the next seventy-two hours." He raised his eyes. "If I remember correctly, Operation Ali was the code name of the project to assassinate you. The Dutch terrorist whom you released revealed that in his first interrogation."

So Mueller had set the date already! Departing from his silence, Jeremiah eagerly leaned forward. "I was not informed of that! When did they intercept?" He stretched his hand toward the Shin Beth report.

"A little after nine." The prime minister pointed at the first paragraph in the Shin Beth report before handing it to Jeremiah.

The Old Man impatiently perused the document. "What's that?" he frowned in amazement. "Fatah headquarters asked for an acknowledgment? And it was radioed back three minutes later? They must be out of their minds."

"What do you mean?" The prime minister looked up in puzzlement.

"This, here," Jeremiah pointed to the document. "Most unusual. One of the basics of undercover work is that operational orders are never acknowledged by radio transmissions. The enemy might pinpoint your transmitter's location and raid your base in a couple of hours. I am sure that Communications is working on that now and . . ." He did not complete his phrase as his eyes lit in sudden realization, and he slowly nodded to himself.

"Anyway, Jeremiah," the prime minister said firmly, retrieving the Shin Beth report, "this is another proof that they are after you. You seem to be the only person in the country who doesn't believe in that plot." He shook his head in exasperation. "You are getting too stubborn, Jeremiah."

Too stubborn and too old. The prime minister did not use the words, but that was what he meant all right.

"Stubborn or not, we are going to save your life in spite of you," the prime minister said with forced cheerfulness. "I have approved Avizur's suggestion that you do not return to your office or home for the next few days until we make sure that the threat on your life has been definitely removed. Your bodyguards are being briefed now on the measures to take."

Jeremiah sighed, crossing his hands on his chest. "It is my official duty to inform you, Mr. Prime Minister, that you are playing straight into Mueller's hands."

The prime minister looked intrigued but not greatly surprised. "What makes you think so?"

"I do believe in the plot to murder me," Jeremiah said tersely. "But I also believe that it is merely a smoke screen behind which another operation is being planned, and that worries me. You mentioned the Dutch terrorist. I released him on purpose, because I wanted Mueller to know that I was on to his game. I expected him to act, and he did." He pointed at the *New York Times* article. "That's the work. Who do you think is 'Salameh's friend' who planned the trap? Mueller, of course. And believe me, the story did not pop up just by coincidence. Mueller wants me out of the way because I may jeopardize his plan. So he leaks a story to the papers. I am automatically blamed, and you remove me from office. And then,"—he slammed his right hand on the second document lying on the desk—"he radioes a totally unnecessary order in an easily broken code setting a deadline for my assassination. You get concerned about my life, of course, exactly as he wants you to, and you decide to stow me away for a while. So I am not only removed, but I am also deprived of my freedom of movement. Don't you see? Now that I am not in his way anymore, he will be free to carry out his real plan without being disturbed." He resumed his former position, erect in his chair, arms crossed, chin aggressively thrust forward. "The *New York Times* article and that radio exchange are the best proof that I was right all along." He sank back into a challenging silence.

The telephone on the desk buzzed, and the prime minister picked up the receiver. "Yes, I am leaving in a moment," he said calmly, then looked back at Jeremiah. His voice was firm, laden with authority. "I have been thoroughly briefed on the Mueller affair, I want you to know that. I am familiar with your version, and I have been told that most of your department heads disagree with it. But even if you are right, the Mossad is in good hands, don't you think?"

Jeremiah thought of the pampered, well-manicured hands of Rafael Avizur. It was he, no doubt, who had kept the prime minister informed about the Mueller affair all along. Jeremiah had not seen him since his return from Washington.

The prime minister nodded with finality and gathered the documents back into the folder. Now that the worst had been said, he seemed relieved. "I must hurry to the office. The foreign minister and the chief of protocol want to discuss the schedule of my visit to Egypt and the arrangements for the Pope's visit to Jerusalem."

"The Pope?" Jeremiah frowned, cocking his head.

"You knew about that, didn't you?" The prime minister threw a puzzled look at him.

Jeremiah nodded. "I have known for six months that he wanted to come, but I did not know a date had been set."

The prime minister spread his hands. "He let us know only last week. We have had no time for any preparations. Isn't that a headache?" He sighed, and his lips stretched in a bleak smile. "The Pope asked us to keep the visit secret until the last moment. He thought that discretion best suits a pilgrimage to the Holy Places." He started to rise, stretching his hand to Jeremiah. "We haven't seen a Pope in Israel since 1964."

The Old Man disregarded the outstretched hand and coldly switched the conversation back to its original topic. "If you have been so thoroughly briefed about the Mueller case," his voice was sharp, sarcastic, "you know that my department heads have no likely explanation for several of Mueller's expressed intentions like his need for a Jew and his threat of ultimate revenge. They can't explain Mueller's meeting with Caruzzi either."

The prime minister walked around the desk and affectionately placed both hands on Jeremiah's shoulders in a gesture that immensely surprised him. "Jeremiah, in your four years of service under my government and all those years you served my predecessors, it has happened many times that you alone held a theory disparaged by the other intelligence chiefs, and finally you turned out to be right. That's what created the myth," he warmly smiled, "of your unique flair and your extraordinary instincts. You may be right, once again, and they may all be wrong. But you know," he suddenly sighed, an aging, preoccupied man, sagging under the burden of his duty, "there is time for every one of us to step down, to let a new generation take over. My own day too may not be very far away. You can go in peace, my friend, and be assured that I shall personally take care that the Mossad continues to explore every possibility connected with the Mueller case, including the one you just mentioned. I would not forgive myself if we disregarded the advice of the man who has been in charge of our security for more than thirty years."

He strode out of the room, leaving Jeremiah standing awkwardly by his chair, thrown in total confusion by the sincerity and warmth of the prime minister. Maybe it was all acting, Jeremiah thought when he had regained his spirits a moment later; but then, just for an instant, he had been himself subjugated by the magnetic personality that had propelled that man to the helm of the country's destiny.

The former head of the Mossad reached for the telephone. "I would like to be connected with Mally Segev at the Mossad headquarters," he said to the operator. His voice was still hesitant, ill-assured.

"A man went on leave today," the editorial of the *Jerusalem Post* said. "In a few weeks when he will formerly quit office, we shall be at liberty to print his photograph and name, still considered a state secret. Today we can only say that this man, affectionately called the Old Man by his subordinates, founded and has directed the excellent secret services of this country for more than three decades. He was the man who unmasked the vilest enemies of Israel's security, the spies Israel Beer, Efrem Yakobian, and Rudolph Sitta. He personally directed the capture of Adolf Eichmann, the bitter war against the German scientists in Egypt, the fantastic intelligence effort that was a decisive factor in our victory in the Six Day War. He saved the life of President De Gaulle by circumventing a vile assassination plot. This man gained international respect when he managed to obtain the full text of Khrushchev's secret speech on Stalin's crimes before the Twentieth Congress of the Communist Party and predict the dramatic shift in Soviet foreign policy. He was the man who warned the free world of the forthcoming collapse of the Shah in Iran and of the approaching war between Khomeini and the Iraqi junta. Had the West listened to him, the whole strategic situation in the Middle East might have been different and the energy crisis not so acute. He is one of the masters of modern espionage and has been more valuable to Israel's security than a score of divisions. On this day of his departure we salute him with pride and gratitude."

The shadow of a smile fluttered on the thin lips of Alfred Mueller as he laid down the airmail copy of the paper and started unwrapping the big box that had been delivered to him through the good offices of Archbishop Innocent Caruzzi. Inside was a black, cowled habit of a Trappist monk, a Vatican passport, and a flight voucher, confirming that Father Hans Mayer was a member of a group of monks on pilgrimage to the Holy Land for the celebration of Easter. A brochure of the Israeli tourist office describing the holy places in the land of the Bible had been attached with a paper clip to the documents.

As he started dressing in the heavy garment of coarse wool, Mueller cast a glance at the departure date neatly typed on his voucher. His flight was to leave for Israel that very day, Thursday the sixth of April at ten-thirty in the morning.

Chapter 16

"HE IS DEAD, Maureen."

She had known it all along, deep in her heart, and when
Liam whispered the words over the phone, her eyes remained
dry. But there was that missed heartbeat in her chest, and a
sudden wave of chill surged through her body. She gripped the
back of the chair as her knees went weak and she slowly
slipped down to the floor by the bed.

"Maureen? Maureen, are you there? Maureen?"

The receiver was still tightly grasped in her hand. "Yes," she
said faintly.

"Are you okay?" The faraway voice was so anguished, so
desperate.

She repeatedly nodded her head, solemn as a child. But
only after the voice had repeated the question over and over
again did she move her lips. "I am okay. I want to know how
it happened."

"You don't have to . . . "

"Liam, I want to know how it happened." She did not recognize the inert, dispassionate voice as her own.

"He was found in an empty train in the Rome central
station. He had no papers on him and officially hasn't been
identified as yet. But a friend of his saw the body in the city
morgue. It's Patrick, girl."

"What friend?"

"An Italian. The bloke who helped Patrick tail Mueller in
Rome. He had left Patrick near the Vatican Museum on
Mueller's trail. They had agreed that Patrick would call him
every couple of hours. When he failed to call, they started

searching for him. They had to be very discreet because . . . because they are in the same business in Italy we are in Ireland. It took them quite a few days to get into the morgue."

"What happened in the train?" There was a long silence over the line, interspersed with faint outbursts of static. "Liam, I have to know," she said urgently.

"We are not sure, girl," Liam's brogue accentuated his anxiety. "Our guess is that Patrick followed Mueller to the railroad station. They must have met in the empty car, and there was a fight of sorts. Patrick was first beaten unconscious, then strangled."

"By Mueller?"

"Who else, Maureen?"

Black circles were floating before her eyes. She put the receiver down and rose to her feet. The room was spinning. She swayed and reached for the table for support. The phone started ringing again, but she did not pick it up. Her long cape was hanging in the small closet by the door. She snatched it and walked out, slamming the door behind her.

The sky was clear, starry, and the night air was cool. She hurried down Salah Ed Din Street, driven by an overwhelming impulse. Michael. She must find Michael.

She had not seen him since last Sunday when she had run away from his apartment. He might have looked for her throughout Jerusalem, but she had not given him the name of her hotel. When she had reached her room after the Palm Sunday procession, all she wanted to do was to pack her things and catch the first flight out of the country. Then she had bitterly realized that she had nowhere to go. Nowhere and nobody. Liam was hiding outside Paris, Patrick had disappeared in Rome, and Belfast could offer her only a load of painful memories and a broken, hysterical mother. Finally she had stayed in the hotel in the vague hope that in a few days things might clear up or she would be able to make up her mind. She had called Liam several times, but he was as confused as she. For four days she had not left her room, ordering sandwiches from room service, standing for hours by her window dully watching the spring storm fall upon the city. Tonight, the weather had cleared, and for the first time she had started to reemerge from her disarray. She had put on a smart white dress, had made up her face, combed her hair, and had gone down to the restaurant for dinner. Men had looked at her, and she had liked it. She had even exchanged a few jokes with two young Americans at a nearby table. Then the phone call from Paris had come, and she had rushed up the steps to take it in her room.

She hurried through the Damascus Gate, oblivious to the admiring looks of the crowds in the Old City. In spite of the late hour, the streets were still packed with tourists who had come to celebrate Easter in the Holy Land. She had to find Michael and warn him about Mueller. On Sunday he had not believed her. But on Sunday he had still thought that Patrick was alive and that Liam was just imagining things. Now her brother lay in the Rome city morgue, strangled to death. He too had believed in Mueller; he too had considered him his friend. Even she hadn't seen through Mueller before he had turned Michael's head with his revolutionary nonsense. She had called Michael naive, she bitterly recalled, and a dupe. But Patrick too had been fooled by that insane killer. Michael would listen to her now, he must listen to her! She must break the spell that Mueller had cast on him for he might be in danger too. Mueller wouldn't hesitate to murder him as cruelly as he had murdered Patrick. Dear God, she thought in despair, how did we get involved with that evil man?

She turned the corner into the Street of the Jews. She was half running now. When was Mueller supposed to arrive? Michael's words surfaced in her memory, "He'll be here on Thursday, and I'll ask him . . . " But today was Thursday, and midnight was approaching. Oh God, she whispered inwardly, please help me be on time, please let me warn him before . . .

The Batei Mahse Square was peaceful and deserted except for two men standing by Michael's house. They kept in the shadow, their backs turned to her. They were talking softly. One of them moved back into the light, and a surge of immense joy overwhelmed her as she recognized Michael's tall, youthful figure. Thank heaven, he was alive! He was talking to a Trappist monk, his head hooded, his back slightly bowed. Michael seemed exhilarated. She moved out of the shadow and took a step toward him. "Michael!" The name was about to burst from her mouth.

And then the monk turned around, raising his head toward

Michael. His hood slipped, and the soft yellow light from the streetlight fell on his face, and she recoiled, terrified, as a silent scream tore her chest and choked her throat.

The monk was Alfred Mueller.

She had never known how powerful, how all-consuming hatred could be. She had never understood people's lust for revenge, for causing pain to somebody they loathed who had hurt them in the past. Yet it was the raw instinct of hatred that made her move stealthily through the dark streets of Old Jerusalem now, following the elusive silhouette of Alfred Mueller.

It was not what she had intended to do at first. When she had hurried toward Michael's house, she had meant to talk to him, to warn him, maybe save his life. But then she had seen Mueller and watched the whispered exchange between him and Michael. Mueller had said something, and Michael had nodded in response, glancing at his watch before climbing the steps to his apartment; Mueller had waited until he had seen Michael close the door behind him and then had turned and walked away. Without thinking, without hesitating, she had moved behind him.

Why was she doing it? She couldn't explain. Maybe she had to take over where Patrick had been stopped. He had also been following Mueller before the blond man had turned on him and choked him to death. And Patrick had done it for her; he had paid with his life for something that she had asked him that he would not refuse her. Still, there was more in her impulse than mere hatred or an obligation to a dead brother. Mueller was walking through this city disguised as a monk. He was an evil, bloodthirsty man whose only talent was killing and destroying. A man who could savagely slay his best friend just because he might have discovered his plan must be planning something utterly fiendish indeed. And she had to stop him, even at the risk of incurring Patrick's fate.

Following Mueller through Jerusalem turned out to be easy. She was unfamiliar with the exotic city, whose narrow streets and covered bazaars looked so mysterious and scary under the blackness of night, but he did not seem to know the city either and would stop at every corner to consult a folded map that he carried in his large sleeve and peer closely at the signs on the walls. Now and then he looked back over his shoulder, but she was always careful to keep at a safe distance; and there was always a dark porch or a vaulted doorway where she could find instant refuge, her long, dark cape melting with the shadow, her hood concealing the fair sheen of her long hair. It occurred to her that they appeared very much alike: two dark figures in long hooded robes silently sneaking through the sleeping city on their way to a rendezvous with . . . with what? What waited for her at the end of the road?

For a while Mueller seemed to wander aimlessly about the city. He swiftly walked past the ancient St. John the Baptist Church, then stopped by the Muristan Fountain, whose clear water spewed from the gaping mouth of an oval stone mask, its features oddly contorted by the ravages of many centuries. For an instant the black figure blended with the shade of the huge Tower of the Lutheran Redeemer Church. Then he strode down the Khan Ez Zeit market street behind the Holy Sepulchre and slowly climbed the steps of the narrow Via Dolorosa, dominated by the succession of flying buttresses. Maureen followed Mueller along the outer wall of the Coptic convent, up Freres Saint Francis Street, and into the twisting alley leading to the sturdy bulk of the Latin Patriarchate. As he reached Jaffa Gate he suddenly turned back. He passed barely two yards from where she clung to the inner wall of a stairway. He descended the famous David Street and turned back into the Christian Quarter. He had completed almost a full circle, and Maureen realized that he was trying to familiarize himself with the Old City.

He walked into a dark nameless alley. At the corner, he suddenly whirled around, throwing a quick glance behind him. Maureen sneaked again into a doorway. When she came out of it, Mueller was gone.

She couldn't afford to lose him, not now! Forgetting her caution, she hurried into the alley. Only after she had taken a few steps did she stop to think that Mueller might be stalking her, immobile in the blackness, his hands reaching for her throat. If he were indeed, nothing could save her. But there was nobody in the dark, and her groping hands soon touched a cold, humid stone wall. It was a blind alley.

As her eyes got accustomed to the darkness, she retraced her steps. On her right was a narrow entrance that she had not noticed as she darted forward. Over it hung a peeling enamel sign, but she could not read it in the dark. Still, there was no doubt that Mueller had walked in. He had no place else to go.

She squatted in the farthest corner of the alley, determined to wait the whole night if necessary. As she wrapped her cape around her, the bells of some nearby churches chimed twelve times in unison, heralding the birth of April seventh, Good Friday.

As the hours passed and the church bells pealed one and two and three, she remained immobile in her place, shivering with the morning cold, her body stiff with fear. More than once, as she heard quick steps in the nearby street and furtive shadows crossed the patch of faint light at the far corner, did her heart leap in terror and all her instincts awake, urging her to run away. And yet she stayed, prisoner of her own will, in grim resolution to persevere to the very end. Did Patrick also tremble in the dark like her, before he was murdered? And if Patrick failed, what chance did she have? There was no logical explanation for what she was doing. But logic had deserted her that eerie night, and her inborn Irish stubbornness had taken over, subjugating her totally.

When dawn broke she painfully got up. All her body ached from cold and fatigue. Across the street, facing the alley, was another vaulted doorway. She pushed the small iron door, and it yielded under her pressure. She walked into a deserted courtyard and stood behind the door, leaving it slightly ajar. That way she had a good view of the stairway where Mueller had disappeared.

He came out a few minutes before six. All around, the sounds of the awakening city were blending into a slowly increasing hum. Mueller was dressed in the same black habit. In his left hand he carried an attaché case, and in his right, a small bundle, tied with string. He stopped a second at the corner, took in the street in a sharp glance, and quickly walked away in the direction of the Jewish Quarter.

He seemed to be on his way to Michael's house. But before going after him, she decided to explore the place where he had spent the night. She quickly moved into the empty alley, still plunged in shadow. The enamel sign incongruously read in faded English characters: *D. B. S. Suleiman. Dentist.* The upper part of the sign carried an inscription in ornate Arabic letters.

At the top of the steps was a small landing with a single door and two windows blocked with rotten wood shutters. She put her ear to the door. She could hear no sound. Then her eyes fell on the transverse steel bar blocking the door. It was fastened to the wall with a heavy padlock. That meant that there was nobody inside. She grasped the padlock and tugged. It was solidly secured. She turned to the windows. The shutters on the first window were tightly fastened. Those on the second protruded slighty, leaving a gap of a few inches between them and the concrete sill. She slipped her fingers underneath and pulled with all her might. They creaked but moved. She broke a fingernail, and a splinter of wood stabbed her left middle finger. She pulled again, and the shutters gave way, flinging open. She peered through the glass window, but the room was dark. Without hesitating, she took off her cape, wrapped it tightly around her right fist, and smashed the window. The glass pane shattered, and shards of broken glass rained to the floor with a sharp, tinkling sound. She paused a second, but nobody seemed to have heard the noise. Over her head, the steep stone walls, round domes, and flat roofs remained deserted. With quick gestures she stuck her left hand through the hole in the glass, found the handle, and opened the window. She heaved herself to a sitting position on the sill and jumped inside. She landed on broken splinters of glass and groped her way to the right. The light switch was by the door as she had expected.

The old-fashioned chandelier cast a yellowish light upon the room. She looked around her. A few old sofas and armchairs, some of them covered with faded brocade, a threadbare carpet, a table, a few chairs. The room didn't seem to be in use. She had no doubt that it was a safe house irregularly used for sheltering terrorists and weapons. She knew enough about such places from her experience in Ireland.

By the massive oak chest at the far corner was another door. She yanked it open. The second room was in disorder.

A few blankets were piled on the floor beside an iron bed that had been slept in; a couple of half-empty food cans and some crumbs of bread lay on the table; and two Kalachnikov submachine rifles were propped in the corner beside a crate of ammunition. But it was not the guns that made her freeze on the threshold, thunderstruck, her eyes wide with horror, her gasp dying in her contracted throat.

It was the face on the poster she saw hanging on the opposite wall.

A beloved, admired, worshipped face. The face of the man whom she and countless millions of others cherished more than any other human being.

Below, and to the right of the energetic, powerful visage at the very place of the heart, three concentric circles had been drawn with obscene red paint. And the center of the so-formed target was a gaping hole with jagged, scorched edges.

So that was the man they wanted to kill. That was the crime they wanted to commit, the most despicable of all crimes.

As she stood there, stunned, sudden flashes of understanding darted through her mind. Now she grasped why Michael had been picked by Mueller. Why the Irish had been banned from the operation. Why Patrick had been killed in Rome. And then the unthinkable consequences of the projected murder slowly dawned on her.

Good God, that must never happen!

She turned on her heels, rushed to the window and down the steps to the street, and ran through the colorful streets of Jerusalem as the first rays of the rising sun tore golden holes in the night shadows.

When she reached Michael's apartment, the door was locked. A friendly neighbor, an aging fat woman with a round face and kind blue eyes, looked at the distraught, wild-eyed girl with deep concern. Yes, she spoke a little English, the lady said. Would she like some coffee, she looked so upset. No, she had missed Mr. Michael Gordon by a few minutes. He had just left in the company of a young monk. But Mr. Gordon was Jewish, wasn't he, the lady asked gently.

Maureen shook her head and ran away.

She paused at the corner of Bet-El Street to regain her breath. Where should she go? She was alone in Jerusalem on that Good Friday, carrying in her heart the terrible secret of Mueller's evil plan. And she did not know what Mueller had done to her beloved.

Jeremiah Peled moodily contemplated the towering ramparts of the Old City wall, sharply etched against the spotless blue sky, and moved away from the large bay window. He felt utterly ridiculous in that luxury suite at the top of the King David Hotel where they had put him against his best judgment. What was he, for heaven's sake, a witness in a Mafia murder case protected by the police from some hired assassins? They had wanted to move him to Tel Aviv or Haifa, but he had insisted on staying in Jerusalem because, though he did not tell them—what was the use with that inflated Avizur calling the shots—he was sure that when something happened, it would happen in Jerusalem, and he wanted to be close by. The Hilton was filled to capacity—all those tourists and the Egyptian delegation here for the autonomy talks—so they had discreetly sneaked him into the presidential suite of the King David. It was a magnificent apartment with its blue curtains and pearl-gray carpets, the Scandinavian leather-covered furniture, the breathtaking view over the Old City. But he disliked the lavish surroundings—he had never been able to get used to luxury—and felt trapped in a sort of golden cage. Golden indeed, but a cage all the same.

In the next room, two of the boys were playing cards. They had closed the door, irritated by his disapproving glances. Two others had dragged a couple of chairs to the corridor to screen anybody approaching the outer door. Early that morning, after the Shin Beth had discovered the terrorist base, a couple of guys had been posted on the roof as well.

The terrorist base had been located exactly as he had predicted in his conversation with the prime minister. The ultra-sophisticated listening devices of Communications—most of them developed in the Mossad electronics lab—had analyzed the acknowledgment transmission radioed from within the Israeli borders in response to the execution order from Beirut. Although it had been a very short burst of letters and numerals broadcast on a very high frequency, the computers and the triangulation devices had pinned its origin down to a region of two square miles. The transmission had come from the southern outskirts of Bethlehem. The Shin Beth had fed that information into the central intelligence data computer, running it against all names and addresses of suspected Fatah sympathizers living within that area. Shortly before midnight the area had been sealed, and a dragnet had been launched with the help of the army. They had discovered the base two hours later, an isolated house off the road to Jericho belonging to the parents of a goldsmith from East Jerusalem. The transceiver was found in the attic together with an impressive cache of weapons, maps of Jerusalem, and some rather amateurish reports about the behavior pattern of Jeremiah Peled. Besides the lawyer, the Shin Beth had arrested a Turkish terrorist, a young man by the name of Adnan Koglu. The Turk had broken under interrogation and admitted that the attempt on Peled's life was scheduled for today, Friday. But the other six participants in the operation, Koglu revealed, had left the base the previous evening on their way to carry out the plan. Peled was not supposed to live through the day.

Rubbish, he grunted to himself furiously, all that was utter nonsense. That's what Mueller wants us to think, and the Mossad has swallowed his bait. Why couldn't they think straight, for God's sake? He knew that Mally shared his views; he had talked to her yesterday, but she had no decision-making authority. What had happened to Roth? What had made Avri Tour so blind? They should have understood by the very exchange of radio signals between Beirut and Bethlehem that Mueller wanted them to find the terrorist base. Arafat would never send operational instructions by radio; he was too clever for that! Furthermore, he had no reason to do so. The target date of a covert operation in enemy territory was always set in advance with authority for change delegated to the commander on the spot. That was routine practice. A radio signal would be broadcast only in one single case: if headquarters decided to cancel the coup altogether. And that acknowledgment nonsense! It was equivalent to

256

suicide, and they knew it. Mueller would know that the Mossad would locate the base within hours of a transmission. Mueller. His face sailed again before Jeremiah's eyes. Where was he now, the wretched son of Kurt Kolaichek and Eva Schwendt? He could not be far away, maybe a few hundred yards from the King David, maybe more, but definitely here, in Jerusalem. There was no doubt in Jeremiah's mind that Mueller had gotten into the country and was lurking close by preparing his most fiendish stroke. He could not imagine Mueller staying away while his ultimate revenge against the Jewish people was being carried out. He was here, perhaps putting the last touches on his plan, perhaps getting his Jew ready, perhaps pressing a button, a trigger, foretasting the heavenly elation of his revenge.

But where was he? What was he planning?

There was a light knock on the door, and one of his bodyguards, a squat, muscular man of Russian origin, walked in the room. "The newspapers, Jeremiah," he said in his heavy accent.

"Thank you, Boris," he nodded and spread the copy of *Haaretz*, Israel's most popular daily, on the large rosewood desk. He methodically scanned the headlines with the faint hope of discovering a hint that would help him solve the enigma. The main headline dealt with a new Soviet threat to Poland. Another fat heading heralded the possible collapse of the government coalition. The opening meeting of the Egyptian and the Israeli foreign ministers in the Hilton Hotel had not brought substantial progress in the implementation of the Camp David accords . . . difficulties at the last moment had blocked the election of an autonomy council in the West Bank. Jeremiah's eyes fell on a last-minute dispatch: "The private pilgrimage of Pope John Paul II to the Holy Land will start today, when the Holy Father visits . . . "

He suddenly became very still. The pilgrimage! Broken bits and pieces madly sped through his mind, falling into a horrifying pattern. The Pope. The Holy Places. Jerusalem. "I need a Jew." "The ultimate revenge." "Afterward, nothing will be the same." Could that be the plan? But how? Mueller could not know the date! What had the prime minister said? It had been kept secret till the last moment . . . but somebody must have known, if not here, then in Rome . . . Caruzzi!

Good God, Mueller had almost duped him again. It could happen any moment now. He had no time, he might be too late!

The terrible truth engulfed him, freezing his blood in his veins.

His face livid, he reached for the telephone.

The man who was bound to die spent most of the night in prayer. Wearing a simple cassock and a small zucchetto skullcap, Karol Wojtyla knelt for long hours in an austere cell at the Bethlehem Church of the Nativity, his lips softly murmuring. As dawn broke he rose from the stone floor, removed his cassock, and washed his athletic torso in a basin of ice-cold water, drawn from a nearby spring. Then he meticulously dressed for his pilgrimage. He first put on a long-sleeved, French-cuffed shirt made by Gammarelli, the Vatican tailor. Over it he donned the long white cassock and a gold pectoral crucifix on a narrow chain. On his feet he put a pair of red satin slippers, embroidered with fine gold thread. The weather was crisp, but he discarded the lambswool cardigan he wore under his vestments in winter. Over his head he slipped the large-sleeved surplice that fell to his knees. Next came the white, gold-edged chasuble. He draped his shoulders with the symbol of his reign, a white wool pallium adorned with six crosses. Then he put on his head the tall, pointed miter embellished with a pattern of leaves embroidered in gold thread and small bunches of flowers, in vivid red. The same pattern was repeated on the long narrow lappets, lined with red silk, that descended from the miter to his shoulders. Finally he took in his left hand his heavy crosier topped with a silver crucifix. Outside his cell his private secretary and the *maestro di casa* were waiting. They genuflected and kissed the gold ring with the Seal of the Fisherman he wore on his right hand. A group of cardinals, representing the Roman Curia, were standing in the bare hall. Attired in red-piped black cassocks, lace surplices, scarlet capes, and red birettas, they bowed deferentially at his passage, kissing his ring and murmuring subdued greetings. "This way, Your Holiness," the Vatican *camerlengo* breathed, and he walked into the modest, white-domed Franciscan church to celebrate the morning mass. After the service, he headed toward the courtyard where hundreds of priests, nuns, monks, and choirboys had been standing for hours, awaiting his appearance with growing anticipation. And there he stood, on the threshold of the Church of the Nativity, the morning sun bathing his robust, white-and-gold robed figure in radiant light. The crowd broke into a spontaneous cheer, saluting the leader of their faith, Vicar of Jesus Christ, Bishop of Rome, Successor of the Prince of the Apostles, Supreme Pontiff of the Universal Church, Patriarch of the West, Primate of Italy, Archbishop and Metropolitan of the Province of Rome, Sovereign of the Vatican State, Pope John Paul II.

From the right side of the courtyard where they had been standing apart from the crowd, a small group of ecclesiastics approached the Holy Father. Leading them was a tall, bulky man with a long grizzled beard, wearing a heavy brocaded robe, richly embroidered with intricate gold and silver patterns. On his head he wore a round, bejeweled crown. He was surrounded by several other bearded priests in white robes; others, in black soutanes and cylindrical, flat-topped hats, stood at a respectful distance behind their leader. The crowned man was the Greek Orthodox Patriarch of Jerusalem, who had come to greet the august visitor to his city. Both men warmly embraced each other.

When Pope Paul VI had met the Ecumenical Patriarch Athenagoras on the Mount of Olives in Jerusalem in 1964, the five-centuries old schism between the Eastern Orthodox and the Roman Catholic churches had begun to heal. John Paul II had even visited Constantinople the last December, and for the first time in nine hundred years, he had joined in an Orthodox eucharistic service with the Ecumenical Patriarch.

According to the express wish of the Pope, no other dignitaries had come to greet him this morning. As he had agreed with the Israeli ambassador in Rome, his meetings with the president and the prime minister of Israel were to take place only after he completed his pilgrimage. The Israeli minister of religion, who had greeted him yesterday night at Ben-Gurion Airport, had assured him that all the arrangements had been carried out according to his requests. He had insisted that no police or soldiers be positioned along the path of his pilgrimage in Jerusalem.

He intended to walk through Jerusalem by the Via Dolorosa up to Golgotha, following the footsteps of Jesus. He chose Good Friday for the pilgrimage, the day of the torture and crucifixion of Jesus. On the path where a martyred Jesus had carried his cross, exposed to the insults and the abuse of the angry mobs, his Vicar should be humble enough to refuse any protective shield of soldiers and weapons. In spite of the recent attempt on his life at St. Peter's Square, which had left several scars on his body, he had turned a deaf ear to the repeated pleas of his security advisers. He had even refused to have police barriers along the streets to keep the crowds away. He would walk among the people, and they would open a path for him without coercion. It had to be a true, modest pilgrimage as he had conceived it in his dreams. That was why he had decided, for the first time, not to take journalists aboard his plane; that was why he had asked for secrecy and discretion until the last moment. Still, he could not refuse the most eminent Princes of the Church, the high-ranking cardinals of the Curia, the privilege of accompanying him; neither could he reject the hospitality of the Franciscans, the custodians of the Holy Places, nor the warm welcome of the heads of the main Christian churches represented in Jerusalem. Therefore, when his long motorcade reached the courtyard of the Omariyeh College in Jerusalem, the starting point of the Via Dolorosa, a huge assembly of priests and nuns, assembled in distinct groups according to their orders, were waiting to join him on his way to Golgotha. The vast courtyard was a magnificent patchwork of vivid colors: the red of the cardinals, the ivory of the Greek dignitaries, the black of the Armenians, the brown of the Dominicans, the immaculate white of the sisters of Zion. In an unprecedented demonstration of Christian unity, the representatives of the diverse currents of the Church were to follow John Paul II on his pilgrimage.

The Old City, as well, was submerged by throngs of people. The word of the Pope's presence in the Holy Land had spread throughout Jerusalem, and thousands upon thousands of excited Christians, Muslims, and Jews pressed along the Via Dolorosa and the adjacent streets, clustering at windows and on balconies and rooftops, hoping to catch a glimpse of God's deputy on earth walking the tortuous path of Jesus to the site of his crucifixion in the Church of the Holy Sepulchre.

The beautiful, palm-shaded court of the Omariyeh College was bathed in sunshine. As he embraced with his kind regard the multitude of believers who were enthusiastically waving and cheering him, John Paul II felt himself transported back two millenniums to the time when at that very place rose the huge ramparts and towers of the Antonia Fortress, built by Herod the Great in honor of Marc Antony. Here, in the very Court of Antonia, Jesus was condemned to death by Pontius Pilate, scourged and crowned with thorns by Pilate's legionnaries.

The crowd parted as the Supreme Pontiff walked the short distance to the neighboring Condemnation and Flagellation Chapels. His lips soundlessly murmured the verse of Saint Mark: "And so Pilate, willing to content the people, released Barabbas unto them, and delivered Jesus, when he had scourged him, to be crucified." He stopped again at the Second Station of the Via Dolorosa, murmuring a prayer with deep emotion. Only a few yards away, in the courtyard of the Ecce Homo Basilica, stretched the Lithostrotos, the pavement on which Roman soldiers had engraved the designs of their pagan games, from which they had mocked Jesus as a false king and prophet. Here Jesus had received the cross. The Holy Father strode forth, passing under the Ecce Homo arch, the first of the many arches spanning the Via Dolorosa. " 'Then came Jesus forth,' " he whispered in the words of Saint John, "wearing the crown of thorns and the purple robe. And Pilate said unto them, *Ecce Homo*, 'Behold the Man.' "

Behind him the huge procession stirred and slowly crawled on its way. Close to him, but tactfully remaining a few steps behind, walked the Greek Patriarch of Jerusalem, accompanied by his entourage. They were followed by the personal staff of the Pope and the seventeen cardinals who had flown with him from Rome. Behind them strode a tightly knit group of Franciscan monks, closely followed by a multitude of nuns clad in immaculate white robes. Next came two old men in dark-blue, gold-buttoned uniforms wearing red fezzes on their heads and ceremoniously tapping the pavement with sleek silver-topped staffs. They opened the Armenian section of the procession, a compact group of black-robed priests, faces shaded by their strange triangular hoods, huge pectoral crosses hanging from their necks. An old, venerable Armenian was carrying a big ornate cross of dull old gold. After them came skinny, dark Ethiopian monks, Syrian Orthodox priests, Copts, Poles, Russians, Dominicans, Benedictines, and Carmelite nuns. Another group of Franciscans closed the colorful cortège.

The Holy Father stopped at the Third Station. A relief engraved over the entrance of the small Polish Chapel represented Jesus stumbling under the weight of the cross. Here the Pope stood for some moments, eyes closed, hands clasped before his chest in deep meditation. Here, Maureen O'Donnell, frantically pushing her way through the crowd, caught a first glimpse of his white-robed figure. She had been wandering about the Old City since early morning, feverishly searching for Michael. As the thrilled crowds had filled the street, she had overheard the excited conversation of three elderly French ladies about the Pope's pilgrimage. He was here, walking the streets of Jerusalem! Since that moment, she had been driven by an overwhelming obsession: Find John Paul and save his life. Even though she didn't know how. Asking directions, running at first, then fighting for every inch of her way through the packed streets, she had reached the Via Dolorosa. Somewhere along the road, she had lost her cape in the tumult. She did not care. Save the Holy Father, that was all that counted. Now, when she spotted him by the Third Station, she redoubled her efforts to approach him. But she could not get nearer; her way was jammed by a dense, wildly cheering crowd. Nobody paid any attention to her distraught face, to the tears streaming from her eyes. "Let me through," she shouted in desperation. "Please, let me through." But her voice was swallowed in the happy roar of the crowd. Beside her, an aging, obese woman fainted and collapsed on the pavement. As she watched three men carry the woman to the shade of a nearby porch, Maureen made an effort to think clearly. What use was there pushing her way through that crowd? She could never get close to the Pope, and what would she do if she did? Warn him? Stop him? But how? And Mueller would not be here in the middle of the crowded, narrow street; because if he tried something—she thought with horror of the three red circles on the Pope's poster—he could never get away. So where was he, good God? And Michael, what had he done with Michael? She could not think of any answers, so she plunged into the crowd with a redoubled effort, elbowing her way along the procession, darting into parallel streets and alleys whenever she saw an empty stretch, crying, gasping, pushing, but keeping close to the white-robed figure.

On the opposite side of the Via Dolorosa, Jeremiah Peled felt the same frustration as he watched the Pope's progression amidst the enthusiastic crowds. Peled's four bodyguards formed a human shield around him, plowing a path through the human swarm, brutally shoving aside anybody who stood in their way. Only after an angry exchange in his suite had he succeeded in imposing his authority on them to make them escort him over here. But how could they protect the Pope? In these crowded streets a shot could come from any window, any roof, any of the sleek belfries and minarets dominating the skyline of Jerusalem. In vain did his men sweep the windows and balconies with watchful looks, striving to detect a suspicious movement, a rifle barrel, a slightly budging window shutter. Jeremiah himself had alerted the police and the Shin Beth as soon as the horrible realization had struck him. They had promised to send all available men to the Old City. He knew that Amos Hefner and some of the boys were madly speeding on the highway from Tel Aviv, and the anti-terrorist unit had been alerted. But what could the police and the secret services do in that human sea, in those narrow streets, without any idea where the attack would come from? The only possible way to protect the Pope would be to snatch him from the middle of the Via Dolorosa and rush him away to safety. But that was unthinkable.

So they continued their painful progression in angry despair. Two of Peled's men urgently whispered into their walkie-talkies, vainly trying to establish contact with other Shin Beth agents.

And in the small room opposite the Church of the Holy Sepulchre, facing the very site of Golgotha, Mueller waited.

Chapter 17

ALFRED MUELLER LOVINGLY caressed the Remington XP-100 that lay in the inner sill of the window, ready for use. The pistol had been thoroughly checked, cleaned, and reassembled, the sight securely clipped on its grooves, the deadly Fireball bullet snugly fit into the chamber. Mueller glanced back at Michael Gordon who was staring at him with fear-glazed eyes. Michael was securely tied to a chair, his hands pulled behind its back, his mouth gagged. Mueller stepped around the chair, crouched, and looked out the window over Michael's shoulder. Perfect. From his position Michael had an excellent view of the square, the rectangular facade of the Holy Sepulchre Church, its round dome, the twin horseshoe windows, the majestic arched portal. And of that flat stretch of stone in the square's eastern corner where John Paul II would stand immobile and offer his chest to the slug that would rip his heart. "Excellent," Alfred whispered in Michael's ear, "you have the best seat. You'll enjoy the spectacle." The stupid Jew would die seconds after the Pope, of course. Yet Mueller thought it a subtle touch of refinement to make him watch the execution. After all, Michael was supposed to appear to have killed himself to escape any punishment for his assassination of the Holy Father.

Mueller chuckled softly. He was wildly exhilarated; feverish anticipation pulsated in his blood, charging his entire body with a terrific sensation of power and of mad, boundless joy. He had done it. The Plan had worked to perfection. Another half hour, maybe less, and he would have accomplished the sweetest revenge in history.

He had been as successful this morning as he had been throughout the previous stages of the project. Michael was waiting for him outside his apartment when he came to pick him up at dawn. He had fed him the story that the march on Jerusalem was today, and the naive Jew boy had swallowed it whole. It was true that today was Friday, the Muslim day of worship, and he had told Michael back in Paris that the operation would start when the Palestinians came out of the mosques on a Friday morning.

He had no trouble luring Michael to the room either. He intended to establish his command post there, he had explained, and Michael had to come along with him, just in case the landlord saw him and asked embarrassing questions. Once he got inside the room, Mueller said, Michael would leave and join his friends from the Jewish Defense League. He should stick with them and keep his ears open, ready to hurry back and warn Alfred if they planned anything dangerous.

They had been among the first to enter the square when the Greek priests unlatched the iron door blocking the western entrance of the Holy Sepulchre compound on St. Helena Road. According to tradition, the compound and the square, actually the church courtyard, were closed at night to outside visitors and reopened at sunrise. Michael and Mueller had walked in separately. Mueller had noticed with satisfaction that Michael's entry had been remarked by the young Greek priests, while nobody paid any attention to the Trappist monk who sneaked in a few minutes later. They had met by the house entrance on the square facing the church, and Michael had led the way up the stairs to his room. Nobody saw them entering. The rest was simple, almost routine: the quick movement behind the unsuspecting young man, the stunning chop on the exposed neck, the trussing and gagging of the Jew. He had brought the thin nylon rope in his bundle together with everything else he needed for the coup. Arafat had meticulously followed their plan. In the safe house that the Fatah people had prepared for him in the Old City, Mueller had found the locked attaché case containing the Remington, and on the table, a letter in Hebrew composed by a Fatah Hebrew expert in Beirut but signed "Michael." The letter was in a sealed envelope, and he had carefully examined it before breaking the seal. It had not been tampered with. The most important factor at the Jerusalem end of the operation was that no visual contact had ever been established between Mueller and the Fatah cell that had prepared the safe house. They had not seen him enter; they did not know what was in the attaché case or what the contents of the letter in the sealed envelope were. Before they came back to the safe house tomorrow, he would have removed all clues to his identity and already left the country in the same way he had come in: as one of a large group of Trappist monks, carrying their prayer books and rosaries. The Israeli immigration officers had been very solicitous, even deferential. The only loose end in the whole operation had been the disappearance of that little Irish tramp, Patrick O'Donnell's sister. He had not found her in Paris when he returned from Rome. Maybe she had panicked and run away when her brother disappeared or even returned to Ireland before that. In any case, she represented no danger to the success of the Plan.

Michael tried to move his head, and a muffled groan escaped through his gag. Mueller leaned toward him, a sardonic grin curving his mouth. "Restless, Jew? Curious? Want to know what's going to happen?" He ran his tongue over his lips. "Why not? You are fully entitled to know. It's you they are going to remember after today. Forever. It's your name that will be on everybody's lips all over the world in a couple of hours. And they'll never forget it." He sneered. "No, Jew, never. I am going to make you a great historical figure, like . . . like Pontius Pilate . . . or Judas Iscariot. Iscariot is better. For you are going to kill God's deputy, do you hear me, kill God's deputy on earth for a second time. Hear me, Jew? I am going to use you for my revenge against your filthy people. My ultimate revenge."

He was breathing shallowly now, and the words that had been treasured so long in the locked recesses of his mind, the details of his cunning, marvelous Plan, were streaming out of his mouth. It felt so good to tell the story, to describe the Plan, to watch the reactions of the Jew as he learned Alfred's secret before he died with it. "This will be the ultimate revenge," Mueller said again, tasting to the full the hacked, cadenced utterance of the words, "the end of all you Jews. After today you will be hunted, persecuted, beaten, exterminated all over the world. Like vermin. Like an epidemic. Nobody will lift his little finger to help any of you. Remember the pogroms?" His hands clutched Michael's shoulders. "Remember the rapes? The massacres? It will all come back, Jew, and it will be worse."

His own words were like dope, exquisite, high-quality stuff, sending him soaring high in a marvelous, orgasmic trip. "See the crowd over there, Michael? They are waiting for somebody. The Pope. John Paul the Second. The Vicar of Christ, God's deputy on earth. He is on his way here, and he will stop here to pray." His hand jerked toward the immured second portal of the Holy Sepulchre that closed off the entrance to Golgotha. His fingers were slightly trembling. "He will say a prayer on the place where they crucified Jesus. Now this here is a Remington. The best weapon ever. I'll shoot him. I'll shoot him dead with one single bullet. Through the heart. I shall not miss. I never miss." He paused, wiping the flecks of froth from the corners of his mouth. The coarse fabric of his sleeve felt good to the touch. "As soon as he dies, I'll feed another bullet into the Remington, and I'll shoot you. In the mouth. Here." He gently pressed the cold barrel of the pistol to Michael's gagged mouth, and the young man shuddered in fear. "It will be done in seconds. Then I'll untie you, and I'll be out and away." He was standing over him now, watching him closely, his breath gushing in hot bursts over Michael's face. "Nobody'll see me. When they come, they'll find your prints all over the Remington. They'll find it still clutched in your hands, your thumb in the trigger, the barrel stuck in your mouth. Suicide. And they'll find that letter on the table. In Hebrew. Know how to read Hebrew, Jew? It doesn't matter. It is a very simple letter; it says, 'I killed the Pope, that enemy of the Jews, to avenge the injustice that the Christian church has done to the Jewish people. To avenge the persecutions and the Inquisition and all the massacres that have been inflicted upon us in the name of the Christian faith.' That letter is signed Michael Gordon."

He took a deep breath and slowly shook his head, anticipating the question that might arise in Michael's mind. "No,

267

nobody in the whole world could prove that this letter is fake, not in a million years. You have never before written a letter in Hebrew, have you? There is no handwriting of yours to compare it with. So you see, the whole wide world will believe you assassinated the Pope. It suits you, right? You are an active member of the Jewish Defense League, you are a crazy Jewish fanatic. It's logical that somebody like you would do it. If your leaders wanted to blow up the Al Aksa Mosque, why not kill the Pope?"

Michael was writhing in his chair like one demented. It was not simple fear that filled his eyes now; it was sheer, utter horror.

"Think, Michael, think what the Pope's death will mean for your people!" Mueller hissed. Michael's terror was sweet, so sweet, to him. He understood. Yes, the Jew boy understood. Triumph vibrated in Mueller's voice. "For the second time in two thousand years, the Jews will be blamed for the death of God's messenger on earth. They killed God once, here in Jerusalem. And two thousand years later, they are killing God again, in the same city of Jerusalem, on the same hill of Golgotha. Could you think of anything more symbolic, Michael? More terrifying?" He paused, stepped toward the window, threw a quick glance outside, then stepped back. "That death down there will be the final proof that you Jews are a cursed seed, unworthy to live on this earth. Christian countries will cut their ties with Israel. Israel will be expelled from the United Nations. Pogroms will erupt all over the world. Nobody will try any longer to stop Arafat and his people from exterminating you." He was in a trance now, whispering urgently, hoarsely. "The worst acts of terrorism will be justified. Nobody will sell weapons to Israel, and Israel will collapse, Michael. It will not survive. You and I will wipe it off the face of the earth."

He stood up. "The Jews are killing Jesus for a second time," he said. "They are raising a second cross at Golgotha. Till the end of time, they will carry a double guilt." He breathed deeply, his face flushed, his forehead moist with perspiration. "A double cross. You and I will do that, Jew."

Michael stared at him, his mind still paralyzed by the tremendous shock. It can't be true, an inner voice was soothing him, this is a nightmare, a bad dream, the fruit of your sick imagination. The black-cowled figure of Mueller swaying in front of him like a sorcerer at a black mass, his mouth spewing a demonic tale, could not be real. But behind Mueller he could see the patch of blue sky and the ancient facade of the Holy Sepulchre and the excited crowds filling the square. Why were they there? Whom were they waiting for? And as he gradually emerged from his daze, sinister thoughts shaped in his mind, pointing to the inevitable conclusion. The people here were waiting for the Pope. Like Mueller said. It was real, it was all real, not a nightmare, and John Paul was on his way here. And the pistol was real too, resting on the window sill, its barrel gleaming faintly. So Mueller was going to use it, he was telling the truth!

The frightening realization jolted him out of his daze. Mueller meant what he said. He was a madman, he was a murdering, cunning maniac, and he was going to do it. He was going to shoot the Pope. Nothing could stop him now. Nobody knew about that room. Nobody knew that Mueller was here with him. God, what a fool he had been all the time. If he had only listened to Maureen!

And that evil man was right to the last detail. If he carried out his project, the world would fall upon the Jews. Flashes from old documentary movies rushed through Michael's mind. Burning synagogues, debased rabbis, shopwindows covered with signs: *Jews! Buying forbidden!* Crowds loaded with hatred assailing the Jewish quarters. Raped women, blood in the streets. God Almighty, there were still enough backward places in the world, in South America, in Europe, even in the United States where ignorant people could be roused to action by that kind of poisonous propaganda, by that satanic accusation!

A word kept echoing in the back of his mind. A word he had not understood when he had first heard it in the crowded buffet of the Gare de Lyon. "Noka." That's what Mueller had answered in a fit of rage when he had asked him why Patrick and Maureen could not participate in the operation. "Noka," Mueller had begun, but had suddenly fallen silent. Of course. He had started to say *No Catholics.* He knew that no Irish, Italians, or South Americans would ever take part in a cold-blooded scheme to murder the Pope. But Mueller had needed Michael Gordon because Michael Gordon was a Jew.

What could he do? He desperately tugged at his ropes, but he was tightly bound, Mueller had taken no chances. He watched in morbid fascination as the hooded man slipped on a pair of thin gloves, took a small towel and carefully wiped his prints off the Remington. Then Mueller moved behind him, and Michael felt the cold touch of steel, the smooth surface of the pistol butt, as Mueller pressed his fingers on the weapon. That was the proof he needed, the key to his revenge.

His heart leapt in his chest as a sudden cheer rose from the courtyard below. Mueller swiftly strode to the window, crouched behind it, and calmly raised his arm.

The Pope was coming.

"Jeremiah, I have contact. I got them on both frequencies." Boris, the Russian-born Shin Beth agent, waved his walkie-talkie at the Old Man. They were still stuck in the middle of the crowd, close to the Eighth Station.

"Whom did you talk to?" Jeremiah asked. He was sweating profusely.

"Police headquarters, Special Branch. They've sent over all their reserves, about fifty border police and plainclothesmen. What should I tell them?"

"Give me that," Jeremiah snapped, reaching for the tiny transceiver.

"Here. Our call word is . . . "

"Never mind the call word," Jeremiah broke in impatiently. He pressed the transmitter button, "Do you hear me, repeat, do you hear me?"

"Loud and clear," the answer came in a whiff of static. "Loud and clear, over."

"This is Jeremiah Peled," the Old Man spoke firmly, disregarding security precautions. "Our man is on his way to the Holy Sepulchre. There are two zones of high danger—the square of the Holy Sepulchre which is an open space between several tall buildings and the interior of the church where the five last stations of the Via Dolorosa are. Somebody might be hiding inside, behind a column or in a chapel, I don't know. Do you hear me?"

"We hear you, sir," the voice was respectful but slightly tinged with panic.

"I want your police—on the double—on top of all the buildings overlooking the square. Redeemer's Church, up on the tower. Minaret of Mosque of Omar, Belfry of the Sepulchre. Roofs, balconies, windows. And I want all the plainclothesmen inside the church covering all the remaining stations: Golgotha, Greek Chapel, Latin Chapel, Rotunda, Vestibule, Tomb."

"But how shall I get them in, I mean . . . "

"I don't care how, just do it!" Jeremiah roared. "Dress them in cassocks if necessary!" He thrust the walkie-talkie into Boris's hands. "Let's take a shortcut," he grunted, "straight to the Holy Sepulchre."

They elbowed their way into the square by the Eastern entrance on the Dye Market barely ahead of the Pope. The Pontiff had just moved away from the ancient pillar marking the spot where Jesus had fallen for the third time. Several priests angrily shouted at Peled and his bodyguards as they rushed for the narrow doorway ahead of the Holy Father. As he squeezed his body through the entrance, Jeremiah had a fleeting glimpse of a tall, striking girl in a white dress. She had just broken her way into the square, using her arms and elbows. Her red-blond hair was disheveled, and her face looked strangely distressed.

Jeremiah reached the middle of the square, surrounded by his men. His back to the church, he took in the skyline with a slow sweeping glance. The disorderly facade of buildings facing the Holy Sepulchre dominated the square and abounded with flat roofs, domes, balconies and windows, all perfectly suited to an assassin's needs. Each was a position for a sharpshooter, Jeremiah thought worriedly. "What about the police?" He turned to Boris. "There's nobody on the minaret or the Redeemer's tower."

Boris pointed to the left where several familiar green berets reassuringly appeared on top of the St. Abraham's Monastery. A moment later, another string of quickly moving green specks darted onto the flat roof of St. James's Chapel. A police helicopter, flying low, emerged from the south and started circling over the roofs. Jeremiah looked sharply to the left, as shouts and applause broke by the eastern entrance of the square. The cheering crowds stirred, and a wavelike movement rippled through the human mass that parted to open a path for the Pontiff. He was quite close now, and Jeremiah got a good look at his energetic broad face with its large Slavic cheekbones and the stubborn square chin. As the Pope passed by him, their eyes met and locked for a short second. The Pope's face was slightly flushed, and his eyes glittered with emotion. He vaguely smiled at the white-haired man staring at him so insistently.

"One more minute," Jeremiah murmured to nobody in particular, "one more minute and we'll only have to worry about the interior of the church."

The Pope, who had seemed headed for the dark portal of the Holy Sepulchre, suddenly turned to the right. The startled crowd parted at his approach. "What happened?" Jeremiah muttered. "Where is he going?"

The Pope purposefully walked to the far eastern corner of the square, then veered back. The Greek Patriarch and the Cardinals took places on both his sides. He was now standing next to the church wall, barely a few yards from the site of Golgotha. He raised his hands, and a hush gently descended on the square. "Let us pray," the Pope said in Latin and fell to his knees. In a slow, harmonious movement hundreds of Christians knelt on the pavement, while Jews and Muslims moved back, so as not to interfere with the prayer. Jeremiah stared at John Paul II, horror-stricken. "Dear God, what a target," he rasped. The Pope was kneeling totally immobile, arms outstretched, chest unprotected, in a position that was the dream of any assassin.

Jeremiah turned around, his eyes urgently scanning the roofs and balconies around him. The green berets were now all over the place. Suddenly he pointed at two windows, straight across the square. The left one was tightly shuttered, but the one on the right, protected with white-painted iron bars, was open, the interior dark. "What's that?"

"It's all right, Jeremiah," one of his bodyguards answered reassuringly. "That building belongs to the Greek Gethsemane Convent. Quite secure."

"Secure, is it?" the Old Man groaned, his eyes glued to the dark window. He was squinting in the sun, cocking his head back, to get a better look. The sunbeams, bathing the square in light, barely touched the bottom of the windowsill where the bars were fastened to the concrete slab. Just for a split second, something glinted dully over the sill. "There!" he suddenly shouted, and before his mind had even digested the meaning of the fleeting sight, he breathlessly leapt forward, brutally shoving aside whoever stood in his way, dashing toward the arched entrance and the steep narrow stairs. His bodyguards raced after him, all except Boris, who had not even noticed the commotion. Bent over his walkie-talkie, he was listening to a dramatic flash about the capture of a terrorist commando team that had attacked Jeremiah Peled's house.

By the eastern wall of the square barely thirty yards away from the Pope, Maureen O'Donnell stood petrified. Her feet seemed to be made of cotton, and she was shaking badly, unable to kneel, unable to move. She watched the immobile Holy Father as in a dream. And her tortured mind again projected on the Pope's chest the red concentric circles she had seen painted over his picture back in Mueller's room. They were going to shoot him now, she knew it! Holy Mary, they were going to kill him, they had been waiting for this very moment. She gasped for breath.

Up in Michael's room, Mueller gripped the Remington with steadily, unwavering hands. The crosshairs of the telescopic sight gradually moved over John Paul's torso. The Pope was exactly where he had expected him to be, in the right place, at the right distance, in the right position. Nobody but a few confidants had known that the Pope intended to stop for a prayer outside the church in order to share his pilgrimage to Golgotha with the thousands of fellow Christians who had come to Jerusalem. Archbishop Innocent Caruzzi had been among the few to know and had revealed the secret to Mueller in good faith, not suspecting the motive behind his question.

The crosshairs were in place now, stabilized on the left side of the Pope's chest. Mueller felt the smooth trigger starting to yield under his crooked finger.

"No!" The scream burst from Maureen O'Donnell's chest, jolting her out of her stupor. And she hurled herself forward.

She darted across the square between the kneeling figures of nuns, monks, and cardinals, so quickly that nobody could stop her. She threw herself at the kneeling Pope as he was spreading his arms, facing the domes of Jerusalem, his body resembling a human cross. And as she dashed toward him she opened her arms too, and for the infinitesimal portion of a second as they faced each other, their bodies erect, their arms outstretched, they were like two human crosses, like a double white cross. It was just a split second, as the moving cross flashed and covered the immobile one, the same short pulse of time when Mueller's bewildered eyes registered the startling scene, but his finger, already commanded, was squeezing the trigger; and a crimson rose blossomed at the right side of the girl's back, as the echo of the shot rolled through the silent square and reverberated in the vaulted passages and dark alleyways of the Eternal City. Pandemonium broke over the square as hundreds of frightened, screaming people hurled themselves in all directions. Some found refuge in the Holy Sepulchre Church, its huge open gates offering the protection of its vast dark halls. But most of the throng stampeded toward the two narrow exits, madly struggling to get out of the holy place that had become a death trap.

As the girl slowly collapsed on the pavement before the Pope, Mueller bit his lip and quickly fed another bullet into the chamber of his rifle. He raised the Remington again, then heard the door crash and the steps behind him.

"Kolaichek!" a voice lashed.

The secret name, his real name, made him gasp, and his finger froze on the trigger. And before he could turn, before he could use his pistol, somebody leapt on his back and crushed him on the floor, locking both his arms in a deadly grip.

He was trapped. He had failed. And they knew who he was, they knew his name! He was in Peled's hands, and the Pope was down there alive. "Kill me!" he suddenly screamed, jerking his head back. The Shin Beth agent held him tight. His sprawled legs were helplessly kicking, his features were distorted, his madly rolling eyes looked at Peled for the first time in his life. "Kill me, don't wait, kill me!"

But Peled was just standing by the door, a little white-haired man watching him thoughtfully, and Mueller realized that now it was Peled's turn to take his own revenge.

Peled glanced out the window at the scene below. Panicked people were running in all directions while frightened screams echoed throughout the square. Some fist fights had broken out by the west entrance where badly scared tourists frantically hurled themselves at the tiny doorway, striving to get out. On the eastern side, a throng of clergymen of different orders was trying to get to the Pope, in spite of the efforts of a few Greek priests to contain them. A tall, thin cardinal was trying to calm an aging nun who had gone into a fit of hysterics. She was staring at the Pope, her body trembling, her strident screams slowly decreasing.

The only quiet people in the square were John Paul II, who had not moved, and the girl in the bloodstained dress lying in a heap at his feet.

"Jeremiah!" a familiar voice called, and the Old Man turned to the door where an ashen-faced Amos Hefner was moving past the Shin Beth agents. He was followed by a sweating Rafael Avizur, his hair uncombed and his beard untidy. One of the bodyguards was deftly untying Michael Gordon from his chair.

Peled addressed Avizur in English. He wanted Mueller to understand every word he said. His loud voice was firm, commanding, "I want Mueller's picture taken, here, with the pistol and the Papal procession in the background. Later we shall take a detailed deposition from this young man." He pointed at Michael Gordon. Avizur was nodding meekly. "Keep the press away from those two."

As the Shin Beth man unfastened the rope binding Michael's legs to the chair, he leapt forward, tearing the gag from his mouth. His face was white, his lips bloodless. For a second he gripped the window bars, staring in horror at the blood-covered girl below. Then he abruptly turned back and darted toward the door. Two Shin Beth agents moved to stop him, but he struggled like one possessed. "Let me go!" he groaned fiercely. "She is dead. Let me go!"

So these two were connected, Peled realized. He nodded to his men. "Let him," he said softly. "He won't go away." The handsome young man rushed to the sunny terrace and down the steps.

In the square the shouts had subsided, and the increasing

wail of an ambulance siren came to a stop. In the sudden silence Peled turned back to Mueller. "I shall not kill you," he said calmly. "I shall turn you. You are going to double-cross your friends now. You'll work for me, and you'll make a better double agent than your father." Then he added, his voice almost a whisper, "We can get your mother, you know."

There was no triumph in his voice, young Hefner noticed, only weariness and a hint of sadness.

From below rose the clear, harmonious singing of a male chorus. The Greek priests, custodians of the Holy Sepulchre, had clustered by the dark portal, softly chanting a hymn. The crowd gradually calmed down, and the shouts faded away. Jeremiah could see the nun who had been hysterically scream-ing before sitting on the pavement, nodding her head as the tall cardinal soothingly spoke to her. He recognized several police plainclothesmen who had joined a group of priests and thrown a protective cordon around the Pope. Then he saw Michael Gordon suddenly sneak behind the priests and kneel over the wounded girl. The Pope too was bent over her, holding her hand. Maureen's eyes were closed, but she was clutching John Paul's strong fingers. She was conscious. Jeremiah watched the golden-haired girl being carefully laid on a stretcher. Michael Gordon kept close to her, holding a plastic bottle of plasma over her left arm.

The Pope smiled at the wounded girl. His right hand gently stroked her face, then made the sign of the cross over her body. He turned back to the crowd that was standing, now silent and grave, facing him. "Benedicat vos," he chanted, "Omnipotent Deus, Pater, et Filius, et Spiritus Sanctus."

The bells of the Holy Sepulchre broke into a clear, melodi-ous peal, swiftly joined by those of the thousand churches of Jerusalem. The Holy Father turned away and walked into the church, following the last steps of Jesus Christ.

Jeremiah followed the holy figure of the Pope with his eyes and suddenly visualized what might have happened if the unknown girl in the white dress had not been there. The voice of his father, Rabbi Piladski, rose from his memory, and he saw him standing in his synagogue, chanting the bless-ing for one who had escaped danger. Jeremiah's lips whis-pered the old Hebrew verse, "Baruch ata Adonai Elokeinu

276

Melech Haolam shegemalani kol tuv" . . . Blessed art Thou Who doest good unto the undeserving, and Who hast dealt kindly with me."

And then, Jeremiah recalled, his father would step back, and the congregation would respond, "He Who hath shown thee kindness, may He deal kindly with thee for ever, Amen."